HER SOUL FOR REVENGE

BY HARLEY LAROUX

The Souls Trilogy
Her Soul to Take
Her Soul for Revenge
Soul of a Witch

Losers
The Dare (prequel)
Losers: Part 1
Losers: Part 2

Dirty First Dates (short erotica series)
Halloween Haunt
The Arcade
The Museum

HER SOUL
FOR REVENGE

Harley Laroux

KENSINGTON
PUBLISHING CORP.

kensingtonbooks.com

CONTENT NOTICE: Some contents within this book may be triggering or disturbing to some readers. Reader discretion is advised.

This book contains drug use, loss/death of family, scenes of trauma, anxiety, PTSD, mentions of suicide and domestic violence, and depictions of "hard" kink/edgeplay.

This book is not intended for anyone under the age of legal adulthood. The activities depicted within this book are dangerous and are not intended to depict realistic expectations of sex, BDSM, or fetish-related activities.

The kinks/fetishes within this book: knifeplay, gunplay, body modification including piercing and scarification, derogatory language/degradation play, flogging, blood, public play, voyeurism, bondage, primal play.

*To all those who have ever felt
lost in darkness.*

WELCOME BACK TO ABELAUM, dear readers!

I'm Harley Laroux—author, cat guardian, plant collector, and candle enthusiast. Thank you so much for picking up *Her Soul for Revenge*, book 2 in the Souls Trilogy!

I'm so excited to be working with Kensington Books for these gorgeous print editions of the Souls Trilogy. Each book will contain an all-new bonus epilogue, and beautiful updates to the covers' original designs!

Inspired by the stunning natural beauty of Washington State and my fascination with all things spooky, the Souls Trilogy follows three fierce women and the demons who love them as they fight to survive in a small town full of monsters, magic, and mystery. These adult paranormal romances are extra spicy, with a diverse cast of queer characters and themes that are sex- and kink-positive. They are stand-alone but interconnected, each following a different couple as they unravel the dark mysteries of their town's past.

The nights are darker, the monsters more dangerous, and the stakes higher than ever in *Her Soul for Revenge*. After spending years on the run, hiding from the cult that tried to sacrifice her as a teenager, Juniper Kynes makes a deal with a demon. Zane will grant her his help to destroy the cult, but in exchange, her soul is his for eternity.

But her soul is not enough. Juniper's fractured spirit drew the demon to her, but it's her heart that makes him stay.

When I first wrote Juniper's story, I knew this was a character who carried so much pain. She was a survivor, a fighter. An imperfect woman fueled by rage who could captivate a creature as powerful as a demon.

When depicting a character like Juniper who lives with PTSD, it was imperative to me that her healing be celebrated not as her final destination, but as a journey. As someone who has struggled with my mental health for most of my life, it is my wholehearted belief that love should embrace even the most damaged and difficult parts of ourselves. True love will be there through the healing journey, not waiting at the end of it. That is what I hoped to depict with Zane and Juniper: love through healing, through brokenness, and through pain.

Love that is truly eternal.

I'm so grateful for the opportunity to share this story

with you. I hope you find just as much love, adventure, and excitement while reading these books as I did while writing them.

WITH LOVE,

Harley Laroux

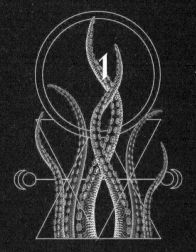

JUNIPER

GRANDPA USED TO tell me never to answer if I heard my name called from the woods. It didn't matter if it sounded like my mother calling, or my brother, or even my best friend. He drilled it into my head from the time I was a little girl, barely old enough to toddle around the yard, let alone the woods.

If the woods call your name, don't answer. Run.

He never explained why. He didn't need to. The rule stuck with me into my teenage years. Every time I rode my bike down the winding road, the trees whizzing by on either side, I'd listen to the boughs creaking and the pine needles rustling. Sometimes, I'd imagine my name was called and I'd peddle faster, my heart racing until I reached school and was safely behind the iron fence surrounding the campus.

Dad claimed it was all bullshit. *Ain't a thing in these woods you can't kill*, he said. *Don't you forget that, Juniper. You just keep your wits about you. Don't go wandering around after dark.*

No matter who you were, if you lived in Abelaum, you held a strong belief about the woods. About when you should go out, when you should hike, when you should lock your doors. Everyone would tell it a little differently, but the general belief was the same: the woods weren't safe.

The threat, whatever it was, was never put into words. There was a general sense of unease about the pines, the kind of thing that made people avoid certain trails and certain roads. Older folks made little charms out of twigs, twine, and fish bones, and would hang them up outside their houses or around the edges of their yards. Grandpa kept them on his fence posts, around the field where his horses grazed, right at the edge of the trees.

There still came a year when one of the mares went missing. He kept them in the stable at night after that.

By the time I was fifteen years old, I realized the superstitious stories were only good for scaring little kids. From the trailer park where we lived, it was a four-mile bike ride to school if I took the road. But it was only a mile and a half if I cut through the woods. I started taking the shortcut when I was fourteen, peddling as fast as I could through the trees.

I wasn't afraid of the woods. But something felt wrong about lingering under the trees too long, as if the longer I stayed in their presence, the more irritated they'd get to have me there. I rode through quickly and didn't linger. No point in pushing my luck.

Even with the shortcut to school, I was usually late, especially when Mom was fighting with her boyfriend all night, and I couldn't drown out the yelling enough to sleep.

My breakfast was an energy drink I'd grabbed from the back of the fridge, which I chugged outside the classroom as I waited for the bell to ring for lunch. I'd missed the first three periods completely, and I wasn't about to walk into Mr. Thorne's class halfway through and get reprimanded with yet another lecture on tardiness.

The bell rang, and I tucked myself into the alcove near the water fountains as the crowds of students flooded the walkways. Finally, I spotted Victoria's high brown ponytail bobbing away and I sprinted through the crowd to catch up with her.

"Girl, you're late again?" Victoria's eyes went wide as she looked over at me. "I swear, Mr. Thorne is going to end up calling your mom again."

I shrugged. "As if she ever picks up the phone. I think her line got disconnected." I poked her arm eagerly. "Soooo? Did you get it?"

"Shhh." She quickly glanced around, then reached into her purse as we walked out to the lunch area. Keeping her hands low, she held up a plastic ziplock bag just high enough for me to see a tiny square of folded tinfoil within.

I grinned, and she smiled widely as she singsonged, "Almost time for a little trip with Lucy!"

The benches spread over the lawn were almost entirely filled. The sun was out, a few puffy white clouds drifting lazily across the crisp blue sky, unusually pleasant weather for October. We wound our way between the tables as Victoria argued with herself about whether or not we should walk off campus to get iced coffee. But another conversation had my attention instead of her caffeine dilemma.

"There's an entire network of mine tunnels out here, man. For all we know, they're right beneath our feet. Nobody knows how deep they go." Nervous laughter followed, and I spotted Victoria's twin brother, Jeremiah, holding the rapt attention of the two new transfer students. "But that was where everything went wrong—they drilled the old silver mine too deep. They hit an underground river system, and the whole mine flooded. Cave-ins trapped most of the workers inside."

"Holy shit," one of the girls murmured. She had a bite of food paused halfway to her mouth, too distracted by Jeremiah's story to keep eating. Typical Jeremiah; as if he didn't already get enough attention on the soccer team, he also had to scare the new girls with local legends.

"So they're all still down there?" the other girl said. "Like, they didn't get them out?"

"Only three came out alive," Jeremiah said darkly. "They survived for two weeks by eating their friends' corpses."

"Ewwww!" both girls shrieked, and I prepared to give Jeremiah a good scare of his own as I came up behind him. He leaned forward, lowering his voice for effect, and Victoria glanced over at me and rolled her eyes.

"But the miners attributed their survival to something *else*," he murmured, and his audience went still with nervous anticipation. "Legend says that as the mine was being dug, something very old and powerful woke up. Some say it's a monster. But the miners said it was a God, a God that granted them mercy, in exchange for—"

"Would you stop with the scary campfire stories already?" I grabbed Jeremiah's shoulders, nearly making him spill his soda and getting some unhappy looks from his audience. Victoria sat down on the opposite bench, gave the two girls one of her signature smiles, and they both quickly scurried away.

No one fucked with Victoria—or with Jeremiah, for that matter. Their father, Kent Hadleigh, was a major donor who'd had an entire wing of the high school dedicated to him for his generosity, so Victoria and Jeremiah could do whatever they damn well pleased.

I didn't know why they wanted to be friends with me, especially since making friends wasn't my strong suit. Most people considered me a bitch, either because they'd pissed me off at some point, or they'd talked to someone who'd pissed me off. Being known as a bitch and having a reputation as a partier were really the only two things me and Victoria had in common.

But she always had a hookup with a dealer, regardless of what I was trying to get, and her family was very generous with their money. Her mom had taken me shopping for new clothes last year when she'd realized I was still wearing shoes with holes in them.

"Goddamn it, did you really have to be such a cock-block?" Jeremiah groaned heavily. "I was going to get both their numbers!"

"Oh no, Jeremiah might miss out on some pussy," Victoria said, her voice dripping with mock sadness as she pulled out her mirror and reapplied her lip gloss. "What a tragedy." She paused, her eyes focusing beyond me, over my shoulder. "Ugh, God. Weirdo at twelve o'clock."

"Hey, guys."

I turned. Everly Hadleigh stood behind me, her long blonde hair forming a wispy mane around her face. She usually spent time with the art kids and was wearing a long, loose black smock with white paint flecked across the skirt. Her hands were clasped behind her back, and her voice was so soft I could barely hear her over the other conversations happening around us.

Victoria popped her lips, looking around. "Did you *hear* something, Juniper? Or is it just windy over here?"

I laughed, but I didn't feel good about it. I didn't have a problem with Everly. She was weird as hell, and way too soft to ever be friends with me, but Victoria *hated* her. I knew why, of course. Everyone knew why.

"Can I borrow some money?" Everly said, her voice softening even further. "Meredith forgot to give me lunch money this morning."

"Mom has a lot on her plate, you know?" Victoria said, rummaging in her purse. "Her focus tends to be on her kids, after all."

I winced. Mrs. Hadleigh—Meredith—wasn't Everly's mom. When someone as illustrious as Kent had an affair with his own secretary, rumors were bound to get around. When a child resulted from that affair, it only got worse. People said Everly's mom wasn't stable, and that was why Everly lived with Kent and Meredith.

But her mom still worked at the Abelaum Historical Society with Kent. It had never made sense to me, but I wasn't one to judge anyone else's weird family situations. It wasn't as if mine was any better.

"Please?" Everly pulled her hair over her shoulder, her fingers plucking at her dress. "I'll just get something from the vending machine."

"Ugh, *fine*," Victoria groaned, pulling a five-dollar bill from her wallet. She held it out, but just as Everly was about to take it, she snatched it back. Everly sighed, her shoulders slumping.

"I'll do your math homework," she said. "For a week."

Victoria smiled, placing a hand over her heart before she finally handed over the cash. "Aww, Ev, that's so sweet of you to offer!" Her smile vanished the moment Everly turned away. "By the way, Jerry, I'm using the car later."

Jeremiah glared at her as I snuck chips off his plate. "Uh, no, me and Brendon are going to Hyper Bowl."

"Then Brendon can pick you up." Victoria shrugged.

"No way, you used the car last time! Have Mom give you a ride!"

"Jerry, I'm using the car, and I'm either going to use it with your body in the trunk, or without."

DESPITE AN ARGUMENT that drew out over the rest of the lunch hour, we got the car that afternoon without needing to murder Jeremiah in the process.

"Where did you tell your mom you were going?" Victoria said, turning the music down just enough to speak. I'd let her pick the place where we'd drop acid tonight, and she was driving us north along the bay, where the trees were thick and houses were few and far between. I thought staying at a hotel or a friend's house would have been better for our first trip, but she insisted being outdoors would be more "magical."

"My mom will be hungover at least until tomorrow," I said. "She wouldn't notice if I was gone for a week."

"Lucky." Victoria pouted. "My mom micromanages *everything*. I told her we were spending the night at Kim's."

Victoria pulled the BMW X5 off the asphalt, driving along a narrow, rutted dirt road. The ground was bright green with moss, with ferns clustered around fallen logs and massive roots. She parked, rolled down the windows and opened the moonroof, turning off the engine. The sounds of the forest were all that remained: the wind in the trees, the singing birds, the groan of the boughs overhead.

"Here," she said. "This is perfect."

I wasn't sure when the acid kicked in. Between the time I put the tab on my tongue and the time that the colors around me began to slide into a bizarre amalgam, time had lost its meaning. "You Are a Memory" by Message to Bears was playing from my phone, and

I swore the song had gone on forever. For hours and hours.

We got out of the car, and as I stretched my arms toward the sky, I was certain I could touch the clouds. I could feel every little crackle of the dry bark beneath my fingers as I climbed up a fallen tree. The air was so crisp—crisp, like overly carbonated soda—and the sensation made me giggle. Then I kept giggling, because I couldn't stop, and everything I looked at just made it funnier.

"Are you feeling it?" Victoria sounded like a tape recording playing too slow, and that made me laugh more. I nodded and laughed, laughed and nodded, and she began to laugh too.

Time kept changing. I could measure it in steps, in breaths. I could measure it in those bizarre waves that rose up in my chest, tight like a band but filling me like air under the wings of a bird. Acid could come in waves, but were those waves minutes? Hours? Eternities?

The sun had dipped low, and I was lying in the grass, watching the kaleidoscope of trees overhead against the pale pink sky. Everything was rippling, oozing, and changing.

Victoria's face appeared above me. She looked strange, but *everything* looked very strange.

"Juniper, we should go for a walk."

I shook my head. I hoped she could see it too: the colors, the swirling, how everything was *breathing*. She reached down her hand, and I had a funny thought that her hand and her head weren't connected at all.

"Let's walk. Come on. I want to show you something."

I wanted to lie there on the grass until it grew over me, until I became like the fallen pine covered in lichens and little patches of moss. But Victoria was pulling me up, so I took her hand and trudged with her, deeper into the woods.

The sun had set. The light was gray, and clouds were filling the sky. I looked at my watch, for the first time in forever, but the numbers didn't make sense. They were just digital marks on a screen, hazy and oddly three-dimensional, as if I could stroke my fingers along the edges of them. I put my wrist down hurriedly, and the moment I did, I saw where Victoria was leading me.

"We're not supposed to be here," I said as the old spires of St. Thaddeus cathedral loomed ahead, towering amongst the trees. Sober, I never would have been afraid of this place. The legends surrounding it were just that: old stories, made up. The paint had faded from its exterior long ago, leaving the wood dark and stained with the damp. Lichens and fungi grew from the old boards. Beneath the three spires that adorned its front, a massive stained-glass window depicted a woman standing beside the sea, her hand upstretched, holding a dagger.

This place had a story, like everything else in Abelaum. It was close to White Pine, the deep mine shaft where rescuers were once able to pull the only survivors of the mine's cave-in back up into the light of day. It was said the three rescued miners stopped here, and dedicated the cathedral to the God they claimed spared their lives in the deep, dark, flooded depths.

The Deep One, they'd called it. Every now and then, you'd still hear the old folks mutter about it. But to our generation, it was just a creepy story. Like Bigfoot, or the Jersey Devil.

History and myth intertwined in this town, utterly inseparable from each other.

The old church should have been dead, like bleached bones, but the air around it rippled like heat off the roof of a car in summer. I stopped abruptly, tugging back against Victoria's hand, and she stared at me with wide eyes.

"Why not?" she said. "You've been in there before, Juni, we both have." She shrugged. "It's the same old church."

"Not . . . not now," I said, and tried to pull my hand from her grip, but either I was weaker than I thought or she was gripping hard. "Not when we're tripping. Let's go back. I want to go back to the trees."

Victoria shook her head. "Just a little while. Please? I just want to walk through it."

Something felt so unexplainably *wrong*. I could smell smoke, like a campfire. As the darkness around us deepened, and we got closer to the cathedral, I could see a glow within the grimy window. The crickets should have been chirping, but the woods were so silent.

But Victoria was my best friend.

The cathedral's front doors weren't chained shut like they usually were. When Victoria and I had been there before, to drink or smoke or do whatever our little rebel hearts desired, we'd had to break in through a back entrance. But the chain was gone, and right before Victoria pushed the doors open, I knew we weren't alone.

Someone was inside. Someone was waiting.

For the first time in my life, from behind me, from the woods, I heard a whisper.

I heard the woods call my name.

I WISH I could forget the things I remember.

I wish the nightmares would stop.

I wish I could erase that night.

That night, when something called my name, I learned why I should have run.

THE CHURCH'S ROOF had caved in years ago, forming a gaping hole that streamed moonlight onto the pile of rubble below. But the pews still stood in their places, in nice neat rows, waiting for congregants to fill them.

As Victoria pushed open the doors, I realized the pews were filled.

Two dozen pairs of eyes turned to watch us enter. Two dozen familiar faces stood as we walked inside. I looked at them in utter confusion, wide-eyed, convinced the acid was making me see things all wrong. They were all wearing white robes, and as I walked past, row by row, they placed masks shaped like stag skulls over their heads.

Mr. Thorne was there, and so was my history teacher, Ms. Malcolm. Mike, who worked at the gas station. That weird old lady, Mrs. Kathy, who lived by the university. A massive bonfire had been built in the center of the church, and Victoria led me around it. I felt like I was stuck on a bizarre amusement park ride, watching the oddities around me with detached fascination.

Until we rounded the fire and stood in front of the pulpit.

Kent Hadleigh stood before us, dressed in white, hands clasped in front of him. Meredith stood off to the side, and Jeremiah beside her. The woman who stood next to Kent was familiar, but I couldn't remember her name.

Until, in the shadows behind the pulpit, I spotted Everly.

The woman standing beside Kent was none other than Heidi Laverne—Kent's receptionist, his mistress, Everly's mother.

I frowned. Victoria let go of my hand, and went to stand beside her mother and Jeremiah. She smiled at me, but the acid in my brain warped her expression into something sinister. I could measure time now in heart-beats. *Ba-dumb, ba-dumb.* Every throb in my chest hurt. Every beat tried to push adrenaline into my limbs. Half my brain was convinced this was all a hallucination. This wasn't real. This was just another wave.

But the other half of my brain was certain something was very, *very* wrong.

I had to leave. I had to leave *now*.

But I turned to find the church doors had been shut, and the congregants, in their masks and white robes, had moved closer. I faced a barrier of masked figures, the dark sockets of their eyes staring at me coldly.

Outside, the gathering clouds unleashed the first crack of thunder.

"We've been waiting for you, Juniper," Kent said. I turned back to him, slowly. Victoria had been given a white robe she was slipping her arms into. I shook my head as her face disappeared behind a mask like the others.

What the fuck was this? What the hell was going on? Was I hallucinating all of this?

I began to back away, quickly, stumbling over debris on the ground. But I didn't get far. Kent nodded his head, and suddenly both my arms were seized, gripped tight by masked figures who forced me back up toward the pulpit. I didn't know what was happening, but I hated strangers touching me. I thrashed against them, pulling back, digging in my heels. Why was everyone just staring?

"Let go!" I jerked against them, their masks looking far too real from behind the veil of psychedelics. It was like they didn't even hear me. They forced me up before Kent and pushed me to my knees.

The moment my knees hit the dirty wooden boards, it was as if reality smacked me in the face. This was real. Holy shit, this was all *real*.

"Don't worry, my dear. All is as it should be." Kent's voice was calm, almost soothing. He smiled down at me and lightly touched my cheek with his cold fingers. I jerked away, tugging against the arms still holding me in place.

"What the fuck is this?" I yelled, my voice shaking. "Let me go. Tell them to let me go."

Kent shook his head, like I was a child making a ridiculously unreasonable request. "God has called you, my dear. It has waited for you for a very long time."

I laughed, but it wasn't funny. None of this was funny. My heart felt like a fist pounding against the inside of my ribs, trying to escape its prison of bones. "Stop," I said. "Stop it. This isn't funny. This isn't *fucking* funny."

Kent turned, lifted a mask from the pulpit behind him, and placed it over his head. He became another empty-eyed skull, and the woman in black peered down at me, examining me carefully.

"What is your name?" she said.

"Juniper! Juniper Kynes!" I struggled, panting. "And I know you! You're Heidi Laverne! I know all of you!" I shouted at them, hoping it would rattle them. I didn't know what they were doing, but I knew their names, their faces. I could tell someone. I could name them guilty.

But guilty of what?

Heidi nodded slowly. "She is the one It seeks. It calls her name."

"It calls her name," the entire congregation murmured in unison behind me.

My mind was spiraling. There were bizarre patterns on the walls, infinite looping geometry in the floorboards, in the pores and freckles across Heidi's face. She stepped back, and from within the folds of her black dress, she drew out a knife and handed it to Kent.

It was like a part of my brain turned off. Some part of me, the part that still had logic, saw what was coming and flicked a switch, shutting me down.

It shut down the part that wanted to scream.

It shut down my frantic struggling, so I wouldn't waste my energy.

I went still, and silent, and yet hot tears streaked down my face.

"Brothers and Sisters!" Kent's voice boomed through the space, echoing amongst the rafters. "Long has God blessed us with Its mercy and patience, long has It awaited this night! Tonight, we begin to fulfill the oath of our ancestors. Tonight begins a new era upon Earth. Tonight, the first sacrifice goes to the Deep One."

"Amen," the congregation said in unison, and a deep shudder of revulsion went straight to my core. I could only stare at the knife, its blade catching the fire's light as Kent turned it slowly in his hands and knelt before me.

"Mr. Hadleigh." My voice was a trembling whisper. "Please."

"Do you know the story, Juniper?" he said, his voice as light and happy as if he were speaking to a little child. "Long ago, three men were rescued from the tragic flooding of the mines. Only three. The only survivors amongst dozens."

"I've heard the story." I was weeping, staring at the blade. Knowing something awful was going to happen, and I could do nothing to stop it, had turned my limbs numb with dread. "My grandpa used to tell me, because his great-grandpa was down there—"

"And his great-grandfather *survived*," Kent said. With one smooth motion, he cut open my t-shirt.

Humiliation rushed through me, unbearably hot on my skin but sickeningly cold in my stomach. I squirmed against the hands that held me as they tugged the ruined shirt off me, begging softly, "Please, please, no, please . . ."

"Your ancestor was spared. God's mercy must be repaid," Kent said with a firm voice.

And then he began to slice into my skin.

My mind went black. Only Kent Hadleigh's voice permeated the void I'd fallen into.

"Your soul was promised to the Deep One, my dear. Six generations have passed, and the oath must be fulfilled. Three lives spared, three souls given."

The congregation echoed, "Three lives spared, three souls given."

I was screaming, my voice ragged, "No, *no*, it's just a story, it's all just a story, it's not real! It's not real! There's no God in the mines. It isn't real!"

Why were they doing this? Why? Adults weren't supposed to believe the stories; they told them to scare little kids. Teenagers told their own scary variations as they drank cheap beer in dark places. It wasn't real.

The cuts burned, searing into my skin as if the knife was blazing hot. My own blood was smeared across my chest, and the sight made me so light-headed that I fell deeper, deeper into that protective dark void.

The next thing I was *truly* aware of was being carried through the rain. It was freezing cold on my skin, washing rivulets of blood from the cuts across my chest. What had they done to me? What the hell had they *done*?

Were they going to kill me?

I was tossed down into the mud. I tried to crawl, tried to move, but perhaps they'd drugged me again because my muscles wouldn't budge. My hands were seized up, clenched like claws, tight and aching. There was a sound like splintering wood amidst the pouring rain. The white cloaks surrounded me, and I reached out for them, clenching my muddy fingers on the cloth, hoping, *begging* for help.

There was no help. I was fifteen years old, and they watched me in silence. Dozens of them.

No one would help me.

No one cared.

"Victoria!" I screamed her name into the faceless masses. "Victoria, help me!"

But she didn't help. She didn't care. She'd brought me here.

"Send her to God."

As I was dragged through the mud, the wooden frame of a dark, open mine shaft loomed up ahead of me. I clawed at their hands; I fought them with every bit of strength I had left.

There was nothing I could do.

They shoved me down into the dark.

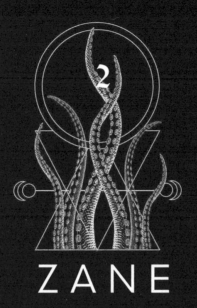

ZANE

THREE YEARS LATER

THERE ARE PLACES on Earth that are cursed all the way down to their roots. Places that hold pain, that tasted blood and can't get enough. Places where darkness grows, and even in daylight, they lie under a shadow.

Those places feel a lot like home, and I suppose that's why demons are attracted to them. Not to say Hell is some wretched, unpleasant place. To the contrary, Hell is endlessly fascinating, even to an immortal. It's vast, far more vast than Earth. It holds darkness, it holds pain and, in some places, misery and agony beyond words. But Hell is inhabited by those who have existed for centuries, for millennia. It has seen wars, uprisings, the growth and destruction of cities, of cultures. It is full of magic and memories.

Abelaum, like Hell, was built on a foundation of magic and memories. It was beautiful; it drew in curious minds and ensnared them, like a spider weaving its web. Some humans stayed there forever; others swiftly left.

But Abelaum had something not even Hell did: Abelaum had a God.

Gods and demons had never gotten along. We'd taken Hell back from Them, and They'd ended up on Earth, weak and asleep. But always, inevitably, curious little humans took things too far. Curious human hands went digging, and curious human minds woke something up.

Humans and Gods were a bad combination. Give a human knowledge, and he thinks he's wise. Give a human magic, and he thinks he's strong. Give a human religion, and he'll think he's right.

Demons were better off avoiding Gods, despite the intrigue a town like Abelaum held. Yet there I was in Abelaum, back again after several years away. I always came back, and I'd keep coming back, as long as Leon was there.

We demons didn't take our bonds lightly. When one of our own was summoned and held captive by some wretched human magician, we didn't simply abandon them. Leon and I had sworn our bond to each other centuries ago, and that bond had never broken. It never would. We may not have been lovers as we once were, but relationships that lasted through hundreds of years had to ebb and flow like the tides.

"That fucking hurts," Leon hissed, baring his sharp teeth as I cleaned the burns across his shoulders. I didn't know why his summoner had punished him this time. Leon was volatile, and I couldn't blame him for that. He'd always been unlucky, and getting summoned and kept captive by that wretched family—the Hadleighs— was just the latest in his string of terrible circumstances.

"You don't need to clean it," he grumbled. "It doesn't matter."

"It matters." I shoved his head back down when he tried to raise it to stand up. Even his blond hair was burned. His summoner wielded brutality like a weapon, using pain to force obedience. "I know you'll heal, Leon, but you can't pretend this physical body doesn't need to be cared for. You'll heal faster if it's clean."

"Fucking Kent," he muttered. "I swear I'll kill him. I swear it."

Kent Hadleigh—a man whom God had given knowledge, magic, and religion. A dangerous trifecta, leading to a man who fancied himself untouchable.

"What was it for this time?" I tossed the bloodied rag away. I returned to Abelaum so often that I'd gotten a house here, and it was useful even outside of giving Leon a place to recover. Humans were far more likely to trust you if you had a house, a car, the illusion of money and grandeur. As a soul hunter, gaining humans' trust was part of my job.

"The girl," Leon said. "They let her out today. Three years later, and Kent's still furious she ever got away. Told me to find her . . . Fuck him. Fuck his orders. She can run for all I care. He can break every bone in my body, but it won't bring her back." He chuckled bitterly.

The girl. I knew the story, only because Leon had told it to me: how Kent had his daughter lure the girl into the woods, how he and his followers had gathered in the old church, how they'd cut the girl before they'd thrown her down into the mine.

Their first sacrifice to their wicked God.

But the girl escaped and ran, and not even Leon had been able to catch her.

How the hell a fifteen-year-old mortal girl had managed to escape from Leon, I'd likely never know. How she'd endured her escape through the woods—bleeding, lost, and drugged—made no sense.

"Why did they lock her up?" I said. "Last I heard, the police were all over her case."

"She tried to kill Victoria Hadleigh." Leon leaned his head back on the couch, closing his golden eyes. "Kent has the cops under his thumb. Fucking humans. So goddamn easy to corrupt." He sighed. "They locked the girl up in some hospital, called her delusional. I don't think she was too upset about it. Kept her safe for the last three years. But now . . . she's out on her own." His voice was getting softer, weaker as sleep took over. Demons didn't sleep often, but when we did, it was because it was desperately needed. "The God has her scent. It'll keep hunting her. She's in for one hell of a wild ride out there." He yawned. "Going to rest my eyes. Just for a minute. Just a minute . . ."

He was out cold.

FROM CURSED PLACES come cursed humans. I was fascinated with them: humans who had been broken and survived; humans who had just turned out *wrong*. I liked to hunt oddities, souls with heavy histories and heavier scars. They fought the hardest, and that made it even sweeter when they eventually became mine.

This girl, the one who had escaped from Kent Hadleigh's cult—she was an oddity, certainly. But if being outcast from society didn't kill her, then the monsters hunting her certainly would. I could smell them lurking in the trees—the Eld beasts. They'd be lured to the magic lingering around her, hungry for a taste.

She likely wouldn't even survive the night.

Since Leon was resting, I wandered. There was too much energy in the air, a tingling at the back of my head that warned me things were shifting. The boundary between Earth, Hell, and all the numerous other realms felt thin. That boundary waxed and waned like the moon, and some thought it would eventually disappear altogether, plunging reality into chaos.

I didn't know if I believed all that, but I did believe there were other demons in Abelaum, demons that hadn't been here only a few days ago. It was their scent I followed curiously through the night.

It led me to an old diner perched at the water's edge, its blinking neon sign advertising that they were open 24/7. I lit up a joint in the parking lot, trying to get a good look inside through the windows. Three demons sat within, all apart from each other. Two I recognized as soul hunters, so I could only guess the third was the same. They knew I was there, shooting me wary glances out the window as they sipped their coffees and poked at plates of food they had no interest in eating.

What the hell were they here for?

As I smoked, the wind shifted. The skunky, herbaceous odor of weed was wafted away from me, replaced instead with a sharp scent of iron and rot. I turned toward the trees, staring back into the shadows. Deep in the darkness, a howl pierced the night: the kind of wretched, animal scream that sounded almost human. I took a long drag, exhaling slowly. First demons, and now the beasts . . . all gathering here.

I wandered inside, and the other demons quickly put their heads down. I'd been around long enough to have made a name for myself, and I'd taken enough souls to have earned a reputation as a hunter not to be trifled with. These demons were young, inexperienced. Eager for their first soul, perhaps, but whose?

I went up to the counter, tapping it to get the nervous waiter's attention. His eyes were wide, his fingers twitching. He didn't know the guests gathered in his restaurant were all unearthly creatures, but his primal instinct knew and would be warning him of the danger.

"Coffee, no cream," I said, and watched his hand shake as he filled a mug from the coffeepot. "Slow night?"

He shrugged. "Weird night. Something's not right about it." He glared out the windows as he handed me the cup. "Did you hear those howls out there? We don't usually get wolves around here."

"It wasn't wolves," I said. I could hear someone sprinting outside, distant but coming closer. Bad night to be out for a run. "Make sure you don't walk to your car alone."

"The hell is that supposed to mean?" he said. Suddenly his eyes widened even further, staring behind me. "What the fuck?"

The sprinting feet were coming closer, closer—

The door burst open, the bells dangling from its handle jangling erratically. I turned slowly, sensing the tension rising in the air. There, standing inside, was a young woman with long, messy brown hair. She was tall and lanky, wearing a backpack and muddy boots. All her clothes were stained with mud—mud . . . and blood.

She froze, scanning the room. Every eye was fixed on her, and three pairs of them were hungry. Her scent was intoxicating, sweet with lingering magic. But the blood on her wasn't her own. I knew the smell of it immediately.

It was the beasts' blood. She'd been fighting the Eld beasts.

"Hey!" the waiter called sharply. "Hey, I know you! Juniper Kynes! You—you're supposed to be locked up! You tried to kill that girl!"

She took a deep breath, and wiped a splatter of blood from her face with her sleeve. She walked across the dining area, heading toward the corner where the bathrooms were. The waiter likely didn't hear her mutter, but I did.

"She tried to kill me first."

She locked herself in the bathroom. Every demon in

the place was tense, their eagerness for her palpable. I chuckled softly, taking a sip of the steaming coffee. Young soul hunters like these were always desperate for easy prey, eager to make a deal with someone who they didn't need to convince that magic and monsters were real.

This girl already knew. She'd seen the worst of it. But that wouldn't make her easy, no. Far from it.

"I should call the cops," the waiter said, staring warily at the bathroom. The sound of running water from within cut off, and the door opened again. Juniper trudged out, her wide eyes flickering around the room. She moved like a frightened animal on the verge of sprinting. Like a wolf . . . a little wolf, left without a pack, alone and hunted.

She really was fascinating.

She came up to the counter, eyeing me. "I need food."

The waiter shook his head. "No. No, you gotta get out." He was reaching slowly for the phone.

She whipped out a pistol and aimed at the waiter. With her other hand she pulled a knife from its sheath on her thigh, and pointed the blade toward me. I raised my hands innocently.

"Don't do anything funny," she hissed, her voice shaking. "Just give me some fucking food. I don't care what. Just put some food in a bag. Now."

The waiter nodded, his face white as a sheet as he disappeared back into the kitchen. Juniper kept the knife pointed at me, shooting nervous glances in my direction and at the demons seated behind me. She couldn't have known what we were, of course. We all wore our human disguises in public.

"You know he's going to call the cops while he's back there," I said. She jumped at the sound of my voice, her breathing quickening as she looked rapidly between me and the door leading back to the kitchen.

"Fucking hell." She climbed over the counter and reached beneath it, hurriedly collecting bags of cookies and tiny packets of oyster crackers that she stuffed into her bag. She vaulted back over, right as a shout came from the kitchen, and ran out the door.

"Cops are on their way!" The waiter crept out from the kitchen. The cook stood behind him, a massive man with a frying pan wielded in his hands like a baseball bat. That vicious woman had really put some fear in them.

I liked that.

With their prey on the move, the demons were moving too, all of them heading out the door. I sighed, and gulped down the rest of the coffee. I wasn't interested . . . or at least . . . I *hadn't* been. But with so many other hunters after her, and that desperate, vicious look in her eyes when she'd brandished the knife at me, I couldn't help but feel intrigued.

I left the restaurant faster than I should have. To the confused waiter's eyes, it would have looked as if I simply vanished, leaving an empty mug behind. The hunters were in the lot outside, heading toward the road, laughing amongst each other and betting who would reach the woman first. I got ahead of them.

They stopped abruptly, their human disguises instantly

slipping. Three pairs of golden eyes watched me cautiously, claws extended, and the hunter I didn't know
bared her teeth. I smirked.

"Don't growl at me, darling, it's rude," I said, and the
hunter beside her gave her a hard nudge in the ribs. "All
this fuss for one little mortal woman, eh?"

"You know she'll be desperate for a deal." Amiria
was the one who spoke up. I knew her to be a fresh soul
hunter, yet to make her first bargain. She was hungry
for it; I could see it in her eyes. "But we were here first,
Zane. Let a novice get a soul for once."

I cocked my head, stepping toward them. With only
one step of mine, they all jerked back. I chuckled at their
nervousness. "I don't think I will. There's plenty of souls
out there, fledglings, trust me. Find someone selfish, someone greedy, someone eager for life's riches with no care for
the afterlife. *That's* an easy bargain. But this one . . ."

I let my body change. My veins ran black, like trails
of ink beneath my skin, as my teeth grew sharper. I gathered energy around me, condensing it, creating a shroud
of darkness. It was petty, perhaps, but it was a warning.
It let them know how much power I had at my disposal:
enough to destroy all of them, here and now, if they
dared try to argue with me.

"This one is mine."

JUNIPER HAD COVERED a lot of ground in the time it
had taken me to disperse the other demons. I spotted her
along the winding road, her pistol still in her hand. She was

walking in the middle of the road, her head jerking from side to side. The forest had grown right up to the edge of the asphalt, and thick blackberry bushes formed a wall of tangled thorns on either side. The trees loomed high, and beneath their boughs, monsters lurked in the shadows.

I could hear them scrambling through the trees.

The woman heard them too.

She turned, her weapon aimed. The bitter scent of fear surrounded her as adrenaline coursed through her. It got my heart racing, that pungent odor of terror. She faced the darkness, eyes wide. The stench of rot was in the air, growing stronger as the beast under the trees crept closer.

It fled the moment I drew near. One Eld beast alone wouldn't face me.

"You need to shoot for the head. It's really the only way to kill them."

She nearly jumped out of her skin at the sound of my voice. She aimed the gun at me, clutching the small pistol with both hands, her extended arms shaking. "Who the hell are you?" she said, then she narrowed her eyes. "You . . . you were in the diner. You followed me."

"You have quite a few things following you, little wolf, and they all wish you a lot more harm than I do." I looked off into the trees. More of the beasts were encroaching on our position, their silhouettes scurrying through the dark. They had long, boney limbs, and vile, hunched bodies. They resembled spiders as they moved. "You need to get indoors. If you're going to travel at night, use a vehicle."

She didn't lower the gun, but curiosity began to creep

over the fear on her face. "Those things . . . do you know what they are?"

"Eld beasts," I said. My golden eyes were hidden behind brown and I had sheathed my claws. I would appear as just a normal human to her, at least for now. No point in scaring her even more. "They're elder monsters, from when the world was young. But magic can stir them from their slumber. Magic . . . and Gods."

Her face looked stricken. She cocked the gun. "You're one of them, aren't you? One of the Libiri?"

I shook my head. "No, I'm not part of Kent Hadleigh's little cult. I have no interest in sacrificing you to an old God. That would be such a waste of your soul." I looked her over, catching a glimpse of her scars at the neckline of her shirt. They were ritual marks, cut into her flesh as she was offered up in sacrifice. "And what a beautiful, damaged soul it is."

She began to back away. "What the hell are you then? What do you want?"

"For now, I want nothing at all." I let my eyes shift, and her entire body went tense. I let my claws come out, and my teeth sharpen. She nearly stumbled as she backed away, barely keeping her feet. "But someday, little wolf, I may want everything."

She fired the gun.

The bullet struck my shoulder. It felt like nothing more than a pinch. I looked down at the wound curiously, poking my finger in to dig out the bullet. She watched, in horror, as I dropped the bloodied bit of metal onto the ground.

"My, my, so flirtatious." I chuckled. "Do that again, Juniper, and I might think you want to play."

"What the *fuck* are you?" She was going to run at any moment. She was shaking her head, her brain unable to process what she was seeing.

"You'll see me again," I said. "Survive a few years, Juniper, fight for your life. I like fighters. They make better prey. Survive, and the next time you see me, I may have an offer for you."

"I don't want your offers," she said. "Stay away from me!"

I *tsk*ed. "You say that now. But as the years go on, and the danger keeps coming, you may change your mind. Or you may not." I shrugged. "The choice is always yours. But I *will* see you again. Now, get inside. Get away from the trees. Wait until morning to travel. Juniper Kynes . . ." I crossed the space between us in a second. I stood over her, her wide eyes defiant and terrified as they looked up, and I smiled with a mouthful of sharp teeth. "Run."

She did run, sprinting down the road. The Eld would keep following her, but I'd hold them back, at least for tonight. May as well give the little wolf a fighting chance.

She had more viciousness in her than I'd thought. So much fire, for a human so burned. I'd hunted enough souls to afford to be picky, so I could hunt by my whims rather than necessity.

She would be a fascinating hunt, indeed.

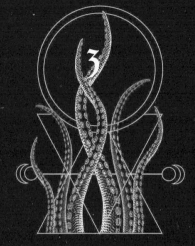

JUNIPER

WHEN ENOUGH PEOPLE tell you you're crazy, you begin to question your own mind. You pick apart your memories, bit by bit, unraveling them until they're disjointed and stained, rearranged, every second doubted. The story I'd told so many times—to rescuers, to police, to my mother, my brother, over and over with increasing desperation—was woven throughout my mind, stitching together who I was back then . . . and whoever I'd become now.

Most people have fantasized about danger: how they would escape, how they would fight, how they'd be too smart to be hurt. But those fantasies are nothing compared to the moment it happens. Sometimes, you can watch danger coming at you like a freight train, and all you can do is stand there. All you can do is let it overtake you.

Sometimes, there's no running, no fighting. Sometimes, bad shit happens.

The bad shit changes you. You can't look at the world the same. You realize that manners, morals, culture, society, friends, and family are all fake. They're ideas we cling to, to make existence bearable. When that's ripped away—the fake optimistic bullshit—the only thing you have left is survival.

Survival is messy. Survival has no morals or kindness. Survival isn't black and white, good versus evil. Survival is shades of red; it's blood taken and blood lost.

My survival was a gun, liquor was my sustenance, and rough sex was my painkiller.

THE DINGY BAR was the closest thing to a club I could find that night. Neon signs hung on the bare wood walls, old license plates were nailed to the ceiling, and pool tables took up the majority of the floor space. I hadn't seen a town for miles on the road, but there must have been one close by because the bar was crowded.

It was late, and the Misfits tribute band playing on stage was almost too drunk to keep singing. I stuck out, about a decade younger than most of the people in there. But I had a gun at my hip and I could whip their asses at pool, so no one had messed with me. Winning those bets on my games was the only way I'd have the money to get gas in the morning, so I was playing a little underhanded to make it happen.

Lie, steal, run. Survive. Survival didn't care about morals.

I lined up my shot, the pool cue perched against my

finger. Someone pressed up against my ass, their hot breath on the back of my neck. A rough hand slid down my arm to rest thick, dirty fingers against my wrist.

"Third game in a row, girl," he said. It was the guy I'd been playing against for the last hour, Will. Big guy, farmworker, bald head and a trimmed beard. "You know, I don't take kindly to giving my money over to a cheater."

I tried to straighten up; his body bent over mine didn't allow it. I sighed heavily and said, "I'm not a cheater, Will. You're just a sore loser."

He yanked me up, gripping my denim jacket tight as he forced me to face him and pressed me back against the table. His friends chuckled, and as my eyes scanned the bar, I saw people looking, but not a single person getting up.

Figured. I'd find no help here.

"Don't you try reaching for that gun, bitch," he said, his breath reeking of liquor and chewing tobacco as he noticed my hand edging for the pistol. "This can go down nice and easy, understand? You can keep all that money, but you're gonna earn it. Hell, my friends and I would love to have you *earn* a little from all of us." Still gripping my jacket, he pressed his fingers against my lips, hard, forcing them into my mouth.

Dumbass. Did he actually think I wouldn't bite?

He jerked his hand back with a yelp, and I spat his blood on the floorboards as I grinned at him. But the hand I'd bit came back with a vengeance, his bare knuckles striking hard against my cheekbone and sending me crumpling to the floor.

Perfect.

"Fucking bitch!" he huffed, wiping his bloody fingers on his jacket. "I'll teach you to fucking bite me—"

I pulled out the gun, aimed, and pulled the trigger.

The back of his head burst open like a watermelon, and chaos erupted around us.

His friends came for me, people ran for the door, and the drunk-as-hell band kept playing as if someone hadn't just been murdered in front of them. But Will was only the first to go down. A pool cue swung toward my head, and I fired again, hitting my mark in the shoulder before my second shot hit between the eyes. I dodged a punch from another, kneed him in the balls, and as he doubled over in front of me, my bullet found its home in the back of his skull.

It didn't matter who died. It didn't matter how much blood was spilled. There was only ever one thing on my mind: survive, in whatever fucked-up ways I needed to.

One bar fight had a way of inspiring others. I was surrounded by mayhem, broken bottles, gunshots, screaming, and cursing. The perfect opportunity to make a quick escape. I rummaged through the pockets of the men I'd shot down, found another hundred-dollar bill and a twenty, and stuffed them in my pockets before I hugged the wall to make my way toward the door.

I'd nearly reached the exit when I was shoved hard from behind—hard enough to knock the wind out of my lungs and send me to the floor. I tried to crawl away, but a hand grasped my ankle and dragged me back.

"You think you're going to get out of this so easily, you fucking—"

The voice choked off into frantic screams, and the hand that had been gripping my ankle suddenly released—only to drop down beside my head, severed, leaking blood across the stained floorboards.

What . . . what the fuck?

I turned. The man who'd grabbed me was gripping his arm, screaming at the stump that remained where his hand had been, but his screams cut off with a gurgle. His throat was slit, leaking blood down onto his white shirt. I stared, wide-eyed, as he dropped to the floor, and the man responsible gave him a little nudge with his foot.

"Well, that's a bit of a mess," he said. He was tall, broad-shouldered, the front of his jacket stained deep red and his hood pulled up. Honey-brown eyes, strangely bright, peered at me from beneath his hood. There were snakebites in his lower lip, the silver rings shining in the light, and a barbell through his eyebrow. His throat, and I assumed the rest of him, was tattooed. He absent-mindedly scratched his bloody fingers on his cheek, before he extended them to help me up. "You good?"

Those eyes were familiar. It tugged at some old memory in me, something hazy and nearly forgotten. Had I met him before?

It didn't matter. I leaped up, ignoring his hand, and sprinted out the door. I didn't have time to exchange words with a hot-as-hell murderer. No, sir. It was time to fucking *go*.

The air outside was hazy with dust, as bar patrons took off from the dirt parking lot at high speed, their trucks tearing down the long, dark road. I ran for my Jeep, yanked open the door, and cranked the engine, pumping the gas to get her going. I set my pistol on the seat, and as I threw the Jeep into reverse, I glanced back at the door . . . and saw the bar owner come outside in a rage, a shotgun in his hands.

Fuck. *Fuck.*

I slammed on the gas, the Jeep's massive tires gaining traction on the dirt, and peeled out onto the road. The bar was in the middle of nowhere, but that meant there was a long, straight drive ahead where I could push the old girl as fast as she could handle.

The trees closed in as I drove, cypress and pine enclosing the road beneath their boughs. The cicadas' song filled the night, and with no streetlights along the old road, only my yellow headlights lit the way. I put a mile between me and the bar, then three, then five. Only then did my heart stop pounding.

The only radio station that came through was playing Delta blues, and I let it play softly as I drove with the windows down, the cold air on my face. I planned to drive through the night; I'd try to make it until noon tomorrow before I stopped. Some people pursued exercise to ease their stress, but I pursued exhaustion. If I could tire myself out utterly and completely, my brain would be too tired to dream.

Too tired for the nightmares.

The jolt of something ramming into the side of the Jeep slammed my head against the door and sent me careening off the road. I slammed on the brakes, managing to bring the vehicle to a stop before I crashed into a tree. I'd hit my head hard enough to bleed, and my vision was spinning as I reached into the backseat, fumbling under the blanket until my fingers touched the cold, smooth barrel of my SPAS-12 shotgun.

Something told me the 9mm pistol wasn't going to cut it for this.

I jumped out of the Jeep, leaving the headlights on so I'd have a little visibility in the dark. The radio was still playing, the slow sad strum of the blues sounding eerie in the darkness under the trees. I searched the shadows, resisting the urge to wipe at the blood slowly dripping down my face. There were too many noises in those trees. Everything creaked and groaned, the cicadas' song forming a chorus with the crickets and the hoot of an owl.

Maybe what had hit me had only been a deer. I'd been driving fast and not paying attention. Maybe . . .

The forest went utterly silent. Only the creaking of the trees remained. The wind shifted, and with it came the smell of death, pungent and sour on the cold air.

I readied the gun as a hulking, misshapen form lurched toward me in the dark.

The Eld looked different everywhere I went. In Abelaum, they resembled bizarre mutated wolves. In New York, they were like massive bloated rats. Here . . . here they looked like goddamn crocodiles.

The creature stepped into the beams of my headlights, its large maw gaping open, lined with rotten teeth. The smell of it was overpowering, like meat left out in the sun in the heat of summer. Its body was long, covered in thick scales, but hunched, as if it wanted to walk upright. Its front legs were too long—bare bones and scaly, moldy flesh. Its back legs were thick, muscular; the thing could probably jump faster than I could shoot.

I had to shoot first.

The shot went off, ringing in my ears, and the beast jumped at me just as I'd anticipated. It gave a deep, guttural snarl as it skidded past me, only barely missing me as I threw myself back. I fired again, the slug striking the monster in the shoulder. I'd waste all my ammo sinking bullets into the beast's body; I needed to hit the head.

I ran, trying to get some distance between us. I thought I was running for the road, but I'd gotten turned around and found myself running deeper into the trees. The Eld beast was right on my heels.

I brought my weapon up as I turned, but I didn't have enough time to aim. I pulled the trigger, and the beast jolted as the bullet hit home, tearing a huge hole in its side and sending gore splattering. It slammed into me and pinned me to the ground as it roared, its jaws snapping inches from my face.

I had to use the gun to hold it back, pressing it against the monster's throat as I tried to get my legs up to kick. I'd underestimated it; these Eld were bigger than the ones I'd encountered before. Its noxious breath wafted around my face, putrid gray saliva dripping from its long, black tongue. My arms were beginning to shake. I couldn't keep this up. I just—I just had to—

I managed to get my leg up, and kicked my boot as

hard as I could against its wounded side. It stumbled away, giving a high-pitched shriek so loud it pierced straight into my eardrums. I scrambled up, but the beast was already lunging for me again.

I fired.

JUNIPER

THE BLAST SPLINTERED the beast's head apart. It went down and curled like a bug, twitching violently before it was still. I exhaled heavily, catching my breath as I watched its body dissolve in mud and worms. They all died the same, these beasts; everything but their skulls rotted away within seconds.

Facing them used to fill me with cold panic. It used to make my heart beat so hard it hurt. But I'd been fighting the Eld for years. I'd once thought they were unique to Abelaum, but no, the Eld were everywhere.

They were drawn to me like flies to honey, but they didn't scare me anymore. There were worse monsters out there, far worse. Monsters like—

"You can hold your own. How cute."

I whirled around, gun at the ready. I didn't know what to expect, but I certainly hadn't been expecting *him*.

That hot murderer from the bar. His clothes were even more bloodstained than before, and there was a dirty smirk on his face as he stepped out of the shadows—the I'll-eat-you-alive-and-laugh-while-I-do type of dirty.

I frowned. "Of course I can. I had myself handled back at the bar too, if you hadn't interrupted."

He held up his hands innocently. Even his palms were tattooed, with elaborate pentagrams and strange runes. "I didn't doubt you. I just wanted a little trouble for myself."

I snorted, but I didn't put the gun away. I knew better than that. "Well, you got it, didn't you? You seem awfully calm for a man who just murdered someone. You do that often?"

He shrugged. "Not often enough to lose that fun, tingling feeling inside. You don't look like you're any stranger to killing either."

I looked down at the mess of fragmented bone, mud, and worms that remained of the Eld beast. The Eld weren't common knowledge. The only people who knew they were real were those unfortunate enough to have encountered them. And if you encountered them, you rarely lived to talk about it.

I glanced back at him skeptically. "Are you familiar with these things?"

"I've seen them around," he said. "You know, if you take one of those skulls in to be examined, they'll tell you it's just a regular old crocodile?"

I nodded. In desperation, I'd collected the skull of an Eld I'd once killed and taken it to a local veterinarian to be examined. If I could prove the monsters existed, then maybe people would start believing me about everything else too. But I had no such luck. The vet told me it was nothing more than a highly decomposed wolf skull.

"You look like you could use a smoke." He held out a slim, hand-rolled joint, but he was smart enough not to take a step toward me. I really needed the high. My alcohol buzz had worn off, and my mind was racing. This guy was a weirdo, and I didn't understand how the hell he'd ended up out here in the woods. But he'd technically saved me back there at the bar, even if I'd never admit it. I didn't see any weapons on him, at least not at a glance, and just one shot from my SPAS would rip him apart. I guess there was no harm in sharing a smoke with him.

I nodded. "Let's get away from here at least. My Jeep is just back there."

"The bayou is up ahead," he said. "Short walk. It's a nice view with the moonlight and all."

I glared at him, adjusting my weapon. "Trying to get me out in the dark alone, pretty boy?"

He held up his hands innocently. "Hey, you're the one with the gun. Pretty sure you've got the advantage."

I pursed my lips in thought. "Lead the way then. But don't try shit. I'll blast your head off too."

"I'll be chaste as a saint," he said, pressing his hands together in a mock prayer as I followed him. I rolled my eyes. Typical. A hot liar. What a shock.

It took only a few minutes to reach the water. The trees opened up and the marshy river stretched out before us, shimmering with silver moonlight. He sat down near the roots of a cypress and leaned back against the trunk, pulled out a lighter, and lit up.

"What's your name?" he said, as the herbaceous odor of marijuana wafted around us.

"What's yours?" I didn't like giving out personal information, even so far from home. No matter how far I went, my past would follow me. I dreaded speaking my name only to see recognition in someone's eyes.

Juniper, the girl who went missing? I thought you were locked up. I thought you were crazy. Seen any monsters lately? Didn't you try to kill—

"Zane," he said, passing over the joint. I took a long, slow drag, savoring the taste. It had been too long since I'd had good weed. "And you don't need to tell me, if you don't want to. I get the need for anonymity."

"Are you local?" I said, coughing a bit as I passed it back. He shook his head.

"Nope." He let the smoke cascade from his lips, around his face. It was probably just the weed talking, but damn, he looked good. Those honey-brown eyes, so oddly familiar, seemed to glow with golden flecks. He passed the joint back, and gazed out across the water. He had a strong jaw, and there were more tattoos beneath his buzzed hair.

"Where are you from then?"

"Here and there. Everywhere. Hell, originally."

I shook my head, but I couldn't hold back a smile at the smartass bastard. "Oh, yeah? Why'd you leave? Couldn't take the heat?"

He shrugged. "All the monsters are here on Earth. Figured I'd join them. What about you? Where are you from?"

I hesitated. "Washington."

"Beautiful place. I have a friend there. He's a lot like you actually."

The weed was making my head pleasantly hazy, the usual ache melting away from my muscles. It was the closest I'd felt to relaxed in a long time. "Like me? How's that?"

"He's been through shit," he said. "It made him bitter. Angry. A little murderous." He shrugged. "But damn, all that anger makes him a good fuck."

I laughed. I couldn't help it. "There's really nothing like a hate-fuck, is there?"

"No, there really isn't."

We sat for a while, sharing the silence and what remained of the joint. Between the moonlight on the water, the crickets chirping in the brush, and the high, I was feeling really damn good. So good that I began to let my eyes wander over that fine-as-hell body seated next to me. He'd kept his word; he wasn't getting handsy. But when I looked, I could see the bulge in his jeans. And goddamn was it a *bulge*.

"You're really not going to make a move, are you?" I said.

He glanced over at me. In the strange light, between the silver moon and the red cherry on the joint, I could have sworn his eyes were molten gold, like the sun right before it sets.

"Why?" That filthy grin was back on his face. "Are you just waiting for me to take advantage of you?"

I rolled my eyes and ran my tongue over my lips. "Why don't you find out?"

He shifted. I was seated on the ground, cross-legged, and he moved so that he was crouched next to me. He was tall enough that he could still look down at me like that. "Dangerous words, from a woman with a gun."

I smirked, picked up the weapon, and aimed it at his head. "Scared?"

Oh, that grin was *wicked*.

He grabbed my ankle and yanked me. I found myself flat on my back beneath him, as his one hand pinned my arm that held the gun and the other gripped my throat with just enough pressure to keep me in place. He leaned close, his lips inches from mine. His scent was intoxicating, like weed and whiskey, like brown sugar and smoke.

Below the silver barbell through his eyebrow, I noticed a tiny tattoo of St. Peter's cross. His gaze burned over me until it settled, smoldering, on my eyes. "Are you really prepared to face the consequences of what you just said?"

"Please don't hurt me, mister," I said, a smile on my lips despite the squeeze of his hand. "I'm just an innocent girl."

He chuckled, deep in his chest. "Oh, you're anything but innocent. And hurting you is exactly what I'm going to do."

It's strange to be haunted by dreams of pain and death, only to wake up and desperately seek the same things. Call it a kink, a fetish, whatever—I couldn't escape the desire to take the very things that had hurt me and make them mine, control them, *use* them. Maybe someday it would make them less frightening. Maybe one day it would make the nightmares stop.

Monsters were real and Gods were evil, so the world was already going to Hell, regardless of my weird sexual turn-ons.

His mouth pressed to mine and my lips parted for him, drinking in his taste like it was the first shot of whiskey on a cold night. He squeezed my throat as he kissed me, his nails digging into my skin, far sharper than I'd expected. His tongue moved against mine, and I could feel the smooth, rounded metal of a tongue piercing— not one but *two*—and gave a soft moan as he bit my lip. Breathless, our mouths parted, but only so he could whisper, "Aww, did you really think I'd be that gentle?"

He reached down, his hand still tight around my throat as he tugged at my jeans, popping the buttons open. He rubbed his palm roughly over my panties, squeezing his hand tighter around my neck as he growled, "I feel that wet spot down there, girl. What a sick little slut. You really wanted to get taken advantage of in the middle of the woods by a stranger? Such a badass little bitch until you've got dick on your mind."

If he'd said that to me back at the bar, I would have slapped him. But being degraded as he slipped his hand into my panties, his fingers encountering the wetness soaking through the cloth, was just one more bizarre thing I could add to my list of fucked-up turn-ons. He rubbed his fingers over my clit, my legs twitching as the stimulation jerked at my nerves.

When he pressed two fingers inside me, slick with my arousal, I gasped sharply and choked back the whimper that tried to escape. He pressed his forehead to mine, so I couldn't avoid his eyes or the sight of that wicked smile, pumping his fingers into me as he said, "Don't close your eyes now, girl. Are you trying to hold back those cute little sounds from me? Hm?"

I didn't understand how the hell he knew I was holding back, but when his fingers curled inside me, any attempts at silencing myself were useless. He pressed against that deep spot that instantly tightened my abdomen, my legs squeezing together at the stimulation. He slid his knees out, using his legs to spread mine and *keep* them spread out. He hadn't even gotten my jeans off my ankles and he already had me soaking my panties, about to orgasm on his fingers.

The sounds he was forcing out of me were pathetic, and they were increasing in volume. The louder I was, the more he began to laugh, and the more I began to think that his teeth looked a hell of a lot sharper than they had before. But it was dark, every nerve in me was throbbing, and because I'd tried so hard to hold back, my orgasm only hit me harder when it came.

For a moment, I forgot how to breathe. He didn't stop pumping his fingers into me, he didn't stop massaging his palm against my swollen clit or curling his fingers up to hit that spot. I couldn't stop myself; I gushed over his hand. God, the way he laughed at me, taunting me for breaking apart as if I had a choice, was too goddamn hot. He withdrew his fingers to suck the digits clean in his mouth.

"Fuck, you taste good," he murmured. He pressed his fingers past my lips, over my tongue, so I could taste myself on his skin. I moaned as he pushed his fingers deep into my mouth, far enough that my eyes began to water and I tried not to choke at the depth.

"Too much for you yet?" I gagged and he pulled his fingers back to slap them against my cheek—a sting that instantly made me smile. "Tell me to stop if it is."

If I'd wanted him to stop, I would have bashed him across the head with the gun, but stopping was the last thing on my mind.

I was about to mouth off, about to challenge him, but it was as if he sensed it coming. He flipped me over to my stomach, straddled me, and ground his hips down against my bare ass as he scratched his nails down my back. God, even through his jeans, I could tell he was thick, and I could have sworn the man had claws from the scratches he left behind.

"I'm going to fucking wreck that little pussy." He brought his voice close to my ear, and gripped my ass tight. I tried to look back at him, but he forced my head down against the dirt.

"I've heard that one before," I said breathlessly. "I'll see if you can actually follow through."

As if he hadn't just made me soak my panties squirting. As if I wasn't still dizzy from the orgasm.

"Oh, is that how it is?" He chuckled, low and dark. "If I don't follow through, feel free to shoot me in the fucking head, because frankly, I deserve it if you get up with that bitchy mouth of yours still capable of speech."

I heard the movement of his belt, the sound of his zipper sliding down. With one hand keeping the nape of my neck pinned, he used the other to tug my hips up, forcing my lower back to arch before he pressed that thick cock inside me.

I cried out and bit down on my wrist curled beneath my head at the stretch of him entering me. *Fuck*, his size wasn't normal. Even slick as I was, so turned on I could hardly think straight, he was almost too big to fit. Every inch stretched me; every inch ached.

"Ah . . . fuck . . ." My voice broke on the words, and he reached around to grip my face as he pressed fully inside me.

"Going to beg for mercy?" he growled, squeezing my cheeks.

I would have snapped at his hand if his grip wasn't so tight. But all I managed to grind out instead was, "No."

All preamble was gone now. He pounded into me and I squeezed around him, throbbing on that knife's edge between pain and pleasure. The hand he'd used to grip my face now forced my mouth open, and two fingers pressed on my tongue. His opposite hand slipped beneath me, teasing my clit as his cock punished me, another orgasm swelling uncontrollably. My cries heightened in pitch; every effort I made to stay quiet only made it worse—better—I didn't know anymore.

He bit down on my shoulder, hard enough to break the skin. The sharp, stinging pain made me moan, and

I shuddered as his tongue moved hungrily over the bite. My legs were shaking, my deep gasping breaths weren't enough. His cock throbbed inside me, an animalistic growl rising in him with every thrust. The thought of him coming inside me, filling me, turned me on too much. Pulling out be damned, I wanted this freak's cum dripping out of me for the rest of the night.

His brutal cock and his fingers on my clit had me writhing in the dirt. He was close, because he released my face to pull up my hips with both hands, fucking into me with urgency. With my head no longer restrained, I looked back at him right as I came, right as his cock throbbed inside me.

I wanted to see his face. I wanted to see the pleasure on it. I wanted to see how he looked as he fucked me.

What I saw instead was that his honey-brown eyes were molten gold. There were rows of sharp teeth between his pierced, parted lips. There were thick black veins in his hands and neck. The angles of his face were sharpened, his muscles swollen. Sharp dark claws dug into my hips, rivulets of blood dripping down from where they were sunk into me.

"Fuck—"

I saw what he was and I still orgasmed on his cock. I still shuddered uncontrollably as he spilled inside me, gripping me tighter as he reached his own peak. But the moment his hold loosened, I kicked myself out from under him and scrambled back, trying to catch my breath as I shouldered the shotgun and aimed.

I remembered him. I knew where I'd seen him before.

He knelt there on the ground, his head tipped back, a smile full of sharp, wicked teeth on his face. His cock . . . fuck, no wonder it had felt so unnatural. *Everything* about him was unnatural, but his dick was thick and ridged, swollen on the sides and beneath, the head slightly slanted and cherry red. I shook my head, cocking the gun as he opened his eyes and fixed me with that gaze.

"Remember me now, little wolf?"

Cold dread rose in me. The night I'd fled Abelaum remained in my memory in only bits and pieces. I'd gone into a diner. I'd pointed the gun I'd stolen from Mom's trailer at the poor waiter, because I was so hungry and had no money, and I didn't know what the hell to do. I'd been followed that night, the Eld stalking through the woods alongside me. I hadn't known what they were at the time.

He'd told me. This man, this . . . *monster*. He'd told me what they were.

"Aww, what? Do I scare you?" He opened his mouth, and extended his tongue. I was right about the piercings, but it was more than that: his tongue was forked, and each side was pierced. "I really hate that disguise. It's such a fucking bother. But if I didn't use it, all you humans would be running away from me, screaming." He paused. "Oh, wait . . . I like it when you run and scream."

I couldn't pull up my jeans and aim at the same time, so I sat butt-naked on the ground and didn't lower my gun. "Tell me what you are, now, or I'll blast your head off."

"You can't kill me with that thing. You should know that from last time."

Last time, I'd seen my bullet enter his body and it hadn't even made him flinch. I'd watched him dig it out like he couldn't feel pain. But I didn't lower my weapon. "I can damn well try. This gun is a hell of a lot bigger than the last one."

He stared me down, that shit-eating grin on his face. "It's been a few years since you last saw me. Surely, you've done your research. I think you *know* what I am."

I swallowed hard. I tried not to think about it. I tried not to remember. But he wasn't the first of his kind I'd encountered. Those golden eyes, the sharp teeth, the claws . . .

The night the Libiri had tried to kill me, the night I'd crawled out of the darkness of the mine and fled through the forest, a being like him had pursued me through the dark. Relentless, merciless; I knew Kent Hadleigh had sent it after me to take me back.

It would have dragged me back to the mine if it had caught me. It would have thrown me back into the dark.

Of course I'd done my research. I had combed through old websites, locked forums, dusty long-forgotten books in the backs of libraries. I'd hoarded those rare gems of knowledge from amongst the rubble of conspiracy and hearsay, trying to make sense of this fucked-up world I lived in.

"Demon," I said, spitting out the word. "You're not the first one I've met. Is that the *friend* in Washington you mentioned, hm? Do you serve Kent Hadleigh too?"

"I told you last time: I work for me, myself, and I," he said. He rose to his feet, and I scrambled up too, trying to tug up my jeans and aim simultaneously.

"Juniper Kynes," he drawled. "The girl who got away. The sacrifice who . . . wasn't. A soul who escaped from a God." He chuckled. He was walking toward me, and his face was changing as he did. The molten gold in his eyes cooled to honey-brown. The thick black veins in his throat disappeared, his teeth shortened and lost their sharpness. His claws disappeared. I was backing away, trying not to trip over gnarled roots and fallen branches.

But he took it one step further; even his tattoos were disappearing. His eyes were widening. He was just some boy-next-door, pretty and innocent, wide-eyed and sweet. But his smile was filthy, no matter what he did. "I've kept my eye on you, since that night. Does this face look familiar? Maybe you've seen it in a crowd, in a club, on the side of the road. But you probably didn't even notice, did you?"

He'd been stalking me. All this time, these last three years, he'd been following me. It was horrifying that a monster like that could blend in so perfectly, but of course he could. Predators had to camouflage themselves to get close to their prey.

Demons disguised themselves to make people feel safe, they made themselves attractive to draw us in—only so they could manipulate us, their prey, into giving up everything. Body and soul.

"I didn't think much of you when I first saw you, Juniper. Frankly, I didn't think you'd survive this long. But I told you we'd meet again. You really are a fascinating little mortal specimen. You should have died so many times, and yet . . . you just . . . keep . . . *going*. Impressive. Very impressive."

I stumbled, but my back struck the trunk of a tree and I pressed myself there. There was nowhere else to go.

I couldn't run. He'd catch me.

I couldn't hide. He'd smell me.

I could shoot, but that wouldn't kill him.

He sauntered up and leaned one hand against the tree over my head. The muzzle of my gun was pressed against his chest, and he didn't give a fuck.

"What the hell do you want?" I said. I should have shot him right then and there, but something kept me from doing it, something I didn't fully understand and definitely couldn't explain.

"You."

That simple word felt like a block of ice had been dropped on my stomach. He leaned down, and again, I could have pulled the trigger. I should have. Perhaps some bizarre curiosity kept me from doing it, but it wasn't fear.

The thing was, if he'd wanted to kill me, he would have done it by now.

He leaned down and whispered in my ear, "I've made my intentions clear. Now it's your turn. When you're sick of running, come find me. Until then, stay alive, little wolf. I want to play with you again."

I DROVE THROUGH the night in silence, the radio off, the windows up. My rage was growing, slowly, the pressure building until it burst. My pussy ached, my clit throbbed with lingering ecstasy. I slammed my fist against the steering wheel. "God fucking *damnit*!"

I'd done a lot of risky shit in the last few years, but tonight took the cake. I'd grown so numb to danger and risks, sometimes the fairly obvious ones went right over my head: like fucking a stranger in the middle of the woods at night. Most people would balk; I'd begged for it.

I hadn't even brought up a goddamn condom, even though I always had a few stored in my glovebox, just in case. I spent too many long nights in bars and clubs to not come prepared, not that it had done me any good tonight. When I reached the next town, I stopped at the first twenty-four-hour pharmacy I could find and picked up a pack of morning-after pills. The last thing I needed was to get knocked up with some demonic baby, if that was even possible.

He'd been following me. He'd followed me all this way from Abelaum. How many places had I encountered him, without even knowing? How many times had our eyes met? How many times had he gotten close and I'd been none the wiser?

It should have been terrifying, and yet, he didn't scare me. Not in the way I expected.

It was only in daylight, as I reached the next city and finally slowed the Jeep's speed, that I noticed a small white scrap of paper tucked against my dashboard. I pulled into the next gas station, and as it was pumping, I plucked up the paper and found words scrawled messily across it. *For business or pleasure. When you're ready to make a deal, call me.*

A phone number was scribbled beneath it.

A deal with a demon. A deal for anything I wanted, in exchange for all that I had left. I should have thrown that scrap of paper away. I should have forgotten all about him and kept running. Running, like I always had.

But I kept the paper. I tucked it away in my wallet, and when the nights were darkest and I was drunk and alone, I thought about it. I thought about what would be worth a deal with a demon.

I thought about his taste, his smell, his tongue, far more than I should have.

I thought about revenge, and I thought about home— the place I swore I'd never go back to.

But I would go back. A lot sooner than I thought.

JUNIPER

THE HOSPITAL ROOM felt stagnant, stuck in a loop of the same soft sounds: the steady beep of my heart monitor, the tap of the rain on the window, the shuffle of the nurses' shoes as they walked through the hall. They rarely came in to check on me anymore. They were quick and silent when they did. They gave me pills to make the nightmares stop, pills to help me remember what really happened to me.

But the nightmares didn't stop, and my memories didn't change.

If I could just talk to the police again, they'd believe me. They had to. If I could just talk to another doctor, they'd realize I wasn't imagining this.

I jerked my head toward the door, but it wasn't a nurse who had just walked in. It was Marcus, his hands shoved into the pockets of his windbreaker, hesitating before he walked any closer.

"Hey, bro." My voice sounded so weak. I needed water. I'd needed water for the last hour, but no one responded when I pressed the call button.

"Hey." He came over to the bedside, his eyes roaming around like he didn't know where to look. He'd always been a good kid: quiet, studious. Nothing like me. When Mom yelled, he didn't yell back. There was a chair behind him, but he didn't sit down.

"I'm surprised Mom let you come." I tried to smile, to lighten the statement, but it still felt as heavy as a brick. Mom hadn't been here, not since the first day I'd woken up. Not since I'd overheard her conversation with the doctor in the hall, and heard her say desperately, "Well, how the hell am I supposed to afford that? Just having her here is putting me into debt, now I'm supposed to keep her medicated?"

"Mom doesn't know." He glanced back toward the door. He was only thirteen; he'd probably ridden his bike here. "Are you feeling any better?"

"Getting there." I scowled down at the IVs in my arm. "I'd be a lot better without all these fucking needles."

He was shuffling his feet as he pulled his hand out of his pocket, handing over a snack-size bag of Hot Cheetos. I grabbed it as if he'd brought me a bar of pure gold. "Nathan said that they wouldn't let him have Hot Cheetos when his appendix was taken out, and I know how much you love these things . . ."

"Holy crap, yes!" I tore open the bag, tossing several of the puffed, spicy snacks into my mouth. "Oh my God. You're a lifesaver."

He smiled tightly, finally sitting down, perched right at the edge of the seat. "So, uh . . . are you . . . I mean . . ." He swallowed hard. "Are you feeling okay to come home?"

"I have to talk to the police again," I said. "They thought I imagined it because of the acid, but it wasn't the acid." I shook my head. "I know what happened. I remember it, everything." I nodded quickly, even though talking about it made my chest tight. The heart monitor had begun to beep more rapidly. "They'll believe me this time. They will."

Marcus was biting his lip. He wasn't looking at me. My heart sunk. "You . . . you believe me . . . don't you?"

His foot was tapping anxiously against the floor. "I don't know, Juni. It's . . . you know . . . everyone says . . ."

"Who's everyone?" I snapped. "Who the hell is everyone, and why do you believe them instead of me?"

He looked stricken. He fumbled for a moment, and pulled out his phone. When he held up the screen for me, a video from the local news was playing. The heart monitor sped up even more. It was Victoria, speaking into the microphone held up to her face.

"She just ran off into the forest," she said. Her eyes were wide, innocently confused. Her makeup was pristine. She was wearing a goddamn blazer. "We just wanted to experiment, you know? I thought it would be chill, but she started acting like things were chasing her. She was screaming at me to get away from her, saying I was trying to kill her. Then she started cutting herself, it was—God." She choked up, covering her mouth with her

hand. Fake. Fucking fake *tears. "It was so awful. I just want her to be okay."*

I clenched my jaw as the video ended. Marcus still wasn't looking at me.

"I didn't do this to myself, Marcus," I said softly. "Please. Please believe me. I didn't." He got up, his phone shoved back into his pocket. He walked fast, his head down, back toward the door. "Marcus, please! Don't . . . don't leave!"

He stopped. The fluorescent light above my bed was flickering, giving off an annoying buzz of electricity. Marcus sighed heavily. "It's too late, Juni."

I shook my head. "No . . . What are you talking about? It's not too late, I—"

The light went out. I stared up at it, utterly confused as I watched the faint, lingering glow of the fluorescent bulb behind its thin plastic cover. The room was quiet. Way too quiet.

My heart monitor had stopped.

I stared at its blank, empty screen. Beyond the monitor, rain was no longer falling against the window. Instead, condensation was rapidly growing across the glass. The water dripped down, collecting along the sill, beginning to leak to the floor.

I could smell seawater. Mold. Wet dirt. I looked back at Marcus, and he wasn't facing away from me anymore. He was looking directly at me, and his eyes were white . . . his jaw was slack. I screamed as I looked down and realized that thick gray tentacles were coiling up his legs, around his chest, engulfing him—

"No!" I tried to tear the IVs out of my arms. I tried to get up from the bed to help him, but I was strapped down. My arms, my legs. I couldn't reach him. "Marcus, run!"

"It's too late, Juni." The voice didn't even come from his own mouth. It echoed all around me as the tentacles pushed into his open mouth, into his eyes. "It's too late."

I JOLTED AWAKE, panting, sweat chilling my skin. It was just before dawn, the wide-open sky colored pale yellow and cold blue. My back ached from having slept in the Jeep, but I was too tense to stretch. My heart was pounding. I was freezing.

I turned on the engine and cranked up the heater, leaning my head against the steering wheel. I'd slept early the night before instead of putting it off as long as possible like I usually did. But I'd been hungry and the money I had left covered my gas, but not food. Sleeping seemed like the only good way to stave off the hunger, but it meant I had more hours to dream.

God, I hated the dreams.

My hunger was back with a vengeance too. My stomach felt like it was trying to consume itself, but after that nightmare, the thought of food was nauseating. It would be better if I just started driving. Maybe after a few hours, my stomach would settle.

I glanced over at my phone, sitting on the passenger seat. A text notification greeted me on the screen and I picked it up with a frown. Probably some stupid spam message . . .

It was Mom.

My mouth went dry. I'd honestly thought she'd lost my number a long time ago. She never texted. She never called. I could have died years ago, and she wouldn't have known or cared. I think, in her mind, I died the night I went missing in the woods.

Part of me didn't even want to read her text. Part of me just wanted to ignore it.

Part of me really, desperately, hoped that maybe my own mother still cared about me.

I unlocked the screen and read.

I don't know if this is even your number anymore.
Marcus is dead.
If you care.
Funeral is Sunday. Don't cause any fucking problems
if you show up.

I think I blacked out, there on the side of the road, staring at the vast fields surrounding me but not seeing them at all. I think I forgot how to breathe. My lungs closed up, and my mind emptied, and all I could see was my little brother, standing there helplessly, telling me it was too late as those tentacles wrapped around him.

No. *No.*

My fingers numb with dread, I looked up Abelaum's local news and saw him emblazoned across the headlines.

Abelaum University's Promising Soccer Captain Found Dead.

Murder on Abelaum University Campus, Investigation Ongoing.

No Suspects in Brutal Campus Stabbing.

The scream of rage that came out of me felt like it was physically ripped from my chest. The sobs that followed took the air from my lungs. They smothered me. They weren't enough to release the helpless rage inside me. I beat the steering wheel with my fist until my fingers ached, until purple bruises began to bloom on my skin.

No suspects. No fucking suspects. Such absolute bullshit. My brother had been stabbed multiple times, in the middle of a university building, and they dared to say they had no suspects.

The police didn't need to be suspicious because they *knew*. Marcus had always been good; he'd never gotten into trouble or gone running into dangerous situations like I had. But he was my brother, and when the God demanded blood, It would get blood.

The Hadleighs were behind this. I *knew* they were.

All these years I'd been running, I'd thought I'd outsmarted them. They'd never find me, they'd never track me down. As long as I kept moving, as long as I laid low, as long as I didn't tell anyone my name, I'd survive.

But now . . . now I'd survived, and Marcus had died in my place.

The police would drop this investigation the moment they could. They were already in Kent Hadleigh's back pocket. I knew how it went; I'd been through it. I'd told them my story again and again, until it was all mixed up in my head, and they told me it never fucking happened.

They told me the church never happened; there were no white cloaks and skull masks. They told me the mine never happened; the shaft had been boarded up for decades. They told me there were no monsters in the dark and no demons pursuing me; it was only the drugs, and I had a problem, and I needed help.

But they were wrong. It had been real. I had the scars to prove it.

It should have been me. As I dug my nails into my palms, sobs wracking my chest, that thought sunk its cruel claws deep into my head: *It should have been me. It was supposed to be me.*

I didn't have to go back, but that was the direction I started driving. Dead was dead, and I didn't want to see my mother. I didn't want to cry at a funeral or see my brother's waxen face in a casket.

I didn't want to go back to Abelaum to mourn. I wanted to go back to do what everyone else refused to do. Accusations didn't help. Authorities didn't help. I'd been running for years thinking I'd gotten away, but God finds a way to take what It wants regardless.

It took my brother. The God, the Hadleighs, all their sick little followers—they operated without fear. They killed without hesitation. They hid in plain sight because they thought no one would dare defy them. After all, they had a God on their side. Who could dare defy a God?

Me. I could. I'd defied It before, and I'd do it again.

There would be no justice unless I took it myself.

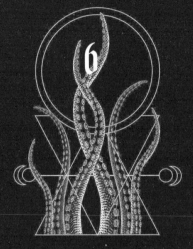

JUNIPER

IT WAS ANOTHER world in Abelaum.

The mist lingered in the streets longer than it should have, rebelling against the sun and blocking out its warmth. The brick buildings dripped with the damp, moss crept over the sidewalks and clung to the houses. The bay was still, its surface like glass, a mirror image of the trees that surrounded it cast upon its surface.

From the outside, Abelaum looked like a safe, peaceful place to live. But behind the facade of hip cafes and microbreweries, there was an unease that had people scurrying inside after dark. Rumors of missing hikers were passed around over brunch. Elementary school students traded local legends like Pokémon cards.

The trees, too, were strange. It was the way their gnarled roots coiled up out of the earth, as if they were trying to escape. I knew what lurked beneath those trees.

I knew the danger that waited for sundown, that hid in shadows. But danger didn't only wait in darkness. It walked in daylight too, in expensive Italian suits, with a charming smile and a pristine family, always above suspicion.

This town was full of monsters.

RAIN POURED DOWN during the funeral. The thunder that reverberated overhead and the flashes of lightning in the clouds felt like God was laughing: laughing at my fear, my pain, my useless struggling. Like a cat toying with a mouse. This was perhaps the greatest joke of all: no matter how far I'd run, It still made me come back here.

I kept my distance from the funeral. I'd scaled the iron fence that guarded Westchurch Cemetery, but stayed beneath the trees, the hood of my black raincoat pulled low over my head. From there, I could look down on the lines of plastic chairs sheltered beneath white canopies, overlooking the rectangular hole cut into the grass.

The tears that wanted to come were locked inside, behind a wall of fury so thick not even grief could slip through.

I watched as they closed the casket and lowered Marcus down. From a distance, his face looked normal. Like he was sleeping. It had been years since I'd seen him in person. I'd only seen his photos on Facebook, his pictures from prom, his wide smile when he got promoted to soccer captain. I should have known how much danger he was in. Jeremiah Hadleigh was on the team with him.

I'd seen their group photos together. I'd seen them tag each other in Facebook posts.

I should have known. I should have warned him.

But he wouldn't have believed me.

My mother was there, seated in the front row, her long brown hair streaked with gray. She was thinner than I remembered her, hunched in her seat, silent and still as she stared at the coffin. She'd done the same thing when Dad left: just sat at the kitchen table and stared, stared as if whatever life that had been inside her was gone.

I think when you lose someone, a little part of yourself goes with them, and never returns.

But where Marcus had gone—no life, no love, no peace could wait for him there.

Nearly all the kids in Abelaum knew the legends, but I knew they were *true*. A God in the mine had made a deal with three men: they could live, but in six generations, they had to pay back God's mercy. Three lives spared must one day be three souls given.

The survivors lived on. They had their families. They had children, grandchildren, great-grandchildren. On and on. Abelaum had been built on that old mine, so half the town could trace their ancestry to its workers. The survivors' story became myth. But always, in the shadows, those who were devoted to the Deep One continued their work. They gathered new worshippers, they watched and waited. They waited for the day the sacrifices could be given.

And now, here we were: The sixth generation. The sacrificial lambs.

As the mourners got up from their chairs and began to disperse, my mother stood alone by the grave. She buried her face in her hands, and my stomach twisted as someone came to her side. Tall and slim, with slick silver hair and a fitted black suit, Kent Hadleigh put his arm around her shoulders and let her weep into his chest.

I was armed and I was confident I could make the shot. My hand wouldn't shake as I took aim at his head, my finger wouldn't hesitate to pull the trigger. It wouldn't end it, but it'd be a damn good start.

My fingers brushed against the pistol strapped to my side, caressing its cold surface. God, the satisfaction I'd feel to see his blood and brains sprayed out on the ground. I couldn't look at him and not see him as he had been that night: cloaked in white, fitting a stag-skull mask over his head, merciless to my cries.

I was meant to be the sacrifice, but when they couldn't have me, they'd taken Marcus.

I lowered my hand. I left the gun alone. Killing Kent now would start a war I wasn't prepared for. At least not yet.

AROUND MIDNIGHT, THE clouds began to clear. The cold starry sky stared down at the little graveyard, the damp grass, the mist creeping in from the trees. I hated funerals: the sobbing, the ceremony, the empty words given by preachers, the choked-up speeches. But in the quiet night, watching my brother's grave from afar, I felt like I could truly say good-bye.

Marcus, after all, had always been quiet. It hurt to think that I didn't know if he'd stayed that way. But as a child, he'd always been careful with his words. He'd never been quick to anger. He'd been thoughtful; the kind of kid who'd pluck dandelions and give them to me on my birthday. I'd always believed that living with Mom would break him, enduring her anger and her sadness. I thought he'd get caught up in that same cycle of pain.

I'd never know if he was happy. I'd never know if he stayed kind. Part of me hoped he hadn't changed, and maybe that was selfish of me. People never stayed how you found them. Over minutes, hours, months, years— the people you've met become strangers, and you have to meet them all over again.

It was strange, honestly; the pain I felt was based on memories of a person I didn't know anymore. He and I only had a past.

They'd taken everything. The Hadleigh family, and the cult they commanded, didn't need to kill me to take my life. I was a dead woman walking. What was left? A mother who hated me, no future, no home, no hope. Just a fury so deep and dark and burning that it could rival a God.

I was getting tired, but I didn't want to sleep. I planned to stay out under the trees all night, and in the morning, maybe I'd have some semblance of direction again. I'd never had a plan in life, because plans couldn't account for Gods and monsters. But now, I felt like I needed one. I needed something solid, something to grasp, something to light up the dark.

The dark had been closing in for so long I couldn't even see out of it anymore.

The mist had crept in across the grass, shrouding Marcus's grave. It was late in the night, and the streets were empty. It was probably safe for me to go down and sit with him for a while, but it felt too intimate. I didn't deserve to be so close to him.

Then, near the grave, something moved.

I went utterly still, every muscle tensing. Goose bumps prickled up my back as I watched a dark figure move across the lawn. Blond hair . . . tattooed skin . . . golden eyes.

Panic burst through me. My limbs twitched and every nerve tingled, demanding I run. My lungs felt like they were being squeezed between cold, rough hands. I didn't dare move. If I even breathed too hard, he'd hear it.

What the hell was Kent Hadleigh's pet demon doing here?

I kept every breath as slow and measured as possible, despite my initial instinct to hold it. I rested my hand against my gun, despite knowing that a bullet wouldn't kill him. My mind was racing: run . . . hide . . . fight . . . or wait.

I waited, keeping myself still in the shadows. He'd see me if he glanced my way. Wild paranoia that Kent had sent him after me made my heart pound painfully, but Kent couldn't possibly know I was back in Abelaum; not even my mother knew.

The demon wandered, glancing at graves as he passed them, before he reached the freshly turned earth that was

Marcus's resting place. Anger made my skin burn as he stopped and read the headstone . . . and began to dig into the grave.

I bit my tongue in an effort not to yell. My nails gripped tight against the tree behind me, as if I could anchor myself there. If I ran at him, if I tried to fight him, he would make quick and careless work of me. Fantasies of shooting him, of managing to kill him, abounded in my mind, but they were only that—fantasies.

I had to be patient. Now, more than ever, I had to bide my time.

The demon kept digging, his eyes like beacons in the night. I heard those wicked claws scratch into the wood when he reached the coffin, and I had to force myself not to look away as the demon pulled my brother from his grave and hauled him over his shoulder.

"Wakey, wakey," he said, and crawled up from the hole to dump Marcus limply in the grass. "Just give me a minute here, buddy. Can't have your mother knowing her son's grave has been desecrated."

God, it made me sick. I'd kill him for this, I'd blast his fucking head off. But even in my fury, I knew the demon was merely a tool. Kent Hadleigh commanded him.

But why steal his body?

The demon hauled Marcus over his shoulder, as if he were nothing more than a sack of meat to be thrown around. My stomach twisted, and rage burned in my throat, but I had to shut it out. I had to keep still, I had to wait and watch. Only when the demon was gone, long out of my sight, did I allow myself to slam my clenched fist against the tree trunk, choking down the screams that wanted to come out with it.

The Hadleighs had sealed their fate when they failed to kill me. They pounded the first nail into their own coffin when they killed Marcus. They hammered the second one home when they stole his body.

I was going to kill them all. No matter what it took. No matter what I had to give up.

No matter what deals had to be made.

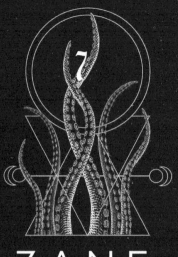

ZANE

I'D BEEN HUNTING souls for over five centuries.

It was lucrative work, and had a way of becoming easier the longer you've done it. Bring one soul back to Hell, and you gain power. Bring two souls back to Hell, your power doubles. And so on.

Collect enough souls, and Hell begins to afford you certain luxuries: human money, specifically. It became far easier to convince humans to trust me when I could impress them with expensive things.

But the best hunts weren't easy. I didn't want them to be; I welcomed the thrill of a challenge. Perhaps that was why I'd become so drawn to the oddities, the weirdos, the murderous little freaks. Perhaps that was why I longed for their souls most of all.

Dear fucking Lucifer, I did love a killer.

Human or demon, it didn't matter: a being with blood

on their hands and a smile on their face just did it for me. Vicious little mortals were rarely a threat to *me*; but damn they were cute, and their souls had a unique weight to them that I adored.

I liked *cute* things. I liked to crush them and break them and see what would become of all the jagged little pieces. Perhaps my definition of *cute* was just a little different.

Juniper Kynes, for example. Adorable. Murderous. Vicious. And bound to be mine.

I'd been hunting her for four years now. I wouldn't call myself *obsessed*—that sounded messy. *Intrigued* was more accurate. *Determined*, perhaps. After all, there came a point in every hunt where it was up to the prey to make their move. I couldn't simply take her soul; she had to give it willingly.

I'd waited years for my little wolf to stop running. I knew she would. She couldn't resist forever.

A wolf needs a pack. A wolf can't hunt alone.

All she had to do was text me four simple words: I want to talk.

I smiled when I saw the message pop up on my cell.

Business or pleasure? I'm a busy demon, no time for small talk.

Fuck you. I laughed aloud, and waited. She wouldn't make a second of this easy, and that's what I liked: a challenge. I wanted to fight for it.

Then, I want to make a deal.

It was a good thing I was alone, because my human disguise instantly slipped. I couldn't hide my claws when I was so eager to get them into her. Name the time and place.

Joanie's Bar, in Blackhook, near the coast. Come late.

I SUPPOSE SHE felt safe in the tiny town she chose. It was miles from Abelaum, hugging the cold coast, a few streets of houses and several old businesses, half of the buildings abandoned. Fishing boats lined the small marina, and Joanie's Bar was perched above that.

I was too eager, and I got there before she did. It was a tiny place, the walls lined with photos of fishermen with their catches. I took a table in the back corner, where I could survey the room, watching as the humans mingled at the bar and quietly sipped pints in their booths. They'd given me a few odd looks, but no trouble. Instinct told them to keep their distance.

Blackhook was nearly two hours from Abelaum, but it still wasn't exempt from the God's influence. The Deep One's tainted essence could still be felt here, pungent in the air, like an ever-present odor of mold and rotten fish. Those who lived here likely didn't even notice. But Abelaum's rot had spread, as rot always does.

Especially now that Kent and his Libiri had succeeded in offering their first sacrifice.

All of Abelaum was talking about it: the sad fate of Juniper's brother. I could assume his murder was what brought her back here, but I was curious what she'd want. A new life, perhaps, somewhere far from Abelaum. Maybe she'd want money. Maybe she'd want Kent Hadleigh killed, which I certainly wouldn't mind doing, although it would prove tricky. There was a reason Leon hadn't already killed him.

The best hunts were difficult, but the best deals were simple. After all, once a deal was done, the idea was to quickly move on to the next. I had places to be and souls to collect, humans to fuck, pleasure to be had. Although I couldn't help but wonder what it would be like to linger with her for a while, to squeeze a few extra benefits out of the deal for myself.

She was a damn good fuck. Beautiful and dangerous. An anomaly born of blood and pain, terror and sacrifice. A human who, against all odds, flouted God and destiny, and emerged, bloodied and broken, to be made into something new.

My own little wolf, a beast in human form. A fragmented piece of destiny.

I sensed her long before she reached the doors. Her smell was absolutely irresistible. Like honeysuckle blooming in the morning, like earth after the rain, like pine needles crushed underfoot. Wild and invigorating, once it got inside your nose, there was no shaking it. When she entered the bar, it was like watching a storm pass over the mountains.

She wore ripped jeans, hiking boots so worn the laces were fraying, and a black hoodie with *Thrasher* emblazoned across the front. Her long, wild brown hair was pulled into a ponytail, revealing the shaved undercut on the side of her head. And her face . . . fuck. The heart of the storm was in those dark eyes and dripped to her full, liquor-tinted lips. Her skin was browned by the sun, and a slim pale scar—like the slice of a knife's blade—ran along her jaw.

She stood just inside the doorway, swaying slightly, not bothering to wipe the mist of rain from her face.

She was drunk. I couldn't blame her.

She spotted me as her eyes swept the room, and lightning flashed in her storm. There was a moment of fear, of indecision, but she didn't turn back. She didn't come up to me right away either. Instead, she went up to the bar, where she embraced the older woman serving drinks, and companionably grasped the shoulders of a few grizzled fishermen hunched over their drinks.

She was surrounded by friends here, and wanted me to know it.

I leaned back, grinning in my chair. How cute! She thought a bar full of humans would actually have a chance of stopping me. She was lucky I didn't want to hurt her; at least not in ways her dark, twisted heart didn't desire.

After a brief conversation with the bartender, she made her way over to me. Her eyes were wary but her walk was confident, and she settled in the chair across from me.

"You remembered what I look like this time," I said. "I feel so special."

"Don't," she said flatly. Her voice was deep and a little husky. But I knew how it sounded when it softened with pleasure, when it heightened with pain. "I always try to remember useful things. Hopefully, I'm not wrong in assuming you're going to be useful."

"Hopefully, I'm not wrong in assuming the same of you." I nodded toward the bartender, who was watching us like a fucking hawk, and held up two fingers for drinks. She glared at me as she began to pour.

"That's Joanie," Juniper said. She'd folded her arms, her shoulders rigid. "She and her wife have owned this place for twenty years. Most of the people in here wouldn't hesitate to shoot you if you try anything."

I smirked. "I know. You came here when you first left Abelaum. Joanie gave you a job and a place to stay for a little while. You stayed until the Eld tracked you out here." My smirk widened as her jaw tightened with anger. "When they started swarming around this place every night, you decided to leave."

She swallowed hard, her eyes locked on me. "Why the fuck have you followed me all this time? What makes me so goddamn special to you?"

"A good hunter tracks his prey," I said, "and waits for just the right moment to take his prize." I smiled as Joanie brought over two beers, slamming mine down a little harder than need be. As she walked away, I said, "What the hell did you tell her anyway? Am I an awful cheating ex, an unpleasant cousin?"

"My business is my business," she said. "They don't care about who you are. All they care about is that I leave here alive."

"And you will. What a waste if I were to just *kill* you after all these years. I guess you could say I've gotten attached." I leaned forward over the table, not missing the way she tensed as I got closer. "But you came here to discuss a deal, so let me tell you the first thing about deals: they *hurt*. They're supposed to. But deals with me? They hurt even more."

Her eyes narrowed. "Why?"

"Because I want them to. I happen to enjoy making humans suffer for what they want. And by the time a human is ready to make a deal with me, it is *very* much what they want."

She snorted. "Try working in a BDSM dungeon. Sounds like what you're looking for."

"Oh, I already did. They found my methods a bit too . . . extreme. But I only cater to what the masochists want. Who am I to tell someone, *No, I won't sew your mouth shut and make you scream*, after I've been *begged* to do exactly that?"

Her expression didn't change. "You talk too much. Sorry to burst your bubble, but pain doesn't scare me."

"You shouldn't tell me things like that, Juniper." I kept my smile reserved, but I was all tingly. There was nothing more exciting than a challenging human, nothing sweeter than a mortal who pretended they weren't afraid. "It sounds an awful lot like a challenge."

"I'm not interested in your games. I want to make a deal, Zane. What are your terms?"

"You tell me, little wolf." I waved my hand. "Tell me your heart's desire, and I can make it happen."

She narrowed her eyes, silent for a moment. Then, "I want to destroy the Libiri."

Ah. Well. I hadn't quite expected . . . *that*. "Destroy . . . right. You mean kill Kent Hadleigh?"

"I want to kill Kent. I want to kill Jeremiah, Victoria, and Meredith. I want their family wiped off the face of the Earth, and then, I want the same for their followers. I want their most loyal slaughtered. I want anyone who has ever supported them to spend the rest of their miserable lives shaking in fear that I might find them." She leaned back, folding her arms. "And I want to do it myself, with my own hands. I just need backup."

"That's . . . extensive." And time consuming. *Very* time consuming. Time that I could be spending starting my next hunt.

She plastered a cocky smirk on her face. "Are you saying you can't do it?"

"I'm *saying* that what you want is going to be a lot of trouble. Destroying the Libiri would mean eradicating half the town of Abelaum."

She shrugged. "I don't have a problem with that. I'll make it simple: we'll just drop a nuke on the whole place. Easy."

I laughed. "While I admire that your idea of simplicity is me giving you access to nuclear bombs, I'm afraid there are in fact limitations on what I can do for you. In this day and age, I can't simply wipe a town off the face of the Earth. Hell's Council would have a fit if I took a deal like that. Wouldn't you rather have a fresh start? A house somewhere far away, money for whatever your heart desires . . . a new life?"

"There is no *new life* for me. They killed my brother."

She nodded slowly, and although she rapidly blinked them away, tears welled up in her eyes. "There's no fresh start from this. If you don't dig out the rot, it will only keep spreading. The only thing my heart desires is revenge." Her hands were clenched into fists on the tabletop. Her voice lowered. "I don't care what you want from me. My soul, my suffering . . . I don't care what it takes. You say your deals hurt. Well, so do mine. And I'm not afraid. Are you?"

This woman. This goddamn *woman*.

"Oh, Juniper." I shook my head. "You don't know what you're asking for."

The rain was pouring, tapping heavily on the bar's old roof. It was late, and the only ones who remained in the bar was the bartender herself, a few drunks, and us. Juniper closed her eyes a moment, her lips pressed into a thin, hard line. She wanted a hard deal, so she'd get one. If I was going to be responsible for helping her enact her revenge, I was going to require more than her soul.

I tapped my fingers on the table, and when she opened her eyes to look at me again, her expression betrayed no fear.

"I don't care what you want," she said again. "I'll give you my soul. I'll damn myself for this. Torture me. Fuck me. Hurt me. It doesn't matter. I want them all dead."

Thoughts of doing all three to her made it goddamn hard to maintain my human disguise. I shifted in my seat, readjusting my rigid cock in my jeans. "Your soul is merely the down payment. It's a heavy price for a heavy task."

She had a good poker face, this one. Any emotion was so rapidly buried, it was as if it had never even been there to begin with. "Try me. What's your price?"

I sipped my beer, slowly, savoring it for a moment. Human alcohol did nothing for my kind, but the taste was pleasant enough. "Your soul is the start," I said. "Your body will also be mine. Your pleasure, your pain—and your submission. *Mine.* In exchange, I'll help carry out this revenge you seek."

It felt like an adequate price for the task. After all, if I was to be tethered to her to carry out her wishes, I was going to make sure I enjoyed myself. She was silent for a moment, her mind turning. I was good at reading humans, discerning their emotions, determining if I was pushing too hard or not hard enough. But she was tricky. She hid everything so carefully.

Finally, she said softly, "I won't submit."

"Then I'm afraid we don't have a deal."

Thunder boomed outside, rattling the bottles of liquor behind the bar. Juniper hissed, turning her face away in fury. But she didn't get up. She didn't storm away. With her eyes fixated on the rain streaming down the bar's front windows, she said softly, "I can't. I *can't.*"

"*Can't* is a little different than *won't*, isn't it?" I grinned.

"All I know is how to fight." She looked up, and behind the anger in her eyes, there was desperation. How funny to find that one little word was her sticking point. But I wasn't that picky.

"Then fight me," I said. "Fight to your heart's

content, and know that you'll lose, every single time. Know that no matter how hard you fight, you're mine in the end." Her eyes flickered across my face, searching for a trap. "And if you can't bear it, beg for mercy. We demons may be cruel, but even we understand the concept of necessary mercies."

She scoffed, her desperation vanishing and pride taking its place. "I don't *beg*."

"Under my claws, you will," I said. "If you ever *do* ask for mercy, I'll grant it. If you can agree to my terms, you'll have what you want. We'll kill the Hadleighs. We'll destroy the Libiri. Anything they attempt to accomplish, we'll destroy." I gulped down the last of my beer. "I haven't had a deal like that since the Middle Ages. I used to get bargains for wars and assassinating kings. This is honestly a little nostalgic."

She clenched her jaw so hard I could see the pale blue swell of a vein down the side of her face. She didn't like my fond reminiscing, but I didn't care. Gaining access to play with her as I pleased was well worth the time it would take to complete this deal.

"It's a big decision," I said, as she glared in thought. "Your body and soul for revenge. I want it *all*, Juniper. Make no mistake, for a deal like this, I will own you in every possible way. You say you're not afraid of pain . . ." I leaned closer, and watched her entire form clench up again, her body getting ready to fight. "But I think you've forgotten how to feel it."

I reached out, brushing my finger lightly against the barely visible line of a scar peeking from beneath the neckline of her shirt. Her skin was so soft for such a hard woman. She held my gaze without flinching.

"They hurt you once," I said softly. "So you decided you would never feel pain again, didn't you? If you can't feel it, then you won't fear it."

She smiled slowly. "Almost. But not quite. They hurt me once, so I decided pain can't hurt me anymore. I decided pain feels really damn good. Pain keeps me going. Sometimes pain is the only thing that reminds me I'm alive."

"Then I think we'll get along just fine, Juniper Kynes." I stood up, and she flinched at the scrape of my chair against the wooden floor. "Go home. Sleep off your liquor and think about it. If you want the deal, go into the forest tomorrow night, as deep as you can. I'll find you."

She looked at me with wide eyes, which quickly narrowed in suspicion. "The forest . . . why?"

I grinned. "Because out there, no one can hear you scream."

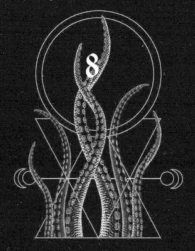

JUNIPER

I STAYED AT the table after he'd left, nursing my beer. I was already drunk as hell; it was the only way I'd managed to get the courage to meet him here. The whiskey I'd sucked down earlier clashed with the beer in my stomach, and I leaned heavily on the table, head hung low, trying to keep myself from vomiting.

What the hell had I done? I'd thought he'd get it over with. I thought he'd snap up my soul the moment I offered it. I'd come here ready to brute-force my way into bravery, but he'd told me to sober up and *think*.

There was nothing to think about. I knew what I needed to do. There was nothing else left for me, nothing but this: a deal to damn my wretched soul, a deal that would bring me under the mercy of a monster.

I jumped at the touch of a hand on my back. But it

was just Joanie, her long brown hair tied back, with a glass of water in her calloused hand.

"You look like shit," she said, in her usual straight-forward, no-time-for-niceties manner. "You've been drinking too much."

I shrugged. "Too much? Too much for what? For my fucking health?"

She narrowed her eyes. "Don't get smart with me now. I'll still whoop your ass."

I believed her. I picked up the water, sipping down as much of it as I could bear. She leaned against the table as she watched me. "I heard about your brother. I'm really sorry, Juniper."

Words like that were supposed to be a comfort. Instead, they felt like a needle being slowly, meticulously pierced into my heart. I nodded slowly, and chugged down the rest of the water. "It is what it is."

She shook her head. "Don't be doing that to yourself, now. I know you're hurting." She sat across from me, hands folded on the table. "It's been a long time, Juniper. You know you can always call us. If you ever need a place, Alice and I would be more than happy—"

"I'm okay," I said quickly. "I got a place."

She nodded, but she didn't look like she believed me. She knew my story, or at least she knew it the way the news had told it, the way gossips had framed it. By the time I was let out of the hospital at eighteen, I'd learned better than to try to make anyone believe me anymore.

"Did that, uh . . . *friend* of yours give you any trouble?" she said.

I shook my head. "Nope. But I'll be trouble for him."

She chuckled, clapping me on the shoulder as she got up. "That's my girl. You give 'em hell, Juniper. Don't worry about hurryin' anywhere. I've still got all the cleanup to do. Just let me know when you're heading out and I'll unlock the door."

She went back to wiping down the bar, and I drank down the last of my beer. I'd give them hell, alright. Hell was just the beginning.

DAD LEFT WHEN I was ten, but I think he and Mom separated long before that. I had no memories of him living in the trailer with us. Instead, the days I could remember spending with him were in the little stone house in the woods.

It wasn't truly a house, but I'd called it that as a child. It was a hunter's cabin, built of stone. It sat on a half-acre of land that Dad claimed had been in the family since Abelaum's founding. Isolated and quiet, it overlooked a creek and was surrounded by woodland on all sides. He would go out there a few weekends out of the year to hunt and fish, and he'd usually try to bring me and Marcus with him.

Dad taught me how to use a gun. He taught me to hunt, how to clean a fish and butcher a deer. He taught me not to be afraid of the dark, because there wasn't a damn thing out there I couldn't learn to protect myself from.

I was eleven when he died. It was the first funeral I'd ever been to. Marcus had cried, and Mom had been so silent. But I felt like someone had punched a hole in my chest. It was a great aching void, irreparably raw. The grief never left, it just grew numb.

Dad left me the cabin and the land it sat on. One of the things I'd made sure to do before I fled Washington was ensure the place was signed over into my name. I think Dad had hoped I'd sell it and go to college, but instead I'd clung to it. It was my last anchor to home, my last tie to him.

I was lucky I had the Jeep, because the narrow dirt road toward the cabin had gone so long unused it was almost entirely overgrown. The cabin itself was far more run-down than I remembered. The front window was shattered, and graffiti was sprayed across the walls. Inside, rats had eaten away the couch cushions and chewed holes in the bed in the loft. Luckily the well hadn't gone dry, but the spigot sputtered and ran brown for a few minutes when I turned it on.

I'd stayed in worse places. The cabin was a mess, but it held memories. Here there had been warm fires and Dad's hugs. Here there had been s'mores and ghost stories, fishing in the river, running around the yard with Marcus. Here my dad had put a rifle in my hands and said, *Juni, don't let your hands shake. If a bear is coming down on you, you don't have time to think. You stay calm. You take a deep breath. And you pull that goddamn trigger.*

I collected some wood from around the yard and got a fire going. I had no idea how I'd manage to sleep, even as exhausted as I was. A thousand thoughts were swirling in the murky alcoholic soup in my head: demonic deals, the price of a soul, the cost of revenge.

Revenge had been a long time coming.

It had taken nearly forty-eight hours for search parties to find me after I crawled out of the mine and ran blindly into the woods. I was dehydrated and barely lucid when I was finally found, strapped to a gurney, and wheeled into the back of an ambulance. When they let me out of the hospital, with a bottle of pills and a therapist's recommendation that I be "watched carefully," I returned to school with a kitchen knife in my backpack, went straight up to Victoria Hadleigh in the middle of second period, and tried to slit her throat.

She'd tried to kill me. It had only seemed right I return the favor.

So much of what happened after the police found me was a blur, smeared like paint. I hadn't been sleeping, I'd barely been eating. I was doubting everything I'd seen, everything I'd heard. I'd sat there and had doctors so *calmly* and *patiently* tell me I was delusional. I'd had police laugh at me. I'd had friends and family turn their backs on me. All the while I'd lie awake at night, terrified to close my eyes because I knew the nightmares would close in, terrified to leave the house because I could still hear that *voice* calling me.

There were months of court cases, meetings with lawyers, meetings with psychiatrists. Evaluations, tests. My mother telling me how lucky I was the Hadleighs were being so *understanding*. Then, finally, commitment. Sent to a hospital with locked doors and quiet hallways. More pills. Watched 24/7.

At least in there, I hadn't had to endure my mother looking at me like I was a rat that had crawled into her house. At least the woods were on the other side of a large brick wall, and although I'd sometimes hear howls in the night, there was no more scratching outside my window. At least in there, I managed to survive until I was eighteen, and they told me I was "rehabilitated."

But three years in the hospital had given me a false sense of security. The Eld beasts couldn't reach me in there. Only once I was out did I realize just how persistent they were.

Wherever I went, no matter how far I ran from Abelaum, they came. I had to learn their weaknesses, their vulnerabilities, where to shoot, to stab, to crush. I learned the dark was never safe, but daylight usually was. I learned how to sift through the myriad of legends and myths to find nuggets of truth—truth I could use to protect myself, truth I could use to make sense of what had happened.

No matter where I ran, no matter how far I went, the God knew. It clung to me like a stain I couldn't wash away. It came to me in dreams. Grasping tentacles. Endless darkness. Visions of impossible things, of a twisted world beyond reality.

God owned the Libiri, and the Libiri owned Abelaum. Like fungal roots, spreading far and wide, choking out all they encountered, so too was their reach. They recruited in whispers, in nudges. They captured curious minds and reassured fearful ones. *The Deep One is watching. The Deep One is merciful. The Deep One will rise.*

Complete the sacrifices. Free the God. Serve with loyalty as humanity falls under the rule of an ancient deity.

Marcus was only the first. Two more sacrifices were meant to follow. Two more tragedies. I wouldn't let them win. I wouldn't let them make those twisted visions I saw in my nightmares a reality.

They'd tried and failed to make me their victim. What remained of me was what they'd made of me: a shadow of their evil, an echo of pain, a storm of their own creation.

A storm that would destroy them, even if it meant destroying myself in the process.

JUNIPER

I RAN THROUGH the dark, lungs burning, legs aching. The ragged wounds on my chest were still bleeding, covered in mud. Twigs and stones cut my bare feet, branches whipped at my face. I didn't know where I was or where I was going. The woods were endless, the darkness so potent that I couldn't see more than a few feet in front of me.

I'd crawled out of the mine. I'd ripped off fingernails trying to grip the muddy, slick walls of the shaft. I'd screamed my throat raw calling for help.

This wasn't a nightmare. This was all too real.

I stopped, my stinging feet stumbling as I came to a halt. The darkness was full of vague shapes, my terrified mind creating phantoms out of shadows. But there, ahead of me, a pair of golden eyes glowed in the dark.

I was rooted in place, my limbs frozen with fear. I didn't know what it was, but I knew it wasn't human.

I was still being hunted.

IT HAD BEEN a long time since I'd last set foot in Abelaum's woods. The rich scent of the damp loam was tinged with mold, the sharp smell of the pines triggering a tightness in my chest that made it difficult to breathe. I stood at the edge of the trees, staring into the shadows, and all I wanted to do was run the other direction. The impulse overtook the entirety of my brain, a frantic scream I was unable to block out, every limb tingling with the sense of danger.

I waited, listening to the wind whisper through the boughs of the towering trees. I listened for the voice that would call to me. I waited for the cold shiver up my spine that told me when Its eyes were on me. The Deep One was trapped underground, but Its influence reached far beyond that: a network of roots that grew ever farther, greedy with hunger.

At least for tonight, the woods were quiet.

I was stone-cold sober. Tonight, I'd seal the deal. I knew now that it wasn't just about my soul. Sex, power, domination—this demon was playing some sadomasochistic game where I was both the prize and the pawn. If that was what the demon wanted, if that was what would secure his help, so be it.

It sickened me that I felt attracted to him. He wasn't something I should have enjoyed; he was something I should have dreaded. But I could so vividly remember how he'd felt inside me, how he'd *tasted*. My treacherous body craved the pain I'd experienced with him, the exquisite agony of being taken by a monster.

With a deep breath, I stepped into the shadow of the trees. My heart hammered against my ribs, aching with every step I took. This feeling was suffocating, but it wasn't only fear. It was excitement. It was a bizarre thrill. It was erratic anticipation.

It was hunger and lust, and—strangely—hope.

I'd struggled for years to survive. I'd learned how to make myself into a weapon. But soon, I'd have a new weapon. I'd have the power to rival my enemies.

The demon hadn't given me specific instructions. The longer I walked, my senses on high alert for the slightest unusual sound, the more my uneasiness grew. Every step was an internal struggle, a battle against my own mind. The darkness wasn't safe, and I'd gone years knowing that once the sun set, I would be hunted.

But this hunt was a little different. This time, I needed to be caught.

The rain muffled all sound behind a haze of white noise. I kept my pistol at the ready, because despite the demon lurking on my heels, there were other monsters eager to have me too. Besides, if I happened to shoot Zane if he snuck up on me too suddenly . . . it would serve him right. I'd seen that wild joy in his eyes when he talked about pain and suffering.

Two sick fucks who enjoyed pain—one mortal, one immortal. What a goddamn pair we'd be.

There was a rustle of leaves overhead, and I almost fired off a shot as a bird beat its wings against the pine needles, scattering thick water droplets. I cursed under my breath, wiping the excess water from my face. I moved the flashlight over the thick brambles nearby, but the beam couldn't penetrate far enough into the dark.

A chill crept up my spine. I wasn't alone.

"Poor little wolf. Nervous, are we?"

I whirled around, gun cocked. Empty darkness greeted me, and I grit my teeth as I willed my pounding heart to calm. "Don't fucking play with me," I muttered.

Laughter echoed through the trees. It came from all around me, but the voice that followed sounded as though it were spoken right in my ear, "Oh, Juniper, playing with you is *exactly* what I'm going to do. I've just got myself a new pet; it would be a *waste* not to play with her."

I didn't turn. He wouldn't be there anyway. I lowered the gun, forcing myself to slip it back into its holster despite my twitchy fingers' desire to pull the trigger. More laughter followed, and out of the corner of my eye, I saw fiery eyes flare to life in the dark.

"Don't tell me the little wolf isn't going to bite?"

I turned my head, slowly. Zane stood between the trees, his body giving off enough heat that steam was rising from his skin in the rain. He had one hand leaned against the cedar beside him, and as he stepped toward me, he sliced his claws through the wood and left deep gashes in the bark. I stood my ground as he suddenly increased his speed, moving so fast he seemed to vanish for a split second. When he reappeared, he was standing over me, one large hand wrapped around my throat, claws digging into my skin.

"Are you ready, Juniper? For a deal sealed in blood?"

I nodded rigidly, trying but failing not to stare at his teeth so close to my face. They were vicious fangs, designed to tear into flesh. A predator's jaw. I forced my eyes back up to meet his and said, "The terms first. Tell me the terms."

I knew demons could twist one's words. Deals with them were risky, because they would do anything to find loopholes around fulfilling their end of the bargain. It suddenly occurred to me that I should have come more prepared. I should have written this down. If I could have afforded a lawyer, I would have had them draw up these terms for me. If any such lawyer existed that wouldn't think I'd absolutely lost my mind.

But instead, it was just me, my uncertain words, and the demon grinning over me.

"Alright," he said, not giving me even an inch of breathing room. He was wild tonight, his last efforts at pretending to be human having fallen away. He looked at me with hunger, with rabid desire. "I offer my help, in whatever ways I am able to give it, to destroy the Libiri cult. I offer to not end your mortal life by my own hand. I offer not to cause you harm beyond the harm that you want."

I considered every word. I tried to find any possible loophole for him to wiggle his way out of, but my mind was preoccupied with the scent of him, so dangerously close. How could I think clearly with his hand around my throat, or with his body pressed against mine? "Part of the deal is that you won't kill me? Really?"

"It's a formality," he said softly. "One you should appreciate."

"And not causing me harm, except what I want? What the hell is that?"

He grinned, all sharp teeth. "You know exactly what that is. Think of it as a built-in safeword. I won't hurt you if you don't want it."

I was overthinking, but I couldn't help it. I was about to sign away my *soul*. There was no coming back from this. My heart thundered, as if it wanted to burst from my ribs and run: run from these woods, from this town, this state. Run and run, as I'd been doing for years.

But this would never end if all I could do was run.

"And in exchange?" Zane widened his eyes. "What do you offer, little wolf?"

"My soul," I said. Then, baring my teeth at the nastiness of it, I said, "And my body, to use as you please, unless you would cause me harm . . . beyond what I want."

His claws tightened, and I forced the whimper that wanted to rise out of me back down my throat. "Would you also care to include an offer not to kill me?"

"No. That's not a promise I'll make."

He *tsk*ed, shaking his head. "Ooh, dangerous. I'll never know if you'll try to murder me when I least suspect it." He shuddered dramatically. "What a thrill."

I tried not to look down, but it was hard to avoid

the sight of the bulge in his jeans, especially when it was pressed up against me. "You're one sick fuck."

"That's what keeps things entertaining: sick fuckery. Just wait until you get to Hell. We've built entire cities around maximizing everything sick and fucked." He chuckled, and I had the feeling that I was missing out on a joke. Probably because I'd never seen Hell.

I'd never seen *his* Hell. I'd seen a Hell all my own.

"So . . ." He drew closer, his lips mere inches from my skin. "Are you ready to bleed for me?"

Anticipation gnawed at my stomach, and my hands would have shook if I hadn't clenched them into fists. My emotions were a tangled knot, tightening uncontrollably. I'd fought with everything I had to keep my soul, and now . . . now I was giving it away, like mere currency to be exchanged.

I'd faced worse. I couldn't back down now. "How do we do this?"

"Demonic bargains are sealed with blood," he said, and his hand eased away from my throat. I breathed out deeply, slowly. "Such a brave little wolf you are. I wonder if you'll cry when you bleed."

"You'd like that, wouldn't you?" I scoffed. I reached down to where I kept my knife tucked into a sheath strapped to my thigh, and tugged it out. "Fine. Where do I—"

"Put your little toy away," he said, his voice deepening, as it had when I first arrived, to reverberate around me, seemingly directionless. He stepped back, held up a clawed hand, and the air morphed between his fingers, like heat over the road in summer. From within the vague shimmer, the shape of a blade appeared, slim and iridescent, smooth as glass. I blinked rapidly, certain my eyes were tricking me.

He grinned at the shock on my face. "What? Never seen a blade formed of aether before?"

"I don't even know what the hell that is."

"It's the same matter I influence when I do this . . ." A sensation pressed against my back, like fingers playing over my skin despite no one touching me. The phantom fingers trailed up my neck and tangled in my hair, the sensation so real that I twitched away and reached for the back of my head.

"Some call it the fifth element," he said. "It takes practice to form anything solid with it. Practice, several centuries, and a few dozen souls claimed for Hell. It's a talent, really."

God, he had an ego too. Considering the knife in his hand, I tried not to roll my eyes. "What now? You cut me and we're done?"

He took a step forward—and I took one back, automatically, instinctually. He stopped, eyes narrowed, and extended the blade toward me. He tapped the sharp tip beneath my chin, the surface as cold as ice, tingling lightly on my skin. It shone with pale, innate light, even in the darkness beneath the trees.

"I'm going to take my time with you, Juniper."

That simple sentence sent a shudder over my entire body.

"You've had your soul offered before, to another," he

said, staring at my chest as if he could see the scars there through my shirt. "It was an unwilling offering, but the method is not very different, whether one is offered to a God or a demon. You were marked with Its name, your blood was spilled for It. But since you weren't willing, God would have had to have you in Its clutches to claim you. Here, tonight, you're willing." His eyes met mine, and that vicious hunger in them seared into me. "You will spill your blood for me. You'll mark *my* name in your flesh. And it will be done."

"I have to do it myself?" I tried not to keep looking at the blade, shining at my throat. I hated the way my stomach twisted at the sight of it, I hated the panic creeping up in my gut. My mind screamed with the memories of another knife, in another time.

"Are you scared?" His voice softened, almost tenderly. What the hell did he care if I was afraid?

"I'm not scared." I swallowed hard. "It's not fear."

It *wasn't* fear, no. It was my clenching gut, my cold lungs, my trembling hands and light head. It was a battle I fought in silence, a war against my own mind. I couldn't back down now, I had to face this.

"Don't you want control?" Zane stepped back and flipped the blade so that the handle faced me. He watched me curiously, as if I'd presented a puzzle he couldn't figure out. "It's not required to be done by your own hand."

"Then you do it," I said quickly. "I can't. My mind won't let me, it . . ." I had to pause. My voice couldn't shake. Not now. Get it together. "Bad memories."

"Mm, I see." He began to pace slowly, flipping the knife. He'd catch it by the blade, then by the handle, over and over. "I can do it for you, if you wish. But can you bear to let me?"

My eyes fixated on the blade, but I wasn't truly seeing it. Instead, I saw my own blood. I heard my own screams of pain. I saw the old beams of the church around me. I could smell the fire and the dust. I could still feel the cold disregard of all those who had watched in silence as I suffered.

My head was spinning. I dug my nails into my palm in an effort not to pass out. Suddenly his heat drew closer to my back, his breath on my neck.

"You came here willingly, Juniper," he said. "But unwilling memories are all you can think of."

He was right. I was spiraling, and I couldn't pull myself out. I squeezed my eyes shut, but it didn't help. I clenched everything as tightly as I could, focusing on every muscle, reminding myself of where I was. Clench tight, hold. Relax one muscle at a time.

But I couldn't run from memories. I couldn't hide. I couldn't erase the sight of that knife slicing open my skin, my blood running down—

A claw traced along the nape of my neck, caressing my spine. It jolted me back to reality so hard that I gasped, my eyes flying open. I could hear the wind in the trees again, and the sound of the rain falling around me. The drops were blessedly cold on my flushed skin.

"Allow me to help you defeat your first enemy, little wolf."

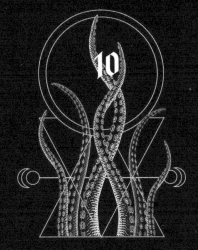

JUNIPER

"DO YOU FEEL regret when those memories grip you?"

I nodded. I was so cold, my breath was forming clouds of condensation as I exhaled. Zane stood behind me still, his presence warm on my back, and some silly part of me longed to lean back against him. Losing myself to memories was draining, like all my energy was being sapped away in those hard, painful heartbeats.

"I wish I'd run," I said. "I wish I'd fought harder. God, I . . ." I stopped myself. I had to. I knew better than this, I knew better than to spill my guts. A demon like him would just use it against me, so I bit my tongue. "Of course I feel regret."

He circled around and stood in front of me. The blade vanished from his hand, dissolving into the air, and for a moment, I was terrified that he'd changed his mind. He was going to reject me, he was going to refuse the deal, and what the hell would I do then?

Instead, he asked, "Would it ease your mind if you ran this time? If you fought? Would you feel better if I took your willing offer by force? If you run now, and I catch you . . ." He reached out, and I braced myself. His claws traced lightly over my throat, following the lines of my throbbing veins. "It will be exactly what you want."

It made no sense to *want* to be overpowered, to *desire* being taken by force. But I knew what he meant. I'd sought out rough, kinky sex long enough that I understood it. I found comfort in being overpowered, so long as I'd chosen to be. I could pluck out the horror in my memories and reimagine it, make it mine.

Maybe my brain was even more shattered than I wanted to admit. But sometimes survival was fucked up, sometimes it was messy and broken. This world was full of strange things, full of pain, fear, and viciousness. I'd learned to take those things as my own.

"You want me to fight you," I said. "But you know you'll win."

"As do you. You know how this game will go. You know the stakes. You know how it will end. But right now, you're tangled up in knots of the past. You're fighting your memories far more than you'll fight me."

It was as if he *wanted* me to feel safe. As if he wanted to find some way to make this comfortable for me. But that made no sense.

"You're not trying to do me a kindness," I said. "This is for your own gain."

"Do my reasons matter? We're both here because we want to be." His pupils had swollen as he looked at me: the golden color in each of his eyes was merely a slim ring around a black void. "Giving up your soul is a form of destruction. Ripping yourself apart so that something new may come of it. That's what you've chosen to do. I'm very fond of destruction, Juniper. When you belong to me, I get to destroy you again and again. Destroy the pain . . . the fear . . . the regret."

How could I kill what couldn't bleed, what I couldn't grasp? I didn't face my memories; I buried them.

I smiled bitterly. "You can't fix me, you know."

He shook his head as he stepped back into the shadows of the trees. "Fix you? Ah, little wolf, I have no desire to fix you. I just want to see all your broken edges shine. I want to feel how sharp you are." He was shrouded in darkness now: all I could see of him was his eyes, and his sharp grinning teeth.

Slowly, I took my knife back out from its sheath. I didn't trust him; the idea was absolutely ludicrous. Yet I was still here. I was still offering my soul. Was there trust in that? "I can't pretend to fight. If you tell me to fight you, I will."

"I hope so. I want to see my little wolf bite."

I'd been alone for years. Not once, in all that time, had someone reached out to my disastrous, broken self and said, "This one is mine. This one is what I want." I was only fit for Gods and monsters, and I'd always run from them.

But this monster was something different. Something

strange. This one I couldn't escape from, because I didn't want to.

So I ran.

RUNNING OPENED THE floodgates, and panic swept in.

It gripped every inch of me. It took my muscles and squeezed them, like cruel fingers digging into me, painful and unshakeable. It placed an anvil on my lungs, so every breath was too shallow, and the air wasn't enough. My head was cold; cold and light like a balloon on the verge of popping.

Panic is a strange thing, when you've felt it for so long. It never feels normal; it feels *familiar*. It becomes an unpleasant friend, one I wanted to leave behind but was also alarmed by the absence of. To not feel panic would have been suspicious. It would have meant I'd let my guard down too much, I'd let myself get too comfortable.

Panic kept me safe. Panic kept me angry. Panic kept me fighting.

It wasn't even Zane I feared. It wasn't the deal I'd asked for that filled me with terror like this. It was hooks in my flesh dragging me back through years, back to a place when I'd had no power nor choice . . .

I was trembling with exhaustion as I grasped the muddy wall of the shaft again, sobbing as I tried to pull myself up. But my arms were shaking so violently that I slipped back down. Down into the dark.

I wasn't alone down here. There should have been

no life, no sound, no movement . . . but I could hear their rough breathing, their growling. Their hulking forms moved in the dark, circling me. I clutched my arms around my bleeding chest, shaking violently, whispering to myself, "No. No, no . . . no . . ."

There were white eyes in skeletal heads, black tongues, and sharp fangs that dripped gray, putrid saliva at the sight of me. And in the deepest shadows there were creatures as pale as the moon itself, skin so translucent the throbbing red membranes of their insides were visible through it.

That awful voice was calling my name. Calling me deeper into the dark.

I paused. I pressed my back against the thick trunk of a tree and ground my fist against the rough bark until my skin burned. This wasn't the same, I had to remember that. I was here by choice. It was like my brain had been split in half; one half fighting for reality, the other striving to drag me back into memories.

I wanted this. I *needed* this. I kept running.

It was too dark to see. The silhouettes of the trees stretched on ahead of me, endless in every direction. There was no trail, no path to follow. The ferns whipped my legs as I ran, branches scratched my face. I didn't know where I was going.

The rain came down harder and I paused again, catching my breath as I searched the shadows. I was running from something that could track me by scent, could easily overwhelm my speed, and could hear my heartbeat. There was no hiding. There was no *escaping*.

I didn't have to escape, I had to remember that. It was okay to be caught this time.

Adrenaline couldn't differentiate between this and true danger. I wanted a deal with a demon, and I had no idea if I could trust him. His every word could be a lie. Maybe I was going to die in this forest. Maybe these were the last breaths I'd ever draw.

But the better part of me knew that wasn't true. Somehow, despite all the fear, despite the invasive memories, I knew Zane wasn't going to kill me. He was going to catch me. He was going to hurt me. He was going to make me his.

Somehow, that excited me.

If I was honest with the darkest parts of myself, that even turned me on.

I climbed over a fallen pine and slid down the short ridge beyond it, crouching close to the dirt with the protruding roots digging into my back as I took slow, deep breaths. Always think one step ahead. Don't lose focus. Be prepared to kill. The demon wanted me to fight him, so I'd fucking fight him. He wanted to claim me, but I wasn't going to make it easy for him.

Snap.

I froze. Slow breath in, count to ten. Slow breath out, count to ten. Look up.

Golden eyes gazed down at me with a wide, sharp smile. "Hello, little wolf."

I slashed out with the knife as I threw myself aside to avoid him. The blade made contact, but there was no time to revel in satisfaction. I regained my balance, half-running and half-sliding down the steepening slope, my boots catching on vines and roots as I went. There was a gully nearby somewhere. I'd seen it as I hiked in. But it was nearly pitch black, and in my rush, I'd lost track of exactly where I was.

I found the gully face-first.

I landed hard in the mud, the air knocked from my lungs. I rolled to my back, gasping, water flowing around me. I had to get up, I had to keep running. Zane's deep voice chuckled from above me, his footsteps crunching as he paced just out of my sight.

"Aww, little wolf. Think before you run. Don't panic now."

I shoved myself up. But when I looked over the ledge, he wasn't there. I spun around, surveying the woods on the opposite side of the gully. Nothing. I held my knife up, at the ready, my head light with the cocktail of chemicals flooding my bloodstream.

One hand seized around my throat from behind, the other gripped my wrist with the blade. I flung my head back and hit his face, but I may as well have slammed my skull against a brick wall. The impact dazed me, and for a moment my vision shifted, the forest around me vanishing.

The long, dark mine tunnel. Gray light. Water dripping overhead. Tentacles coiling toward me out of the dark—

"Hey, hey, wake the fuck up."

He slapped my cheek, snapping me back from the nightmares that waited eagerly at the edge of my consciousness. He released me with a shove, and I caught myself on the wall of the gully, turning to face him. "Don't let It overtake you. It will claim every moment of vulnerability you have if you let It. It will take your pleasure, your pain, your *living*. Don't let It."

I blinked rapidly, knife at the ready, or as ready as I could be, considering I felt as if I'd just been jolted out of sleep. "How . . . how do you know that?"

He twitched, as if resisting the urge to seize me again. Instead, he paced, fingers clenching and unclenching at his sides. "Let's just say that Gods and demons don't get along." He bared his teeth, a growl rising in his throat as he said viciously, "It's not allowed to distract you from me, Juniper. Gods are jealous, but so am I. Only I'm allowed to torment you."

He lunged, and I slashed. From his mouth to his cheek, just below his eye, blood welled up and began to drip. I backed away slowly as he raised his hand and touched the gash, then gazed down curiously at his bloodied fingers.

"So the little wolf *can* bite." He chuckled. "Good. Very *good*, Juniper. Fuck. You made me hard."

I shouldn't have looked down. I shouldn't have been curious. I shouldn't have gotten so hot at the sight of his rigid cock pressing against his pants, betraying its unnatural, terrifying size. Something demanding coiled in my belly; a snake with fangs dripping with lust.

I shouldn't have felt lust for him. Not him. Not a monster.

I sprinted away. I had no idea how close he was, I had

no time to think. I used a stone jutting out from the dirt to launch myself up, landing hard against the side of the ravine and scrambling up. Don't look back, don't stop. Just run, run.

He'd gotten ahead of me. I slammed into him so hard it knocked me back on my ass, but this time he didn't give me the opportunity to get up again. He pinned me down as I thrashed wildly with the knife, trying to slash him anywhere I could. He laughed as he caught my hands, pressing them to the dirt and grinding his hips down against mine. His cock pressed against me, hard and thick, separated from me only by thin layers of clothing. The heat in me was spreading, settling traitorously between my legs as Zane smiled, the blood from his cut lip running into his mouth and staining his sharp teeth red.

"What now, Juniper? Shall I let you run some more?" He used his knee to pin my wrist, and with his free hand, he grabbed my face and squeezed. "Open up, little wolf. Taste the blood you've drawn."

Some mad part of me obeyed, opening my mouth for his bloodied fingers. It was sharp like iron but bizarrely sweet, and it made a shudder run through my entire body.

"More," I whispered, and he tweaked an eyebrow, shifting slightly. The slight shift was all I needed. "More!" I wrenched my hand free, plunging the knife toward him. He didn't even try to dodge me. He let the blade slice through his shirt down to his chest, opening up a fresh red line across his tattooed flesh.

But I was still pinned, and it was all too easy for him to take back the control of my arm.

"Oh, fuck, yes." He moaned from between clenched teeth, and held my arm still as he licked his blood from my knife. "That's my girl."

I strained so hard against him that every muscle ached. "I'm . . . not . . . yours!" I bit out every word like a curse, trying to buck up my hips to throw him off. He let me go, leaping back from me with unnatural speed, but it wasn't because I'd won my struggle.

He wanted to play with me a little longer.

He tugged off his torn shirt and tossed it to the forest floor, rolling his shoulders. His chest was a canvas of tattooed art, the detail of the black-and-white pieces astounding. The lines and shadows, the stunningly realistic faces, were mesmerizing—even more so with his blood smeared across them.

He opened his arms, smirking. "More, little wolf? You want more? Then come get it. Hurt me."

I went at him with everything I had left. As if my life depended on it. As if I could actually win. But like running in a dream, my every movement was too slow. He dodged around me like my attacks were nothing more than child's play. He leaped to the side, then behind, and laughed as he shoved my back and sent me down to my knees.

"Come on, little wolf. Bite harder."

My mind was racing, but not with fear. This was a release of every pent-up terror inside me. Most days, I forced myself to silence my own screams, to hold back the desire to fight and the wild urges to run. But not to-night. Tonight, I set myself free. Those knotted memories holding me so tightly had been loosened.

He wanted me to bite harder? Then I'd fucking bite harder.

I swung the knife as he came near me again, and the blade sunk deep into his side. A little wince of pain flick-ered across his face, and I gasped, jerking back, shocked for a moment that he'd let me *stab* him.

"Now, there's a good bite. Fuck, *yes.*"

I'd been a fool to think I'd hurt him. He seized me, my hair knotted in his hand, and forced me to stay there on my knees as he tugged the blade from his flesh. He groaned as he looked at it, but it wasn't with pain; it was with pleasure. He held the blade up to my lips, golden eyes bright in the dark, and hissed, "Go on. Taste your handiwork."

I really was sick to want it. I was sick to feel the heat stir inside me at that, to look at the wound I'd left him with and feel turned-on as hell. I ran my tongue along the metal as he watched, and the muscles in his arm jumped as I licked my lips and gazed up at him.

"How does it taste?" he said.

"Like your pain," I said. "And it's pretty damn good."

"Fuck, that's my girl."

He wrenched me aside, and I had to catch myself with my hands in the mud. His grip loosened, but only so he could press his boot down between my shoulder blades before I could stand. Harder—harder—he crushed me down against the dirt. He knelt beside me, his boot still on my back, grinning, as I glared at him with my cheek in the mud.

"You fought hard, little wolf," he said. The cut across his face was already healing. Little more than a slim red line remained in its place now. The wound in his side would soon follow. "Now it's my turn to make you bleed."

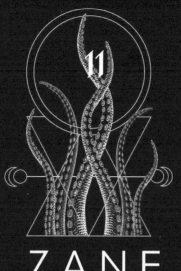

ZANE

THE MOMENT SHE knew the fight was over, the tension went out of her. She sighed beneath me, the rain catching on her eyelashes like glittering jewels as she peered up at me. Not in submission, no, not at all. Her dark eyes were hard with pride, utterly unafraid, but they were calm. The quiet after the storm, the gentle exhale as the chaos passed.

I'd hunted hundreds of humans over the centuries, only to be so often disappointed when they couldn't rise to my challenges. Warriors, murderers, criminals, killers from all walks of life—I hunted them for the challenge, because I didn't want prey who gave up when there was still a fight to be had.

I wanted those souls who got out of bed and went to war against the world, those humans who raged against the futility of their small, insignificant lives. *Those* were the souls I would bring to Hell, those were the souls I would lay my claim to.

Juniper was all of that. I felt electric as I knelt over her, and I couldn't recall the last time I'd experienced such a rush outside of Hell itself. She was vicious, brave, a wild little thing.

And for some reason, when I'd seen the pain in her memories rise to the surface, all I'd wanted to do was take it away.

That wasn't part of the deal. Vicious jealousy had rushed over me when I realized the God still had Its tentacles wrapped around her mind. Her soul was mine—*mine*. Nothing else, no other creature, was allowed to torment what was mine.

I'd never been one for jealousy, but it would make claiming her even more satisfying.

The wound in my side stung as it healed. I wanted to slow its healing if only to feel the thrill of it a little longer. When she stabbed me, fuck, I nearly came then and there. I didn't want to stop, truly I didn't, but if there was one thing I'd learned of this vicious human, it was that she'd exhaust herself before she gave up. So I had to call the end, and seeing the relief on her face stirred up a strange feeling in my chest.

I caressed my fingers over her face for a moment, marveling at the softness of her skin, cool with the rain, before I leaned close to her and nudged the knife against her jaw.

"Last chance," I growled. "Do you still want this?"

She didn't look away. Her skin twitched at the touch

of the blade, but she said, "We have a deal, Zane. Do it. Take me."

Dangerous words for such a breakable creature. I wanted her to scream, I wanted her to *beg*. She could wield the knife so well, but could she take it in return? Could she bleed as beautifully as she fought?

I tossed her knife away. It would have done the job just fine, and perhaps it was just me being a goddamn snob. But willing my own blade into existence, bringing together the shuddering, shimmering wisps of aether to construct something beautiful and deadly, was far more satisfying to me than wielding a bit of pounded metal.

I straddled her back, slicing the sharp blade through her jacket from the collar to the hem. She gasped as the rain hit her naked flesh, and goose bumps lined across her. Her hips pressed up as she squirmed. I groaned, knotted a hand in her long, wet hair, and said, "Keep moving your hips like that and watch what happens. You'll get this cock pounding your cunt."

She was panting as I tugged her hair, and again, this time with purpose, she arched her back and ground her ass up between my legs. "Don't threaten me with a good time," she muttered, and I nearly lost it.

I tugged away the ruins of her clothes, leaving only her black bra. I flipped her onto her back, and gazed upon the scars etched into her skin. Lines and symbols, runes in a long-dead tongue: a devotion to an ancient God. She'd tried to cover them with tattoos, but they were impossible to hide. Her face hardened when she realized I was looking at them.

"They're ugly as fuck," she said. Her voice was rough, as if it was an effort to get the words out. I dragged my claws down her chest, making her arch up and hiss.

"Every inch of you is a tease," I said, bringing my face down close to her breasts. I ran my tongue along one of her scars, following the line across her chest, savoring every inch of that beautiful flesh.

I could see it in her eyes when her mind wandered, when those memories took reality from her, when they stole precious seconds of her ticking mortal life. It was wasteful, and infuriating, and if I could consume the pain from those old wounds, I would.

I sliced the blade through her bra, and the tight fabric snapped back, laying her bare in the cold rain, her nipples hard. They were tattooed, like the rest of her, each one adorned with a Flower of Life. I took the tip of the knife and teased it against her nipple, and then the other, before I closed my mouth over one of them. She gasped sharply as my tongue teased the swollen bud, flicking it and sucking before giving it a little nip with my teeth. The other breast got the same treatment, and she began to squirm, shuddering beneath me.

I moved lower, tugged open the buttons on her pants, and pulled them from her legs. But I had a surprise waiting for me beneath—she wasn't wearing any panties. I glanced up at her with a grin, tracing my claws along her thigh. "No panties, eh? Are you *trying* to make me fuck you?"

I got up, yanking her with me, one hand in her hair,

the other gripping the knife. I brought her to her knees and held her there before me as she looked up at me with utter defiance on her beautiful face. I'd never met a mortal so demonic. Holding back from playing with her as roughly as I pleased was sheer torture, but it played perfectly to my masochism, edging me every time I had to temper my strength.

"I don't really have to try, do I?" she said. "I don't think you have much control over that thing in your pants, do you?"

I laughed. "Really? You think I don't have it under control?" I traced the knife lightly along her collarbone. "If I didn't have control, you wouldn't still be mouthing off. If I didn't have control, that mouth of yours would be occupied with other things."

She laughed too, but hers was sharp with something like fear, wild with something like ecstasy. "So says the demon. All talk and no—"

"This is where I'll mark you," I said, tapping the knife against her chest and watching with satisfaction as the smile melted from her face. "Here, right below that gorgeous face, so no one will ever look at this body without knowing who it belongs to. It's going to hurt, Juniper." I grinned as her throat tensed with a gulp. "Don't pass out on me."

I cut into her skin. She flinched, but didn't whimper, her eyes fluttering closed as fear rushed over her in waves, the scent of it bitterly sweet in the air.

"Stay with me, Juniper. Repeat my words back to me. Remember where you are."

The pain in her memories would swallow her up if I let it, and I wasn't going to lose her for even a goddamn second. To claim a soul was sacred; even when it was filthy, even when it was bloody. I wanted her in this, wholeheartedly. I hadn't hunted her for all these years to have her lost in her mind at the culmination.

I wanted her fear, her desperate pain, her hateful desire. I could see it in her eyes: the struggle against wanting this, the confusion and disgust that she found herself desiring more. She suffered for her own lust. She let herself fall into utter corruption amidst a torrent of pleasure and pain.

A willing sacrifice, for me and me alone. An offering, as ancient and primal as Earth itself. Blood and flesh, lust and need. The Libiri had treated her like a lamb to be slaughtered, but she was a wolf, and a wolf wouldn't bow its head if it wasn't willing.

She opened her eyes. She held on to my arm that gripped her hair, chin up, jaw clenched. "Don't stop. I want this. I need it."

"Repeat back to me, little wolf. Be brave now. I, Juniper Kynes, offer my soul—"

"I, Juniper Kynes, offer my soul . . ."

"By the terms of the deal agreed between us."

"By the terms—" She hissed as the knife edged lower. "By the terms of the deal agreed between us."

It was my own mark I was giving her, my own name. All demons had two names: the one by which we called ourselves, and the one that called to our very beings. The name by which we could be summoned and imprisoned was also the name by which we claimed our offered souls. To claim a soul was to entrust the most vulnerable part of ourselves to another.

"I accept this deal of my own free will."

"I accept—I . . . fuck—" Her eyes closed again as a rivulet of blood streaked down from the cuts. I was careful, cutting only as deeply as I needed to scar. "I accept this deal of my own free-fucking-will."

I grinned. Only one more line. Warmth grew in my chest, like hot strings tugging at my ribs. Her scent was stronger, her mind more open. When I reached out my being, with a subtle nudge to give her the sensation of gentle hands caressing her back, it was far easier than it had been before.

She was binding herself to me, irrevocably.

I gave her the final words, drawing the knife down between her breasts as I did, and she repeated back, "With this blood I spill, my soul is yours, forever, beyond my earthly life, to be claimed by no other, guarded and owned by you alone."

Claiming a soul was nothing short of sheer ecstasy. The words didn't matter, it was the blood and the will that did it. The final moment, when the mark was complete, stole the air from my lungs. She gasped, her nails digging into my arm. A binding like this could heal wounds, it could awaken one on the verge of death.

Two beings bound into one, two forces of life intertwined. It sent tingles down my arms and shivers up my back, and my cock throbbed until I truly couldn't bear it another second.

I tugged down my waistband and wiped the edge of the bloodied knife across my rigid shaft, shuddering at the uniquely cold touch of the blade. She watched me, eyes wide, breathing deeply, her arousal sweet and pungent in the air. I gripped my cock and growled, "Now you're going to use that filthy mouth of yours to show me how sorry you are for fucking *stabbing* me."

"You think I'll apologize?" she said. The blood loss and fading adrenaline had left her dazed, but I could smell the dopamine flooding her system.

"I don't think you're going to say a goddamn word," I snarled. "Because your tongue will be too busy pleasing my cock in apology."

Her eyes flickered to my cock, gripped in my hand. It always pleased me to see a mortal balk at its girth. It wasn't built to enter a human body, but enter it would— no matter if she bled, no matter if she screamed, she'd melt on it.

"Can you take it?" I said softly, as her gaze moved back to my face. She was trembling, the kind of subtle tremors that came over her in little waves. Humans were fragile, and vicious as she was, I wasn't trying to ruin my little pet already.

She held my gaze, rain streaming down her face as she said, "Of course I can."

"Then open up, Juniper."

Her lips parted for me as I pressed my cock against them. I barely fit in her mouth, the squeeze alone making me groan as I went deeper, and her throat convulsed around me with a barely suppressed gag. Her tongue caressed my shaft, stroking over the ridges near my head. I held her steady by her hair, her eyes tearing up as she struggled to take me down her throat.

I'd been slow at first, to ease her into it, but I'd had enough of that soft shit. I fucked into her mouth roughly, hard and fast. She clawed at my arm for something to grip on to, her nails digging into my skin. Every squeeze of her throat spurred me on, her tongue stroking me, eager for me, tasting me like she couldn't get enough. I couldn't avoid her teeth since her mouth was such a tight squeeze, but I was a sucker for pain. She gazed up at me, tears mixing with the rain, lips embraced around me.

"God, you look sexy when you're sorry."

Her mouth was so full, she barely managed to smile. But she did, and her tongue curled around me as I fucked her throat. She felt so tight, so *warm*, and took me well. My balls tightened and my abdomen tensed, ecstasy shooting through me as I throbbed in her mouth and spilled down her throat. She clung to me, unable to swallow as I pumped into her, my cum spilling over her lips. She gasped as I left her mouth, desperately trying to catch her breath as my seed dripped down her chin and I hauled her up to her feet.

"Your mouth got its punishment. Now it's that tight little pussy's turn."

I pressed her to the trunk of a nearby pine, slapping the palm of my hand against her ass, first one cheek and then the other. She gasped sharply, then hissed as the tree's rough bark prickled against her bare breasts. I was careful to ensure the fresh cuts on her chest didn't rub as I secured her wrists in one hand above her head and reached between her legs with the other.

"How are you still hard?" She gaped at me in disbelief as my rigid cock pressed against her ass. I slid my fingers between the slick folds of her labia, wet with her arousal, her clit hot and swollen with need. I sheathed my claws, massaging her roughly until her legs began to shake.

"As long as you're wet for me, I'm hard," I said, my teeth grazing her ear as her eyes rolled back. Her mouth gaped open in a soundless cry as I pressed two fingers deep inside her, her walls throbbing around them as I stretched her open. She moved her hips with me, arching back to give me a deeper angle inside her.

But she was going to get a lot more than just two fingers.

I withdrew my hand and gripped her hips, squeezing my cock inside her. She whimpered with every inch, panting desperately. Her pussy gripped me tightly as I pressed all the way inside—before withdrawing completely and plunging in again. She screamed, the sound choked with frantic need. I pulled her hips back, fucking her mercilessly until her knees buckled and I had to loop an arm around her to keep her upright. I reached between her legs and rubbed her clit, grinning as she shook from head to toe and went limp in my arms, the pleasure shattering her.

"Is it too much for you? Hm?" She managed to shake her head, the defiant little thing.

"Please . . ." she moaned. "Coming . . . make me come . . ."

There was urgency in her cries. Her clit was hot beneath my fingers, her muscles squeezing me as she reached the edge.

"You're going to . . . to . . . make me . . . come . . . fuck . . ."

"Who do you belong to, Juniper?" I hissed, gripping her throat as I kept working her clit. "Say my name. Tell me who fucking owns this cunt."

"Zane . . ." Her voice broke as she cried my name, and so did the rest of her. She convulsed, her breath hitching as I brought her to her peak, shuddering violently in my arms.

JUNIPER

I WAS NAKED, bleeding, covered in mud, and soaked to my bones. My face was covered in cum and so were my legs. I was shaking as Zane turned me to face him, grasped my jaw, and whispered, "Mine. All mine, from now to eternity."

Those words felt like a warm blanket wrapping around my exhausted body. I'd pushed myself to the very edge of my limits, I felt utterly *ruined*. It felt so good I wanted to cry, but there was no way I was showing him tears like that. It was time to collect my pride and be strong again, but I was certain if I tried to walk, I'd pass out.

It wouldn't be an elegant swooning-upon-a-chaise-lounge moment either. I'd collapse face-down in the mud and *really* make a mess of myself.

I had to get it together. Walk back out of the woods. Go home. Sleep. I desperately needed sleep.

Could I sleep after this? After what I'd done . . .

I'd sold my soul. I'd made a deal with a demon. I'd let him do things to me I never thought I'd trust someone to do—ever. I'd let him bring up memories that terrified me, I'd let him hurt me in ways I should have killed him for.

But I'd let him. I'd trusted him to do it.

"Stay with me, Juniper," Zane said, as my vision swam. His body was pressed close enough to keep me warm, and I wanted to nuzzle up against him. I wanted to absorb his heat and curl myself close to it. His arm was around me, and most of my weight was resting against him.

I had to gather the strength to hold myself up. This made me look so fucking *weak*.

I tried to push him. *Tried.* But once again, the resilience I encountered was similar to a brick wall. "Let go. I'm . . . I'm going home. It's done."

"If I let you go, you're going to collapse."

"Fuck you, I'm . . . I'm *fine*. Let *go*."

He did, and my knees buckled. I caught myself on my hands, but my head hung down, dazed and groggy. I was only vaguely aware of his boots in the mud beside me.

"You know, Juniper, I value my possessions. Allowing you to lay in the mud isn't really proper care and keeping of humans now, is it?"

"Shut up." Slow deep breaths. That was all I needed. Just slow deep breaths, and I'd get up. "It's done, just . . . just . . ."

"Just leave you alone in the woods?" He snorted. "Just leave my new human pet to fend for herself after

I fucked her to exhaustion?" He crouched beside me, and his hand tugged up my hair so I had to look at him smirking at me. "I think not, Juniper. I'm taking you home."

My body decided to give up before my mind did. I was too tired, too overwhelmed. It didn't help that I'd barely eaten or slept since the funeral. I was used to pushing myself, but I'd gone too far this time.

As my vision blurred, I expected my face to hit the mud. Instead, I felt him gripping me, holding me, *lifting* me. I wanted to struggle against him—I was *fine*, goddamn it! But once my head flopped against his chest, I couldn't even muster up the strength to say a word, let alone fight. Not even the rain on my face could keep me awake.

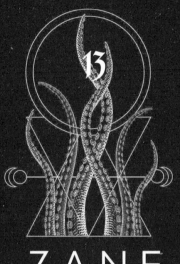

ZANE

MY HEAD WAS buzzing, and my skin tingled everywhere her limp body touched me. I'd wanted to keep going, I hadn't wanted to stop. But I could have gone until it killed her, and killing her wasn't what I wished for.

She was mine. Finally, after all these years of following her, waiting, watching. *Mine*. My new little pet, my broken toy; and I didn't collect toys to fix them. No, broken toys were the interesting ones. They were sharp and dangerous, like shards of shattered glass I couldn't resist running my fingers over until I bled.

I'd be getting off to the memory of her stabbing me for a while: the viciousness on her face, the unbridled primality when she swung the knife at me. Fuck, it gave me goose bumps. My cock was still hard, and I was aching to bury it in that warm, sensitive pussy again the second I could.

Humans were always so *tight*, poor little things. They weren't built for demon cocks, but they were adaptable, stretchy. A little pressure and they'd take it all.

But as I'd told her before she passed out, caring for her had to come first. I was a monster, but I wasn't *wasteful*. I needed her strong so I could play with her again.

She'd been using a little shack in the mountains as shelter. I'd followed her there the previous night and kept watch, to ensure no Eld beasts came along and ruined my bargain before it even happened. But I wasn't taking her back to that place: it smelled like piss and rat shit. That was no place for a human.

No place for *my* human. The sensation of her soul bound to my being was still new and heavy, familiar but strange. Every soul felt a little different: some warm, some cold, heavy or light, soft or sharp. Hers was fiery, dangerously warm the more I pulled toward it. Binding a soul to mine meant the universe tugged at all the little strings around us, tighter and tighter, weaving our threads closer until they were inseparable. Sometimes it felt messy, tangled. Hers felt like a constant pressure, as if her soul was always pulling in another direction.

She was a fighter all the way to her soul. I liked that.

She was soaked by the time I got her home, but not even the cold rain made her stir. She was sleep-deprived, low on calories, dehydrated. Considering she was so skilled at survival, she was absolute shit at actually taking care of herself.

With her soul bound to mine, her body could heal a little faster than usual. The cuts on her chest had already begun to knit together, and the bleeding had stopped. But her swift healing was also contributing to her exhaustion, as her body worked harder and faster than it was built to.

She'd be knocked out for a while, so I wanted to make her comfortable.

My house had several bedrooms, none of which I used for sleeping. The beds in them just kept up appearances, because who the hell didn't put a bed in their house? The only thing I used them for was fucking, but why fuck on a bed when there was literally *everywhere* else? Bed-fucking was unimaginative, but I digress.

I decided to put her in the master suite, give her something nice to wake up to.

But she was bloody and covered in mud. It didn't seem right to lay her on clean sheets like that. I laid her in the tub first and ran the hot water. She stirred, but only a little, her eyes fluttering when the water touched her. Damn, she really was exhausted. I'd thought she'd wake up and do the washing herself, but no luck there.

Well. Fuck. It wasn't my style to mess around with unconscious humans; it went against my principles. There was no fun to be had if they didn't even know what was happening, and sneaking to get a bit of pleasure was pathetic. But it wasn't about that. I wasn't going to put her to bed muddy. There was too much risk of those cuts getting infected, and losing a human to infection was an amateur mistake.

I rinsed her off, using the detachable shower head to get the mud off her skin and out of her hair. I went slow, because disturbing her sleep just felt rude at this point. As I ran the water over her body, I got to take in every little detail of the art inked into her skin. A gray wolf's head was centered proudly on her chest, surrounded by pine boughs, as if it were peering out from the forest. There were white flowers between the boughs, a touch of softness I wouldn't have expected.

They covered her old scars but couldn't entirely hide them. Whoever had inflicted them on her—Kent Hadleigh, I could only assume—had been brutally reckless with their blade. They'd been rough, creating jagged scars. She'd likely been struggling against them, thrashing, causing the knife to slip.

It made me instantly, irrationally furious. I had to pause to force my blinding rage to calm. Just the thought of someone else holding her down, hurting her against her will, taking her suffering when they had no fucking right to it . . .

Fucking Lucifer, it enraged me. No wonder her initial response to seeing the knife had been such terror. I wasn't used to experiencing such a visceral reaction to it; Earth was rampant with violent, cruel, unfair things, and I hardly blinked an eye at them. But when it came to her, when it came to *my* little wolf, it was different. I'd taken care with the knife, so the scars I'd given her would be slim, working within the lines of the art she already had.

They weren't meant to mar her flesh, they were meant to honor it. The sight of my sigil etched into her skin made my cock hard again, a dangerous combination with my anger. I was going to end up breaking something if I wasn't careful. I needed to go for a run. I needed to catch my breath *away* from her.

Why the hell did she have me so wound up?

I toweled her off and laid her in bed. She stirred as her head settled on the pillow, but she only exhaled softly and turned onto her side, clutching the blankets close to her chin. Her skin was so soft, it was like silk under my fingers. And when I trailed my hand over her shoulder, goose bumps blossomed across her skin. I sat back, lounging in the plush chair tucked in the corner beneath the window.

I wanted to keep touching her. I wanted to explore every inch, take my time, follow the lines of every scar, and count the freckles across her back. I longed to feel that soft, warm, mortal skin under my hands.

But I was trying to be good, I was trying to be *polite*. Self-control was a torturously difficult exercise.

Her lips moved with silent words in her sleep, and my claws sunk into the chair's fabric. Those filthy lips around my cock, hungry and eager—I bit my knuckles hard enough to make myself bleed. My cock was aching, straining against the confines of my jeans. *No touching, Zane. No more fucking touching.*

I left her alone, took her clothes downstairs, and put them in the wash—at least the pieces that were still wearable. I would've preferred she stay naked, but she wouldn't go for that.

I had to get my head straight before she awoke.

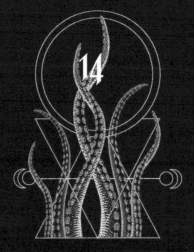

JUNIPER

THE NEXT THING I knew, I was opening my eyes in an unfamiliar room, in an unfamiliar bed.

I lay there and blinked in utter confusion for several minutes. I couldn't remember the last time I'd slept—or fallen unconscious—and not awoken in a cold sweat from nightmares. I hadn't dreamed at all, at least not that I could remember. My body was sore, every muscle aching, and there was a lingering sting on my chest.

The *sting*. That was what brought it back to me: I'd done the unthinkable. I'd sold my soul to a demon, in exchange for mass murder. I was going to kill Kent Hadleigh and his cult, and I had a demon to help me do it.

A sadistic madman of a demon who laughed when he was stabbed and gave orgasms like a serial killer murdering his latest victim—hard, fast, and brutal, with passionately violent glee.

I sat up slowly, letting the covers fall from my chest. I was shockingly clean, my hair still slightly damp. I couldn't remember showering, so did that mean . . .

Did that mean the demon that had chased me through the woods had *bathed* me?

The thought made me instantly squirm. It was hard to believe he'd bothered to clean me up. He'd even taken the time to put me in bed and tuck me under the covers. It seemed too nice, too *caring*. Kindness felt like a trap, and it made me instantly suspicious.

I didn't need to be taken care of; I'd made that clear to him back in the forest. He'd ignored me, of course, but if he'd left me alone like I'd told him to, I would have managed fine on my own. A few minutes of resting my eyes, and I would have been more than capable of walking home.

I sighed heavily, wincing as I tried to run my hand through my tangled hair. I was lying to myself. My pride was berating me for it, but I'd needed Zane's help back there in the woods. I wouldn't have made it to safety without him.

The room I was in was spacious, with a few cushioned chairs, a television, and a large dark trunk at the foot of the bed. Gray stone adorned the bathroom at the far side of the room, and curtains were drawn across floor-to-ceiling windows to my left. I couldn't hear any rain, but the light spilling through was pale and muted.

Where the hell was my gun?

I slipped out of bed, the wooden floor cool beneath my feet. I went into the bathroom, the large mirror over the bronze basin sink giving me a full view of my naked body. It was a body covered in scars, burns, and art; a body I'd often hated and rarely loved. After the Libiri had cut me, the ragged wounds had swollen and scabbed over before they slowly healed to pale scars. I hadn't been able to bear looking in the mirror and seeing them, a constant reminder of the horror, the pain, and the agony that had come after. The agony of not being believed, of being treated like a troubled child making wild accusations.

I'd eventually covered them with tattoos. At least then, I could look in the mirror and see the art I'd chosen.

But there were new scars now, scars that had miraculously healed between last night and this morning. The lines were slim, not jagged and torn like the others. I didn't understand the marks, but they were simple, centered on the wolf's head I'd had tattooed on my chest. The new scars hadn't disfigured the art at all. They flowed with it.

I frowned, tracing my fingers along the pale unfamiliar lines. I'd let a demon take a knife to my skin. I wasn't even sure how I'd been able to bear it, how I'd been brave enough to kneel there and accept it. But I'd done it, and that brought a wave of relief crashing over me. I'd faced the thing I feared. I'd relived one of my greatest terrors and . . .

I was okay. I was alive.

I didn't feel the same nausea seeing these scars as I had when I looked at the old ones. I'd chosen them, not unlike my tattoos. They were strange, but they were mine.

I splashed cold water on my face before I searched the room for my clothes and weapons. But there was nothing in the room that belonged to me, and there were no clothes in any of the drawers. Cursing, I snatched the white sheet off the bed and wrapped it around myself, tucking it in so I could move with my hands free before I eased open the bedroom door.

The hallway extended to the left, and from the landing, I had a view down to the lower floor over the wooden railing. Gray light filtered through large windows above the entry door below, giving me a view of a dirt yard and distant trees. I crept down the stairs and found myself in a hall that branched off into the kitchen on the left, and the living room ahead. I slipped into the kitchen, found it empty, and took the largest knife from the block on the countertop. I wasn't about to walk around a strange house unarmed.

The living room was spacious, with an L-shaped couch in the middle of the space. The carpet felt clean and soft under my toes. The far wall was glass, with a view of the dock extending into the lake just down the back steps. It was beautiful, the kind of view people dreamed of having.

Surely this wasn't *Zane's* house. Did demons have houses? Did they *need* them?

Something moved behind me, reflected in the glass over my shoulder. I didn't move, but I tightened my grip on the knife. The large, dark form moved silently, coming closer . . . closer—

I spun around, slamming the knife down. The blade

was sharp, and it sunk deep, all the way up to the hilt in the bare, tattooed chest in front of me.

Oh . . . *shit* . . .

Zane *tsk*ed, looking down at the knife, then slowly back up to me as I took a step back, and then another.

"Juniper, oh, *Juniper.*" He sighed, grasped the knife, and jerked it free from his flesh. Blood dripped along the blade, but the wound it left behind didn't bleed. He waved the knife at me, smiling tightly. "Playtime is over, little wolf. That hurt, you know."

"Don't sneak up on me," I said, my back nearly pressed against the glass. "You scared me."

His eyes widened pointedly. "Yes, that's what we demons do. We sneak and scare."

"Then you're going to keep getting stabbed."

He rolled his eyes. He was wearing joggers low on his hips, the black band of his briefs barely visible above them. His chest rippled with muscles, every inch of skin covered in ink. Images of men and women bound in shackles and rope, suspended, gagged—it was practically pornographic, and not just because of the art.

The stab wound wasn't even visible anymore.

"Mm, you have to remember something about threatening me." He stepped closer. I had nowhere to run; I could only lift my chin defiantly, staring him down as he caressed the blade along my cheek. "Pain turns me on. Threats turn me on. So it sounds like you're flirting with me." He smirked. "Be good, unless your intention is to make me treat you like you're very, very bad."

I gulped. My pussy seemed to think his words were

good enough to get all hot and clenched over. I squeezed my thighs together, but his smile widened. Goddamn it, he could *smell* me. I couldn't even hide my own irrational arousal from him.

I wanted my knife back. I may have given him my soul, but being around him, unarmed, was unnerving. "Where are my clothes?"

"They're clean and drying. They should be ready soon."

I narrowed my eyes. "You . . . *washed* my clothes? You do laundry?"

"Unfortunately, human society dictates that I'm required to put clothing upon this fleshy body," he said. "So yes, I do laundry. Did you think demons magically stay clean?"

I opened my mouth several times, at a loss for words. "I don't know a goddamn thing about demons. I thought you all just . . ." I waved my hands around. "Disappeared into the air or something when you're not chasing humans through the woods."

He laughed, shaking his head as he turned away and carried the knife back toward the kitchen. I followed, because I didn't know what else to do. "No, little wolf, we don't just disappear. If we're on Earth, we're staying in our physical form the majority of the time. Floating around Earth as just spiritual energy is a terrible idea. It'll get you all mixed up."

I wasn't sure what he meant, but I didn't question it. He set the knife in the sink and leaned back on the counter, the veins in his muscular arms creating drool-worthy lines beneath his skin as he tapped his claws against the cabinets.

Drool-worthy? Oh God, had my brain really gone there?

The demon smirked, as if he could read my ludicrous thoughts. "Are you hungry?"

Yes, I was, in more than one sense of the word. "What's it matter to you?"

"I have an interest in keeping you alive," he said. "Let me tell you a little *fun fact*, Juniper. Soul bargains are overseen by Hell's Council. Think of them as our government. Now, once upon a time, an absolute dolt of a demon decided to convince an entire bar of drunken humans to give him their souls. He then massacred *all* of them, so he wouldn't have to bother fulfilling his end of their deals. The Council doesn't look very fondly upon the bargain-and-murder method of soul hunting. They put a stop to it. So I'm not trying to have you die from something so silly as starving to death, because I'm really trying to avoid the Council's attention. Now, are you hungry?"

I thought of telling him I wasn't going to starve to death after only a day . . . but I *was* hungry. I nodded.

"Oh, *good*. Look at you, admitting you have needs. Bravo." He gave a sarcastic clap of his hands and snatched up a key from the counter, jangling it in the air. "Let's go then."

"I don't have clothes on, asshole," I said as he brushed past me toward the front door. The touch of his arm against my bare shoulder sent a little shiver up my back and a tingle straight down to my core. Goddamn it, the demon was a walking death trap baited with good looks. "And you're barely dressed either!"

"Is that a problem?" He turned, one hand on the front door knob. It caught me off guard, and my eyes immediately darted down—down to the absurd bulge in his pants. I hurriedly looked away, jaw clenched, my arms folded over the sheet I'd wrapped around myself. "Mm, that's what I thought."

I REALLY DIDN'T plan on getting into the bright orange Acura NSX the demon had parked in the yard, but the hunger shakes had set in. I'd be useless soon if I didn't consume some calories. I slid into the passenger seat, begrudgingly noticing just how comfortable the leather was as I settled in. Zane kept looking over at me, a cocky smile on his face as he started the engine.

"What?" I finally snapped, when he wouldn't stop staring.

"You like the car." He didn't even pose it as a question.

"Why does a demon have a car?" I said. "Or a house?"

He pulled out of the yard, onto a narrow road shaded by maple trees. The engine roared, the tires screeched, and the car took off down the winding road, the force of its speed making my stomach flip and pressing me back into the seat.

"Why wouldn't I get a car?" he said, raising his voice over the sound of the engine. "I can run faster than any human, but I can't run around in public. The Council would have a fit if I showed off like that." He leaned back in the seat, one hand on the wheel. "I have to show off in other ways."

I began to recognize the roads as we drove. We were a little north of Abelaum, following the road south along the bay. I wasn't going to admit it, but the car was impressive. And expensive.

"Do you have a job or something?" I said, trying not to look at him so I wouldn't slip up and look *down* again.

"I hunt souls."

"Does Hell pay you for that? You bought the house and the car somehow."

"Hell provides," he said simply. "For those who provide for it in return. Soul hunters are treated generously by the Council."

This was all sounding a bit too much like something out of a fantasy novel. Soul hunters, councils in Hell, the fact that Hell itself was even real. I fell silent, and Zane turned up the radio, blasting "Twisted" by MISSIO through the car's sound system. He nodded his head along to the music, having a fantastic time while I glared in the seat beside him.

He was playing nice, but I wasn't going to forget he was a monster—a monster I'd made a deal with for one purpose, and one purpose only: to bring an end to the Hadleighs and their cult.

But maybe I'd get a few more good fucks out of it, as a bonus. As much as I wanted to, I couldn't deny it. I was so goddamn attracted to him that I got shivers just from looking at him. The thought of his dick made my pussy start doing kegels of her own free fucking will.

He finally slowed as we drove into downtown Abelaum. We passed the university campus, the tall stone buildings partially hidden behind trees. I'd thought I might go there, once upon a time. Back before my reality was shattered, before I realized the university was just another trap the Libiri used to lure in new followers.

We drove past the bars, the boutiques, and the cafes, finally pulling into the parking lot at Dick's Drive-In.

I balked as he got out. "I'm wearing a fucking *sheet*, Zane!"

But he just kept walking, shirtless, toward the order window. I growled furiously, slammed my fist against the dashboard hard enough to hurt—and followed him.

It had been ages since I'd had a good burger; that was the only excuse I had.

Luckily, the sheet I wore was completely overshadowed by Zane strutting up to the window, shirtless. I don't think the woman who took our order even realized I was there, continuing to stare at him even as I told her what I wanted. I couldn't blame her.

Back in the car, the smell of the food had me digging into the bag like a starving animal. I had finished my first burger before I noticed Zane watching me, a pleased smile on his face.

"What?" I said, with sauce smudged on my face and lettuce spilled down the sheet.

"Just admiring my pet," he said. "I thought you might be stubborn and hold back on eating."

"I'm not your fucking pet," I muttered.

"Mm, and yet I clearly remember you telling me I *owned* you the other night." God, he was unbearable. That stupid cocky grin. He looked so *pleased* with himself.

He was eating up the attention I was giving him, so I took it away. I started on my second burger, refusing to even glance in his direction as he hummed along to the stereo. He hadn't ordered any food for himself, just a large soda that he sipped as he bobbed his head.

"What's our first place of attack, little wolf?" he said, as I finished my second burger and leaned back in the seat, obnoxiously full but perfectly satiated. "Where do we hurt your enemies first?"

I had to think for a moment. I hadn't planned this far. Beyond selling my soul and getting a demon on my side, I wasn't sure what to do next. Anger and grief were still clouding my thoughts, so it was difficult to contemplate how best to go after the Hadleighs when . . .

When Marcus hadn't even been safely laid to rest.

"My brother's body was stolen from his grave," I said. "The night of his funeral, someone came and stole him. I watched it happen." I turned to him. "Kent Hadleigh has a demon that works for him. That's who took my brother's body. I need to find out where his body is and get it back."

Zane nodded. "I know that demon. I'll ask him about it."

"Kill him after you're done speaking with him. We need to get him out of the way so Kent doesn't have his protection."

Zane laughed and started the car's engine again. "Sorry, but I won't be doing that."

My eyes widened as I looked at him, my heart pounding. "We made a deal. You agreed to help me kill—"

"I agreed to help you destroy the Libiri," he said. He didn't keep his eyes on the road as he drove. He looked out the window instead, as if he were merely a passenger watching the world go by. It was unnerving as hell. "Leon has caused you no harm, nor will he. He's not one of them."

My heart was hammering against my ribs in fury. This was exactly what I was afraid of: the demon twisting words to get out of his bargain.

"No harm?" I snarled. "No fucking harm? He was there the night they threw me down in the dark! He chased me, he fucking chased me for hours! He would've dragged me back if he caught me, and would have thrown me down there again to *die*!"

I braced my hands against the dash to stop their shaking. The burgers were threatening to come up, my stomach twisting.

"Juniper, listen to me."

I squeezed my eyes shut. Deep breaths, deep breaths. Ten seconds in, ten seconds out.

"I've known Leon a long time—"

"Stop fucking saying his name," I hissed. I wanted to curl up into a ball. I wanted to scream. I hated feeling so irrational, I hated that I couldn't make this panic calm. "I want him *dead*. I'll do it myself—"

"No, you won't."

I opened my eyes, glaring at him across the seat. I wanted to strangle him. I wanted to stab him again. How dare he do this to me? How dare he take *everything* I had left and then *refuse*—

"Leon hates the Hadleighs as much as you do, Juniper," he said, and his voice sounded strange, almost . . . sad. But that couldn't be. "I know, I've heard the story. Kent Hadleigh sent him after you once you escaped the mine. But he couldn't find you. He couldn't catch you and he paid for that dearly. He didn't have a choice."

"He's a sick, sadistic monster."

"The Hadleigh family has kept him enslaved for nearly a hundred years. Imagine enduring Kent Hadleigh *every fucking day*, for years upon years. Imagine him having the power to hurt you, to magically break you again and again. No hope of escape, no hope even of death. Leon would kill that family in a heartbeat if he could."

I couldn't deny it this time; his tone was sad, *pained* even. I didn't get it.

"Why do you care about him?" I snapped. "What does he matter to you?"

"We're bonded." I frowned in confusion, and he stuck out his forked tongue, pointing to the two metal bars pierced through his flesh. "*Bonded*, Juniper. We marked each other. We were mates . . . brothers . . . lovers . . ." He waved his hand. "Fucking semantics. There's not a human word for it. You'll just have to believe me when I tell you he isn't your enemy, as much as you may hate him. You're not going to kill him. Neither am I."

I was too angry to think logically, too furious to take the deep breaths I so desperately needed. The moment we were back at the house, I stormed out of the car, slamming the door behind me.

Zane caught me before I could get inside.

Darkness surrounded me, as if someone had snuffed out the sun. Phantom tethers coiled around my ankles, rooting me in place. Out of the corner of my eye, Zane loomed up behind me, a dark figure with bright narrowed eyes glaring down at me.

"You're a fucking bastard liar!" I said, fists clenched at my sides. I refused to turn and face him. "You're going back on your deal—"

"I'm not going back on shit." His teeth clipped together close to my ear, and the sound sent a jolt of fear through me. "Let's reiterate a few little rules, Juniper Kynes. You do not command me. We have a deal, a *partnership*. As much as it may disgust you that you sold yourself to a monster, you're with me of your own free fucking will. Now stop holding your breath, you're going to make yourself pass out."

I sucked in a slow, bitter breath. The darkness lightened, like mist chased away by the dawn. The tethers encompassing my ankles vanished. His hand reached around my throat, and his claws caressed lightly along my jaw. I shivered at the touch, the coldness of his claws shocking in comparison to the warmth of his skin.

"What happens when we go after Kent and Leon stands in our way?" I said tightly. His fingers tightened too, holding my jaw as if to demand my attention.

"He won't. Leon will do everything in his power not to protect the Hadleighs. You can hate him all you want, Juniper. Plenty of beings hate that murderous bastard." He let me go, and I turned toward him, arms folded. Without his supernatural darkness and dramatic deep voice, he was just a clawed pretty boy with sharp teeth and weird eyes. I scowled.

"Are you done with your theatrics?" I said. His eyes widened at the challenge.

"*My* theatrics? What about yours, little wolf? Are you done throwing a tantrum?"

I kept my mouth closed, angry words caged behind my clenched teeth. My heart rate was slowing, coming down from the mind-numbing panic. *Leon.* I'd never known the demon's name before. A name stripped away some of the terror, like a phantom brought into sunlight.

"I'll get the information you need," Zane said, rubbing his hand over his head with a heavy sigh. "I'll find out where your brother's body is."

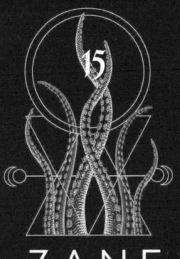

ZANE

WHEN I FIRST met Leon, he was haunting a graveyard in France, jealously guarding the grave of the dead human he'd once loved. He'd fallen for a mortal whose soul he'd never claimed, and death separated them forever. He hadn't been able to bear it.

It seemed ludicrous now, considering that in the centuries since then, he'd developed the habit of killing any human who rubbed him even slightly wrong. But he was a romantic at heart. On the rare occasion he got a liking for someone, his devotion was strong—*obsessive*, even.

It was foolish, loving a human. Humans were fragile, and they didn't view loyalty like our kind did. A bond between demons rarely broke, but humans threw each other away over the pettiest things. I'd told Leon as much. I'd told him he needed to detach his raging emotions. He needed to bury his grief. But Leon was all rage—he was all wildly swinging feelings.

I knew better. Hunting souls had led me to hundreds of humans over the centuries. Some I'd felt affection for, but in the way one feels affection for a sentimental object—it was special, certainly, but ultimately disposable.

Juniper was challenging that outlook.

She was merely a soul, a fascinating endeavor, a pleasurable pet. Except, she was *so damn difficult.* She raged at me, her cortisol shooting so high it even put *me* on edge. I reasoned it was normal enough: her soul had only just bound to mine, so those powerful things she felt could affect me too.

But it was more than that. It was more than just a touch of shared emotion.

I didn't *want* her to be angry. I hated her accusations that I was trying to get out of our bargain, as if I was cheating her out of something. I upheld my deals. I always had.

Did I blame her for her anger? Of course not. But it frustrated me to no end that I couldn't reason her down from it. It was difficult to think of her as a fun pastime when that look of panic in her eyes—utter, heart-aching *panic*—made me feel like a massive stone was pressing on my chest.

I'd always sought the broken ones. It had never bothered me, the terrible circumstances from which so many damaged souls came. Such was life: violent, unfair, cruel. All one could do was find pleasure where they could, hold tight to indulgences, and savor every drop of enjoyment one could possibly suck from the marrow of existence.

I FOUND LEON on the university campus, guarding a building cordoned off with yellow caution tape.

"What's all this?" I plucked at the tape curiously with my finger. "Smells like blood. Blood and magic."

"Get away from it, would you?" He glared at me from the bottom of the steps, arms crossed. "You're making it look like I'm not doing my job. That kid, Marcus, died in there. They can't get the bloodstains out of the stones."

"And what's this?" I pinched at his tight shirt. *PNW Security Services* was stitched onto the front. "Playing security guard, are we? Have you caught any naughty, snooping students yet?"

"Only one," he muttered, peevishly straightening his shirt. "I'm still figuring out how to punish her for it."

I chuckled, lighting up a joint. "Well, if you need help thinking something up, I'll gladly help you brainstorm some ways to make her squeal."

The campus was quiet that afternoon. Students hurried past between classes, and groups of them were spread out across the lawn as they studied. Leon glared at any who dared come too close with undeniable distaste.

Being forcibly summoned and kept, as he had for so long, will change a demon in unpleasant ways. I was fortunate to have never experienced it. After a few centuries of collecting souls and growing my power, a magician would need to be powerful indeed to manage to summon me, *if* they were able to get their hands on my name.

"I'm supposed to tell you not to smoke here," he said.

"Noted. When can you leave? I want to go out somewhere. Catch up. It's been ages since Kent let you out."

"Tonight." He paused, giving a long, heavy glare to a pair of students who'd paused in front of the building to snap a photo with their phones. One glance from him and their faces fell, hurrying away. "There's a festival in town. Kent wants me to keep an eye on things."

"Why?" I groaned. I laid down on the stone steps behind him, simply because it bothered him, and bothering Leon was far more fun than it should have been. "That's such a painfully mundane use for a demon. Doesn't he ever give you anything interesting to do?"

"At least this way, he's not always fucking watching me. Zane." He shot me an extremely perturbed look. "I'm supposed to tell you not to lay on that."

"Good job, gold star, what a very good little demon you are— Hey, hey, woah!" I leaped up the moment he raised his foot to smash it down on my face. "Be nice, be nice, fucker. I'm getting up." I took a long drag on the joint, exhaled in his face, and dodged away before he could hurt me. He looked ready to snap my neck—it was charming, really.

"I'll see you tonight then!" I flicked the joint over my shoulder as I walked away, earning some disgusted looks from a few passing students. I made sure to snap my teeth at them to keep them moving. "That little pub off Main Street! Rose and Thyme. I'll meet you there."

THE STREETS WERE crowded that night, and the bar even more so. Drunken humans bumped against the tables, walls, and each other; their volume growing louder and louder as they all tried to be heard over each other. It was a special kind of chaos, watching intoxicated humans get together. Like puppies let loose to do as they pleased.

Leon didn't look at them quite so fondly.

"The next human that bumps into me is going to get their spine separated from their fucking body," he snapped. He had his back to the wall, his eyes scanning rapidly over the crowd. The beers we'd bought weren't going to do anything when it came to getting intoxicated. But, as with most edible things found on Earth, we consumed them because the taste was interesting, not because they had an effect.

"Easy, kid." I shook my head, relaxing in my chair. "It's all part of the fun. Clumsy, intoxicated humans . . . glasses of their cold, fermented beverages . . . you, staring past my head like I don't exist."

He snapped his gaze back to me. "Got distracted."

"*That* was more than just distraction," I said, glancing back over my shoulder. It wasn't hard to determine where his gaze had been. All I had to do was find the woman staring at him, who quickly snapped her gaze away the moment she noticed me watching her. She was too small for her clothes, her booted feet dangling from her barstool, her eyes enlarged by her thick glasses. She couldn't keep her gaze away for long. It kept dragging back, irresistible curiosity demanding she look again. But she wasn't just some random, curious human.

She was seated at a table with Victoria Hadleigh.

I raised an eyebrow in Leon's direction. "Is the Hadleigh woman going to be a problem?"

He shook his head. "She doesn't care. She's not constantly kissing Kent's ass, unlike Jeremiah. She doesn't give a fuck what I do."

"And the other woman you're staring at?"

"She's a new student at the university. Raelynn Lawson. Bothersome. Too curious. Can't get her nose out of places it doesn't belong."

"I'm guessing she's got it up the Hadleighs' asses?"

"Unfortunately," he muttered. "It's not entirely her fault. Victoria and Jeremiah decided she's their toy of the week. They've been lavishing her with attention." His eyes narrowed. "It's odd. I don't know what the hell they want from her."

"Do you care?" I chuckled, but the sound died at the expression I glimpsed briefly on his face. "Holy shit, you *care*." I looked back again. Tiny human woman, fidgety, couldn't stop glancing in his direction. "Oh no."

"Don't start," he groaned. "I *don't* care. It's just . . . strange. A curiosity."

"That's how it starts, Leon," I said. "One day you *don't care,* and the next you're obsessed. If she's involved with the Hadleighs, she's not good for you." He grunted, my words bouncing off his thick skull like Ping-Pong balls. "Fucking hell, we need to get you out of Abelaum. Away from Kent. This has gone on too long."

He ran a hand through his hair, leaving it even messier than before. "The man is insufferable. His family . . .

also insufferable. I want to murder them. Is that too much to ask for? One little opportunity to slowly and meticulously rip their limbs off, starting with fingers and toes."

"I should bring it up with the Council again. Keeping a demon in captivity for over a hundred years isn't normal. At some point they have to intervene." I paused. As much as I wanted to have a casual conversation, there was still a purpose I had for seeking him out.

There were few things I ever felt a need to keep from Leon, but this . . . this might be one of those things. He didn't exactly have good feelings about Juniper. It wasn't personal on his end—she was just a bad memory. But it felt like a shitty thing to say, if I were to admit I had made a bargain with the woman that eluded his capture all those years ago.

She was supposed to be dead, and he'd paid for her survival dearly.

"What did Kent let you out for anyway?" I said. "Why the sudden guard duty?"

"The Libiri made a sacrifice." He was still staring behind me, utterly infatuated. "The kid . . . Marcus. It was him. The Libiri offered him up to the God and had me toss his corpse down into the mine. So shit is stirring up. Kent wants me to make sure the Eld don't become a nuisance. If bodies start piling up, it'll make things more difficult for him. Fuck, if that's all he needs me to do, what's a little guard duty? It's easy enough. And he leaves me alone, most of the time."

Toss his corpse down into the mine. Oh, Juniper was

going to *love* that. This was going to be a goddamn pain in the ass.

I would have rather heard it was at the bottom of the ocean. That would be easier than going down into the mine.

"Sounds like things are finally going Kent's way then," I said. "I guess that's lucky for you."

"Maybe. The old man has been acting a little strange."

"How so?"

"He's nervous. Stressed." He tapped his fingers against his arm, staring off in thought. "He's still volatile, but he's let me get away with some things I wouldn't have expected him to."

"Maybe he's finally warming up to your charming personality."

Leon snorted. "Oh, sure. It's only taken him a few decades. No, something is going on. Marcus's murder getting so much attention might have him on edge." He gulped down the last of his beer, setting down the cup heavily. "Enough about the old bastard. What about you? Hunting again?"

"I've got a new target," I said. "I'm getting close to wrapping it up." An utter lie: this bargain and all its difficulties was far from over, but that was embarrassing to say. Made it sound like I didn't know what I was doing, like I was a rookie taking desperate, difficult deals.

He smirked. "A difficult one, eh?"

"She'll be fun . . . if she doesn't kill me first."

"And you scold me for getting the least bit interested in a human." He shook his head. "Here you are trying to make bargains with humans who might *kill* you."

"I like things that might kill me. I like things that *try* to kill me. You, for example."

He scoffed. "I never tried to kill you."

"Bullshit, you tried to kill me! Multiple times!"

"You're being dramatic. *Consensually* getting *close* to killing you doesn't count."

"I can list off all the times you've tried to kill me, starting with France—"

"That doesn't count either. I killed anything that got near me back then. You just made the mistake of getting near me."

I rolled my eyes and held up a second finger. "The incident in Toronto."

"That was your own fault."

A third finger. "New York. Outside that club."

He paused. "That . . . I wasn't *really* trying." I raised an eyebrow, and he shrugged. "If I was really trying, you'd be dead."

"I would not. You can't kill me."

He got up from the table. "I need a joint if I'm going to keep up this argument."

I joined him. "I've got three. Outside we go."

His eyes lingered on the woman as we passed her. And the fool said it was merely a curiosity. I'd known Leon far too long to mistake that look for *merely a curiosity.*

I just hoped when all this was done, he could pursue whatever curiosity he wanted. Juniper and I were aligned in that, at least—we'd both gladly see the Hadleighs die.

ZANE

THERE WAS SOMETHING about cold air and marijuana that immediately made me feel at ease. The herb
humans grew on Earth was nothing in comparison to the
plants back in Hell—it smelled similar despite its effects
being minimal. But there was something deeply nostalgic
in it. Smoking reminded me of looking over Hell's Black
Sea from the onyx cliffs high above, lounging the day
away.

That was before I'd started soul hunting seriously;
once I picked that up, I spent most of my time on Earth
searching for my next target.

"Been back home recently?" Leon said, as if on cue.
He longed for Hell so desperately that it ate away at him.
He'd spent so many years cut off from everything that
made a demon's life worth living. The freedom of Hell,
the pleasure of its cities, the beauty of its wilderness—I

missed it myself, but I could return whenever I wished. Leon didn't have that choice.

"Been a while," I said. "Probably about a decade since I last went back."

"Mm." He took a long drag on the joint and passed it back to me, his eyes darting behind me as he exhaled. "Well, well, well. We've got curious ears trying to listen."

I snapped my head back. Raelynn, the tiny woman from inside the bar, was standing on the corner outside, doing a terrible job of pretending she wasn't interested in what we were doing. I chuckled, shaking my head.

"Shall we have a little fun with her?" Leon said. The hunger in his voice was unmistakable: I recognized the lust in his tone. It wasn't even directed at me, and I still got a little chill. Leon had always been a vicious play-mate, one of the few I'd had who could challenge my threshold for pain.

We'd shared before: men, women, other demons. But tonight, my mind was elsewhere.

It had only been a few hours, yet I kept wondering what Juniper was doing.

"Take the lead," I said. "She's all yours." Leon grinned, and I cleared my throat. "Hide the teeth, kid. You're looking a little sharp." A *little* was an under-statement: every tooth in his mouth had gone sharp the moment he noticed her.

Fuck, he had it *bad*.

He calmed himself before he called her over, and she responded far too quickly to hide how closely she'd been listening.

"It'll be easier for you to eavesdrop on our conversation if you come closer," I said as she approached us, her wide eyes darting between us. It was instinctual for humans to be wary of us, even if they didn't know why. But this one's self-preservation seemed broken: she was a little too eager for her own good.

"That's Zane," Leon nodded toward me in introduction. She regarded me carefully, like she'd found something new to study and wanted to absorb every detail.

"Brothers?" she said.

"I don't think most people fuck their brothers." Leon chuckled, shaking his head.

It wasn't like I could pass up an opportunity to try to make the situation awkward. Being the amazing wingman that I was, I said quickly, "Some do. Bros with benefits."

I could *feel* Leon's prickly exasperation in the air. "It's frowned upon."

"As if you give a fuck what's frowned upon." I passed him back the joint. All the while Raelynn stood there beside us, smoking her sweet-smelling vape pen and gazing at Leon just a bit too keenly.

Leon was going to have a problem with this one. He was working himself up just looking at her, edging closer to her before he said, "Why did you come out here, Rae?"

"To smoke." She was a terrible liar, so terrible it made me laugh.

Leon insisted. "No, no, no. *Why* did you come out *here*?"

Poor girl was squirming under his gaze. If she was involved with the Libiri, she certainly wasn't very good at it: she was about to soak through her panties just from Leon looking at her for too long.

"I was curious," she said. "About you. I was curious."

"Curiosity is dangerous," I said. "I've heard it kills pussies . . . Is that the phrase?"

Leon rolled his eyes before he flicked away what remained of his joint. "Close enough. Tell you what, sweetheart. I'll make this game a little easier for you, a little safer. Because I like this game. I like playing with you."

I was about to play third wheel to these two, but I didn't mind. I had a thing for being a voyeur anyway—just watching meant denying myself, and denial was a pleasure as much as a torture. Getting myself hard, enduring the strain, letting myself get more and more turned-on until it fucking *hurt* . . . yeah, I liked that shit. So I let Leon take the lead. I listened to him whisper filthy promises to her until she was shaking. He got her up against the wall and slipped his hand down her jeans.

The first soft sound of pleasure out of her had me hard as fuck—and it had me thinking of Juniper.

I'd moved closer to the mouth of the alleyway to keep watch. Raelynn was whimpering and squirming against Leon, arms around his neck, knees gone weak. My dick was pressed so hard against the waistband of my jeans that I dug my claws into my palm to control myself.

I wanted nothing more than to get back to the house

and fuck Juniper senseless. Her body was mine to break with pleasure and pain, mine to use as I pleased. A woman like her was wound so tight it was a wonder she didn't spontaneously combust. She craved a distraction, a release. She may have hated me, but she didn't hate how I could make her feel.

She couldn't let herself relax . . . but I could make her. I'd seen it when I'd caught her in the forest, when I'd told her the fight was over. Giving me control had relieved her, if only for a few minutes, of the desperate need to fight. I'd gladly give her that relief again.

Just to make myself hurt a little more, I kept watching as Raelynn shook, the sweet smell of her arousal on the verge of making me feral. I inhaled deeply, clasping my hands behind my back because I couldn't manage to hide my claws.

I was going to fucking *wreck* Juniper when I got home. If she wanted information, she was going to scream for it.

Raelynn was losing control, and Leon had covered her mouth to muffle her moans. Fuck, he looked good like that: hands squeezed around her face, his body taut, jaw clenched tight as he worked her to her peak—

What can I say, I was just a horny fucker that wished every day was an orgy. I always needed more: more stimulation, more pleasure, more pain.

Leon had to hold her up as she orgasmed on his fingers, his hand pressed tightly to her mouth, her eyes fluttering closed. He held up his fingers as she leaned back against the wall, catching her breath, and the sight of the glistening arousal on his hand made my mouth water.

"That was fucking gorgeous," I said, slipping my arm around his shoulders as he sucked one finger clean. He offered the other finger to me, and I took just enough time licking my tongue around it to make his breath catch.

"Always the middle finger," I muttered.

He smirked. "For you? Always." He was as hard as I was, and I knew he was aching to bury his cock in her. But that would give his true nature away. We could hide most of our demonic features with a little effort, but trying to make our dicks look anywhere near human was practically impossible. He backed away as she buttoned her jeans with trembling fingers. "Thanks for playing. See you on campus, doll."

We wandered down Main Street, dodging stumbling groups of drunk humans before we turned toward the lake. There were bonfires lit along the shore, and we stood in the shadows near the trees, watching from a distance.

"You're fucked for her," I said, as he stared at his hand like her cum had permanently altered his skin. He shook his head.

"She's just a toy."

"Mm, right. At least make a deal for her soul. Make it worth your time."

He frowned. "It's a little difficult to honor a bargain when Kent's got me by the fucking balls."

We both caught the scent at the same time: the wind

shifted, and the stench of rotting meat rushed in my nose, sickly sweet and cloying. I snorted in disgust, and Leon peered back into the trees.

"Fucking Eld," he muttered. "Fucking humans too, lining up out here like a goddamn meat buffet." His eyes were bright, a shine of gold overtaking the pale green color he usually hid behind. He flexed his claws, teeth elongating.

"Want my help?" I said. He shook his head.

"No, I need to blow off a little steam." He cracked his neck in readiness and gave me one last glance before he disappeared into the trees. "See you around."

He vanished, and it was time I did too. I hoped Juniper was awake when I got back to the house, because I needed to let off a little steam too.

ZANE

IT WAS AFTER midnight by the time I got back to the house, and all the lights were off. It disappointed me far more than it should have to realize Juniper was probably asleep—why the hell did humans need so much sleep anyway? It shouldn't have mattered. I could have gone back into town and found any number of horny, desperate humans eager to play.

But I didn't want any human. I wanted her. I wanted her vicious submission. I wanted her desperate lust. I wanted to see that fiery, furious light in her eyes as pleasure broke her to pieces.

I wasn't enough of an asshole to go in there and wake her up. It was going to be a long fucking night.

I smelled something strange, and didn't realize until I got up to the front door what exactly it was: a bundle of cinnamon sticks and sage sprigs, knotted together and smoldering in a bowl outside the front door. It was scattered along the windowsill too, and on the steps leading up to the porch.

The scent of those herbs could deter the Eld. It wasn't foolproof, but it was an age-old method and better than nothing.

The door was locked too, which caught me off guard. I never locked the door; I had no reason to. And since I never did, I hadn't brought any keys.

Not that it mattered. Simple deadbolt locks were ridiculously easy to open. A little nudge from my mind and the bolt clicked back, and I opened the door to step into the hall—

I smelled her fear in the same moment I saw her crouched in the kitchen doorway, her pistol aimed at my head.

I glanced over at her nonchalantly, grinning as she sighed in relief. "Expecting someone else, little wolf?" She stood, rubbing the back of her neck tiredly, a frown fixed on her face.

"I heard the beasts howling out there as soon as the sun started to set," she said. "I wasn't going to just sit here and hope they don't try to get in."

She hadn't slept at all. She'd been sitting here in the dark, with her gun, waiting for monsters to break down her door. It brought that tightness back into my chest, the same tightness I'd felt when I'd seen her panic over Leon.

Perhaps I shouldn't have left her alone. Perhaps it was cruel to—

No. No, she didn't need me to be her goddamn

babysitter. She'd survived this long for good reason, and my desire to make her feel safe was just my own pride talking.

"Smart girl," I said, closing the door behind me. "But you can relax. They won't be so eager to get near this house with me here. You can keep pointing that gun at me though. Turns me on."

She scoffed. "What *doesn't* turn you on? Something is seriously wrong with you." She kept the weapon in her hand as she walked back into the kitchen and grabbed a beer from the fridge. She must have gone out and bought it while I was away.

"Given my nature, I'm inclined to like fucked-up things. And you're telling me it wouldn't turn *you* on? Come on. I think that pistol is an extension of your arm at this point." She glared at me irritably, but I was feeling good. It was a relief to get back into a private space where I didn't have to pretend to be human. I could let my disguise go, relax my claws and teeth. Making myself look human required constant effort. "Think about it, Juniper: you, pinned to the wall, and me with that gun pressed up inside you . . ." Her eyes narrowed even further, but there was no hiding her scent. Well, well, well. What a kinky little bitch. "That's what I thought."

"I didn't agree, douchebag." She set the gun down on the counter, cracked open her beer, and took a sip. Her eyes were reddened with exhaustion, but she made up for her obvious tiredness with an even stronger attitude. "You talked to him?"

Such an angry little thing; she wouldn't even say his

name. "Yeah. He said Kent has been nervous lately. Something has him on edge, but he doesn't know what. Might be worth looking into."

She nodded. "Might be. And what about Marcus?"

"I have good news and bad news. What'll it be first?"

She didn't look amused. "Bad news. Hit me with it."

"Ah, well, bad news first ruins the impact of the good news—"

"Just *tell me*, Zane."

I sighed dramatically, but really, the more unpleasant she acted, the more I wanted to bend her over the counter and fuck the bitchiness out of her body. "Fine. The bad news is that dear brother Marcus is in White Pine."

Her hand clenched around the beer can, causing the metal to crinkle under her fingers. "Fucking hell. That bastard threw him down in the mine?"

"Yeah. Shame about that, but he is *technically* buried again," I said. "He's underground at least."

If her eyes could have shot fireballs in my direction, they would have. "And what the hell is the good news then?"

"Oh, right. Well, the good news is that I found out where he is." I grinned. "Told you, bad news first ruins the impact."

"I fucking hate you." It was surprising how fast that woman could move. She snatched a knife out of the block and raised it to throw at me—but I had her by the wrist before she could launch her projectile. She growled at me furiously, wriggling, pinned between me and the counter as I leaned over her.

"Don't kill the messenger, little wolf," I said softly. "I'm going to have to start keeping dangerous, pointy objects out of your reach."

"Don't you fucking dare," she snapped. "It's not like it would kill you anyway!" She strained against my hand, but all her strength had nothing on mine. "You'd probably *like* it. You'd just get all horny if I stabbed you again!"

"You've got me there," I said. "Just like how you like it when I take control." My grin widened, as did her eyes, with blazing fury. Her arousal was undeniable. I could feel it when her hips moved subtly against me, the gap between us already nonexistent. My hours of longing for her, only made worse by watching Leon with his eager little human toy, were about to bring me to an absolute explosion.

I wanted her. I wanted her *now*.

Despite her fury, she wanted it too.

I leaned my head down, so my breath brushed along her neck. Goose bumps prickled across her skin, her inhale hitching slightly. "Tell me no, Juniper," I said. "Go on. Tell me you don't want it and I'll stop, no hesitation. No games."

She clenched her jaw, her breath still shuddering as my lips traced along her ear. Fuck, she smelled so good. Her skin was aromatic with sweat, soft and warm. I wanted to bite it. I wanted to taste her blood on my tongue and hear the fury in her voice melt into irresistible pleasure.

I kissed slowly down her neck, letting my breath touch her as much as my lips did. I paused at her collarbone, at the smooth curve of her shoulder, before I nipped my teeth along her flesh. She'd be covered in bruises in the morning, everywhere my teeth touched. Marked all over as mine.

"How cute. Vicious Juniper likes soft kisses."

She tried to scoff; it came out as a gasp. "I . . . I'm not . . ."

"Not cute? Yes, you are. Cute, angry little thing."

She snarled like she wanted to bite my head off, but every little bite made her shudder. The scent of her arousal grew stronger, and my mouth began to water. I wanted to slip my hand down her pants and feel how slick she was, but even more than that, I wanted her to beg for it.

I wanted her to *need* it.

"I'm going to let go of your wrist," I said. "So you'd better drop that knife."

She smirked, watching me out of the corner of her eye. "Why? Scared you might get poked?"

I growled low in my throat, a warning as much as a promise. "If you try to stab me, I'm going to punish you."

Her tension didn't ease, and her smirk didn't leave. The moment my hold on her wrist loosened, she did exactly what I'd warned her not to.

She tried to stab me, well aware of the consequences; perhaps even *because* of the consequences.

If her intentions were to see if I was more than just talk, I'd gladly prove I could follow through on my threats.

I seized her again before she could bring the knife down, and she wriggled so quickly that she slipped to the floor. The knife fell from her grasp, and before she could seize it again, I was on top of her, pinning her to the tile on her stomach.

"Ah, Juniper, Juniper." I *tsk*ed. "What a bad girl you've been. Stabbing isn't nice."

"As if you want me to be nice," she ground out the words, snarling furiously as she thrashed beneath me. She was right—this was exactly how I liked her. Righteously angry, proudly in denial that every choice she made was bringing her closer to what she so desperately wanted: a good, hard fuck.

I secured her wrists firmly against her back in my hand, and dragged my claws across her shoulders. She hissed at the sting and her hips bucked up, wedging nicely between my legs and right up against my balls.

"What do we say if we want it to stop, Juniper?" I prodded, making sure she was still grasping logic and not losing herself in the struggle. "Tell me. Tell me now, or we don't play."

She gritted her teeth, panting for a moment from the effort of fighting against me. "Mercy," she finally whispered.

"There it is. Now . . ." I hauled her up to her feet, hands still restrained, and forced her back toward the counter so she was bent over the edge. "You say something is wrong with me for my tastes, but"—slowly, I laid my hand over her pistol and watched her eyes widen—"our tastes run in the same direction. You're just as fucked up as me."

I lifted the weapon and ejected the magazine before I checked the chamber for any remaining bullets. A quick flick of my finger and the safety was on. Human weapons weren't something I ever needed to use, but I liked to understand the basics of destructive objects even if I didn't personally have a need for them. I caressed the metal down her side, over her ribs and the curve of her hip. Every inch of her was tense, and she held her breath as the weapon neared her thigh.

"I can smell that sweet cunt, Juniper," I said, smiling as her eyes fluttered closed for a moment, only to open harder than ever. God, I loved to see her fight it: her arousal, her own pleasure, how much she wanted this. "Tell me, have you soaked your panties yet?"

"Find out," she said. Her hair had fallen into her face, and her cheeks were flushed. My smile widened.

"You'd like that, wouldn't you?" She shuddered, and her hips pressed back against me. She was arching her back, a subtle plea for stimulation. I tightened my grip on her wrists as I moved the gun between her legs, teasing the cold metal over her thighs. Her legs tightened around it, a tremor going through her as she sucked in her breath. "You wish I'd touch you, pleasure you, make you cum as if you don't have a choice in the matter. Too bad, Juniper." I leaned over her back, curved against her body so she could feel the weight of me on her. "If you want more, you're going to have to beg for it."

"I don't . . . I don't beg." She moved herself against the gun, but the stimulation through her jeans wasn't enough, if her frustrated panting was any indication.

"I think you do," I said, my voice low in her ear. "Look at you, rutting like a bitch in heat. Fucking *desperate*, aren't you? How long can you wait, hm? How long"—I moved the muzzle of the gun back and forth, right where her clit was hidden beneath her clothes— "can you take it, Juniper?"

A tiny sound, the barest whimper, escaped her mouth. She was shaking, doing everything she could to pretend she wasn't losing herself to lust. "There it is," I taunted. "Feels so good, doesn't it? But not quite good enough." I released her wrists so I could tug open the button on her jeans. Her hands clenched hard against the countertop, and she gasped sharply before pressing her lips tightly together again. "I'll keep you on edge as long as it takes. Until I hear that word pass your lips."

"What word?" Her voice broke. Poor, needy little thing. She couldn't keep those whimpers back forever.

"Please," I murmured, nudging the gun up against her, laughing as she ground herself down against it. "*Please*," I moaned the word in her ear, and moved my hips in unison with the gun, thrusting it between her legs. "Please . . . fucking *please* . . ."

She was breathing fast, her heart pounding. She tried to tug down her jeans, as if that would tempt me to move faster. It only convinced me to make her suffer longer. I grabbed her arm before she could pull them down, and she struggled, wrestling against me.

"Aww, really, Juniper?" I wrangled her back under control—her shoulders pressed against me, my free arm wrapped around her chest, hand gripped around her throat. I took the gun and traced the muzzle down her cheek. "Shall I stop? Tell me to stop, little wolf."

"No." She said it like a curse, like it infuriated her. "Don't . . . don't stop . . . fuck . . ."

"Don't stop? Oh, you mean keep taking my time."

I pulled her to the floor, and she swore as I forced her head down against the tile. I kept her hips up, her ass backed against me. She didn't lift her head when I tugged her jeans down, leaving them around her knees. Her panties were damp, pulled tight against her pussy. I nudged the gun against her, pressing it against the damp spot. As much as I savored making her suffer through the wait, it was just as much torture for me. I wanted to get my mouth on her, I longed for the taste of her on my tongue.

"Zane . . ." she moaned my name, and it was like she'd thrown gasoline on that primal fire smoldering inside me. It was practically irresistible, the need to have her taking over every nerve in my body. I dug my claws into her hip, laughing at my own arm trembling.

Damn, she knew how to get to me. She had my dick wrapped around her finger.

"You know what to say, Juniper." I nudged her panties aside with the gun, licking my lips at the sight of her. The metal glistened with her arousal as I caressed it over her, her thighs trembling at its cold touch.

Low and breathless but cruel, she said, "I don't think you can wait. You want it . . . too badly . . ."

My eyes widened. This mortal thought she could resist longer than me? "That's a dangerous game, Juniper."

She spread her legs a little wider, as wide as her bunched-up jeans would allow. "I think . . . we both . . . we both know demons can't resist . . . what they want."

I ran my tongue up her thigh, over the supple curve of her ass before I bit it like a peach. She groaned, but *fuck*. "I want to bury my dick in that hot cunt," I snarled. "But you'll break before I do."

She pressed back a little more, right up against the muzzle of the gun. I wasn't moving it now, just holding it to her, but that was all she needed. She arched her back and pressed harder, moaning as the pistol's muzzle slipped inside. Her pussy hugged around it, slick and swollen with need. She rocked forward and back, fucking herself on the weapon. When I looked down at her face, lying against the floor, she smiled at me wickedly.

"You wish it was your dick," she said, running her tongue over those soft, perfect lips. "But I can still come on my gun. It doesn't make a difference to me."

She just *had* to add that little insult in there. My hand snapped out, gripping her face and squeezing her cheeks as she laughed. I pressed the gun in, deep and hard. "It doesn't make a difference? Is that so? Do you think I'm going to let you come when you keep defying me?"

"That's exactly what you're going to do," she gasped, breathless, dripping down her thighs. "Even if you stop right now, I'm going to lock myself upstairs and make myself come without you."

I leaned over her, tightening my grip as I fucked the gun into her. "You think a lock will fucking keep me out?

I'll rip the door off its goddamn hinges, Juniper. I'll tie you to the bed until you're *weeping* for release."

Her eyes fluttered, rolling back in her head. Fucking hell, she got off on the threats; it only brought her closer to the edge. I didn't even want to stop . . . I wanted to see that glorious pussy clench, I wanted to see it squirt. My dick was so hard it was painful, that pulsating organ screaming at me to sink myself inside her.

"You can't resist." She was just taunting me now, eyes bright, cheeks flushed with pleasure. "You know you want to feel it . . . ah . . . you want to feel how wet it is . . ."

I swear to fucking Lucifer if she kept running her mouth—

"Oh God," she moaned, and I could feel the extra resistance as I pressed the gun into her, her walls tightening. "I'm . . . I'm gonna come . . ."

Like *hell* she was.

I jerked her up from the floor and slammed her onto her back. "Don't you dare call for *God*," I snarled. "It's *my* name you're going to be crying."

I slid the gun away, and it skid across the tile as I tore open my jeans, practically ripping the fabric. She was giggling—the wind was knocked out of her but she was fucking *giggling* at me. I tossed away her jeans and shredded her panties, laying her bare.

I wanted to rip her apart.

I wanted to eat her alive.

Fuck, I wanted to feel that tight, wet hole stretched around me.

I pinned her by the throat, pressing her legs back until her knees almost touched her shoulders. Even still, *still*, she whispered hoarsely, "I knew . . . knew you couldn't . . . resist."

I entered her roughly, mercilessly. I was far bigger than the pistol, and she cried out as I stretched her, legs shaking. Fuck taking my time, fuck waiting. Every cry spurred me on, and when her voice began to shake in unison with her body, it was *my* turn to laugh. "Cocky little slut," I growled, squeezing her throat.

Her bare toes curled. Her eyes rolled back. I squeezed the sides of her neck as she came and watched her face pass from pleasure to sheer ecstasy. I'd given her exactly what she wanted; all her taunting had been right. There was something about her, about the way her body tightened and throbbed around me, the way her nails clawed up my back and her lips parted, that ignited the most desperate parts of me. I couldn't fucking resist it.

I shuddered as I came, pumping her full, savoring her tiny whimpers as my cock throbbed inside her. She was panting, shaking, thighs sticky with her arousal and dripping my cum. I got up, leaning against the counter as she laid at my feet trying to catch her breath.

"I knew it," she said triumphantly. "I knew you couldn't hold out as long as me."

I wanted to snap the marble countertops in half.

She sat up slowly and leaned back against the cabinets, still chuckling, still breathless, still so goddamn pleased with herself. "We're going to White Pine tomorrow. We're getting Marcus." She grinned up at me. "Unless you're too scared."

"I'm not scared of shit," I snarled. I'd come so hard my vision had gone blurry for a moment, and I *still* wanted more. I was addicted, I was goddamn obsessed. And she was so fucking *smug* about it.

This was a problem. A massive problem.

I squatted down, glaring into her smug, beautiful face. "I haven't even begun to wreck you, girl. You think you won this round? You've only made me crave breaking you more."

She grinned, flipping me off from the floor. "I've already wrecked you, demon boy. Round one goes to me."

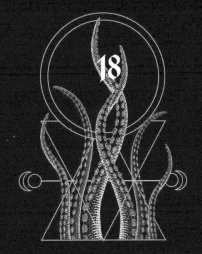

18

JUNIPER

I'D LEARNED TO live a lonely life. It was safer that way. I moved often and didn't linger anywhere too long. I didn't use my real name, and I didn't trust anyone I met. Companionship and pleasure weren't things I encountered often. I already wasn't very personable, so it was hard enough to make friends. But in the years since I'd left Abelaum, I'd learned that relationships were just anchors that would try to tie me down. Getting attached to anyone, or letting them get attached to me, was laughably foolish. I was a danger to anyone I got close to; I was literal walking bait for cursed, magical monsters.

Relationships were hard, but sex was easy. It was my favorite way to let off steam, the only thing I'd found that could give me some brief relief from my constant, crushing worry. But one-night stands could only do so much.

Good sex, sex that left me sore and drunk off the orgasm were rare.

At least, it was rare . . . before.

Zane had turned my brain into lust-filled mush. His smell was so distracting, and it was *everywhere* in that house. I couldn't lay on the couch without smelling him, and my entire body got hot and my stomach got all squirmy every time I saw him. The next morning, as I was trying to cook breakfast to prepare myself for the heavy task ahead, I could feel the weight of his eyes on me as he watched me from the living room.

I couldn't look at that countertop the same way anymore. I glared at it as my eggs fried in the pan, my own pathetic whimpers echoing in my ears. Goddamn it, he'd made me desperate. He'd forced me to make sounds I didn't even think I was capable of. Guns weren't toys, but Christ, he'd had me so horny I'd fucked myself on my own weapon. At least he'd been just as desperate, at least he'd given in first. The satisfaction I'd felt when he—

I hurriedly turned off the stove, having nearly burned the eggs. I swore furiously, but I still plated them beside my toast. I wasn't going to waste perfectly edible food.

I'd genuinely thought that, once our deal was made, Zane would be like a genie in a lamp and vanish until I needed him. It had been an outrageously naive belief. Now that we were bound, our bargain sealed in blood and cum, I couldn't get away from him.

I didn't think I wanted to.

SOMETHING ELSE I'D learned in the years spent struggling to survive was to always appear confident, even
when I knew I was fucked. If I clung hard enough to false
bravado, it might just get me through another day.

So as we drove toward White Pine, the sunlight falling
in shafts through the clouds, my spirits were high. My
adrenaline was pumping, anticipation made my fingers
tap rapidly against the door. I had my pistol strapped to
my hip, my shotgun on my back, my knife at my ankle,
and a demon on my side.

This wouldn't be like it was before. I was older.
Stronger. I wasn't helpless.

We drove deep into the forest. The trees were draped
in vines, ferns clustered around their roots, creating a
wall of vibrant green on either side. Zane kept the radio
turned up loud, playing KennyHoopla as we drove, and I
moved my head along with it.

I tried to think only of what would come after we
were done. I would bury Marcus up at Dad's cabin, in
the yard, where we'd spent so many weekends playing together as kids. It was isolated and quiet. If Kent's demon
came around for his body again, I doubted he would look
there.

But as we pulled off the asphalt onto the narrow dirt
road that wound back into the trees, my anticipation
soured. My stomach was knotted, and there was a weight
on my chest, making it difficult to breathe. The road
ended at a metal gate with a rusted *No Trespassing* sign.

Zane turned off the engine. "You good?" I nodded.
"Don't lie, Juniper."

"I'm fine." I kept my voice clipped and short. I jerked open the car door and slammed it behind me, leaning against it. I'd be fine. I could get through this. I took a few deep breaths, inhaling the crisp, fresh air, but buried beneath the pungent scent of pine was something else. Something sickly and rotten.

It had been here—*right here*—where Victoria and I had dropped acid all those years ago. I'd lain in this grass and stared at the boughs above. I'd wandered through these woods as Victoria led me by the hand.

St. Thaddeus cathedral was beyond the fence, hidden behind the trees. I hadn't been back here since. When doctors had tried to persuade me to go back to the church so I could see it was empty, I'd refused. It didn't matter if the church was no longer filled with white-cloaked cult members. It didn't matter if no evidence could be found of what had happened there.

That church was never empty. It was full of memories, full of pain.

"Juniper."

I jerked my head around, but Zane wasn't even out of the car yet. I guess he'd decided to give me a few moments of space. The wind rustled through the trees, the crisp autumn leaves shaking. I frowned. If Zane hadn't spoken, then . . .

"Juniper."

The clouds moved over the sun, casting me into shadow, and a chill went up my back. I turned slowly, scanning the trees. The greenery was so deep and bright. Every inch of ground was covered with flora, and all around me, the woods seemed to breathe. The wind, the bird song, the creaking boughs . . .

My grandfather's warning echoed in my head: *If you hear your name called from the woods, run.*

The Deep One knew I was here.

I jumped as the car door opened. Zane laid his hands on the roof, watching me expectantly. "Let's try again. You good?"

Confidence. Always be confident. "Yeah. Completely fine." He tweaked an eyebrow slowly. "I'm *fine*. Come on, we're wasting daylight. Let's get up to the shaft."

I led the way, even though every step felt heavier than the last. The trail into the forest was narrow, barely big enough for one person to walk along. I carried only my weapons, plus a small pack with climbing supplies: a harness, ropes, hooks. I'd climbed out of the mine without them before, but it was nothing short of a miracle I'd managed it.

Every fiber of my being was repulsed by this place, every step was a fight against my own frantic desire to turn back. Part of me knew this was foolish: Marcus was dead. Regardless of where his body lay, his life wasn't coming back. But I'd been in the mine before, I'd been in the dark. The horror of that place would never leave my mind, and the thought of leaving my own brother down there was unbearable. It didn't feel right.

It grew colder as more clouds gathered overhead, and it looked unlikely we'd be spared from rain for much longer. My hands were gripped tight around my backpack's straps, my jaw clenched so hard it ached. Parts of the trail were overgrown, and I had to stomp my way through bushes and intruding vines.

The path forked, and I paused. I stretched my tingling fingertips in an effort to get some feeling back into them. To the right, the path sloped down and widened toward the cathedral. Uphill, to the left . . .

I closed my eyes. There was roaring in my ears like distant waves, but amongst the roaring, there was the *silence*. That terrible, suffocating silence of being underground with just the slow, distant drip of water.

"Don't get lost, little wolf."

I opened my eyes. Zane was right behind me, only inches away. He hadn't touched me, but there was the sensation of a hand gripping the back of my neck. Instead of being menacing, it was grounding, almost comforting.

The overwhelming desire to feel his arms around me welled up in my chest. That was something else I'd learned to do without: physical touch, the comfort of an embrace, the intimacy of holding another's hand. Over the last few years, the only times I'd let myself get physically close to another was if we intended to fuck. Sex was vulnerable enough, but allowing myself the intimacy of simple physical contact was far more intense.

I took a deep breath and turned left up the trail. The last place I should have been looking for comfort was in the arms of a demon.

The trees hung low over the path, their roots coiled out of the ground, and I had to move carefully to avoid tripping. As cold raindrops began to fall, the forest grew silent. As if it had taken a breath and held it, the air was tense. I kept an eye out beneath the trees, watching carefully for any unusual signs of movement. The Eld beasts didn't usually come out during the day, but there were other things that could come hunting us.

Something crunched under my foot and I paused. Crushed on the forest floor was a trinket, made of twigs bound together into a triangle with twine. I picked it up, turning over the broken pieces in my hand. Tiny fish bones had been interwoven in the twine, and little notches were cut into the branches.

"My grandpa used to make these," I said. "He'd hang them around the porch and the barn. Said they'd protect the horses."

"They're about as useful as burning a candle to cover the smell of a corpse," Zane said.

I dropped the trinket and kept moving, but I soon noticed more of them in the trees. Just a few here and there, at first. But soon, there were dozens, dangling down from the low boughs overhead, and Zane had to duck beneath them. They swayed in the breeze, the sound of the twigs knocking against each other strangely eerie in the quiet forest.

The trail flattened, and I stopped abruptly. "There," I said. "There it is."

The White Pine shaft was ahead. Set into the hillside, the old boards that framed it were stained with age and burned with markings: odd runes, not unlike the scars on my chest. A faded sign hung from a broken chain, reading *CAUTION: OPEN MINE. DO NOT ENTER.* The opening was boarded up, but the boards nailed across it were clearly newer than the frame: they were pale and rough, with no rust on the nails.

It had been opened recently, likely when they threw Marcus's body down.

Sickening dread wrapped its hands around my throat as we got closer. Cold air seeped from between the boards, icy enough to bring goose bumps to my skin. It smelled like wet stones, like ocean brine and mold. Zane began to break the boards, and as he did, another smell rushed in my nose.

It was sickly sweet, instantly tugging at my gag reflex. The smell of rotting flesh.

Zane peered down into the dark, his lip curled. "Can't say I've ever wanted to be this close to a God. This place is . . ." He snorted. "Well, frankly this place is vile."

Vile was putting it mildly.

As the rain fell harder, I prepared my climbing gear. The shaft had been destroyed by the mine's flooding, the path down mostly eroded. What remained was a short, steep, muddy slope that abruptly fell into the water below. I could remember sliding in the mud, trying to find traction, digging my fingers into the dirt but still slipping down, down—

I shook my head. No thoughts, just actions. No emotions, just survival.

"*Juniper.*"

"What?" I raised my head, but Zane frowned at me. I insisted, "*What?*"

"I didn't say anything."

I moved faster. I couldn't let my courage be shaken now. I tied my rope to a large stone outside the shaft and ensured my harness was secure. I avoided looking down into the dark, and tried not to contemplate what it would be like to rappel down. I clipped my light onto my jacket, tested the rope one last time, and said, "When we find him, you'll have to carry him. I'm not strong enough."

Zane nodded, stretching his arms over his head. "Right-o." He leaned into the shaft, looked down into the dark with an expression of resigned distaste. He inhaled deeply, and said, "Ah, the sweet scent of putre-faction."

Then he leaped down, disappearing into the dark.

"Don't think," I murmured. "Just don't think." I held tight to the rope, keeping it taut as I backed toward the shaft. If I looked too closely at the old wooden frame, I'd find my own nail marks in the wood. If I thought about it too long, I'd hear my own screams echoing in the trees.

My throat was so tight, my tongue like dry cotton. My feet found the edge and I was balancing on it, the darkness at my back. The darkness of my nightmares.

I eased back over the edge, and down.

I let the rope out slowly as I moved. Just one step at a time. The darkness closed in quickly, my light illuminat-ing the smooth, muddy slope in front of me. I found the drop-off at the end, and with a slow, shaking breath, I rappelled down the rest of the way.

I landed in a few inches of water. Most of the cav-ern was filled with it. I unhooked my harness, leaving the rope to dangle there until I returned. Zane had already made his way across the water and was inspecting the branching shafts that led away from the cavern. He didn't have any cheerful, sarcastic greeting for me, and his silence heightened my nerves.

I gave my rope one last tug to reassure myself it was still secure. But as I did, I noticed something sticking out of the dirt wall it dangled against. I frowned as I plucked it from the mud. Thin . . . almost translucent . . . the color of bone . . .

A fingernail.

I dropped it instantly, nauseated. The air was heavy, the crushing weight of the earth around me making my skull prickle with claustrophobia. I waded across the water, lifting my guns to keep them dry. The water didn't feel as cold as I'd thought it would, but that didn't make it any better. Its lukewarm temperature felt oddly sinister.

"Which way?" I said softly. Zane nodded up the shaft he stood beside, his eyes narrowed as he gazed into the dark. My light illuminated the narrow tunnel, but the shadows still lay thick beyond its reach.

"There's drag marks on the ground here," he said. "And I can smell it."

"Smell what?"

"His corpse."

Zane led the way down the narrow tunnel. The ceiling was low enough that he had to bend, and even my head brushed it as I walked. It wasn't long before I could smell it too: that vile rot, like old meat left in the sun. I kept glancing back, unable to shake off the feeling of being watched. It was eerily silent save for our footsteps.

The tunnel opened into a low cavern. Stalagmites jutted up from the floor, and the remnants of an old mine cart track were scattered around. White mushrooms sprouted in clusters from the walls, and they glowed softly when I moved my light away from them. The smell was horrific, and I tugged my shirt up to cover my nose in desperation. Zane paused again, sniffing the air, frowning.

"What's wrong?" My voice was barely a whisper, but even that felt too loud.

"His body is close." Zane turned slowly. "Get ready."

I pulled out the shotgun. We crept forward, our boots splashing through puddles. The cavern opened wider, the stalagmites and stalactites like the teeth of some monstrous beast encaging us within its jaws. As my light moved around the cavern, I noticed odd scratches in the stones. Like claw marks. There were more mushrooms too—across the ground, the walls, even the ceiling.

Suddenly, Zane stopped. I turned my light toward him, then looked past him.

We'd found Marcus.

But something else had found him first.

JUNIPER

MARCUS LAY ON a ridge, atop a cluster of stalagmites, his body bent and broken between the spikes. He
was bloated, his flesh mottled unnatural colors, his eye
sockets empty—plucked clean. My brain couldn't seem
to process what I was seeing. It couldn't connect the
dots between the ruined flesh I saw, and the brother I'd
known.

Then it clicked, and a strange, cold numbness settled
over me like ice spreading through my veins.

Something had dragged Marcus up there, and it—
they—were still there.

They were as still as the stones that surrounded
them. Their limbs were long, as pale as bones. Their
heads—skeletal, with milky white eyes and thin sharp
antlers—drooped from their long necks. They looked
stretched—everything out of proportion, too long, too

thin. Their legs ended in white cloven hooves, and their knees were *backward*, like long-legged birds. Wispy rags hung from their bodies, but the fabric looked disturbingly flesh-like.

They weren't moving. Their arms hung limply at their sides. Only their heads were slightly swaying, so slowly that if I hadn't stared at them for so long, I wouldn't have noticed it at all.

I edged closer to Zane, as quietly as I could. He glanced down at me, and I mouthed silently, "What are they?"

He shook his head and pressed his finger to his lips. Message received, quiet and clear.

Keeping low to the ground, Zane crept across the cavern. He climbed up the ridge, and I raised my gun and kept my aim steadily on the creature closest to him. They still hadn't moved, other than that subtle swaying of their heads. Zane crawled across the ridge, his eyes wide and unblinking, shockingly bright in the dark. He was right next to Marcus now, barely an arm's length from the closest creature. Slowly, he reached over the stones and lifted Marcus from between them. My brother's head rolled back, strange black liquid dripping from his purple, shrunken lips.

"Juniper."

I shuddered, but I didn't turn. The voice had come from behind me, a breathy whisper somewhere above my head. I had to ignore it. Just fucking ignore it. I held my aim as Zane began to crawl back down.

"You've come back to me."

My grip on the gun tightened. I could no longer reassure myself that it was only in my head. I was in *Its*
territory now. These dark, flooded tunnels were the God's
domain. It knew I was here. It *knew*.

"You've defied me for so long."

There was a strange, soft sound behind me, like
something slimy sliding through water. I exhaled slowly,
hardly able to bear drawing another breath because of
the stench. My heart was pounding so hard it hurt, and I
desperately needed more air. But I didn't move. Zane was
nearly back down, Marcus slung over his shoulder, and
the creatures still seemed entirely unaware. We were so
close . . .

"You can't run anymore."

The wet dragging sound was right at my feet. There
was pressure against my boot. Slowly, I looked down.

Thick, gray, slimy tentacles were coiling around my
ankles.

I screamed, scrambling away and tripping over the
uneven ground. I swung the gun wildly, using it like a
cudgel to beat back the creature trying to coil itself
around me. The tentacles kept coming, slithering toward
me, emerging from the shallow puddles, from the mud
itself. Backed against the wall, I started shooting, barely
taking aim. They were slithering up my legs, gripping me,
holding down my arms, covering my mouth as I tried to
bite. I squeezed my eyes shut as they coiled around my
head, remembering my nightmares of tentacles pressing
into my brother's eyeballs—

"Juniper!"

My eyes shot open. Zane crouched over me, one hand pinning my wrists, the other clamped over my mouth. He'd turned off my light. Only the faintly glowing mushrooms provided illumination. His eyes were wide, his teeth bared. Marcus's body lay behind him on the ground.

There were no tentacles. None at all. There were only the pale creatures on the ridge—and all of them had raised their heads toward us.

Click, click, click.

One of them straightened its neck, with a sound like popping joints. I tried to hold my breath, my skin cold with sweat. Were they blind? Could they see us if we didn't move? Seconds passed, as the creatures moved their upright heads back and forth, bobbing them like snakes taking aim at their prey.

Then, one of them *spoke*.

"Who creeps in the dark?" The voice was a harsh, low whisper. The other two clicked their teeth together rapidly, the sound echoing around the cavern. Zane was utterly still, not breathing, not even blinking.

With sudden, jerking movements and that awful sound of popping, one of the creatures scurried down from the ridge. It bobbed its head on that long, spine-like neck, clicking its teeth. "Sweet flesh. Tender, living flesh. Where are you?"

The smell of mold was so strong now, it almost overpowered the stench of the corpse. My head was light—whether from the smell, from struggling to hold my breath, or from fear, I wasn't sure. The creature moved rapidly but with uncertainty, jerking around the cavern as the others swayed on the ridge above, trying to find us in the dark.

Suddenly, the creature stopped. Its white eyes didn't blink, and they reflected the mushroom's luminescent glow. A sound, like a sudden draft or breath of wind, came through the chamber. The temperature had dropped low enough that I shivered.

"The Deep One speaks," the creature whispered, and the other two abruptly stopped chattering their teeth. "It wants the living flesh. Where . . ."

I shifted my gun. I had to be ready to shoot.

But that soft sound of movement was all it took. The creature's head jerked toward me, and it *screamed*.

Zane jerked me to my feet, shoving me toward the mouth of the tunnel. He grabbed Marcus, carrying him as easily as a ragdoll. I stumbled in the dark, unable to see without my light as Zane easily got ahead of me. I fumbled to turn the light back on as I sprinted; but my foot caught on a stone and I went down, landing hard on my side.

With the air knocked out of me, I rolled to my back. My light shone up into the pale creature's face, standing over me.

I fired the gun, the blast knocking it back, but only for a second. The others were right behind it, moving rapidly toward me. Even the one I'd shot shuddered on the ground and rose back up, thick black mud dripping from its head. My bullet hole was swiftly disappearing, melting back together.

I fired again and again, the creatures absorbing the slugs like they were nothing.

I tried to reload, but my hands were shaking and my bullets dropped to the ground, rolling away from me. I scrambled for them in the dark as the creatures surrounded me, their teeth chattering, their heads swaying. My light swung over them, and I realized that mushrooms were sprouting around their hooves.

"Tender flesh," one whispered, and clicked its teeth. "The Deep One calls you."

I found a bullet, rolled under the narrow edge of a rock. I couldn't reach it; my hand couldn't fit far enough. The creature stood over me as I grasped for it, reaching down a pale boney hand that dripped icy cold water—

A roar shook the walls of the mine, dislodging stones and dust. A shape flung itself over me, slamming into the creature and knocking it back. I scrambled up and away, my light swinging wildly over the chaos. It was Zane, pinning one of the monsters to the ground as the others locked onto his back, their hands gripping him so hard that bruises were blooming across his skin. He ripped at them, his claws tearing into their thin bellies and ripping out roots and mud. He ripped another off his back, gripping its skull and slamming it repeatedly against the stones until mud splattered across the walls.

With one monster twitching at his feet, the others jerked back, screeching and chattering their teeth as they retreated into the dark.

Zane turned to me, and I saw for the first time that the whites of his eyes had gone completely black, their golden color showing like a ring of fire in the night sky. He grabbed my arm and pulled me; but when I couldn't run fast enough, he hauled me onto his back, sprinting through the cavern's tunnels at an impossible speed. I didn't fight him, I didn't protest. I didn't care if I had to be carried like a baby—whatever it took to put distance between me and those things. Whatever it took to get out of this awful place.

He let me down the moment we emerged into the cool, fresh air. I wanted to drop to my knees, just to feel the grass under my hands, but I forced myself to stand. The weight of everything was dropping onto me, harder and heavier than I could have imagined. Marcus lay on the grass nearby; Zane had gone ahead and brought him up before he came back for me.

I'd done all this for a corpse. I'd risked my life, I'd risked everything, for rotting flesh.

I swallowed down my shame. I swallowed down the tears that wanted to come, the sobs that wanted to explode out of me. Those things had ruined his body, torn it, *eaten* it. Marcus never deserved this. He deserved better than this.

Zane rubbed his hand over his head, before he paused to examine the deep purple bruises across his skin. His shirt had been torn, and there were ragged bite marks across his shoulder and his neck. I tried not to stare, but the extent of his injuries just kept getting worse the longer I looked. Deep gashes, bite wounds, and as he slowly clenched and unclenched his hand, I could tell his fingers were broken.

He'd come back for me. He'd . . .

He'd saved me.

Why the hell had he done that? Why had he bothered?

"We should move," he said, his voice rough. His eyes were simply golden again, the darkness in them gone. "The Gollums won't stop. They'll keep coming."

"Gollums?" I glanced back at the mine. "They . . . they knew who I was. They said the Deep One wants me . . ."

"They serve the God." He limped over to where Marcus lay and dragged him up, throwing him over his shoulder again. The movement hurt him; I could see it on his face. "Gods are jealous. Gods are possessive. Just because It got your brother in your place doesn't mean It won't still want you. And the Gollums won't stop now that they're awake." He looked at me, a frown deepening on his face. "Did you hear Its voice? Did It speak to you?"

A chill went up my back as I remembered the whispers . . . the tentacles curling up my legs. "I heard It. I saw It."

He swore, turning for the trail. He didn't say another word as we made our way back down the hillside and through the forest. When we reached the car, he put Marcus in the trunk, wrapped in the blankets we'd brought. Only when he was in the car, seated beside me, did he lean his head back for a moment and let out a heavy sigh.

"That fucking sucked."

I giggled—then laughed. It wasn't even funny, but I laughed because I couldn't cry. I was exhausted, all the

adrenaline drained out of me. I was grieving, I was horrified, I was confused. So I laughed because if I didn't, I'd
scream.

"Yeah, it really . . . it really did." I shook my head,
daring to glance over at him. "You smell awful."

"Well, *yeah*, I've got corpse juice all over me!" He
ripped off the rags that remained of his shirt, tossing
it out the window as we began to drive. "Try having a
heightened sense of smell around that shit."

We kept the radio turned off, just driving with the
hum of the engine and tapping of the rain. I leaned my
head against the cold window, but what I wanted . . .
what I really wanted . . . was to lay my head against his
shoulder.

It was foolish. It was weak. I wouldn't do it, but God,
the desire for it ached. The gap between us across the
seats felt a million miles wide, and it had been so long
since I'd just . . . touched . . . someone.

Not for sex, not for pleasure. Just touch.

I stole a glance over at him, and his eyes met mine.
He'd saved my life. He'd injured himself to save my life,
and I couldn't understand why.

"Did they hurt you?" he said.

"No. They didn't." *Thanks to you*, was what I should
have said. *I owe you my life. Thank you. You came back
for me.*

But I didn't say it. I didn't dare.

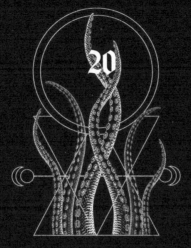

JUNIPER

IT TOOK US a few hours to reach my cabin. The car couldn't make it up the steeper portions of the road, so Zane carried Marcus, wrapped in blankets, behind me up the hillside. My feet felt like they were made of lead, every step dragging me down. I needed to stay awake. I needed to find just a little more strength.

"You can leave us here," I said as we reached the cabin. "I'll bury him."

Zane frowned as he lay the body down, looking around at the tiny cabin. "Do you even have heat here?"

"There's a stove. Why do you care?" I winced. Why did that come out? Harsh words fell off my tongue easier than anything else, tumbling forward without thought. Demon or not, he didn't deserve it.

Fuck, the last thing I needed to be feeling was even more guilt.

"Please," I said softly. "Just . . . just leave me here. I need to be alone."

He kept looking around the yard, his expression far from pleased. "Fine. Call me when you're ready."

He moved fast enough to simply vanish. Not another word, not a single protest. I winced as I stared at the spot where he'd been, digging my nails into my palm. I hadn't even said thank you. Was I supposed to? Was I obligated to? The only reason he'd bothered to save me was because of our bargain, it was because . . .

Because . . .

"Fuck." I slammed my fist against the side of the house as I went back to get the old shovel. The head was rusted and the handle was full of splinters, but it would have to do. I had a few hours until nightfall, but the dark would move in quickly thanks to the cloud cover. I needed this done before sunset, so despite the pain in every muscle, I started digging.

There was an old log at the far side of the yard, a tree that had fallen years ago during a storm. Dad used to say he was going to cut it up for firewood, but it became one of my and Marcus's favorite places to play when we were kids. It used to look huge to me, and in my memories, it still was. A monstrous, moss-covered tree that served as a home for a family of chipmunks and little bugs.

I used to have to climb up the side, imagining I was scaling Mt. Everest. I'd get to the top and reach down my hand to help Marcus up, because he was too little to climb it himself.

I dug his grave there, next to the log.

The hours passed and the darkness grew. My shoulders ached, my back was in knots, but I kept digging. My hands were rubbed raw from the shovel's rough handle, my palms had formed blisters that broke and bled. But I kept digging.

Finally, when it was ready, I pulled Marcus's body across the yard. I had to use the blanket to drag him. I wasn't strong enough to lift him. He'd grown so much, but of course he had. The last time I'd seen him, he'd still been just a boy. His voice had barely started to change. I wished I could move back the blanket. I wished I could see his face. But I didn't want to see what had become of him. I didn't want to see that his eyes were gone and his body had begun to rot.

I didn't want to remember him that way.

I wanted to remember him running around the yard with a stick for a sword, his shoelaces untied, wearing his favorite red-and-yellow Tonka Truck shirt. I wanted to remember him standing up on top of the log and giggling down at the little chipmunks when they emerged from their nest.

I let my feet dangle into the grave, his body beside me. I sniffed, wiped my nose and smeared dirt across my face. My throat tightened. My chest hurt. My eyes stung so badly no amount of blinking could make it stop.

I laid my hand over the blanket. "I'm sorry," I whispered. The ache grew worse. "I'm so sorry."

I hung my head. I let myself cry. I let the ache overtake me. I let the pain strangle me. It hurt, and nothing, *nothing* would make it stop.

THE SPIGOT WASN'T working, so I couldn't wash the dirt off my hands. I always had a supply of baby wipes, because I was used to going long periods without access to a shower, so I wiped myself down with those as best I could. I only had a can of beans left and some crackers. I still hadn't gotten gas for the generator, so the wood-burning stove soon became my only light.

I wanted a hot shower. I wanted a glass of cold whiskey. A blanket, even. I wanted to stretch out on a soft couch. I wanted to wrap myself in clean sheets. God, I wanted to stop crying.

I shouldn't have stayed at the demon's house, not even for a few days. I'd spent years on the road, sleeping in my car, in the open air, in shitty hotel rooms if I could afford it. Letting myself indulge in something comfortable hadn't been worth it. Comfort wasn't part of my life; it simply wasn't. I didn't need it. I didn't even deserve it.

I'd run away and let Marcus die. I hadn't been here to protect him. I hadn't even been able to protect his body. All I could do was make sure the Hadleighs paid for this. No matter how much it hurt. No matter how alone I felt. Tomorrow I'd wake up and figure out what the next step would be. I'd figure out how to hurt them like they'd hurt me.

I curled up near the fire, since it was too cold to sleep across the room in the bed. It wasn't comfortable, but I was too tired to care.

"GET UP INTO the castle! Quick! We'll be safe up there!"

I sprinted across the yard, leaving Marcus in the dust. I hauled myself up onto the mossy log, our "castle," my fingers clinging onto the scratchy bark until I'd pulled myself all the way up. I raised my arms triumphantly, watching as my little brother tried to climb up after me.

"It's too tall, Juni!" He pouted, standing back with his arms folded. "How am I supposed to get into the castle?"

"Your knight will help you, of course!" I got down on my hands and knees, extending an arm to help him. I hauled him up, until he was able to scramble atop the log and stand beside me, surveying the yard from our perch.

I put my hands on my hips. "Our enemies will never defeat us now!"

Marcus wrinkled his nose skeptically. "But . . . what about . . . the army?"

"No army can reach us!" I cried. "We're too high up for them to ever reach the castle."

"What about a dragon?" he said, his face somber. This was, after all, a very important wartime discussion. "What if they have a dragon, Juni?"

"Then your knight will slay it," I said. I whipped my stick out from where I'd tucked it into my belt loop, brandishing it. "Fear not, Prince Marcus! Your knight fears no armies and no dragons!"

He giggled, plopping down on the log. I sat beside him, but kept my stick in my hand. A knight should never be without her trusty sword.

"I'm not afraid of dragons either," he said.

"Good. Remember: we're safe as long as we're in the castle. And as long as you have your knight to defend you."

He giggled again, kicking his feet so his heels knocked against the log. The sun was beginning to set, staining the sky pink and orange, like ice cream melted amongst the clouds. Dad would call us inside soon, and we'd make a wild dash across the yard through enemy forces. Right as we'd reach the house, a dragon would swoop down, and I would defeat it, and our kingdom would be safe.

After all, a knight feared nothing. A knight would never be defeated.

"Juni? What's that?"

I looked up. Marcus was pointing his little finger across the yard, toward the trees that led down to the creek. The sun was getting low, so the shadows were growing. I narrowed my eyes. "I don't see anything, Prince Marcus. Is it the dragon?"

He shook his head. His face looked strange. He didn't look like he was playing anymore. "No, Juni, look."

He was still pointing stubbornly into the trees, and a cold feeling went down my back. I hopped off the log—being the knight, obviously I had to be the one to bravely go into danger. I looked back into the trees, expecting to see a deer or maybe a coyote slinking through the dusk.

But it was so dark.

I shook my head, turning back toward him. "Marcus, I don't see—"

Marcus was gone. All that remained was a long,

narrow strip of upturned dirt at the base of the log, and the cold feeling on my spine came back.

I looked down at my hands: long, calloused fingers, dirty and scarred. It wasn't a stick tucked into my belt loop; it was a gun in my hands. I wasn't a child anymore. This log wasn't our safe castle. And Marcus . . .

Marcus was . . .

Behind me, in the trees, something howled.

I SNAPPED AWAKE, jerking up from the floor. The fire had gone low, and only smoldering coals remained. My hands and feet were freezing cold. I sat there for a moment, breathing slowly, listening. I could hear the wind moving through the trees outside, the groaning of their boughs, the distant trickle of the creek.

I could hear growling.

I leaped up and grabbed my gun, tugging aside the curtain over the window. The clouds had cleared, and silver moonlight lent faint illumination to the yard. Eld beasts yipped and fought amongst each other, their bodies hunched and horrifically ragged as they swarmed the yard. There were so many—*too* many. Six, seven, even more back amongst the trees. They were all gathered at the far side of the yard, around that fallen log . . .

A furious, agonized cry ripped out of me the moment I realized what they'd done.

They'd dug up Marcus.

They'd dug him up.

They were fighting over his corpse, snarling at each

other, rough growls and deep barks sounding as they snapped their teeth at each other. Saliva dripped from their jaws as they tugged at him, as they pulled at his arms and ripped the blanket I'd wrapped him in.

I didn't think. I couldn't think. My mind was a barren wasteland of white-hot rage as I sprinted into the yard.

I fired wildly, erratically, again and again. The beasts scattered for a moment in confusion, but quickly swarmed back. They cut off my route back to the house. Their horrific cries filled the air as they surrounded me, lunging for me. As soon as I'd shoot at one, another would leap in. Their smell was heavy in the air, sickly sweet, turning my stomach.

"Get away from him!" I screamed at them, as if they could understand, as if there was any semblance of humanity behind those dead, white eyes. I struggled to reload, swung the gun to try to force them back. One of them lunged, gripping the stock in its teeth. They snapped at my legs. They were wrestling the gun away—

They ripped it out of my hands and swarmed over me.

Their claws lacerated me, tearing through my clothes. It should have hurt, but all I had left was blinding fury. They couldn't take him. Not again. They didn't get to consume his body like it was mere meat. *They didn't get to take my brother from me!* I still had my knife strapped to my leg and I tugged it free, slashing at them. But their flesh was rotten, and it didn't matter if I stabbed it or ripped it. One got its teeth into my arm and wrenched its head, piercing into me so deep that the pain finally exploded through the rush of shock and adrenaline.

I tried to curl my legs up to protect my stomach. I tried to thrash and fight. I screamed at them and swung the blade at their eyes. But there were too many. There were so many of them on me that they were fighting each other for me, fighting like they had over Marcus. Who would get the best flesh, who could sneak a bite. I curled up, my hands over my head, my legs drawn close. Their claws tore into my back, their teeth snapped near my head. I was surrounded by their stench, choking on it, unable to breathe.

They were going to eat me alive.

ZANE

I DIDN'T KNOW what I was still doing there, hours later, sitting in my car on the side of that narrow, twisting road at the base of the mountain. I should have been home, sleeping off my injuries. I should have been anywhere but here, with my car smelling like a rotting corpse, unable to drive away.

Why did Juniper want to stay in that wretched place anyway? The windows were broken, and it smelled like mold and rat shit. It was isolated, a prime location for the beasts to find her. Yet she wanted to be alone up there with her half-eaten dead brother. She'd wanted to dig his grave in the encroaching dark without any help.

"Fucking hell." I rolled my head back, groaning. I needed to drive away. I needed to go out and fuck someone, remind myself that a bargain was merely a business transaction, mutually beneficial but completely impersonal. At this point, "mutually beneficial" was a stretch to say anyway. Diving into mines where Gods slept, fighting Gollums, fucking with the cult that had practically built Abelaum—the amount of work and danger ahead of us was outrageous.

I should have been half-assing this. If Juniper died, she died. I'd still get her soul. There were plenty more souls out there to claim.

But leaving her up there didn't feel right. *That* was why I was still sitting here, that was why I couldn't just suck it up and go home.

It was cold out, and there was no way in hell she was warm enough in that little shack. She was likely still digging, even though it was dark and she really should have been inside. That look in her eyes before I'd left had been so broken, so wretchedly hurt—it fucking haunted me. I knew the reason she'd told me to leave was so she could weep alone.

Her sorrow was her business, not mine. But the bond between our beings still left me aching, it left me feeling hollow since I'd left her. There was no reason to be so attached, no point in being overly involved.

"Fuck. Fucking fuck. Fuck." I got out and slammed the car door, stalking back up the rutted dirt road. There was no harm in checking if she'd changed her mind about staying out here. She was a fool if she hadn't. What sense did it make to be alone anyway? None. None at all. It was simply more convenient for her to stay with me. We could plan things easier. We could get this deal done quicker.

And if she didn't want to come after all? Fine. I didn't care.

That ache in my chest tightened, and I clenched my teeth. I just needed her back at the house; that was the end of it. It made no sense for her to be out here. It made no sense for her to suffer in some cold, shitty little shack, instead of staying with me.

I paused, sniffing the air. Pine, damp earth, a deer somewhere nearby, and . . . blood.

I listened. The boughs above creaked, animals scurried through the ferns, but no crickets were chirping.

And in the distance . . . howling. Barking. Those wretched, scream-like cries of the Eld beasts.

My veins went cold. It wasn't only the beasts I heard screaming.

I sprinted up the mountainside, reaching her yard in mere minutes. When I broke through the trees next to that miserable little cabin and saw the swelling horde of beasts fighting over something on the ground, it felt like someone had stabbed a hot knife into my chest and twisted it.

Nothing, *nothing* could touch my little wolf and live.

I yelled so loud that the beasts startled, half of them scurrying back from their prize just enough for me to see her. She was lying limp on the ground, her clothing torn to shreds, her blood pooling around her.

There were no cohesive thoughts left in my mind when I saw that. Only vicious, feral bloodlust that dug down to my deepest strength and demanded I use it. The beasts snapped at me uselessly as I grabbed them, crushing skulls and cracking bones, flinging their filthy bodies across the yard. I gathered energy around me, condensed it, and used it to push them back, push them down, and then burst their heads with the pressure. I commanded the energy around me as easily as breathing, far more easily than I'd ever been able to before.

Every soul I claimed increased my strength, but rarely did I flex my full power. But in those moments, that felt like an eternity, I would have done anything to get them off her. Even as I crushed them, tore them apart, their rancid blood splattering my face, I looked back at her continually, desperately, hoping I'd see her move, see her struggle or . . . or open her eyes.

I didn't let a single beast escape. When they realized they were outmatched, and tried to run into the trees, I still caught them, crushing their rotten heads in my hands. Finally, as I dropped yet another corpse at my feet, utter silence fell as its body rapidly decayed into mud and worms.

Not one remained alive.

Juniper lay on the ground, curled on her side, her bleeding arms wrapped around her head. The tightness in my chest grew heavier. My hands were covered with gore, my claws drenched with it. But I reached out, carefully, and laid my hand against her side.

She took one slow, shallow breath, and the tightness in my chest burst.

I picked her up, moving quickly. She groaned, her arms falling away from her face, her fist pounding weakly against my chest. The beasts had torn at her back, bitten her arms and legs. What did a human need to heal wounds like this? A doctor, of course, but who the hell was I to trust with her in Abelaum? The thought of someone else taking her, touching her—fuck, I'd rip their fucking hands off before I let them.

I laid her in the car. I raised her limp head, wiping blood and dirt away from her mouth. Somehow, she'd managed to protect her stomach, but her arms and legs had been torn as a result.

Her lips moved, and I froze. She shuddered, her fingers twitching, her limp arms moving to wrap around her stomach again. Her eyes fluttered, squeezed . . . and opened.

She looked at me with utter confusion, blinking slowly. Then she looked down, at my hand on her wrist, and around the inside of the car, as if she couldn't figure out where she was. I moved my hand off her, but I had to grip the doorframe to keep it away from her as she looked back at me.

"What . . . what happened . . . to Marcus?"

I wanted to shake her for being worried about a corpse when she was bleeding all over my car. I wanted to shake myself for being worried about her at all, for being so breathless with relief that I couldn't even respond to her for a moment.

When I finally managed to say something, it was, "What the hell were you doing fighting that many Eld alone?"

She tried to sit up, but quickly winced and collapsed back again. "What . . . what the hell . . . was I supposed to do?" she hissed, closing her eyes against the pain. "They dug him up. They . . . they were eating him . . ."

"They nearly ate *you*." I had to pause again and calm myself. I was still balancing on the edge of rage. "You need stitches, Juniper."

"No doctors," she said quickly, shaking her head. "Please. Please, no doctors."

She didn't trust them, and I didn't blame her. I didn't fucking trust them to touch her either. I slammed the car door and got into the driver's seat, starting the engine. She was breathing deeper now, breathing quickly, the scent of her fear growing.

"No doctors." She grasped my arm, squeezing weakly. "Don't . . . don't take me to a hospital . . . I can't . . ."

"I'm not taking you to a doctor," I said roughly, the tires skidding out as I pulled onto the road. "I'm taking you home."

I didn't have anything at the house I'd need to care for her, so I stopped at a 24-hour pharmacy on the way. Her eyes were closed, and her head had drooped down, but her breathing was still rapid and frightened even in her sleep. The longer I looked at her, the tighter my hand got on the wheel.

I never should have left her up there. Damn her pride, fuck her determination that she had to do everything herself.

She was *mine*, and I took care of what was mine.

The clerk gave me a long, wary look as I came up to the register with an arm full of various bandages and disinfectants. I'd already slipped behind the pharmacy counter and snatched a few pill bottles that would be useful for an injured human. The clerk's hands fumbled as he rang me up, unable to stop staring at me.

"Are you, uh . . . having a good night?" he said. I gave an impatient nod of my head. "You, uh . . . you got a little something . . . on your face."

I glanced up at myself on the CCTV. I was smeared with blood from head-to-toe. I smiled tightly as I looked back at the wide-eyed clerk. "You'd better just forget I was here."

He nodded quickly, shoving my things into a plastic bag. "Oh yeah. Yeah. No problem."

JUNIPER

BEFORE I SLIPPED into unconsciousness, my last thought was that this was such a stupid, useless way to die.

I'd acted recklessly, I'd let emotion get the better of me. Strange how imminent death can bring such sudden clarity. My anger, my grief, my despair—they were useless to me now. It didn't matter. None of it mattered if I was dead.

I floated in pain, the sounds of the Eld beasts' horrible cries surrounding me. Their cries grew worse, they became an endless cacophony of screams, howling, snarling. And then . . .

Then I heard Zane's voice. I felt his arms around me. The pain got worse and worse, but the howls were gone. I was warm. It was quiet. I drifted deeper to escape the pain.

Death couldn't hurt this much, at least . . . I desperately hoped it didn't.

Something tugged at me, pressing against the awful ache in my side. I weakly tried to shove it away, even though my arms felt like stones dangling from my shoulders. My vision was just a blur. Trying to focus on anything made my head swim.

"Easy, easy. It's just me." Zane again. His deep voice was like a warm fire, a soft blanket, a steaming mug of cider. I wanted to sink into it and lose myself in it. It occurred to me suddenly that he'd probably be really good at reading bedtime stories.

It then occurred to me that I'd lost way too much blood, and it was making me loopy as hell.

He lifted me, holding me tight and close against his chest. God, he was so warm. So, so warm. I nuzzled my face against his chest, even though his shirt felt dirty. It didn't matter that he smelled like blood—*his* scent was still there, buried beneath, rich and comforting.

I wanted that scent in a goddamn candle.

But even his warmth couldn't keep the cold away. I kept drifting in and out of the dark, my eyes too heavy to keep open. I shivered, and as if from a great distance, I heard him say quickly, "What's wrong? Why are you shaking?"

I laughed a little, or at least I tried. It may have sounded more like a gross hiccup. But he sounded so worried, so . . . so concerned. For me. But why would he worry over me? If I died, it just saved him the trouble of having to fulfill his end of the deal; I'd be going to Hell regardless. I managed to get my eyes open and realized we were standing inside, in his living room. All the curtains were drawn over the windows, the lights were on, and he was holding me cradled in his arms.

I looked up at him, frowning down at me. "You're a mess," I said softly. I needed water. My throat was so dry it hurt. "You're all . . . you're all dirty."

He shook his head. "You're one to talk. You look like the leftovers at a meat market."

My light-headedness demanded I close my eyes again. When I next managed to open them, I was lying on the couch, my head propped up on a pillow. Zane was crouched over me, his eyes narrowed in concentration. There was the prick of a needle piercing my skin and a tug as my wound was stitched together.

I looked at him in silence for a long while. His intense concentration was focused on the gaping wound on my upper arm, my flesh ripped open by the Eld beasts' claws. The pain of the needle was nothing in comparison to all the other agony my body was going through.

"I guess I'm not . . . not very sexy like this, am I?" I said, my voice little more than a croak. His bright eyes glared at me before he went right back to tying off my stitches. "Did you . . . did you hear me screaming?"

His face twitched, an expression I couldn't fully understand. He set aside the needle and picked up a cloth instead, using the damp rag to carefully clean away the blood and dirt on my arm. "Yes. I heard you screaming."

The warmth of the damp cloth felt good. His hands on me felt so nice I could have moaned, and not even in a sexy way. It was just that everything hurt except his gentle touches. "Why . . . why did you come back?"

"I never want to hear that sound again, Juniper." He gripped the cloth in his hand, his fingers slowly curling into a fist around it. He was shaking his head, his jaw clenched so tight that a vein in his temple was slowly turning black. "I never want to hear the way you sound when you're in pain like that . . . when you're scared like that . . ." He looked away from me, fixing his smoldering gaze on the far wall. "I slaughtered them all, Juniper. Every single one. I promise you right now that nothing that dares try to hurt you gets to live. *Nothing*." His voice became a growl and he closed his eyes, breathing slowly.

He was so angry I could feel his arm shaking as he went back to wiping down my skin. I didn't understand, and it made me frightened again. My heart began to beat harder, and that awful grip of anxiety tightened its hold.

"Please don't be afraid," he said softly. "Don't . . . just . . ." He sighed heavily. "I need to bathe you. And get you into bed. And give you pills."

It was like he had a mental checklist of how to keep me alive. It was . . . sweet. It was kind. Too kind. Far kinder than he should have been. With a wince, I lifted my head from the pillow and braced myself on my arm. It was far more difficult than I'd hoped it would be. Trying to stand seemed truly daunting.

But I had to do this. I had to get it together. If I was alone, this all would have been up to me, and I knew better than to rely on anyone else.

"I can do it," I said. "I just need a drink. Can you bring me a beer?"

"I'm bringing you water. You need hydration. Do *not* get up." He jabbed his finger at me, stopping halfway to the kitchen. "I swear to fucking Lucifer, don't try to stand up off that couch."

I leaned back against the cushions. Christ, just sitting up made me lose my breath. And I wasn't about to listen to a demon tell me I couldn't drink. "I'll get it myself!" I said, but raising my voice made my head swim, and I groaned, clutching it in my filthy hands.

"You fucking will not." He was already back, offering me a glass of water and two tiny bottles of pills. "You can't drink alcohol with this prescription."

I hated that my hands shook as I reached up to take the pills and water. The pills were each prescribed to someone different—one was penicillin, the other was oxycodone. My eyes almost bulged out of my head.

"Did you steal these?" He shrugged, standing over me like he expected me to run for the door. As if I could manage a single step without falling on my face. I usually avoided shit like oxy; getting used to comfort just made it worse when it wasn't available anymore, and I never had money for doctors. But God, everything hurt. I put one of each pill on my palm and drank them down with half the glass of water. I really had needed the hydration, far more than I'd realized. I drank the rest almost immediately.

"Alright. Let's get you cleaned up."

He didn't even give me the option to walk. He scooped me up from the couch like it was nothing, and I settled my head against his chest again as he carried me up the stairs. His heartbeat was strange, sometimes slow and sometimes wildly fast, like the organ didn't know how exactly a demon was supposed to operate.

"You've got a weird heartbeat," I muttered, and he chuckled.

"Demons aren't built for Earth," he said. "Our shit is a little wonky."

He set me down again on the bathroom floor, running the shower so it would get hot. I felt like a ragdoll, all my limbs floppy, my strength nonexistent. I'd endured serious injuries before, but this . . . this was the worst.

And it wasn't even as bad as it could have been.

"Thank you."

He turned toward me, unzipping his jeans. "What was that?"

"You heard me," I muttered. His sarcastic grin confirmed I was right. "I don't know why you came back. I don't know why you . . . care. *If* you care. But I just—"

He squatted down in front of me, arms resting on his knees. "I take care of what's mine." He reached out, his claws brushing my face as he tucked a wild strand of my hair behind my ear. "It's as simple as that. You're not alone anymore, Juniper. Get that through your thick skull."

There was a strange feeling in my chest as he stood and finished undressing. It felt . . . warm. Warm and soft, squishing around inside me like pillows padding my heart.

"What are you doing?" I said, trying to distract myself from the not-unpleasant-but-definitely-terrifying soft feeling. "Why are you naked?"

"The better question is, why aren't *you* naked?" he said. "I'm filthy, you're filthier. We're getting cleaned up."

I nodded, and tried to strip off my shirt. But halfway over my head, my arms felt like Jell-O again, and I couldn't manage to pull my hair through the neck, so the clothing was stuck like a bag over my face, my arms refusing to tug it any further.

"Fuck. Fucking . . . stupid . . ." The shirt was pulled out of my hands, and Zane tossed it away into the corner.

"I'm not washing them this time," he said. "We're just throwing them away."

He eased off my boots, and then my jeans. He was careful, slowing down every time I hissed in pain. He'd undressed me before, but this felt different. It wasn't sexual, and yet it felt so intimate. When he lifted me again and carried me inside the large walk-in shower, I didn't want him to put me down.

The feeling of his bare skin on mine—not in the midst of fucking but just *touching*—almost brought me to tears.

"Can you stand up?" he said. The water was so warm, washing away streams of blood and dirt down the drain.

I nodded slowly. "If you let me lean on you, I can."

I hated to receive help nearly as much as I hated to ask for it. I'd gotten myself into this mess with my own reckless actions, and I felt like the help wasn't deserved. I'd fucked up, I deserved the pain. Maybe it would make me remember to be more cautious next time.

But I was so tired. I was tired and raw, like a crab yanked out of its shell. I leaned heavily against him as he set me slowly on my feet, my legs trembling until I managed to lock my knees. I lay my cheek against his shoulder, my eyes only half-open, the hot water hitting my aching back.

"There's blood in your hair," he said. He was gripping my arms to steady me, and even in the steam from the shower, his skin still felt unusually hot.

My eyes were fully closed now. I was too tired to keep them open. "I should just shave it off. It's filthy."

"Lucifer's balls, stop being such a fucking martyr. Sit down."

He eased me to the floor. The shower was big enough for him to kneel behind me as I sat cross-legged on the tile, barely able to keep myself awake. He got my long hair wet, tipping my head into the streaming water. He squeezed a dollop of shampoo into his hand, and began to massage it into my hair.

I bit my lip. God, it felt amazing. His claws lightly scratched my scalp, massaging the soap through my hair, working the suds down to the very ends. He took his time, moving slowly, my body becoming more relaxed with every passing minute.

"Don't fall asleep on me now," he said. "I've gotta rinse you."

I closed my eyes as he tipped me into the shower's stream. Dirt, blood, and grime were stroked out of my hair, his hands gentle as they rubbed all over my scalp. The heat had soothed the ache in my muscles, and the oxy was finally kicking in.

"I'm sleepy," I mumbled, my head drooping down

as he squeezed the water from my hair. I wanted to stay awake, but my body had other plans. I didn't even know if I'd make it to bed.

"I know. We're almost done."

He stood up for a few minutes. I could only guess he was washing himself, but I couldn't stay awake for it. I drifted off, nearly asleep when the water turning off stirred me awake again. Everything was a very sleepy blur, painkillers and exhaustion refusing to allow me to open my eyes as a towel was wrapped around my body and around my hair.

He laid me in bed naked, and pulled the clean blankets over me. His hands brushed my shoulder as he covered me, and I longed for more of that little touch. The thought of back-scratches and a bedtime story sounded really damn good to my ridiculous, sleep-deprived brain.

He said something about bandages, but I was too tired to pay attention. I was asleep within seconds.

JUNIPER

THE SUN SHONE bright the next day, in a crisp, cold-blue sky. Zane went with me back up the mountain, carrying me on his back for most of the way. My pride told me I should have limped my way up the hillside, but maybe for once—just once—I could set my pride aside and accept the help.

It would have taken us hours to reach the cabin if I'd been walking. The Eld really did a number on me; my body ached as if someone had beaten me with hammers. The closer we got to the yard, the more my nausea grew. I could still smell the stench of death.

Just at the edge of the yard, Zane set me down.

"Wait here," he said. "I'll get your brother buried."

"I can help—"

He held up a clawed hand. "No, you can't. You don't

need to keep exposing yourself to seeing his body. Give yourself a little mercy, Juniper."

I didn't argue with him. He was right, I couldn't bear the sight again. I'd seen plenty of death through the years, I'd taken lives, I'd inflicted and endured brutal injuries. But this was my brother, and he wouldn't have wanted me to see him like that either.

Give yourself a little mercy. Easier said than done, but I tried.

It was only a few minutes before Zane returned and motioned for me to follow him. There were few signs of the carnage from last night, but splintered trees at the edge of the yard served as evidence something massively powerful had ripped through here. A shiver went up my spine at the memory of Zane fighting the Gollums, and the brutal, untamable strength he could unleash. I had no memory of what he'd done to the Eld, but when he said he'd slaughtered them all, it must have been a bloodbath.

The grave was filled again; Marcus laid to rest once more. But this time, the massive log I'd buried him beside had been pulled over the grave, a barrier against anything that wanted to dig him up again.

The prince was laid to rest in his crypt beneath the castle, and in the castle he's safe.

"Here." I turned to find Zane standing there with my shotgun in his hand. "I found it back in the trees."

I took it carefully, immediately more at ease with the weight of it in my hands. But a gun couldn't save me from foolish actions. I'd let emotion drag me into danger last night, and it had nearly cost me my life. I wouldn't make that mistake again.

"I'll be nearby," Zane said, and he walked away to give me some privacy. I knelt down near the grave, and laid my hand over the dirt. All my tears were drained, the sharp agony now a dull, cold ache in my chest. No matter what I did now, no matter how hard I fought, Marcus was gone.

But he wouldn't be forgotten. I wouldn't let them forget. Those who had done this to him—those who had done this to *me*—would die with our names on their lips.

"I'm coming for you, fuckers," I murmured. I kissed my hand and laid it to the dirt in one final good-bye. Then I went back to the cabin and collected the few things I had. As I left the house, locking the door behind me, the wind picked up and rustled through the trees, tracing a cold chill up my back.

"Juniper . . ."

I turned. Even on a sunny day like this, shadows lay beneath the trees. There would always be dark places in these woods.

"I'll find you."

The voice was a hiss on the wind, but it was also a whisper in my ear. The God had come so close to having me once; It would never forgive my escape. No matter how far I went, no matter where I hid, it didn't matter. It would always be looking for me, grasping for me, trying to drag me back into the dark.

"Find me," I said softly, glaring into the trees, into the shadows where wicked things hid. "I'll be bathing in

your servants' blood when you do. You can't stop me."
The wind blew harder, *colder*. The trees groaned under
the sudden force. "All you can do is watch the destruction."

MY INJURIES KEPT me from moving around much
for the next few days. As it turned out, I was severely
sleep-deprived besides my extensive wounds. I collapsed
into bed mid-afternoon and didn't stir until the next
morning. I woke up only to eat, down an antibiotic and
another oxy, and then fall back asleep for another twelve
hours.

Miraculously, I didn't have any nightmares. My
dreams were disjointed and strange, long looping visions of walking through the woods as it got darker and
darker. But nothing came out of the darkness for me, at
least not yet.

By day three, I couldn't take it anymore. If I had been
alone, I would have already been dead or on my way to
it, and that wasn't acceptable. I hauled myself out of bed,
made eggs and toast for breakfast, took an antibiotic but
skipped the pain pills. I was sore as Hell, but that wasn't
an excuse. I couldn't keep lounging around.

I jogged around the lake, keeping close to the shore. I
had to stop far more than I found acceptable. I was risk-
ing tearing open my stitches, but I was getting anxious
the longer I let myself rest. I was out on the deck, into
my second set of burpees when I noticed Zane near the
house.

I tried to ignore him. He didn't let me.

"The fuck are you doing?" He watched me move up and down, his frown deepening in confusion. "You're bleeding through your bandages. I can smell it."

"I'll . . . deal with it . . . later," I panted. My head was getting a little light, but that didn't matter. I got up for another jump, but Zane grabbed my upper arm before I could.

"Juniper, in general, I find humans to be painfully fragile," he said. "Annoyingly delicate. Bump one of you mortals the wrong way and suddenly you've got broken bones. But you're not going to kill your own mortality by breaking your body again. Opening your own scars won't make them disappear."

"Don't try to be philosophical." I was trying to catch my breath, but damn, now that I'd lost my momentum, the exhaustion was hitting me hard. "I don't deserve to just sit in the house."

"You tell me not to be philosophical, yet here you are imposing arbitrary stipulations on your own healing." He scoffed. "You know what demons do when we're hurt? We sleep. We'll sleep for *years* if that's how long it takes." He shook his head. "What the hell do you mean, you don't *deserve* it? What does deserving have to do with it?"

I was too dizzy to keep standing. I sat on the deck, panting, and realized Zane was right about the bleeding: a large red stain had appeared on the bandage on my right arm. He squatted down across from me, so I knew he wasn't just asking those questions for the hell of it. He wanted answers.

"Why does it matter to you?" I traced my thumb over the bloody stain. I should have been worried about the stitches I'd torn beneath; but instead, when I looked at the blood, all I saw was weakness.

"You need to stop asking that question."

I glared up at him. "Why?"

"Because neither one of us is ready to hear the answer."

That wasn't what I'd expected to hear. But as I looked at him, at those golden eyes with black veins creeping in at the edges, I knew he was right.

"Do you know the story?" I said softly. "About the girl who went missing? The girl who lost her mind?" I looked down at the deck, at the swirls in the old, stained wood. "Do you know the story everyone told, or do you know the real one? You're friends with Leon, so . . . maybe he told you."

"Your story," he said. "The girl who was lured into the woods, captured, tortured, thrown underground to die." He nodded. It was the first time I'd heard another soul acknowledge what happened—what really happened. After so many years of only hearing the lies, to hear the truth from another mouth was stunning. "But you didn't die. You got out. And that's all I know, because that's all Leon knows." He chuckled. "He never understood how you got out of there. How you got away from him. I don't, either."

"I didn't stop," I said softly. "Everything hurt. I was so fucking scared. But . . ."

I HAD TO get out.

I didn't know how long I'd been screaming, only that my throat was so raw my voice was broken. What had happened after Victoria opened the church doors was warped by the LSD, shrouded and blurred by panic and pain.

All those people, faceless, hidden by their masks. Kent Hadleigh with the knife. Victoria, her hand around mine like Judas's kiss. Jeremiah, cold and uncaring. Meredith Hadleigh, watching me in disgust. Heidi Laverne, asking for my name. Everly, hidden in the shadows, witnessing me bleed.

I knew them. I'd trusted them.

I dug my fingers into the mud, dragging myself up the slope with shaking arms. Every breath was a panicked sob; adrenaline had overtaken every nerve, every muscle. Another fingernail ripped off, pain shooting up my hand into my arm. They'd boarded up the entrance to the shaft; I'd heard the hammers pounding as I screamed. Part of my brain thought I was already dead, and I should just lay down and wait for whatever I could hear moving around in the dark to come take me.

I didn't stop.

I found little roots in the mud and grasped them. I flattened myself to the ground, my cheek sliding through the mud, shuddering with pain as I scrambled higher . . .

higher. I couldn't slip down again. I wouldn't be able to make it back up. My strength was failing.

If I fell again, it would be for the last time.

"Juniper Kynes . . . come to me . . . "

"No," I growled frantically, grasping for another handhold. "No, no, no, get away from me!"

I didn't know if the voice was real. The acid was still warping my vision, creating fractals and bizarre colors in the dark. None of this felt real. This was just a nightmare, and any second, I'd wake up.

I had to wake up.

Sobs wracked my chest as I reached the boards over the mine shaft entrance. I grabbed onto them, the first solid thing I'd felt in those long, painful minutes of climbing. There was space between the boards, enough for me to stick my arm through and wave it weakly in the rain.

"Help me." My voice was barely a squeak, even though I tried to scream. "Please . . . please . . . somebody help me . . . " I pressed my shoulder against the boards, my feet slipping in the mud as I tried to get some leverage. The boards didn't even wiggle. I couldn't squeeze between them. Desperately, I dug my fingers into the dirt beneath. I could dig out. I had to.

Then, in the darkness, I saw a white-cloak approaching.

Their hood was pulled up, and I couldn't see their face in the dark. I gripped the boards, my heart hammering against my ribs. I should have known they'd be waiting for me, to make sure I didn't escape. But I wouldn't go back into the dark. They couldn't make me. They'd have to kill me if they wanted to throw me back down there.

I felt like a cornered animal as I swung my fist at them through the boards, growling, "Get away! Don't you fucking come near me!"

"Keep your voice down."

The voice was familiar, but I couldn't put a face to it. Soft-spoken and gentle, it still triggered a deep and smothering panic in me as the figure laid their hands against the boards blocking me in. I thought they were checking their sturdiness, ensuring I wasn't about to escape.

When the boards fell away, as if the nails in them had vanished, I froze in complete disbelief.

But only for a second. Then I was up, scrambling to my feet. I shoved them out of my way as hard as I could, I tried to run—

They grabbed my arm, fingers digging into my skin. I thrashed against them, I tried to scratch their face, I balled up my fists. Their hood fell back as they struggled against me, and I realized who it was.

Heidi Laverne.

I froze for a moment in utter terror, before I went at her with renewed viciousness, snarling like an animal. She'd done this. She'd stood there beside Kent; she'd watched in silence; she'd let them do this to me! But something strange coiled around my arms, some invisible force that restrained my fists and anchored my feet. I spat at her. I cursed her. I threatened her with every violent thing that sprang to my mind.

"*Give me a moment,*" *she said desperately, her eyes wide as she nervously glanced back.* "*Please, child, just a moment.*"

She reached out for me, laying her hands against my forehead. I couldn't move away. I couldn't fight her. But a bizarre moment of perfect calm swept over me, beating back my terror, making my tense arms go limp. Her hand was warm. She smelled like lavender and lilac.

"*You will be hunted,*" *she whispered quickly, still glancing around as if she feared someone would come upon us at any moment.* "*A monster will be sent after you, to take you back underground. He won't see you, child, as long as you run.*"

She let go of me, and the strange restraints released me. I stumbled back, the feeling of calm instantly disappearing and cold fear taking its place.

"*Go,*" *she said.* "*Run. Don't stop. No matter what you see, don't stop running.*"

"I RAN ALL night. I've heard that people can get super strength when they're scared, like mothers pulling cars off their children. Whatever causes that . . . whatever crazy adrenaline rush that is . . . that's what I felt. Everything hurt and I just kept running."

I paused. The last time I'd told anyone this, they'd laughed at me. When I told it again, they told me I'd hallucinated. They even told me Heidi wasn't even in Washington, that she'd gone to visit friends in Alaska so she couldn't have been there in the woods.

But I knew what happened to me. Even if I hadn't known why, even if it made no sense. I hadn't imagined it.

Zane wasn't looking at me with disbelief. He was just nodding, slowly, his eyes narrowed. There was nothing comfortable about telling him this. But there was relief in getting it out.

"She was right—a monster came after me. I kept seeing him . . . seeing his eyes in the dark. He looked terrifying." I swallowed hard. Right in front of me sat a demon with claws, bright eyes, and sharp teeth; but back then, in the dark, I hadn't known anything like that existed. The thing I'd seen chasing me had been a monster straight out of my nightmares. "I should have died. I was meant to. But here I am. Alive, even though I fucked up so many times. That's why I say I don't deserve it. Because every day since then, I've earned survival. I've *earned* staying alive. When I do nothing . . . when I let someone else help me . . . it's like I didn't earn it. And I don't deserve it."

I didn't want him to look at me with pity. I didn't need any sympathy. I just wanted to say it. I just wanted it understood. My brain worked in fucked-up ways, and I didn't know how to fix it. But if I was going to be vulnerable, I figured I'd go all the way.

There was still a part of me that feared he would laugh, and God, that would be worse than pity.

"I shouldn't have told you that," I said quickly. "I don't think this shit would make sense to a demon anyway. Probably sounds ridiculous."

I looked up, finally, my expression hardened so if he laughed, at least he wouldn't get to see that it hurt. But he wasn't laughing. I didn't know what the expression was I saw on his face, only that it felt gentle despite the bright eyes and sharp teeth.

"I've been alive for somewhere near a thousand years," he said. The declaration caught me off guard, and I stared, speechless. "Not nearly as long as some. But long enough to see hundreds of thousands of human lives come and go. The fall of kingdoms, armies wiped out—I've been involved in a few." He smirked, but his expression quickly sobered again. "Deserving has nothing to do with it, Juniper. Whatever force of will that brought me into existence, brought you into existence too. Fuck, what did I do to deserve eternity when your natural life is so short?" He shook his head. "It has nothing to do with what you deserve. Life itself is probably just a spontaneous abnormality in this chaotic universe, but here it is. It's ours regardless. I know you humans like to look for purpose; some demons end up doing that too. We all want to know *why*, at some point."

He was staring out across the lake, his bright eyes softened in the sunlight. "I don't believe in fate or a higher purpose. I believe we take these rare, unusual, nonsensical lives of ours and do whatever the hell we want. Don't waste your life punishing yourself." He looked over at me, a mischievous smirk on his face. "You've got eternity, at the end of all this. Your mortal life will end, but Hell awaits. You'll outlive the Hadleighs, the Libiri. Despite all the pain they caused you, you'll see more than they ever will. Maybe that frightens you. Don't let it. I'd like to see what becomes of you, Juniper Kynes. A human like you, in Hell, can be a powerful thing."

I smiled before I could catch myself. "Ugh, God, I still have to put up with you in Hell, don't I?"

"Oh yeah." He laughed. "You're stuck with me. I get to keep bothering you for eternity."

Seconds passed, with only the sound of the lake beneath us and the birds in the trees. I needed to change my bandage and redo a few stitches, but I didn't want to get up. I didn't want to leave his side.

I felt comfortable there. I felt calm.

I hadn't felt calm in a long time.

"So . . . you're old as shit, huh?" I finally said, breaking the easy silence. He laughed.

"In the eyes of other demons, I've barely hit thirty," he said. "But my kind tend to stay mentally young and obnoxious forever."

"You said you've made deals with kings?"

"Oh, yes. Kings, emperors, monks, priests, chiefs. I never take a dull bargain."

"Tell me about one. Tell me about the most unbelievable, wild bargain you've ever taken."

"Shit, have I got a story for you. It was Japan, 1467 . . ."

I laid down, stretching out my back on the deck. It felt nice to lay there. I was finally breathing easy as I closed my eyes.

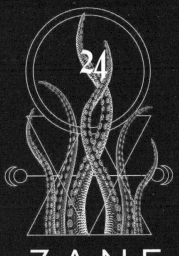

ZANE

IT WAS THE middle of the night, and Leon was in the woods.

I smelled him as soon as he got close to the house. Juniper was asleep, stretched out under a blanket on the couch with the TV playing low, so I went out to meet him. The last thing I wanted was for him to creep inside the house and catch her by surprise. What a fucking mess that would be.

I found him by the water.

"Out for a stroll?" I called, grinning as I came up beside him. "Need a light?"

He nodded, and I lit the joint at his lips. He took a few long drags, his foot tapping impatiently, his eyes flickering out across the water.

"He dismissed me, Zane. I'm free."

I thought I must have hallucinated his words. "You . . . he *what*?"

"Kent Hadleigh dismissed me." He grinned, and it was the kind of grin I hadn't seen on his face for a long time. A killer's smile. The smile that had made my heart beat faster the first time I'd seen it. "I told him I'd crush precious Jeremiah's skull if he didn't. So he made the right choice. Dismissed me."

"Holy shit." I took the joint when he offered it. "A goddamn century later, and finally . . .you can go home. Fucking hell."

"You should have seen Jeremiah's face," he said. "Pathetic little rat nearly pissed himself." Then, his face sobered. "There's a problem though. The grimoire. My name. Kent lost it."

The only way Kent managed to keep Leon under control was because of that old book. It had given him the knowledge to summon and control a demon like Leon—control him through pain, through torture. The fact that he no longer had it made him vulnerable.

It made Leon vulnerable too. His name was out there again, and if it fell into the wrong hands, he'd end up back under the control of another magician.

"Do you remember the woman from the bar?" Leon said, his voice low. "Raelynn?"

"Your little obsession? Of course I remember."

I expected him to protest the *obsession* bit. He didn't. "Kent wants to sacrifice her."

"She's one of the three." I nodded slowly. "Of course. No wonder the Hadleigh brats were clinging to her."

"I refused to take her," he said, his voice even lower, as if he needed to get the words out but didn't want them heard. "And I'm not going to *fucking* let him—" He cut himself off. He shook his head, nervous energy making his muscles twitch. "She has the grimoire, Zane. I don't know how the hell she got it."

"It'll be easy enough to get back then."

"Should be. Might have a little fun toying with her first though." He smirked. "Speaking of toys . . . you have a human in the house."

"Can't share this one with you," I said. "She takes a while to warm up to . . . anything."

He laughed. "How long have you been after this one?"

"About four years."

He rolled his eyes. "You've always been the patient one."

"It's a gift. I just have this insurmountable talent for—" He punched my arm to shut me up. "*Fuck*, for getting what I want. Asshole."

"A *free* asshole." He stretched his arms. "Well, I'll leave you to your little toy. If she ever warms up to it, we'll have ourselves a foursome."

WHAT LEON SAID changed things: Kent no longer had him, and he no longer had the grimoire. Without the grimoire's spells, Kent was significantly more vulnerable; a fact Juniper and I could use to our advantage.

"So he can't use magic anymore," Juniper mused,

pinching her lip between her thumb and forefinger. "Then he's just a sitting duck without his demon." Her eyes narrowed as she looked at the laptop screen in front of her. "God, Victoria is so annoying. Every other photo is her in a bikini on a yacht."

"I've seen your Instagram feed, Juni. Half the people you follow are hot women in bikinis."

She glared at me over the top of her laptop screen. "None of those women tried to *kill me*."

"Every lover I've had has tried to kill me," I said. "Keeps things exciting."

She'd been scouring the Hadleighs' social media for days. With the worst of her wounds healed, she was eager to get back into the thick of things and make her move against them. But choosing where to strike was risky. Even without the grimoire, Kent was hardly helpless.

We still had a big problem to deal with.

"If we take out Kent first, the Libiri will fall apart," Juniper said. "They'll be scrambling. If we can start tracking his movements, we can find—"

"There's something else we need to deal with first." And I wasn't looking forward to it, at all. "Kent Hadleigh still has access to magic, even without his little book."

"We'll take care of that first then," she said simply, setting the laptop aside.

I snickered, shaking my head. "What do you know about witches, Juniper?"

She shrugged. "Broomsticks, pointy hats, *double, double, toil and trouble*." She paused, her eyes narrowing. "Are you . . . are you implying Kent Hadleigh is a witch?"

"He isn't a witch. His mistress and their daughter are."

Her eyes slowly widened, realization coming over her. "Heidi and Everly? Are *witches*?"

"Think about it," I said. "Think back to the night you crawled out of the mine. I've wracked my brain for years trying to figure out how you got away from Leon. But when you said Heidi touched you, it made sense. She hid you from him. Gave you a chance to get away."

Juniper frowned, her muscles twitching with tension as she thought back. Those memories took over her whole body when they came. She braced for them as if bracing for pain. "Heidi was in the church. She stood beside Kent while he . . ." She took a moment. One slow deep breath. "She stood beside Kent while he cut me. She did nothing to stop it. Why would she protect me later?"

I shrugged. "Regret, perhaps. Or a vendetta against Kent. From what Leon has said in the past, Kent never treated her or Everly well. A witch with a vendetta is a dangerous thing. Witches, in general, are very dangerous. No broomsticks, no pointy hats, and no cauldrons. Just very powerful magic. The kind of magic any sane demon wouldn't fuck with." I sighed heavily. "Unfortunately, I'm not very sane, and neither are you."

She grinned. "Damn right. Everly was there that night too. She watched."

"I can only assume she has power like her mother. And while Heidi may have a vendetta against Kent, there's no guarantee Everly will go against her father. They're both risks. They're both dangerous."

"Then we take them both out." Juniper leaned back in her chair. "How powerful are they?"

I rubbed my head, holding back a groan. "Listen. There's very few things demons will avoid fucking with. The first on the No Fuck List is Gods. I'm currently breaking that rule, but in general, every demon knows better than to fuck with a God. The second is Reapers: Hell's executioners. Reapers are to be avoided at all costs, unless you've got a death wish. The third is witches. Witches have the power to discover our true names, and therefore control us by magical means."

Her eyes narrowed. "Meaning?"

"Meaning if we go after the witches and things go south, and they manage to discover my name, they can turn me against you. Granted, they'd need to be incredibly powerful to summon me to their service. But it's still a possibility."

Her fingers tapped rapidly on her thigh, her lips pressed tightly together in thought. "What are their weaknesses?"

"Same as any mortals: guns, fire, knives. They can still be caught off guard. They can still bleed."

"Then we make them bleed."

BUT WE HAD to find them first, and it proved not nearly so easy as locating the other Hadleighs.

"The last time any of the Hadleighs had a photo

with Heidi Laverne was six years ago," Juniper said. We were in my car, sitting in the student parking lot at Abelaum University. "She was in a group photo taken in front of the Historical Society building. She used to work there—she guided our field trip through the museum in elementary school. But she's not listed as faculty on their website. No death records for her."

"No sign of her at their house last night," I said. I'd watched the Hadleigh house from the previous evening until nearly noon this morning, before coming to meet up with Juniper. She'd been so excited to drive the car. By the look of the gas tank, she'd done a little more driving than simply going from the house to the university. "I didn't see Everly either."

"Strange." Juniper tapped her fingers against the wheel. She watched every group of students that passed by, on the lookout for familiar faces. "Everly's social accounts are all locked, so no luck there either. Only one photo of her with the family, from years ago. But she was listed as a vendor for the Main Street Art Fest, so she's still around."

"She's too valuable to Kent for him to let her move away," I said. "If we find her, there's a good chance we'll find her mother."

Juniper nodded, suddenly going tense as she spotted a group of students making their way across the quad. "There's Jeremiah. Follow him. We need to know everywhere he goes, who he talks to. I'll keep an eye out for Victoria."

"Why do I get Jeremiah?" It wasn't as if I'd ever

interacted with the man, but . . . "He's such an obnoxious bastard."

Leon had told me enough. I knew it was true.

Juniper sighed. "Victoria will notice you if you follow
her. If I lay low, she won't notice me."

"Seems like it should be the opposite. You two were
close."

"Just trust me," she said. "Victoria will absolutely notice if some—" She cut herself off abruptly. "Just follow
him."

"No, no, please, go on, Victoria will if . . . ?" She'd
regretted whatever she was about to say, therefore, I had
to know what it was.

She grit her teeth. "Victoria will notice . . ." She
lowered her voice even more, as if she hated to get the
words out. "She'll notice if some hot guy is following her
around."

"Me? A hot guy? Wow, Juniper, you flatter me—"

"Jesus *Christ*, just go follow Jeremiah!"

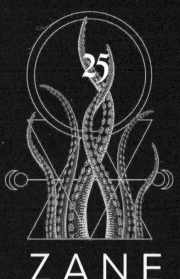

ZANE

FOLLOWING JEREMIAH WAS as unpleasant as I expected.

He smelled awful. He tried to cover it up with some obnoxious cheap cologne, but the resulting odor was just a vile concoction of chemical musk, body odor, and ball sweat. I was certain I couldn't be the only one who smelled it, but apparently humans' sense of smell truly was dull. The gross bastard met up with four different women throughout the course of the day, all of whom gave off instant arousal at the sight of him.

Repulsive. I wouldn't even hate-fuck the little shit.

It wasn't hard to follow him. The man had no awareness of his surroundings. His steps were loud, his voice was loud. It was like trying to follow a bull through a glass shop.

Following him took so little concentration that

instead, I just kept thinking about Juniper and how it would have been far less boring to stay with her all day, listen to her talk through every thought that popped into her head. I think she'd gotten used to talking to herself through the years; she tended to narrate her thoughts as she worked through problems. I didn't even think about fucking her; just being around her was enough as it seemed.

I mean, it was nice to think about fucking her too, but that wasn't the point.

I frowned. There it was again—that aching little soft spot she'd wedged herself inside.

I usually left humans to their own devices once our bargain was complete. Once I'd fulfilled my end of the deal, I had no need to see those I'd claimed again until they died, when I'd escort them to Hell, give them a quick rundown of the rules, and then let them figure the rest out for themselves. I was a hunter, not a babysitter.

But that irresistible drive to keep hunting, to wrap this deal up and move on to the next, wasn't there now. It was fucking weird. Had I lost my touch? Lost my drive? I was one of the most well-known soul hunters in Hell because I was prolific—I made good deals, I finished them quickly, and I kept a steady stream of souls marching through Hell's gates.

I'd never planned on meeting a human who made me feel like changing that. A human that had me so interested even her soul didn't feel like enough.

Why the *fuck* wasn't her soul enough? What more did I want?

At least once darkness fell and the day's last classes were done, things got a little more interesting.

Jeremiah left campus in a Dodge Challenger, the engine rumbling all the way down the road. He headed for the bay, parked in a lot not far from the water, and walked back along the shore. Beyond a thick grove of trees, a bonfire had been lit on an isolated beach. Five people were already there, drinking beers and blasting music from a speaker stuck in the sand. I watched from the trees, out of sight in the shadows.

"Hey, J Boss, we've been waiting for you!" one of them called to Jeremiah as he arrived, offering him a beer. Jeremiah greeted them all as he began to drink, boring small talk droning on until he took a seat on a massive old log near the fire. Clearly the others regarded him as important. They all shut up once he started talking.

"Alright, first things first," he said, tossing his empty can away. "Do you have the box, Nick?"

"Yessir," Nick drawled. He brought over a cardboard box, dirty and stained as if it had been buried. "Everything is still in there."

"Are you sure you should take that back, J?" a blonde woman spoke up, wrinkling her nose as Jeremiah took the box. "Like, isn't it a risk for you?"

Jeremiah laughed as he opened the box. "Trust me, the pigs aren't looking for Marcus Kynes's killer. Now that the journalists don't care, neither do they. I can take back my mementos in peace."

Jeremiah withdrew something from the box that

caught the firelight: a large knife, wrapped in plastic, the blade still stained with blood.

"I should make a shadowbox of this shit," he said. "Put it right next to the soccer trophies."

The blood was old enough that I couldn't smell it anymore, and realization dawned on me. One of the other men laughed, a little nervously.

"That's kinda gross, man. Just saying. You should leave that buried—"

"*Excuse* me?" Jeremiah was on his feet, and the nervous laughter instantly died. "What did you say, Tommy? You wanna repeat that?"

Tommy glanced around, blinking slowly. The woman at his side took a few steps back as Jeremiah got in his face. "You think I should *bury* this, Tommy? Just bury it and let everyone forget what I accomplished?"

Tommy hurriedly shook his head. "No . . . no, man, of course not . . ."

"No one gets to forget this," Jeremiah said, smiling widely, as he pulled the plastic off the knife. "No one in the Libiri gets to forget I did what Dad couldn't do. What Victoria couldn't do." He held up the knife, right against Tommy's throat. "I made the first sacrifice. It was all me. I bled Marcus like God's sweet little lamb." He turned slowly, pointing the blade at each person, one by one. "I'll kill the next lamb, and I'll kill the final one too. God demanded one Hadleigh live, and one Hadleigh die, and I promise you I won't be the one dying. I serve by living."

"That's how it's meant to be," the blonde woman said quickly. "Victoria keeps saying she's having dreams, hearing God's voice." She smirked victoriously as Jeremiah approached her. "Victoria knows she's the one who's meant to die. And J is meant to lead."

"That's right, sweetheart," Jeremiah said, and grasped her face like he was praising a puppy. "Victoria knows what she's meant for. Dad can't see it yet, but he'll come around. It's all about God's will."

Fuck, he had them eating out of his hand. It had been Jeremiah's doing to kill Marcus—in a bid to prove he shouldn't be sacrificed himself. He was planning his own sister's death. And that girl, Raelynn, was meant to be a sacrifice, too.

That meant the Libiri had all their kills lined up, easily accessible. It meant they were far too close to achieving their final goal.

If all three sacrifices were made, and the God was unleashed, Juniper's revenge was out of the question. Humanity would be out of the question. Earth would be lost entirely.

The clock was ticking a lot faster than I'd thought.

"Now, what about Everly?" Her name wrenched my attention back. Jeremiah was seated again, the blonde woman right next to him, her head resting on his shoulder. "Have any of you heard anything? Seen anything?"

Everyone exchanged uncertain looks before shaking their heads. The woman said, "Her phone is turned off. She blocked me on everything."

Jeremiah looked at her sharply. "Why'd she block you? Did you run your mouth and tell her something?"

"No!" The woman shook her head. "Of course not,

I wouldn't do that! She's just a paranoid weirdo . . . she always was . . ."

"Yeah, that's the problem," Jeremiah muttered. "She had to go and throw away all we did for her, after how fucking nice we were." He shook his head. "She belongs with the Libiri. If you see anything, if you hear anything, you bring it directly to me. Not my dad. Not Victoria. *Me*. Got it?"

They all nodded. I'd heard all I needed to.

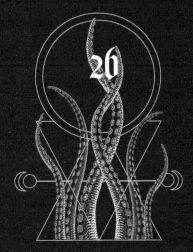

JUNIPER

"I SHOULD HAVE known it was Jeremiah. I should have *known*, the sick fuck!"

I was raging, but I couldn't stop. Pacing up and down the living room, fists clenched so tight it hurt. I wanted to punch something. The fact that Jeremiah had not only killed Marcus, but *gloated* about it to his friends, kept mementos of it, thought it was something to be proud of—God, it made me sick.

Zane was perched up on the back of the couch, legs spread, letting me yell it out. He looked too big to be up there, as if he should have toppled the couch backward. But I guess gravity didn't work the same for demons.

"He's a fool that likes to run his mouth," he said. "And he controls others through fear and false bravado. It's pathetic."

I stopped pacing, forcing myself through a few deep

breaths to make my heart stop pounding. "He's a *dead* fool. Fuck." I squatted down, rubbing my hands over my eyes. "Okay, I gotta focus. Following Victoria got me nothing. But it sounds like Jeremiah spilled all the beans. So now we know Everly is missing."

"Sounds like she ran away. You said she never seemed comfortable with the Hadleighs anyway. Maybe she finally had enough."

"She could be in Australia by now, for all we know." I shook my head. "And no information on her mother. I don't like it."

I could make the call to go after the Hadleighs anyway, even without knowing where the witches were. But rushing into things wouldn't help. I had to take it slow. I had to make sure I was considering this from every angle.

If I went to kill Kent, and he had even one of the witches with him, it could be the end of everything.

But the Hadleighs already had their next sacrifice nearly in their clutches. The last thing I needed was for the God to grow even more powerful. The Gollums were awake, and Zane had warned me they'd crawl out of the mine soon enough. Eld beasts were swarming the forests, and I could hear them howling almost every night. What else would come crawling out of the dark if another sacrifice was made?

"I'll try to track the witch," Zane said. "Witches and their magic have a distinct scent. Everly's will be easier to find since she's younger, less experienced. But it'll take time. I'll have to explore the area, see if I can catch a hint of her scent anywhere nearby. If we find the daughter, we'll likely find the mother."

I nodded. "I'll keep an eye on Victoria and Jeremiah. That girl, Raelynn . . . I'll try to figure out what her deal is. Hopefully she's cautious. The last thing we need is for some happy-go-lucky girl with no sense of danger to get close to them."

Zane snickered. "Look, this girl has a thing for Leon. I guarantee you her sense of danger is skewed . . . or completely nonexistent."

"Well, if he's so interested in her, tell him to make himself useful and keep her away from the Hadleighs."

We had a plan, and that made me feel a little better. I stood, cracking my knuckles. "Once the witches are taken care of, it's time to come down on the Hadleighs, hard. I swear I'm buying a bottle of champagne on the day I get to gut Jeremiah."

"I like it when you get all murderous," Zane said, watching me keenly, a familiar hunger in his eyes.

"Oh, it'll be more than murder." I walked over to him and leaned over the couch so I could rest my arms on either side of the cushions beside his perch. He still had his shirt on, for once. It was a little annoying, actually. "It'll be a massacre. It will be a work of fucking bloody *art*."

There was something about those sharp teeth when he smiled that raised my body temperature and made my heart start thumping harder. "Yeah? Tell me more, little wolf."

It still felt dangerous to be so close to him. He was a beast that could bite at the slightest provocation, but his bite didn't scare me. To me, his danger was a toy. He could mold it to fit my fantasies or wield it to save my life.

This freak had pounded his fist straight through my protective walls and offered a way out, a crack in my otherwise formidable defenses against vulnerability. Did I trust him? I wasn't sure. But I'd sooner put my life in his hands than anyone else's.

"I'll use that knife he's so proud of to carve his intestines out," I said, and Zane eagerly licked his tongue over his lips. "I used to think I'd kill Victoria last, but I've changed my mind. I want to kill Jeremiah last. I want to take my time with him."

"As you should, love." He ran his claws along my cheek, brushing my hair back behind my ear. His hand lingered there, cupped against my head. "I can hear him screaming already."

"He'll do more than scream," I said. "I want him to *beg*. I want him to cry for mercy."

When Zane moved, it was quick, like a predator striking. He kept his hand cupped around my head, and the other hand squeezed against the side of my neck as he got up from the couch, pushing me back several steps as he held me, towering over me. "Yeah? And will you give him mercy?"

I reached down and squeezed the hardness in his jeans. "Never. I just want to hear him cry while I bleed him out."

My words finally unleashed that feral energy. He captured my mouth, his kiss deep and hungry, his grip on me tightening as he backed me up until I was pressed to the large windows that looked out on the lake. I grasped at him, clawing his back and tugging up his shirt. I pulled it over his head and dragged my nails down his bare chest before I wrapped my arms around his neck and he lifted me, my legs wrapping around his waist as he gripped my ass.

He kissed my throat, right where my pulse beat, and he groaned when I bit him in return. I couldn't hurt him, not really, but he liked it when I tried. I bit hard and left my marks on his skin before he pinned my head back by the throat.

"Oh, my little wolf wants it rough, doesn't she?" he growled, and I barely nodded before he slapped my cheek and made me gasp. The sting blossomed beautifully across my skin, tingling, igniting some desperate desire that craved more—more pain, more pleasure, more of his overwhelming desire.

No one had ever looked at my rage and refused to shrink away from it. I was used to being seen as intimidating, threatening, unpleasant: an angry bitch. But it kept me safe, it kept people from getting too close.

Except Zane. He'd never pulled away, no, he'd kept pushing even when I pushed back. What kind of madman looked at my murderous rage and wanted more? What kind of freak didn't find the deep hatred I held to be repulsive?

My anger was my armor. My hatred kept me locked inside iron bars—protection against everything but bars nonetheless, a cage I wasn't even sure I wanted to get out of.

Zane was disassembling that cage, piece by piece. He'd stood outside long enough, looking at the vicious human within, and instead of shaking his head and leaving me there, he wanted to come inside.

"Rougher than that," I whispered, and Zane slammed me back again, his hand tightening around my neck.

"Say that again," he said. "Tell me what you want."

"Fuck me up." I smiled. "Just fucking wreck me."

He threw me back, and the sensation of falling overwhelmed me for a split second before he caught me. He threw me again, this time toward the wall, the force of it taking my breath away. And again, he caught me, inches from slamming into the wall, chuckling as he gripped his hand over my face, claws pricking my cheeks, palm covering my mouth.

"So easy to toss around," he said, his teeth clipping together inches from my face. When he threw me again, he let me hit his target; I fell back on the couch, the impact cushioned, but I was still breathless from the rush as he got on top of me and ripped my shirt. From the neckline to the hem, the fabric tore open in his claws. I wasn't wearing a bra, and he kept me pinned with one hand while he circled a single sharp claw around my nipple.

"Let's hear you scream," he said, and his voice was so gentle, but his claws weren't as they dug into my skin.

I cried out against his hand, half in pain, half in ecstasy at the dopamine rush. I shuddered as his claws dragged over me, leaving trails of red down my belly. I squirmed, struggling beneath him, and he growled and went tense like a dog about to have his bone taken away.

A new sensation, like bands constricting around my limbs, crept up my body. They grew tighter and tighter, until I could barely move at all.

He smiled down at me, running his tongue over his bared teeth.

"A little human could never escape from a demon," he said. "I may let you go, to run and fight and entertain me, but if I really want to keep you still, keep you helpless . . ." He let go of my face, straightening up. Despite him no longer holding me down, I was still utterly unable to move. "Then I can. I can do whatever I want."

Fuck, why did that get me so hot? His power was sexy as hell. After all, part of our bargain was that he wouldn't hurt me beyond what I wanted. I could fight to my heart's content, I could play the game and let myself be the victim, but all the while it would hinge on my will.

With those invisible bands keeping me in place, he pulled down my sweatpants, tracing his claws along my thighs as he did. He hooked his finger in my panties and tore them, grinning up at me as he lowered his head and licked his lips.

"Soaking wet," he murmured. "Sick little slut."

He roughly shoved my legs apart and jerked me toward him. He kept his eyes on my face as he ran his tongue up my inner thigh and set his teeth against me. He bit softly at first, leaving stinging nips along my tender skin. But his bites grew harder, until he broke my skin and sucked at my flesh between his teeth. My thighs were going to be covered in bruises by the time he was done.

All the while he kept his eyes on my face, looking at me like he was daring me to keep fighting him.

Of course I'd keep fighting, no matter how tight he'd restrain me. Or at least, that was what I told myself before his mouth closed over me. Once his tongue was on me, swirling over my clit, every other thought emptied out of my head.

He gripped my thighs as he ate me, forcing them to remain spread. He probed inside me with his tongue, the sensation of his piercings stroking me sending a violent shudder over my body. He groaned, and the vibrations of it made me gasp. He had me nearly to the edge when he suddenly raised his head and smacked my thigh, the sharp pain making me cry out.

"Can you orgasm from pain, sick little slut?" he murmured, keeping me spread in front of him as he traced the red outline of his hand on my skin. "Do you want to try?"

I nodded, my head light at the promise of pain, light in the best of ways. I flinched when he slapped my thigh again, right where it still stung, before rapidly smacking the other. My thighs clenched but couldn't close, and I gripped the couch cushions tight as my groan turned into a vicious growl, following another slap.

"You're dripping wet for it." He laughed, and instead of slapping my thigh again, he slapped my clit.

Fuck, how could something hurt so bad but feel so good? My back arched up, straining against the invisible restraints, and he slapped me again, the sensation throbbing through my abdomen. Fuck, it *was* getting me closer to orgasm. It shouldn't have felt so good, I shouldn't have been getting even warmer and wetter down there. The pain was shocking and intense, but it stimulated those overly sensitive, swollen nerves.

"Let's see how hard you come with my cock in your ass and your clit getting spanked."

In my ass—fuck—holy *fuck*.

He grabbed a bottle of lube from a drawer in the coffee table and stroked a drop of it over his fingers. He kissed me again, grinding his cock between my legs as his tongue moved demandingly over mine. He slipped a finger inside me, pressing past that first tight ring of muscle and probing my ass as I panted into his mouth. As he pumped his finger in and out, and then added another, he smacked my clit again. I moaned as I tightened around his fingers, just two digits already feeling so full. He moved them slowly in and out, leaned over me with a smile, and said sweetly, "Keep your legs open, slut."

When he smacked me, my first instinct was to squeeze my legs shut. But I fought the urge, moaning loudly and gripping the cushions tight. His palm slapped down again, his fingers still stretching me, and I screamed, slamming my fist against the couch.

"Shall we continue?" He chuckled. "You sound like you're enjoying yourself."

"Yes, God, yes." I groaned as he withdrew his fingers. He squeezed more lube onto his shaft, slick as he pressed that dangerously thick head up against my hole.

"What did I tell you," he said darkly, "about calling God's name? I should punish you for that."

"Fuck . . . fuck, fuck, fuck," I murmured, the word becoming a mantra as he pressed inside me. I could feel every ridge and swell on his monstrous cock as it squeezed deeper. My legs were shaking, and he was halfway into me when he raised his hand again.

"Ready, slut?"

God, that name made my insides shudder in the best of ways. I would have killed anyone else who dared call me that, but him? From his lips, it made me feel filthy, it made me feel desperate. I nodded, biting my lip as I braced for the pain, for the throbbing, agonizing pleasure. I screamed when it came, my muscles tightening around him, squeezing until he groaned and his eyes fluttered closed for a moment.

"Fucking hell." His pupils swelled as he opened them again, the blackness spreading to encompass nearly all of those bright golden rings. "You feel so fucking good."

He entered me fully, leaning over me as my legs shook and I gasped, breathless at the stretch of having all of him inside me. "There's my girl," he growled in my ear, with a sudden hard, cruel thrust into me. "You take the pain so fucking well."

I was so full, but my pussy was aching for him. It was swollen, dripping with need as he said sweetly, "Spread your legs for me again, love. I'm going to make you come."

My breath came in rapid, desperate gasps as I obeyed, holding my own legs open because if I didn't, I wouldn't be able to keep them spread through sheer force of will. He slapped my thighs, leaving me shaking, before he spanked my pussy again—and again. The growing knot of pain was intertwined with swelling pleasure. They were inseparable, every sharp slap making me clench tighter and tighter until—

I shook from head to toe as I came, throbbing as he fucked my ass and gave me one last slap that was nearly unbearable, my clit pulsing with stimulation. The orgasm gripped me so tight I could barely breathe, and my pleasure made him move faster. My legs were pinned back, shaking violently as he used my ass until I felt his cock swell.

"Does the little slut want my cum in her ass?" he said, grinning as he gripped my face and shook it hard. "Say it, slut. Say what you want."

I was too high on pain, still drowning in pleasure. It was easier just to growl at him, and snap at his hand like a feral thing, than to manage words. But he dodged my bite and came back harder, smiling wide as he hooked two fingers in my mouth.

"Go on and bite me," he growled. "Fucking *bite* me like you mean it."

God, his words got me hot. I bit down, hard, hard enough to have broken a mortal man's fingers. But it only made Zane more vicious, it made him groan in pleasure as he fucked into me at a punishing pace.

"This ass is mine," he growled, tugging my head forward. My bite had broken his skin, and his blood dripped over my lips. "All mine, don't you ever fucking forget it."

I released his fingers and spat his blood back in his

face. He laughed—wildly, hungrily—and smeared the bloody spit over his face with his still-bleeding hand.

It was enough to push him over the edge.

His cock throbbed repeatedly, the subtle change in its thickness making my eyes roll back again. He pumped inside me, hot cum filling me. He eased me down, tucking back my hair as I closed my eyes and caught my breath. He caressed my thighs, touching softly where they stung, and leaving gentle kisses over my hot skin.

"Fucking beautiful," he murmured. "So beautiful."

And I actually felt like I was.

JUNIPER

WALKING AROUND DOWNTOWN Abelaum felt
like trying to move barefoot across a floor covered in
thumbtacks, without making a sound. Every smiling face
alarmed me. The laughter of passersby seemed sinister.
Not even the most innocent actions were safe.

I could feel their eyes on me, prickling up my back,
pressing against my skull. I was lucky the weather was
rainy, because I could walk with my hood up. Hiding my
face was the only way I could stay calm.

I would have preferred to have Zane with me, but he
was off trying to track down the witches. I could reach
him by cell—thank God demons accepted modern tech-
nology—but not having him immediately nearby felt as if
I'd left my guns at home and gone out without a weapon.

I'd left this place for a reason. Abelaum wasn't safe
for me. At least when I'd been out of Washington, I'd

known the chances of me encountering a member of the Libiri were slim. Here, they were everywhere, hiding in plain sight.

And unless I could kill them, I didn't want to encounter them.

But I still had work to do. Just as I'd suspected, Victoria was focusing most of her social time on that girl Zane had told me about, Raelynn.

There was no mistaking her; Zane's description had been spot-on. A tiny woman, barely five foot, with big glasses and bobbed black hair. She made a strange companion for Victoria, who sat there with her Coach bag, sleek white raincoat, and perfectly manicured nails. Little miss Raelynn was wearing a denim jacket two sizes too big, the front lapels covered in band pins and the back covered in a massive Bad Religion patch.

She didn't look familiar to me. I had to wonder how she'd ended up here, how the Hadleighs had managed to suck her in. Probably the same way they'd gotten me. Victoria would turn on her charm, make you feel special. She had a way of making you feel like the fortunate one for getting her attention. I'd considered myself lucky when I'd gained her friendship in high school. No one else had liked me but her.

The coffee I'd been drinking turned in my stomach. I was watching the two women from across the cafe, seated behind Victoria and in a corner so she couldn't get an easy look at me. The woman who'd tried to kill me was only feet away. Her voice was all I could hear. There'd been a time when we'd been so close. Or at least . . . I'd felt close to her. I'd told her everything. I'd told her about my parents, about my dad leaving, and the pain of his death. I'd told her about my mother's hatred of him, her boyfriends, her drinking—everything.

And she'd told me about her dad's affair. How Everly had been born just a few months before she and Jeremiah were. How she'd seen her mother crying in the garden. How she felt like her dad was always pitting her and Jeremiah against each other, telling them both to "make daddy proud" as if it was all a game to earn his love.

Now I knew their competition had been very real. How fucking sick, to plan to sacrifice one of your children for some wicked God's promises.

My hands tightened on the porcelain coffee mug. I didn't feel sympathy for Victoria. She was carrying on the same murderous tradition as the rest of her cult. She lured people in, made them trust her, and then she manipulated that trust for her own gain. All in the hope that her own life would be spared.

Fuck her. Play stupid games, win stupid prizes. From what Zane had heard, her own brother was already plotting her death.

This poor Raelynn girl looked oblivious as hell. She kept glancing out the window, a little restless in her seat, chugging down an iced black coffee at a rate that would have given me a heart attack. She smiled and nodded politely as Victoria carried on about some asinine story. Did she have family here? Other friends?

People who would realize if she went missing?

I was so focused on the two of them, it took me

nearly a minute to notice the woman with long blonde hair standing outside the cafe. But eventually, she stood for so long in my peripheral that my eyes flickered over to her. The rain dripped down her hood, dampening the strands of her hair that had been plucked out of shelter by the wind. Bright blue eyes, a long black skirt . . .

It had been years, but I knew her face.

Everly.

She'd been watching Victoria and Raelynn, but the moment recognition clicked in my brain, her eyes darted over to me.

Her eyes widened. Her face was stricken with fear.

And she ran.

I followed her immediately. I didn't want to make a big fuss as I left, but the moment I was outside the door, I sprinted down the sidewalk. I barely caught sight of her jacket whipping around a corner ahead. The rain was pouring now, and most people had taken shelter inside so my way was clear as I chased after her. She was always one corner ahead, dodging down narrow side streets, taking an ever-more-convoluted path in an attempt to lose me. But I was faster, gaining on her with every step.

She turned again, and I was only a second behind her. But the moment I turned, I stopped. It was a dead end.

She was gone.

I frowned. The narrow path stood between three buildings, with no way out but *up*. The old stone and brick buildings had fire escapes, but the ladders were pulled up, and it would have been easy to see her if she'd somehow gotten up there. There were a couple small trash cans, a pile of cardboard boxes—nowhere a fully grown woman could hide.

How the hell?

I walked down the alley, looking even in the places she couldn't possibly fit. There were no doors, no crawl spaces, no vents. I stared up at the building at the end, frowning. There was no way she'd gotten up to the roof in merely seconds. It was impossible.

There was a strong scent of berries in the air. Berries and sugar. It was overbearingly sweet, and the hairs on the back of my neck stood up.

The bricks in front of me looked strange. They were slightly misaligned, their edges not quite lining up properly, the surface of some of them strangely smooth. I reached out toward them, eyes widening in disbelief. There was no fucking way . . .

As if from behind a curtain, Everly reappeared, her back pressed to the bricks. Something hit me, a pulse that compressed my chest, shoving me back and giving her the room to run past me. I grabbed for her, seizing the strap on her bag. She pulled back hard against me, her eyes wide with fear. Her bag burst open, spilling contents across the wet ground, but she was free of my grip.

This time, when I got to the mouth of the alley, I had no idea where she'd gone.

"Goddamn it!" I scanned the entire street, but there was no sign of her. She could have been right in front of me, *invisible*, and I'd have no fucking idea.

I wasn't too surprised by weird, magical, paranormal shit anymore. But if these witches could turn themselves invisible, that was going to be a real problem. Everly had always been so quiet, so timid—at least in high school. But that meant nothing now. She'd been there that night in the church. She'd watched with all the rest. Just like her parents, she'd learned to turn a blind eye to pain and torture if it was for her God.

Back down the alley, I examined the items that had dropped from Everly's bag, and pulled out my cell to call Zane. But I hadn't even managed to unlock the screen when I was suddenly aware of someone standing behind me.

He was already here.

"What have I told you about sneaking up on me?" I said.

"Awww, the mortal can't hear massive footsteps on a wet street." I tried to smack him in the balls, but he turned so that my palm smacked his ass instead. "Ooh, yeah, do it harder next time."

"You completely missed the witch," I said with a heavy sigh. "She was right here."

"Why do you think I'm over here?" He picked up a tube of chapstick, sniffed it, and carelessly tossed it away. "She used magic. I could smell it a mile away." He paused as I picked up a damp, folded piece of paper from the ground. "Did she hurt you?"

"No. She looked scared." I unfolded the paper as carefully as I could, but it was soaked from the rain and ripping at the slightest touch. I laid it down on top of a metal trash can lid, and my eyes widened as I realized what it was.

A map of Western Washington, covered in scribbles of blue ink. The ink was blooming from the rain, but I could make out little notes, X's, and lines through vast sections of empty forest.

"Jackpot," I said softly. "I don't think you're going to need to track her anymore, Zane."

JUNIPER

THERE WAS A marking on the map, a tiny X with a dotted trail leading away from it, deep into a vast expanse of forestland a few hours northwest of Abelaum. The trees were thick, their roots tangled and covered with the thorny brambles of blackberry bushes. We passed a few hiking trails, with dirt lots beside them where hikers could park before they began their journey, but Zane said the areas didn't feel right.

"It won't be that simple," he said, eyes scanning the trees as we kept driving. "We need to find the right way in."

I wasn't sure what the hell that meant, but considering we were dealing with witches and magic, I was going to assume Zane knew more about all that than I did.

When we finally stopped the car, I didn't need any assurance we'd found the right place.

The trees had grown utterly wild. Many of them were bent, as if they'd endured a heavy wind as they grew. Some were twisted over each other, their boughs hanging low to brush the ground. It was late in the year to bloom, but thick clusters of wildflowers stretched back into the trees: purple, white, yellow, and pink. These flowers shouldn't have been blooming at the same time, let alone in the same place. Every inch of the ground—every rock, limb, and fallen tree—was covered with a thick blanket of moss.

It was like staring into a terrarium: everything was too thick, too clustered. As if the forest was trying to draw itself together, creating a cocoon around whatever was inside.

Zane sighed heavily, shaking his head. "This is a bad fucking idea."

I nodded. "Yeah. Probably."

A narrow, winding dirt trail led back into the forest. The thick, gnarled limbs of the maple trees curved over the path, their mossy limbs dripping with the drizzling rain. Goose bumps prickled over my arms, and I nervously laid my hand over the knife strapped to my thigh. The rain collected on the leaves above and formed heavy drops that dripped slowly to the ground. That was the only sound in there: the dripping rain. The trees didn't groan, they didn't move in the breeze, the birds didn't sing. There was just the slow, steady drip of the rain.

Zane stepped ahead of me. "Stay close," he said. "And be cautious. Not everything you see is as it appears."

Fabulous. Exactly what I wanted to hear.

We walked for an hour. Then two hours. Neither of us spoke: not because we had nothing to say, but because we didn't dare to make a sound. It was too quiet, and breaking the silence felt sacrilegious—or dangerous.

I hadn't seen or heard anything, but I still felt like we were being watched.

The smell of the wildflowers, pleasant at first, was unbearably heavy in the air. It was cloying in my nose and made my head ache. The vibrancy of the greenery around us was dizzying. Was I imagining it, or did everything look the same?

We'd been walking for two hours, but this looked . . . familiar.

"We must have passed it," I finally said softly, and paused to rummage the map out of my backpack. Zane kept walking.

"Don't stop," he said sharply. "Stay close."

I didn't miss the note of alarm in his voice. I jogged to catch back up with him and popped open the top of my pistol's holster to be ready. The noise made Zane flinch, and he glanced back, wide-eyed.

"Whatever you do," he said, "don't take that fucking gun out."

I blinked rapidly in disbelief. "Don't . . . *don't* take out my gun?"

He shook his head rapidly. "No. Don't do it, Juniper. Don't do anything threatening."

"Why?"

"We're being watched."

That seemed like a damn good point at which to pull out my gun. My fingers twitched with the need for it, and I grit my teeth as I fought the urge. "What the hell does that mean, Zane?"

He didn't say anything. His claws were out, he was walking fast, and his movements were twitchy. We weren't moving nearly as fast as he wanted to, and that scared me more than anything. If Zane felt the need to run, then what the hell was—

He stopped abruptly. A massive tree was bent low over the trail ahead, curved into an arch. Flowers were clustered everywhere, their perfume unbearably heavy, but there was another scent too: like iron and coal.

Zane growled low in his chest, and I followed his gaze up to the tree curved over the path. Someone—some-*thing*—was crouched on the mossy trunk. Long limbs, pale skin cut through with a webbing of ink-black veins, and black eyes. Solid black eyes and long sharp teeth.

Zane managed to get out a single word.

"Fuck."

The creature moved. I blinked and it vanished, and Zane was suddenly thrown back. He slammed into the trunk of a tree nearly fifty yards away, cracking it, the violent sound of splintering wood ringing out in the eerily silent forest.

I reached for my gun, but I wasn't fast enough.

The creature slammed into me, knocking me flat on the ground and flinging my pistol from my hands. I scrambled up, gasping for the air that had been forced from my aching lungs, grasping for my weapon. The

forest had plunged into darkness and I was discombob-
ulated, stumbling. There was yelling—ragged, pained
yelling—and then something seized me from behind.

One hand on the back of my skull. One hand on my
jaw. Claws digging into my skin. My head throbbed, as
if a speaker had been turned up full-volume against my
head and was pounding bass into my skull. The voice
that chuckled in my ear, so deep and dark it couldn't possibly be human, said, "Lights out, girl."

I was going to die.

It was going to snap my neck.

There was another impact, and this one ripped the
creature off me. I was thrown to my stomach, and I
couldn't see my gun in the dark, but I could see Zane
locked in combat with the creature. Not just a creature—a demon unlike any I'd ever seen.

It threw Zane off and slammed its foot down on his
face with a sickening crunch. Laughter reverberated
through the forest, laughter that was utterly cold and
cruel. Suddenly the demon was right in front of me, black
eyes staring into mine, its teeth too long and sharp to
fully shut its mouth.

Leathery black wings extended from its back, cocooning me into total darkness. It smelled like the flowers
were burning.

"He was right, you know. Coming here was a very
bad idea."

I was struck hard, and darkness enveloped me.

JUNIPER

THE BIRDS WERE singing.

I stirred, aware that something soft was beneath my head, but the rest of me was lying on something cool and hard. I wasn't outside anymore. I couldn't feel any moss beneath me or any wind on my skin. My backpack was gone. There was a sweet smell, like caramel, berries, and new grass. Another smell too, familiar but distant . . . tea. It was Earl Grey tea.

A piano was playing. It intertwined with the birdsong, creating a symphony unlike anything I'd ever heard. It didn't arouse my memories, it aroused feelings: the feeling of curling up close to my dad near the fire. Of hugging Marcus. Of my mom reading a bedtime story.

Of Zane. Looking at me. Kissing me. Holding me.

Zane. Where the fuck was Zane?

The piano stopped. There was a soft clinking sound and a little sigh. I wasn't alone.

I opened my eyes. It took a few blinks for my vision to fully come into focus, but as it did, I realized I was lying on a pale tile floor. A knit sweater had been folded beneath my head like a pillow. Vines dangled above me, and I was surrounded by potted plants and raised garden beds. There were trees, flowers, bushes—everything fragrant and vibrant with life. I was in a large greenhouse, with a domed glass ceiling high above where birds fluttered through the air. I shook my head dizzily, trying to raise it from the ground.

"Be careful. He was rough with you."

I stiffened. Her voice was so familiar, even after so many years.

"Everly Hadleigh?" She looked almost the same as she had in high school. Her blonde hair was longer now, trailing down her back to her waist. She wore a long black dress, the bodice covered in lace, and her feet were bare.

"Everly Laverne, please," she said softly. She had a porcelain teacup in front of her, set upon the metal table she was sitting beside. She sipped from the cup slowly, her hand slightly shaking. "My father never wanted me to have his name anyway."

I sat up slowly, and winced as my head throbbed. When the darkness of those wings had enveloped me, I'd truly thought I was going to die. Especially after seeing the way that thing had thrown around Zane . . .

"Where's my demon?" I said sharply. I thought of the

creature's foot crashing down on his face, the force with which he'd been thrown—a sick, cold feeling of dread coiled in my stomach. "Where the hell is he?"

"With Callum. He's alive," she added quickly. "Callum won't allow him near me, so . . ."

"What the fuck is a Callum?" I lurched to my feet, wincing at the ache. I must have been curled up on the floor for a while: every muscle was stiff. Everly looked significantly more nervous now that I was standing up.

"He's the . . . he's . . ." She frowned slightly, as if she was grasping for the right words. "He's *my* demon. He's the guardian of this place. Of . . . me. I didn't mean for him to be so rough with you. With either of you." Her hands clenched in her lap. "But your demon . . . Zane . . . he's fine. I mean . . ." She shrugged. "They heal quickly."

"Don't you fucking talk about him like it's not a big deal that *your* demon bashed his fucking face in," I hissed. That moment consumed my every thought, fueling my rage. Wherever the hell her demon was, I wanted to fucking kill him for touching Zane like that.

Everly's face was somber, her mouth pressed into a thin, hard line. "Did you come here to kill me, Juniper Kynes?"

The birdsong stopped. The greenhouse was deathly silent and suddenly cold. She knew who I was—but of course she did. It was a dangerous time to tell the truth, but I'd found the truth was dangerous more often than not.

"You remember me," I said. "You looked terrified when you saw me in Abelaum. You looked like you'd seen a ghost."

"Memories are far more frightening than ghosts." Her finger traced slowly along the plate beneath her teacup, following the delicate curves of the porcelain. She'd averted her eyes and was chewing her lower lip.

"Memories," I repeated bitterly. "Oh yeah, I know all about how frightening they can be. You want to talk about scary memories? We share one: you, me . . . and your mother. Is she here? Is Heidi Laverne here?" I raised my voice, and it echoed around the eerily quiet greenhouse.

Everly seemed to shrink under my raised voice. "My mother is dead," she said softly. "Her mistakes . . ." She paused and cleared her throat. "I can't apologize for her. An apology probably isn't even what you want to hear. She regretted everything. She tried to make things right."

"She tried to *make things right*?" I laughed. I needed a weapon. I needed my gun back, my knife, something, anything. But even armed, even if I managed to kill her, there was no way in hell I'd escape her demon. "What have *you* done to make things right, Everly? You were there too, hiding in the shadows like a fucking coward!"

I lunged toward her, too furious to think straight. But something smooth and cool whipped out and snapped around my wrist, jerking me back. I looked down and found a green vine coiled around my arm.

"What the fuck is this?" I tugged at it, and suddenly my other wrist was caught too. I was yanked back, prevented from getting any closer to her by the shockingly strong vines.

"Please don't be violent," she said.

The sickening realization that I was trapped here made my stomach lurch. Trapped, separated from Zane—and although she claimed he was safe and un-harmed, I didn't believe that. Not for a second. He could be injured, he could be . . .

He could be dead. I swallowed hard, the thought hit-ting me so brutally that for a moment I couldn't breathe. Zane could already be dead. She might have taken the only thing I had left, the tiny spark of joy I'd found in this darkness.

His warmth, his protection, his ridiculous sarcastic jokes, his massive fucking ego—if she'd taken that, if she or her demon had harmed him—

I clenched my fists to stop their shaking, forcing my-self to keep breathing slowly. I had to keep it together.

But the rage was bubbling up. Not just rage at Heidi, at Everly, at the Hadleighs or at the Libiri. It was rage that I lived with those memories every day. Rage that so many parts of me were irrevocably broken. No matter what I did, I couldn't escape what had happened. No amount of vengeance would bring my brother back. No amount of blood I spilled could drown out the memories.

"Don't be violent? *Don't be violent?* You listened to me scream for help and did nothing!" I yelled. Everly flinched, and she looked like she was going to be sick. "Was it *fun* for you, Everly? Did it make you happy to see some innocent girl suffer for your God? Did you—"

"I don't serve that God!"

Glass shattered somewhere above, and Everly flinched at the sound. Her breathing had grown rapid and she quickly looked away from me, gripping the edge of the table. It was like she was fighting with herself, struggling to hold something back.

"I spent years with your family, Everly. Victoria was my *best friend*," I spat out the words, sickening as they were. "I trusted your father. I trusted your mother. I trusted *you*. You never warned me, you never told me to stay away. You never even tried, and your mother didn't either. You both are fucking sick. You both deserve to die for what you let them do to me!"

"I can't make it right," she said. "I was supposed to be inspired, that's what they told me. I was supposed to witness something beautiful and be left in awe of God's power. All I saw was torture. There wasn't a day I could look at my mother after that and not see it." Her eyes shone with tears for a moment, only for her to rapidly blink them away. "But she's dead. And I am not my mother."

I wanted to break something, hit something. I wanted to scream. It felt mocking, that she had witnessed the worst thing that had ever happened to me but felt like she could remove herself from it, like she could be *distant* from it. She had the memories too, but she didn't have to be trapped by them. She didn't have to see the scars every day.

I curled my lip in disgust. "But you are your father's daughter."

"He didn't raise me like them," she said. "He raised me, but not *like them*." She stood, and a rumble like thunder moved through the floor. "He was clear, always, that I was not the daughter he *wanted*; I was only the one he *needed*. I wish I could change it. I wish I hadn't been afraid. I wish I hadn't spent so many years *afraid*."

The porcelain cup shattered, splattering tea everywhere. It dripped down the table, pooling on the floor, and Everly sighed heavily. She let go of the table, staring at the shattered glass with bitter resignation.

I'd had no idea what to expect coming here. But this woman in front of me wasn't the coldhearted, Evil-God-worshipping witch I'd imagined. She wasn't even the heartless Hadleigh I'd imagined. She was something else.

A storm. A storm like me. A bomb on the verge of exploding.

"What are you going to do, Everly?" I said softly. "Turn your demon on me? Or kill me yourself?"

"I don't want you dead, Juniper. I need you alive. I need you to finish what you set out to do."

I tested the strength of the vines again, but they still didn't budge. "And what is it you think I set out to do?"

"Kill the Hadleighs. Destroy the Libiri. Make sure they can't complete another sacrifice." She stepped closer to me, and goose bumps prickled up my arms. There was something about her, something I only noticed once she was close. The air itself was charged around her, as if electricity was coursing from her. "That's why you're still in Abelaum, isn't it? I can only guess that your brother's death brought you back . . . but revenge made you stay. That's why you're out here, isn't it? You came out here to kill me."

"Well, I sure as hell didn't come out here for a god-damn tea party," I said. "Are you trying to bargain with me?"

She shook her head. "I'm trying to make it clear I'm not your enemy."

I frowned. "You mean you've turned against the Libiri? Against your family?"

"They're not my family," she said. "They were never my family. The blood of the coven is thicker than the water of the womb, and I am the last of my coven. Our goals are intertwined, Juniper; yours and mine."

"What's your goal then?"

"To end all this," she said. "To kill the God."

For a moment, I thought I must have heard her wrong. "How is that possible?" I said. "It's a *God*. It's . . . I don't even know if It's a physical thing . . . and you think you're going to kill It?"

"I'm going to," she said firmly. "I have to. I'm the only one left who can. But if the Libiri complete their sacrifices, and the God is set free, then there will be nothing I can do. Earth, as we know it, will end. Humanity will end."

She waved her hand and the vines holding me captive let go, retreating back to their planters. I rubbed my wrists, resisting the urge to lunge at her again.

"My mother realized her mistakes too late," she said. "She trusted Kent's preaching more than her own knowledge for too long. She hurt people. She hurt *you*. I don't blame you for hating her, or for hating me. She went back for you that night because she wanted to try to take it all back." She turned away, leaving herself vulnerable, her back turned to me. Was it an extension of trust, or was it a trap? Was she trying to lure me into attacking her, so she could retaliate and hurt me?

But if she'd wanted to hurt me, she'd easily have already done so.

"My mother couldn't bear the mistakes she made. She couldn't face them." Everly's shoulders swelled and then sank with a heavy sigh. "I can't erase her mistakes. But I can refuse to make the same ones she did."

She seemed sincere. When she glanced back at me, the pain on her face was undeniable.

"I'm not trying to save the world, Everly," I said. "I'm not a hero. I'm . . . angry. I'm only angry. What I'm trying to do isn't deep, or selfless, or courageous. It's bitter. It's *selfish*. It won't fix anything or bring anyone back." I shook my head. "Look, what you're trying to do is noble. And probably impossible. I can't help you."

"Yes, you can," she said. "Because all you need to do is what you've wanted to do all along: kill them. Kill them all, before they can destroy anyone else's life. They're moving to take the next sacrifice, Juniper. You know they are. You've seen it."

"Raelynn Lawson," I muttered. "She's not my problem."

"But stopping the Hadleighs before they kill her is in your interest," she said, a note of desperation in her voice. "If they make another sacrifice, the God's power grows. It'll be even harder for you to kill Kent, harder to kill any of them."

She was right. But I'd set out to do this for myself; I couldn't pretend it was for any other purpose. This wasn't a mission to save humanity, this was no hero's journey. This was for me. It was the only way forward, the only path I saw for myself. I couldn't just move on from the pain. I couldn't start over, I couldn't *live*, because the shadow of the Libiri was always over me.

The only thing I cared about in this fucked-up world was *me*. I'd survived because of how hard *I'd* fought.

Except . . . that wasn't entirely true anymore, was it? Down in the mine, trying to get Marcus out, I should have died. Up on the mountain, fighting the Eld, I should have been torn apart.

I wasn't fighting alone anymore. And as much as it frightened me . . . I no longer cared *only* about myself.

I cared about Zane too.

He was the first thing I'd thought of as I woke up. He was the first thing I'd feared losing. Even now, my nails were digging into my palms with the force of the anxiety that he wasn't with me. I still didn't know if he was okay.

Even if it was only in the most minuscule way, my actions weren't just about me anymore.

"I'm not trying to recruit you to a cause, Juniper," Everly said. "I'm not asking you to forgive me, or forgive my mother. But you can't kill me." Her voice hardened, taking on an edge that caught me off guard. "If you try, Callum will destroy you. He'll destroy your demon too. Don't make me your enemy."

I narrowed my eyes, regarding her carefully. I doubted I could trust her, but what would she gain by lying to me now? How did it benefit her to formulate this whole story instead of just killing me?

She'd had her chance, and her demon could have easily done it too. The only thing I could assume was that she was telling the truth.

"So I kill the Hadleighs," I said. "Just like I planned. I destroy the Libiri, and you destroy the God. Is that the deal?"

She nodded. "Kill them. Make them all suffer. And we'll see this end." She picked up a bit of shattered porcelain from the ground, slicing her finger as she did. She watched the blood drip down and laughed softly. "Callum will smell me bleeding. He'll worry. Let's walk together."

THE WITCH'S HOUSE was massive. Walking through its long halls, I felt as if I'd stepped back in time. Some of the walls were richly papered with a dark filigree pattern, others were paneled with wood. But there were some walls that looked even older, made of carved stone. It was the kind of place that should have felt dilapidated, but there was no dust, no cobwebs. The floors shone, and the rugs and tapestries were rich in their colors, as if they were new.

"If you want to kill Kent, you'll get your best opportunity on October 31st," she said. She kept sucking the cut on her finger and pressing it against her dress to stave off the bleeding.

"Halloween. How fitting."

"Victoria still throws a Halloween party every year," she said. "I remember you came to a couple."

No one who'd been to a Hadleigh party could ever forget it. I'd attended the first one when I was thirteen. The Hadleighs' massive house would fill with people, drinks would flow, drugs would be passed around. In crowds like that, it was easy to make someone disappear.

"They always claim their parents go out of town," Everly said. "But they don't. Kent will be there to keep an eye on things, especially if they're going to try to take Raelynn. And I think they will. She has no family in the state. She has a close friend who isn't involved with the Libiri, but that doesn't offer her much protection." She chewed her thumbnail, obvious worry on her face. I sighed.

"I'll try to keep her away from them," I said. "*If* I see her. But I'm not going out of my way to do it."

Everly smiled in relief, nodding her head. "Thank you. Trust me, the party will be a good opportunity for you. If you can find Kent, he'll likely be alone. It'll be noisy, everyone will be drunk."

"No one will notice a few gunshots," I said.

"Exactly. And another thing." She paused in the middle of the hall, her eyes narrowed in thought. "If there's one thing Kent is paranoid about, it's demons. Keeping Leon made him nervous—he always suspected the demon would try to kill him at the slightest opportunity. He was right, of course. But Leon ended up going after Jeremiah, since he couldn't get at Kent."

"So Kent is protected somehow," I said. "Will Zane be able to get near him?"

"Kent carries an amulet that prevents most paranormal entities from harming him," she said. "But if you can get the amulet off him, your demon won't have a problem. Kent has other artifacts too, old ones his grandfather brought out of the mine nearly a century ago, and things my mother gave him too. I don't know what most of them do, and I don't think Kent does either. The family has a lot of magic at their disposal, if they figure out how to use it."

"Got it. So we go to the party, prevent human sacrifice, kill Kent. Sounds like a good night."

"Once my father is dead, the Libiri will be left scrambling. They'll be vulnerable." She paused, and I wondered if it felt strange for her to talk about killing her own father. She didn't speak about the man with any affection, but still. She blinked rapidly and turned away from me to look back down the hall. "Don't be afraid. Callum is coming."

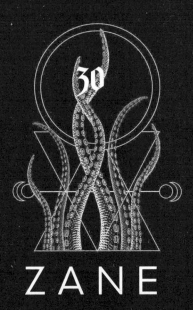

ZANE

"WHERE DID YOU take her? Where did you *fucking take her*?"

The Archdemon narrowed his eyes at me from the doorway. Black eyes, as dark as the empty expanses of the night sky. He picked a claw between his long teeth, as if he was already bored with the sight of me.

"Don't growl at me, hellion. It's rude."

"Rude? Fucking rude? *You took my human!*"

Usually, I could reach out my mind and feel Juniper's presence: like reaching toward a fire and feeling its warmth. Her soul's tie to me was a silver thread when I closed my eyes, the brightest of all the threads from every soul I'd collected. But I couldn't feel her here. It was like everything was muted; her soul hidden from me.

The realization was nothing short of terrifying. I wasn't used to feeling out of control, to feeling so ripped by emotions that I couldn't even think straight. But they'd taken her. They'd fucking *taken her*.

I thrashed against the chains he'd used to bind me to the floor, but they didn't budge. The room was cold, with stone walls and a carved stone floor. The carvings were huge, but easily recognizable as a summoning circle. It was a powerful one, the kind of thing that would require a massive outpouring of magic to use.

The kind of magic that could summon an Archdemon.

Creatures like him had been alive so long and claimed so many souls that they had risen through all of Hell's ranks to achieve something near royalty. Hell's Council was made up of Archdemons, but there were hundreds, if not thousands, of them in existence.

They were rarely seen, let alone on Earth.

We were in deep fucking shit.

"I swear to Lucifer, if you hurt her—" I strained against the chains again, my veins bulging and blackening as I tried to break them. The damn things were ancient, the manacles worn smooth by time. They wouldn't budge, they wouldn't even bend. Whatever magic infused them was beyond my strength. "If she comes back with a single fucking scratch on her—"

The Archdemon crossed the room in a blink. He crouched over me, chin resting on his palm. "I hit her head so hard she fell unconscious," he said coldly. "And I'd do it again if my lady wishes it. I'll make you watch me tear her apart, piece by piece, if my lady wishes it."

I wasn't good at being at another creature's mercy. I was a significant if not deadly threat to most things I met,

so having the tables turned was nothing short of madden-
ing. All the threats that wanted to spill out of me were
useless. The more I sat there yelling at him, the more energy I expended that I should have been focusing toward
healing the injuries he'd caused me.

I'd thought I was going to die. I *still* thought I was
going to die. But fuck, the least I could do was hold out
hope that this bastard's "lady" wasn't as merciless as he
was. Relying on a witch to spare my life—and Juniper's
life—was a miserable predicament, but I wasn't seeing
another way out of this.

I sat back, letting the manacles fall limp, and the
Archdemon grinned. "There's a good boy. I really
would've *hated* to have to restrain you further." He
paused for a moment, and snapped his fingers as if he'd
suddenly remembered something important. "Ah, wait,
no, I really wouldn't have hated that. It's so much more
entertaining when you fight. Then I get to watch you fail
again . . . and again . . . and again."

Don't take the bait, don't fucking take the bait. He
was tapping his claws impatiently on the floor, watching
me with such hyper-focused, pent-up energy I was surprised he wasn't literally vibrating. I sighed heavily.

"Just don't hurt her," I said. "Tell your lady . . . whoever the hell she is . . . not to hurt her."

"Why?" He was conjuring a ball of aether in and
out of existence, tossing the opalescent sphere between
his hands. Damn, and here I'd felt special that I'd finally
gained enough power to do that; it was nothing more
than child's play to this bastard. "You've got her soul,

don't you? I assume that's why you're following her around. The only life you should really be concerned about is your own."

I wasn't about to explain myself to this asshole. I tried not to look at him as he paced around the room, tossing that little ball back and forth. He was dressed in a fitted black suit, his shoes sleek, shining leather that tapped on the floor.

"Personally, I hope she wants you both dead."

I hung my head down, clenching my jaw. *It was bait, it was just fucking bait.*

"It's so much fun to kill the stubborn ones. I get to see how long it takes for you to cry."

Nope. Don't say a word, Zane. Mouth shut. Not worth it.

"Now that I know you're soft for your little mortal woman, I have a feeling it won't take you long at all."

He'd paced closer—*very* close. Close enough that I knew it was just more bait, dangling tantalizingly in front of my face.

I took it anyway. Like a complete idiot.

I SPENT THE next hour in even more pain, and it was my own damn fault. Squashed between the floor and his shoe was significantly worse than just being chained. He'd even pulled up a chair to make himself comfortable.

"You know, buddy, at this point I've just accepted that I'm not going to beat you in a fight," I muttered, my mouth a little difficult to use considering I had a shoe pressed against my cheek. "Maybe you could remove the foot? Hm? It seems intentionally condescending."

He laughed. It wasn't a pleasant sound—it got a little too deep in my bones, and echoed off the stone walls. "I'm pretty damn comfortable with you as a footrest, actually. Can't say I'm eager to move."

He had music playing on an old gramophone in the corner, but the occasional snapping of his fingers wasn't in tune with it. He was operating on some other timeline, some other reality, and it was frankly unnerving.

"You got a name?" I said. "I mean, since we're just going to sit here and get to know each other . . . I figured . . . an introduction might be nice." I really should have shut up, but my energy was building up and my nerves with it. With every moment that passed without Juniper, I grew more restless. I had to distract myself. "So . . . uh . . . I'm Zane."

Not even so much as a grunt in return. Alright, Captain Unpleasant. If you were going to torture someone, at least have the decency to have a little conversation. Take me to dinner first. I prefer to be courted properly prior to torture.

"Have you been here long? Odd place, Abelaum. A little Hellish, isn't it?" *Snap, snap, snap* went his fingers. I rolled my eyes. "Where's that witch of yours? I mean, I'm assuming she's yours. I don't think a witchling could have summoned a lovely being like you . . ." There was a shift, and although I couldn't see, I could *feel* his glare on me. "You two have made a deal, eh? Lucky you, getting a witch's soul. I've heard they're sweet as heaven—"

His shoe pressed a little harder—hard enough to make my bones protest. "You know nothing of witches, hellion. You talk too much."

"I've been told that before. It's a personal fault, I'll admit. How old are you anyway? I've heard rumors some of you royal types have been around since before humans—is that true? Personally, I think the claim is bullshit, but—"

He stiffened suddenly, and for a moment, I thought I'd *really* pissed him off. Moving rapidly, he unlocked me from the manacles and hauled me to my feet, my body tingling everywhere he touched me.

Then, keeping a tight hold on my arm, he forced us to teleport.

I'd never liked teleporting; it made me queasy. Dismantling one's heavy physical body, throwing one's spiritual form through space, then hurriedly reassembling a physical form again? Highly unpleasant. But teleporting with someone else, dragged along with them, reached a whole new level of awful.

By the time we stopped, and my physical body was back together again, I doubled over and gagged.

"Let him go, Callum. They won't harm us."

The voice came from a tall, blurry figure nearby. My eyes didn't want to focus, so I squeezed them shut for a moment. The sugary-sweet scent of magic rushed in my nose, but it wasn't just the witch nearby.

Honeysuckle and pine. The scent of a wolf.

It was Juniper who touched me, without a doubt. The relief that rushed over me at the feeling of her hands on my back was so profound it made me laugh. She was alive.

I could feel her mind's pulsing uncertainty and worry. I could smell her sweet scent and feel her soft skin.

I leaned into her. Her arms tightened around me.

"What the fuck did you do to him?" Her voice was vicious. "You said he wouldn't be hurt, Everly!"

"He's fine." I could hear the eyeroll in the Arch-demon's words. "He's just being dramatic."

I was being dramatic, yes. But I'd gotten Juniper to be all soft over me as a result, and that was immensely satisfying. The vicious little thing actually *cared*. If we lived, I'd be sure to tease her about it for the rest of eternity.

My vision was finally focusing. We were in a hallway, one side all large windows that looked out on the forest, the other wall lined with paintings. I got up, slowly, as my equilibrium returned. I dragged Juniper closer to me as I did, wrapping my arms around her. The cold tightness in my chest was fading just having her close.

Damn, I had it bad. The bastards would have to kill me if they wanted to take her away again. I was lucky Juniper hated having vulnerable conversations, because I didn't know how the hell I'd explain this in words.

No . . . that was wrong. I knew what words to say, I knew what I was feeling. But fuck, I wasn't going to admit it.

"Are you hurt?" Her voice was muffled against my chest.

"Just a few cracks in the bones," I said, giving her a careless grin. "No big deal."

I let her go, but she stayed close. I could see the witch clearly now, although she was partially hidden behind

Callum. She seemed timid, looking at me like she feared I would lunge at her at any second. The smell of her magic filled the room, and the air pulsed with every beat of her heart. It was a feral magic, chaotic, bursting at the seams.

"Then we have an understanding," she said, her voice soft as she rested her head against Callum's side. "Don't we, Juniper?"

"I kill the Libiri, you kill the God," she said, and my eyes nearly bugged out of my head. "And we stay the hell out of each other's way."

"A God-killer, eh?" I said, looking at Callum, who appeared painfully bored with our presence. "Were you in the wars?"

He smirked. "I was. I've killed my share of Gods."

"But with an army at your back," I said. "Still so confident when it's just you and the witchling?"

Everly looked up at him, her eyes wide, and she laid her hand against his chest. It was a warning: a reminder. It was like the violence seeped out of him with one touch. He looked at her with those black eyes and laid a kiss on her forehead, and I very nearly laughed out loud.

No one in Hell would ever, *ever* believe I'd just witnessed an Archdemon chastely kiss a mortal. It was ludicrous.

"I don't need an army, hellion," he said simply. He nudged his head up against Everly, whispering softly, "Make them leave."

She nodded. "I'm sure you're both eager to go. Good luck to you . . . both of you. If we meet again, may it be in a better world."

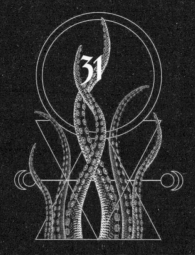

JUNIPER

THE WALK OUT of the woods was far faster than the journey in. The path seemed wider, the trees were no longer overbearingly thick. It was like the forest had opened, like the trees had released the breath they were holding and decided to let us pass by.

My backpack and weapons had been returned to me before we left. As we walked, Zane stayed close to me, his arm brushing mine, still looking around the forest like he expected to encounter another attack.

I'd never been the little girl who dreamed of being swept off her feet by fairy-tale royalty. I'd never dreamed of a family or a partner, after seeing what a mess my own family was. I'd considered myself better off alone, even before Victoria betrayed me and really drove the point home. I didn't need anyone else. I didn't want anyone else. I didn't need romance. I didn't need devotion. I didn't need love.

I didn't need love. It was a silly thing to think about anyway, especially now, when my future was damned. I was a murderer, planning to murder again. I'd sold my soul. My mind was broken in more ways than I could count, in ways I didn't think could ever be fixed. Dreaming of a future, of a partnership, of . . . of peace, of calm—it was useless. There was no point.

Especially to find those things crossing my mind when I looked at a demon—I was a fool.

But God, when I'd seen him appear in the hallway, dragged along by that Archdemon freak, all I'd wanted was to be next to him again. I didn't need a rescuer, I didn't need a guardian; he wasn't that.

He was my comfort. Comfort in the face of the world's madness. He was the one being who'd seen me weak, who'd seen me break down, who'd seen me vulnerable, and had never tried to exploit that.

He was a *demon*. Exploitation was exactly what he was supposed to do, wasn't it?

We were silent until we got back to the car. I was reaching for the door handle when Zane laid his hand against the door.

"Are you alright?" His voice was low, his gaze intense on my face. My mind was already in a million different places.

"I'm fine," I said quickly. "Just . . . fine. That didn't go down how I thought it would, but . . . Everly told me some shit about Kent that may help us."

He was nodding. "Good. That's good."

"Yeah, it'll at least help us prepare for our next—"

"I don't give a fuck what the witch said. I meant it's good you're alright. It's good you're not hurt. It's—" He paused, and winced as if in pain. "It's good they didn't hurt you. Because I don't know what the fuck I would've done."

He was . . . glad I was . . .

Oh.

I wasn't great with words, but that silenced me completely. My throat closed up, and my heart began to pound. My hands were sweaty. He'd positioned himself close to me, and that had a ridiculous way of making me flustered. I needed a drink. Several very large drinks, because my mind wasn't right.

What he'd just said shouldn't have made me feel *that* way.

"I . . . I mean . . . I guess it doesn't really matter if I die though, right?" I was staring hard at the door handle, my one escape from these words that were rushing wildly out of me. "You've got my soul, so . . . no loss to you . . . if I . . ."

He grabbed my neck, long fingers curling into my hair to cradle my head—and kissed me.

My eyes were open, but I couldn't see. His lips were soft but his grip was hard. His touch was hot and his other hand grabbed my waist, pulling me closer, and I closed my eyes as I wrapped my arms around him.

I didn't know what the hell this was. It was too frightening to contemplate, too complicated to try to understand. Why did he get to break down my walls again and again, dismantling the cold, unattached safety I'd surrounded myself with? Those walls were all I had, they were my protection. They kept me safe from pain, from heartbreak, from betrayal.

I didn't want to think about what these feelings meant.

But I could think about that kiss. I could lose myself in the sensation of his hard chest against mine, and the muscles in his back as my hands wrapped around his neck and my nails dragged along his skin. His forked tongue caressed around mine, and he kissed me like he was starving.

These were soft, tender feelings that remained in the rubble of my walls. They were bruised and beaten, trembling in the light that touched them, striving to crawl back into the dark. They'd been ignored and unnurtured for so long, they curled away from freedom.

Zane kept dragging them toward it.

It shouldn't have felt like this with him. I shouldn't have wanted him to tear me apart and hold me tenderly. I shouldn't have wanted him to hold me at all. I was setting myself up for disaster. He was a monster, and I'd seen enough of them to know they could only cause pain.

When he broke the kiss, pulling back mere inches from my mouth, I was pressed back against the car. He kept holding me, caressing me, keeping me close. How was I supposed to put the wall back up? I was vulnerable as hell. I was shaking.

"Why are you scared?" he said softly. I shook my head, but he grasped my face again and made me look up at him. "What are you scared of, love?"

Love. He'd called me that before. I'd brushed it off. It felt different now, it felt heavy. I was breathing hard, and I wasn't even sure why. It was like panic without the pain. He lifted my hand, watched my fingers trembling— and he kissed the back of it, kissed my palm, kissed my wrist and let his lips linger there.

"What are you scared of?"

"This," I whispered, and he smiled against my skin. "I'm scared of this . . . whatever . . . whatever this is."

He looked up at me, with his head still lowered as he held my hand. It was strange that a monster could look gentle, especially when he smiled at me with teeth sharp enough to rip me apart.

"And what do you think this is?"

This was usually the point at which I'd end the conversation. I'd met my fair share of people that had grown close to me over the years—men and women who'd somehow decided they wanted more from me—and those questions were always the ones that made me run.

But Zane and I were bound together. Eternally. There was no getting out of it. A damning bargain was all it was supposed to be.

"A bargain," I said softly. "It's . . . just a bargain."

He took both my hands, and kissed the other one just the same as he had the first, before he laid my palms against his chest. "Juniper Kynes, a storm manifested in human form, is afraid of a bargain?" He leaned close and kissed my neck, pausing with his lips barely brushing beneath my ear. "No, you're not. You're afraid of something far bigger than that. And I'll tell you something,

Juniper—this is a hell of a lot more than a bargain. I'm not fucking around. I don't fuck around when I find something I want."

"But you already have me." My voice sounded desperate. As if I was pleading with him to be callous, to tell me he was just joking.

"Body and soul. But I decided I want something else too." He laid his hand around my neck and pressed his thumb against my pulse. Every beat was emphasized as it throbbed against his finger, hard and fast. "That right there. I want that next." He lowered his voice, a shiver-inducing whisper in my ear. "And I'll have it. Just wait."

He left it at that. He let me go, left me standing there shaking as he got into the driver's seat. And when I got in after him, he started the engine and turned up the music, bobbing his head to the beat like he didn't have a care in the world.

Except he did care. He cared far too much, and I did too.

JUNIPER

AS WE ARRIVED back at the house that night, I was overcome with the strangest feeling of coming home.

We flicked on the lights, and everything was warm. It was quiet—it felt safe and familiar. As soon as the door clicked shut behind me, and I threw the deadbolt into place, I sighed. The tension in my back eased.

"Damn," I said it softly, barely even realizing I'd given voice to the word. But Zane turned back toward me, curiously.

"What is it?"

"It's just . . . it's good to be back," I said. He walked a little closer, with a curious, mischievous curve at the edge of his mouth.

"Is it?" He tucked a stray lock of hair back behind my ear and rubbed his fingers over the short fuzz of my undercut. "Why is that?"

I narrowed my eyes, barely restraining a shiver at his gentle touch. "You know why."

"Oh, do I?" He pressed me back a little more, his body up against mine. "I'd rather hear you explain it."

"I'd rather you shut up." I couldn't even manage to say it viciously. Damn, I'd lost my touch. He chuckled.

"I can't properly harass you if I shut up, now can I?"

"Oh, I'm sure you'd find a way." He stroked his fingers down my face and under my chin, and I grabbed his wrist. But as I did, I noticed the bruises there that I hadn't before: dark purple marks across his flesh, faded to yellow in spots but still angry in others.

It twisted my stomach. Even knowing he was here and safe, it made me furious to see the marks lingering.

"It wasn't the first time I've been in chains, little wolf," he said, grinning as he captured my attention back from staring at his bruises. "But I'd rather you restrain me any day than that winged asshole."

I shook my head in disbelief. "Is that what you were thinking of while we were separated? You were off somewhere in chains, wishing I was the one pushing you around?"

"Something like that." He lowered his head, looking at my fingers around his bruised wrist. "What would you think of that, hm? I demanded your body and soul when we made this deal. I demanded your submission." He laughed, as if he realized now just how impossible that particular demand had been. "What if I wanted your dominance too?"

I looked at him skeptically, certain he was fucking

with me. "You would want *me* to command *you*? I have a hard time believing that."

"Why? We demons crave all stimulation. We crave the new, the unusual, pain and pleasure both. You know I like pain, Juniper. I think you can understand why pain can be ecstasy . . . and why it can be a relief. Why entrusting control to another can feel freeing."

He put into words what I couldn't. After so many years clinging to control, gripping it as if it was my single lifeline, giving it up to him felt like taking a heavy sigh, like untensing my body after a long day. It was strange to think he understood that.

But perhaps that was part of why I'd learned to trust him. He understood what he was doing. He knew how it felt, he understood my unspoken desire intimately because he experienced it too.

"I can't control you," I said. "I'm just a human."

"Control isn't all about physical strength now, is it?" He took a step back, and I followed him into the living room. The warm interior lights made the outdoors black as ink, and he pressed a button on the wall that drew all the curtains closed over the massive windows. He turned to face me again, and in the lamplight, I could see even more of his injuries. It wasn't just the bruises on his wrists, but on his throat and his face too.

"Control is about force of will," he said. "It's about your will, and my will, in unison for what we desire. You're fierce, Juniper. Not even a God could force your submission, so I certainly can't." He chuckled softly. "It's not about that. You've given me control because you've wanted to. I can do the same." The lingering smile on his face sobered for a moment. "They put me in chains to keep me away from you. That's not a feeling I enjoyed. It's still there." He traced the bruises on his wrists, curiously, a frown on his face. "I'd prefer to replace that feeling. I'd prefer that you help me do that."

Suddenly, he was pressed against me again. His hands cradled my head, his sharp teeth smiled down at me, as he said, "Tell me why you sighed with relief when you walked in that door, and I'll give you control tonight. I think we both could use the outlet."

I'd never imagined he'd even offer that. I'd played both roles in the past—I could submit when it felt right, I could dominate when allowed. They both fulfilled something different—different but intertwined, two halves of the same coin, two faces for the same deep need. The way he'd put it felt right to me: these games we played weren't about physical strength, even though that could play a part in it. They were about willingness and desire. They were about relief and release.

But of course he had to be difficult about it. He had to demand I give a little of my precious, protected vulnerability before he gave me his.

"This house feels like home," I said, holding my chin up in defiant pride. "I haven't had that in a long time. So I sighed. Because I feel good. Because I feel happy." That last sentence came out viciously. I'd gone a damn long time without daring to say anything like that, so now that I claimed it, I'd defend it. I'd wield my happiness like a bludgeon to hurt anyone who dared to try to take it. "I'm happy we're alive. I'm happy we made it out. I'm happy that . . . that I finally . . ." I swallowed. "That I finally feel like there was a reason I survived."

He nodded, his pupils swelling with pleasure the longer he looked at me. "My little wolf gets braver every day," he said. "You're brave enough now to be as viciously happy as you are angry. Now . . ." His eyes darkened, and my core tightened with need. He stepped behind me, just out of my sight, his words a breath on the back of my neck. "Do you still want me to shut up?"

I grinned, my anticipation growing. "Always."

He was gone and back before I even realized he'd left. He dropped something heavy on the coffee table, turned to me with a smug smirk, and said, "Make me."

I was staring at the item he'd dropped, wide-eyed: two black leather straps attached to a shining silver ball. "Is that a *metal* ball gag?"

"You're not the first being to want me to shut up," he said.

"Are you trying to break your teeth?" I picked up the toy, turning it over in my hands curiously. It was beautiful, but not something I'd ever put in my mouth. Clenching metal between my teeth? No, thank you. I couldn't afford a dental bill like that.

Zane chuckled. "I'm a demon, love, remember? I practically teethed on metal binkies."

"Really?"

"No." He shrugged. "But I could have."

Imagining that gag in his mouth was getting me absurdly warm. Muffling that dirty, sarcastic mouth of his would feel so fucking good. Restraining a being as powerful as him, in any way at all, gave me a little shiver up my spine. "You've had this in the house all this time? What other toys are you hiding?"

He gave me a look that told me I was in for a surprise. I followed him upstairs, to the master bedroom, where he gave the large black chest at the foot of the bed a tap with his shoe. "Take a look."

I crouched down in front of it and opened the lid. There were floggers, shackles, clubs, paddles, and chains. There was metal, leather, and wood. Some of the items were studded with metal spikes, some with sharp spines. I shook my head in disbelief, picking up a pair of thick metal shackles. As I turned back toward him, I had the shackles in one hand and the ball gag in the other. "None of these toys look very comfortable for humans."

He gave me a long look up and down, and his forked tongue slid hungrily over his grinning teeth. "Most of these things aren't meant for humans."

"You should have told me these were here earlier," I said, walking toward him. "I could have shut you up weeks ago and saved myself the headache."

He sniffed and leaned his towering height a little closer to my face. "As I said, love . . . make me."

The idea that I could, in fact, *force* him to do anything was ludicrous. No number of whips and chains could amount to me overpowering him, but that wasn't the point. This absurdly powerful being had decided to lay down his power at my feet, and that gave me a serious head rush. It made the lingering stress of the day, the gripping fear of having faced death, suddenly melt away.

All that mattered was right here, in this house, in this home. All that mattered was he and I, together again, ready to fight another day.

"Get on your knees," I said. "Now."

He knelt in front of me, and holy shit, seeing those bright eyes staring up at me, waiting for an order, made my heartbeat quicken. Shit, this was a being that could kill me in a second if he wanted—instead he was on his knees with a hard-on already visible in his jeans.

"Shirt off."

He tweaked an eyebrow at me. "Trying to get yourself a good view, eh?"

I narrowed my eyes. "I gave you an order, not a suggestion."

He tugged his shirt over his head and tossed it aside, giving me a cocky smirk. He knew how damn good he looked. He knew that the slight sheen of sweat over his muscular chest got me hot. He knew it made my mouth water when he rolled his shoulders and flexed his hands, emphasizing the thick veins running down his arms.

"Anything else you want me to take off?" he said.

"No. Open your mouth."

A full set of deadly fangs greeted me, wickedly sharp. Curious, I dared to touch a finger to his teeth, right over the edge, testing it like a knife's blade. His forked tongue brushed against me, teasing me, and my breath hitched for a moment as he took my finger in his mouth and sucked.

When he opened his mouth again, it was to say, "You're blushing, Juniper."

I glared down at him. "Shut. *Up*."

I fit the ball gag in his mouth, securing the straps behind his head. It felt bizarre to see a metal ball fitted between his teeth, even knowing it couldn't hurt him. The shackles didn't lock, but were securable with a nut and bolt. I circled him, enjoying the view before I said, "Hands behind your back."

He moved his arms back, and I gave myself a moment to enjoy the tightness in his shoulders, the way his muscles swelled when he moved. I crouched down, locking the shackles into place around his wrists.

"I guess you could break these if you really wanted, couldn't you?" I laughed softly. "Oh, wow, you're actually silent for once. What a good boy."

He side-eyed me as I stood, the shackles secured. Gagged, in chains, on his knees—fuck, that was a sexy thing to see. I stood in front of him again, and scratched my nails lightly down the side of his face. His pupils had swelled, and he moved slightly to tug against the chains, keeping his eyes on me all the while.

"Let's see how well you can keep quiet, hm?"

He mumbled something as I walked back toward the chest. I shook my head, even though his muffled sounds around the gag elicited an excited warmth deep in my stomach. "Are you failing already? Is it just too hard to resist the smart-ass remarks?" I had no idea what he'd tried to say; I could only assume it was something sarcastic because, well, of course.

When I turned back to him with a new toy in my hands, he managed to smile even around the gag.

"Do you like the look of this?" I let the flogger I'd selected swing from my hand as I approached him. The handle was leather, but the tails were slim pieces of metal chain. It was the kind of piece that could cause damage if wielded hard enough, but he'd already told me these toys weren't here with humans in mind. I ran the metal tails up his arm, over his shoulders . . . and whipped it down.

His breath hitched for only a moment. The chains left behind beautiful red marks, growing brighter across his skin with every passing second. I hummed appreciatively and whipped it down again. His shoulders tightened, and I scratched my nails over the fresh marks.

"So quiet," I teased. "Not so hard to silence yourself once it's a challenge, is it?"

I put more force into my next lash. He exhaled heavily, readjusting himself, spreading his legs slightly. "Jeans getting a little tight there?" I brought my lips close to his neck, let my breath tease up his skin to just below his ear. "Poor boy. Doesn't look very comfortable." His hips twitched forward, and he took a deep, slow breath as I stood back and raised the flogger again. "Does the sting make your cock twitch?"

I whipped the chains down, and he growled as the reddened marks bloomed across his skin. Every step I took left me viscerally aware of how wet I was. I'd taken command in sex before, with other partners, but there was something particularly exciting about someone as powerful as Zane submitting to me. Even knowing he was a masochist hadn't prepared me for him to *actually* let me take command.

I draped the flogger around his neck and pressed my foot against his crotch. His thick, hard length twitched against me, and I giggled as I applied a little more pressure. "Should I set this greedy cock of yours free?" I ground my foot down and he groaned, the veins in his arms beginning to run black. "I think I will. I just don't know yet if it'll be to make you feel good . . . or to hurt you."

I crouched down and pulled open the button on his jeans. The head of his cock was glistening with precum, having pushed past the waistband of his briefs entirely. I rubbed my fingertip in slow circles around his slick cherry-red head, savoring every twitch.

"You're looking a little tense, Zane." His half-lidded eyes were fixed on me with such predatory hunger that I wondered if he was going to lose his patience and break out of the cuffs. The sight of his fangs around that thick silver gag, sharp against the bright metal, made my stomach squirm with desire.

I'd tamed a monster all my own, a monster who knelt for me from sheer desire.

I pulled down his zipper and tugged down his briefs so his cock sprang free, straining toward me. I gripped it in my hand, too big to be fully encircled by my fingers. I stroked along it slowly, marveling at the ridges and swells of its ridiculous girth. Another bead of precum dripped from his tip, and I caught it with my thumb and sucked it in my mouth.

A shudder ran over him as he watched me, his hips jerking forward.

"What?" I said sweetly, dragging the flogger from around his neck. "Do you want more?"

I walked behind him, lashing him again before I stripped off my shirt and tossed it over his head to land in front of him. Another lash, and then my bra followed. Another—and I tugged off my jeans and threw them into the pile. Only my panties remained, damp with my arousal, along with my sheathed knife on my thigh. His back was beautifully reddened, a few small welts forming amongst his tattoos.

"You've been so quiet, Zane," I said softly. "You can manage to shut up after all. I think I should make it more difficult for you."

I slid my panties down, and dangled them in front of his face. The moment he saw the dampness glistening on the fabric, he groaned.

"Do you want a little taste?" I circled him, naked, and trailed my finger down my chest, over the soft hair between my legs. "Should I let you taste?"

He nodded eagerly, every muscle tense, nostrils flaring with the effort of keeping himself obediently on his knees. It had to be sheer torture to control himself. Those chains on him were nothing: it was the self-restraint, the shuddering control, that truly kept him in his place.

There was something so cathartic in this. My anxiety had melted away when I'd trusted him enough to submit to him—this feeling was different, but no less intense. I was in awe of his self-control and enamored with my own power. I didn't need any weapons to be powerful here.

I slipped my finger between my legs, sighing softly as I rubbed over my clit. His eyes were fixated on me, and he stared at my fingers as I drew them away, glistening with my arousal. I crouched down and stroked my finger over his lips. He was practically shaking with the effort not to break through those chains.

I straddled him, teasing my pussy against the thick head of his cock and trailing the flogger up his back. "Too bad about that gag, boy. You can't taste me with that in your mouth."

When he groaned again, it was closer to a growl, and he tried to mutter something around the gag. I whipped the flogger down, grinning at the brief flicker of pain across his face. "Complaining, are we? Behave yourself, or this is all you're going to get."

I slid his head inside—just the head, and even that stretched me. I bit my lip, savoring the tightness as he watched me. It was a struggle not to take all of him. I teased him for how turned on he was, but I wasn't doing any better. His cock twitched eagerly inside me, throbbing at my entrance, and I laughed softly.

"Do you want this pussy, Zane? Do you want more?"

He couldn't move his hands to touch me; he used that weird little mind trick of his instead. It brought the sensation of fingers stroking through my hair and caressing down to grip tightly around my neck. I whipped the flogger against his back again, and he chuckled victoriously around the gag.

"Don't get fucking cheeky with me," I hissed. "I'll use this flogger on your cock if you can't behave."

His eyes widened slightly, a glint of masochistic joy brightening them. Of *course* he liked the idea of that. Figures. But I understood it too well—after all, I was also the type to feel like threats of punishment were really just offers for a good time.

We were far too alike sometimes; alike in ways I'd never thought I could share with another being.

I got up, leaving his cock straining and glistening with arousal. He jerked toward me: eager, almost desperate. I shook my head at him, even though waiting to have him fill me was damn near torture for me too.

"You know, Zane, I let you carve your name in my skin." I walked around him, swinging the flogger idly, the chains clinking together softly as I kissed it over his shoulders. "I'd really like to do the same to you."

I pulled my knife from its sheath on my thigh, leaned over his shoulder, and held up the blade in front of him. His eyes widened with excitement, his jaw squeezing tighter around the gag. The thought of getting to mark him like he'd marked me—leaving my name in his flesh, scarring him so every demon who crossed his path would know a mortal had laid her claim on him—made desire tingle over every inch of my body.

"Should I do it?" I whispered, right in his ear. He didn't hesitate for even a second. His eager nodding made me laugh. "Damn, you really want me to cut you up, don't you?" I walked back around in front of him and tapped the knife under his chin. "Fucking sit up straight. And don't you dare come until I say you can."

I braced my hands on his shoulders, and lowered myself down onto him. He groaned as my pussy squeezed around him, tight even though I tried to relax to fit his girth more easily. I sheathed him fully inside me, panting through the last couple inches. It didn't get any easier, fitting that monster inside.

His every muscle was taut as he watched me. I'd never thought I'd see a demon try so hard to behave. But of course, the only time he could manage to be good was when he was doing something so bad.

I traced my knife lightly along his skin, just beneath his collarbone. There was a gap in his tattoos there, a space between the dark, serpentine designs along his shoulders and the elaborate piece that adorned his chest.

That was where I'd mark my name.

I kissed his skin before I cut it. I kissed it slowly, taking my time, inhaling his scent with every touch of my lips against him. I looked up, and found him watching me longingly, his eyes bright with the anticipation of pain.

"You made a deal to own me," I said softly, my lips inches from his. His cock throbbed inside me, and I barely held back a groan. "But I own you too."

I sliced into his skin. Zane's breath hitched around the gag, and he tipped his head back, his eyes closing as he savored the careful, stinging cuts. I formed the first letter of my name, and then the second, my gaze flickering back to his face every few seconds. His cock throbbed again, and I moved myself slowly along his shaft, riding him as I continued through the letters.

"Fuck, you feel so good," I murmured. I paused half-way through my name, watching the blood drip down as I pleasured myself, fucking myself on his cock with one arm around his neck to hold myself up. "You get even harder when I cut you." I paused, his cock buried deep inside me, and slapped my palm against his cheek. His eyes opened again, and he muttered something incomprehensible around the gag.

"Don't close your eyes," I said, as I set the knife back against his skin. "Watch me."

He watched, his cock throbbing with every cut I made. He was shaking as if cold, but his body was feverishly hot. As his breath came harder, the room grew darker and so did his eyes. He was thrusting fervently into me as I reached the end of my name. That feral need couldn't be caged for much longer.

I wanted it too badly to hold back anymore. I carved the final letter into him, smiling at the sight of my name etched in blood across his chest. But I only had a moment to truly admire it. There was a loud snap, and suddenly I found myself on my back, pinned to the floor, and Zane was gripping my thighs as he angled himself deep inside me.

He'd *broken* the shackles. He'd snapped them like they were nothing more than brittle glass.

My gasp choked off into desperate moans. He pounded into me, still gagged, the chains dangling from his wrists as he held my legs up and fucked me hard. I clawed his neck, leaving long red scratches across his tattooed skin, and he gripped my legs hard enough to bruise.

Every inch of him was tense, shaking, pushed to uncontrollable need by my slow teasing. I cried out, squeezing around him as pleasure shattered me into pieces. When the bliss contorted my face, he watched with veneration, with longing, as if he'd witnessed something unspeakably holy.

"Zane!" My voice shook, my body enraptured by that perfect ecstasy. My toes curled, my mind dazed and empty as he thrust into me with ravenous urgency. The sight of my scratches on his neck, the welts from the flogger on his shoulders, nearly made me come again then and there. I was riding high on an endless wave of euphoria, only brought higher as his cock throbbed inside me.

He growled around the gag and slammed his fist down, his claws ripping into the carpet as he came, pumping me full with his seed. He leaned into the crook of my shoulder, his hot forehead pressed to my skin, sucking in his breath sharply with every pulse of his cock inside me.

We lay still, panting, twined together like that for several minutes as we caught our breath. Slowly, with shaking arms, I unbuckled his gag and took it from his mouth. He chuckled softly and laid his head back down against my shoulder, working his jaw for a minute to get the tension out.

"So, what do you think of it?" I said softly. "Now you have my mark too."

He sat up, smiling as he looked down at the fresh cuts on his chest. The bleeding had already stopped, the wounds swiftly healing. "I'll make sure they scar," he said. "It's an honor to be marked by a wolf."

He pulled me up against him, holding me close. I hadn't thought my marks would stay. I thought they'd be fun for the few minutes they lasted and nothing more.

But it felt right. I was glad my name was there.

I didn't know what the hell would become of us. I didn't even know if we would live another day or die. For now, it didn't matter.

For whatever it was worth, regardless of what these twisting, confusing, frightening emotions meant—I'd given myself to a demon, and he'd given himself to me in return.

JUNIPER

I'D DONE A lot of weird shit on October 31st, but I'd never made plans to crash a Halloween party and kill its host before. Every morning, I woke up with a ticking clock in my head. A countdown that seemed to drag slower and slower the closer it got to zero.

This was it. Kent Hadleigh was going to die.

I had no idea if we'd be successful. Any number of things could go wrong, the possibility that we'd fail never left my mind. But finally, after so many years, I was close. My tension was a knot pulled tight in my stomach, squeezing inside me from the time I opened my eyes until the hour I finally managed to close them.

But as nervous as I was, it was hard not to have fun when Zane was so goddamn excited about it.

"All the best parties end in murder," he said, trailing behind me as we wound through the Halloween store, browsing the messy rows of costumes. "That's what keeps people talking about it."

"Are you an expert on parties?" His chatter was distracting me from how irritating it was to shop: there were screaming children running everywhere, the aisles were too crowded, and all the costumes were too small.

"Yeah, actually. I've been to hundreds of parties across nearly ten centuries. And I can guarantee you, all the best ones had a murder."

"I think that's just because you like murder."

"Are all Halloween stores like this?" He dodged two children that sprinted past, nearly smacking into him. He shot a quick look back at them, and the child in the lead tripped, falling so abruptly that the kid chasing behind tripped over him too, and they fell into a pile. He smiled smugly as he looked back at me.

"Tripping children?" I said. "Really? Are you proud of yourself for that one?"

"Very. It was hilarious."

I rolled my eyes and had to look away before he saw me laugh. Not that I could really hide it from him; he'd probably smell it or something, since he could smell everything else. "But yeah, welcome to twenty-first-century capitalism, Halloween edition. All year, there's no Halloween stores—then October hits, and suddenly every empty building has one."

"So many foam skeletons," he said, brushing past several that were dangling from a display. He picked up a French maid costume encased in a plastic bag. "These costumes look like lingerie."

"Yeah. That's kind of the point."

He grinned. "You should buy this one."

I scoffed. "*You* should. I'd look ridiculous."

"Fuck, I'd look hot as hell in this," he said. "And I'd still dick you down good. Demon maid at your service." He thrust his hips, and the image of him doing that dressed as a maid almost broke me.

"God, stop. Please." I had to turn away because I was trying too hard not to laugh. But I quickly added, "Buy it in your size, but you are *not* wearing it to the party."

THE MORE NERVOUS I was, the harder it was to sleep. I'd killed before; I knew what it felt like to take a human life. But killing Kent Hadleigh *meant something.* Facing him again, standing before him of my own free will, meant something.

My anxiety felt like an open door, a gap in my defenses through which any number of awful things could slip in. If I didn't plan carefully enough, if I wasn't cautious enough, or if I was too cautious entirely—this could all end in failure.

That open door of worry was an invitation. It was a beacon. I just didn't realize it at first.

I was running through exercise drills near the dock. The sky was gray, but the rain was a mere mist, cooling my skin as I sweat. The breeze was cold, and the water lapping against the shore formed a meditational rhythm I synced my breathing to.

Breathe in—punch—breathe out—kick—breathe in—

"Juniper."

"What?" I yelled back at the house without turning. One of Zane's favorite pastimes was to tease me relentlessly any time I tried to work out, claiming he was just helping get my heartrate up.

But there was no response.

I paused, panting between my sets, and looked back at the house. No sign of Zane at all. I straightened up, slowing my breathing so I could better hear around me. The wind picked up, the lapping waves on the lake coming faster, seeping up the pebbly shore. I scanned the trees, but the only movement I could see was a small flock of birds fluttering between the branches and the ground.

There was nothing there, nothing at all. But a chill still ran up my back. It suddenly felt like it would be a lot safer inside.

I'd left my water bottle at the dock, so I jogged back for it. The water had come up enough to grab it; it was floating a couple yards offshore.

"Damn it." I sighed heavily as I waded in. The water was cold, but it felt nice after working up a sweat. The pebbles were smooth beneath my feet as the water came up to my waist, and I snatched the bottle before it could bob further out.

I froze, the bottle gripped in my hand. There was something in the middle of the lake, poking up above the water.

A blood-red face. Perfectly round, wide, staring eyes.

It was looking at me. It was looking *right at me*.

It slipped back below the surface with the barest ripple. The wind stilled. The waves calmed around me until the lake became eerily glass-like. I backed out of the water, keeping an eye on the depths around me, my eyes constantly flickering back to the spot where the head had disappeared.

The pebbles crunched under my feet as I reached the shore. It was colder now, and I shivered in my wet clothes. I knew better than to trust everything my eyes saw, even when I was awake. Nightmares didn't restrict themselves to my sleeping hours.

But I heard nothing. I smelt nothing. So I turned.

And found myself face-to-face with the blood-red being.

It had no eyelids, it had no lips. All its skin was pulled back and it loomed over me, like a spider over a fly. It reached out with three long, knobby red fingers—

I GASPED, JERKING upright, panting as I looked around. I wasn't on the shore; in fact, the lake was nowhere in sight. Neither was the dock, or the house.

I was underground, in a narrow, dimly lit tunnel. Water dripped slowly from overhead, the smell of damp dirt and fungi heavy in my nose. I was in the mine.

I shook my head, squeezing my eyes shut tight. No, no, no, this was impossible.

"Juniper . . ."

Laughter followed the whisper, and I opened my eyes. Darkness waited for me in either direction, completely impenetrable. This was just a dream. Just a dream, nothing more. I must have passed out. That creature must have knocked me unconscious.

But how? And why? I'd never seen anything like it before—

Shlop . . . shlop . . . shlop . . .

I stared into the dark. Something was coming. Something was taking slow, heavy steps through the mud. I had no weapons. I had no light.

"Wake up," I whispered softly, digging my fingernails into my arm. "Come on, Juniper. Wake up. *Wake up.*"

"There is . . . no . . . waking . . ."

The voice hissed out of the dark. It was more than an echoing whisper now, more than a mere breath on the wind. It had form, it had weight. It was real. It was *here*.

Deep in the darkness, a strange shape was lurching toward me. There was a sound like something slimy sliding over the wet ground. I took a step back, and then another, terrified to run into the dark at my back, but too fearful to remain here.

Thick gray tentacles reached out of the shadows. They were coiling outward from the strange shape, which was slowly morphing before my eyes. It shrank and grew, burgeoning outward and then collapsing into itself, as if its form wasn't solid. Icy fingers wrapped around my heart, squeezing, the cold aching in my ribs.

"I've found you, Juniper. I've found you at last."

I began to hyperventilate. I couldn't wake up. Why the hell wasn't I waking up? This was all in my head, I had to remember that. It was all just in my head.

The tentacles were coming faster. They were nearly at my ankles. The shape in the dark came into the dim gray light.

It was a human, but It . . . wasn't. It was a being beyond beauty, so horrifyingly exquisite that one physical form alone could not contain It. It was made of light and darkness, flesh and bone, an ever-shifting amalgamation of air and energy. Its tentacles were so long that they wrapped around the mine shaft's walls, coiling toward me.

Eyeballs blinked over every inch of Its skin, and they were all staring at me.

I shook my head slowly. "You're not real," I whispered, the words trembling out from between my lips. "This is a dream. Just a dream. You're not real."

When the God spoke again, it was with a thousand voices all in unison. A thousand voices, barely masking a thousand screams. *"You think this is not real, and yet, you don't know where you are."* The being smiled, Its lips pulling back from rows upon rows of teeth. I was still backing away, but I had no idea what lay in the dark behind me. *"Where are you, Juniper? Where does your body lie? In the woods? In the dirt? On the shore?"* Its smile widened. *"Are you in the water, Juniper? Are you drowning?"*

It was right. Where was my body? Where the hell was I? Had I managed to walk back on shore, or . . . or had that red creature dragged me under?

What if I wasn't waking up because I . . . *couldn't?*

Panic gripped me. I had to run. I had to—

My back hit a dirt wall. I was at the end of the tunnel. I had nowhere else to go.

"You can't take me," I whispered desperately. "My soul isn't yours. It's never been yours."

The tentacles coiled around my ankles and wrapped up my legs. The God stood back, Its face half in shadow, Its numerous eyes blinking at me.

"*I cannot take your soul . . . but I can take your mind.*"

The tentacles were around my chest now, squeezing tighter and tighter. I clawed at them, digging my nails into their slick, slimy flesh, but they couldn't be moved. Then they were around my shoulders . . . around my throat. They were squeezing until I couldn't breathe.

"*You never should have defied Me. You stole yourself away from Me. But I will have what's Mine.*"

The tentacles coiled around my face. I squeezed my eyes shut as they probed at my lids, at my mouth. I couldn't breathe—*I couldn't breathe*—

"JUNIPER!"

I thrashed, screaming, striking with my fists, kicking hard, struggling until the shock of cold water jolted my eyes open. I was crouched on the shore, pebbles beneath my hands. Zane stood over me, golden eyes narrowed in confusion as he watched me. I scrambled to my feet and turned in circles, looking everywhere, my heart pounding in my ears.

"What the hell happened?" His voice was dark,

vicious. The sound of it made me finally remember to breathe.

"I, uh . . . I . . ." My voice caught. I was shaking violently with cold. I didn't know what to say. I didn't know how I could possibly explain that. Finally, I choked out, "The God found me. It found me."

EVEN KNOWING HE would believe me, the fear was still there: the terror of being laughed at, of being told I'd imagined it all. Even as I explained what I'd seen, the words pouring out in a flood, I was second-guessing myself. Had I exerted myself too much and passed out? Had I been hallucinating? Had I seen the red creature at all?

But when I'd finished telling it all, Zane's face was hard with worry.

"It was a Watcher," he said. "They're parasitic monsters, attracted to the prey of other creatures."

I frowned, shivering again beneath the blanket over my shoulders. "Why? What the hell does it want?"

"To feed. Watchers seek out the prey of larger, more dangerous creatures. In Hell, they're known to follow Reapers around so they can feed on the fear of their victims. That's what sustains it: fear. It will aid whatever is hunting you to increase your fear, your panic. By itself, there's little it can do to harm you. But it can make you vulnerable. It can overwhelm you, distract you—that's how it hunts."

I'd never encountered anything like that. The sight of those wide, lidless eyes staring blankly at me wouldn't leave my head. It twisted my stomach, burned into my mind.

"What can I do?" I said. "How can I kill it?"

"I don't know if you can." Zane rubbed his hand over his head in thought. "The best thing you can do, if you see it again, is ignore it. Pretend it isn't there, don't give in to the fear."

Far easier said than done. Fear was a fact of life. I'd learned to operate despite it; erasing it entirely was impossible.

"When I was unconscious, the God said It *found* me." I bit my lip, hardly daring to ask the question. "Does that . . . does that mean It knows where I am? Does that mean It can . . . take me?"

Zane moved closer to me, tugging me into his warmth. I curled against his side, still shivering, trying to ease down my lingering panic.

"When the Libiri cut you and threw you down in the dark, the God got Its influence deep in your mind," he said. "Demons have a similar power: I can give you the sensation of phantom touches, or create the illusion that you're restrained." Those phantom fingers traced along my neck as he spoke. I'd gotten used to that little mind trick of his, although I still didn't understand how it worked. "Gods can do that too, but of course, their power is usually greater than a demon's. They can create far more powerful, frightening sensations."

I didn't want to close my eyes. I was afraid that if I dared, for even a moment, I'd find myself back in the dark again, with those tentacles curling around my body.

"It's an illusion, Juniper," Zane said. "I know it feels real, but it's just the God pushing Its influence over your mind and forcing you to feel things that aren't there. That's why It waits for you to be vulnerable, that's why It comes to you in your sleep. The Watcher will try to give the God more opportunities to get to you. If it can panic you, if it can find a way to terrify you, it will. But the God is still trapped, Juniper. It can't reach you. Remember that: no matter what It says, no matter what awful things It shows you, the God can't touch you."

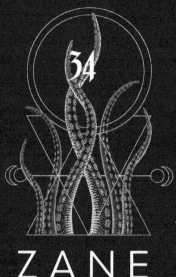

ZANE

IF I HAD to choose one thing to do on Earth—besides collecting mortal souls—I'd choose to party.

Don't get me wrong, a party on Earth was never going to compare to what went down in Hell. A mortal wouldn't even survive a Hell party; if the recreational substances didn't immediately kill them, sheer exhaustion would. Hell could rage for days on end, for *months* if the company was good enough.

But human parties were so earnest, so sweetly desperate. The pungent stench of alcohol, of sweat, of needy horny mortals all hoping for the opportunity to fuck. Humans couldn't hold their liquor for shit either. All of them would be stumbling around like toddlers within a few hours, losing control of all emotions and bodily functions.

It was cute. They wanted stimulation so badly, but

once they had it, their little mortal brains couldn't handle it.

To say I was looking forward to the Hadleigh party was an understatement. I was frankly ecstatic.

Juniper was a bundle of nerves, but I fucked her good and got a shot of whiskey in her, and she mellowed out after that. But her excitement lingered in twitchy hands, fingers rubbing together, clenching, continually running through her hair.

The Watcher had her spooked, and I didn't blame her. By demonic standards, they were generally harmless creatures, regardless of how unpleasant they were to look at. But Juniper was exactly the kind of being they'd want to prey on. She was brave as hell, but bravery didn't mean she wasn't afraid.

She lived with a deep, dark well of fear within her, and it was a precarious balance she walked day after day to not fall into the depths.

Every time I found something that helped calm her, I felt like I'd won a goddamn medal.

I'd been honest with her: I wanted more. Body and soul was fun and games; but having her mind, having her heart, that was something else entirely. It was beyond mortality, beyond bargains. It wasn't just business.

I wanted to claim her smile, her laugh, the way she looked when she sighed after a long day and laid her head back, eyes closed. They were unclaimable things, things without names, things that wouldn't bring me power or glory. Things like the storm that raged in her, the nervous energy in her long fingers, the way she bit her lip in thought.

Humans sought to fulfill so many different needs in their mates, whereas demons took mates as a matter of devotion and fascination. Juniper was short-tempered, selfish, a woman of few words, stubborn, anxious, aggressive.

I wanted all of it. All her messiness, all her sharp edges and fragmented pieces. I wanted the sharpness. I wanted to cut myself on it again and again. I wanted to move her pieces around until they all made sense.

And she needed to let her walls down. She needed to be as messy as she pleased without fear of being alone.

"WHY DO THEY do these tutorials so fast?" she grumbled, skipping back nearly a minute in the video she was watching on her laptop. "It's like one of those stupid How To Draw things: step one is a circle, and step two is a fully formed drawing of a horse."

I chuckled and let her struggle with the makeup for a few more seconds. Our costumes for the party were simple: fitted black suits, boots, bow ties, and skulls painted on our faces. It was subtle enough to not attract too much attention, but the thick face paint would do the trick to keep Juniper's identity hidden. The blazers made it easier for her to hide her weapons too, and she was coming well-armed.

"Alright, alright, I've seen you struggle enough," I said. "Sit your ass down, I'll do the makeup."

She looked at me skeptically. "Really?"

"Yes, really." I snapped her laptop closed, cutting off the video. "I've had hundreds of years to do whatever the hell I please. You think in all that time I've never gotten artistic?"

She sat down on the toilet lid so I could smear the black and white paint across her skin. She had a hard time sitting still, so I took my time to make sure she squirmed.

"I'll spank you if you keep fidgeting."

"You fucking will not," she said, but her skin got hotter. I grinned.

"You'll cry all your makeup off and I'll have to do it again."

"Ha! Oh, you wish—"

"Close your mouth. I need to paint on the rest of your teeth."

Instead of closing her mouth, she snapped at my fingers. I didn't make idle threats, and she'd asked for it, but she still put up a fight as I wrestled her up and under my arm.

"Was that a good idea, Juniper?" She hadn't dressed yet and was just wearing a pair of tight gym shorts. The bounce when I smacked her ass was extremely satisfying.

"I'd do it again and actually bite you next time!" she yelled, stomping on my toes but certainly not getting me to move. A few more smacks and she was hot as hell, her angry yelling taking on a slightly higher note of desire. Only with her properly needy did I let her go, pushing her ass back down onto her seat.

"Now sit still." I leaned over her, brush in hand. "Or I'll find a way to punish you that doesn't make you horny."

She didn't stop squirming. "Yeah, good luck with that."

"I'll find something," I said. "There's something out there you hate. Maybe a paddle instead of my hand."

"You're just going to turn me on more talking like that."

"Mm, maybe I'll smother you instead."

"Smothering is just lazy choking, and you know I'm into that. Try again."

"Needles."

Her eyes widened as I moved the brush along her jaw. "What?"

I smiled. "I should be more specific: piercings. I'll put a few needles through that tender skin of yours and see if you still get turned on."

She'd gone very still, her mind turning. Her arousal hadn't gone away. In fact . . . "Goddamn it, I'm into it."

I laughed. "Don't sound so angry about it. I'm not complaining. And you're done, so you can squirm all you like."

"Damn, I've got a fucked-up head," she muttered, standing to examine her face paint in the mirror. I started on mine next, hiding my face behind the layers of paint.

"Not fucked up to a demon, love," I said. "We use piercings as marks of loyalty and devotion. When we take a mate, we'll pierce them to lay our claim. It's pretty damn normal for Hell."

"You're really selling me on Hell." She watched me in the mirror. The striking paint on her face made her brown eyes look even richer. "Personally, I'm looking forward to trying out a whole new dimension." She paused. "Is it a different dimension?"

"A different reality. But there are books in our libraries there that'll explain it much better than I could."

She stood at my side for a moment. We'd chosen subtle costumes, but there was nothing subtle about her face, her body. Even hidden behind paint, her beauty demanded appreciation.

She frowned. "What are you grinning for?"

"Thinking about piercing your tongue," I said. "You'd look so damn good with my metal in you. And fuck, it would feel good on my cock."

She shoved me. "I already let you cut up my chest. You really want to make me bleed again?"

"You cut me up too," I said. "So we're even there." Not a day had gone by since she'd carved her name in my chest that I didn't find myself admiring the sight of it in every reflective surface I passed. I could've let it heal entirely, erasing it from my skin—but like the piercings and the tattoos, it was a part of me now. "We can talk about it again after we kill Kent. Give you some time to think about it."

"We'll see. Hurry up, Mister Artist. We've got a party to crash."

She smacked my ass on her way out. I exhaled heavily through my mouth, shaking my head as I resisted the urge to snatch her up for another fuck. Maybe she thought I was kidding, but I wanted my metal in her. I'd be asking her again.

THE LONG, PAVED driveway was full by the time we arrived at the Hadleigh house. Cars were parking in the grass along the road, but we parked even further than that: along a narrow dirt road a half mile past the house, where Juniper's Jeep could sit hidden amongst the trees.

I'd wanted to take the NSX, but she'd insisted, "Your car will stick out to them. Clean, expensive—and we don't want their attention. No big entrance. We go in quietly."

I *loved* making an entrance, so this "subtle" thing wasn't exactly easy. Still, it was cute Juniper thought we could slip into the party without catching attention.

She looked hot as fuck. Her long hair was pulled back in a high ponytail, the suit fit her perfectly. Her cold, disinterested gaze did nothing to dissuade people from staring at her. As we neared the house, half the people we passed looked twice.

But when they looked back, I made sure they saw me first. I made sure they *knew*.

Don't touch.

The property was encompassed by a large stone wall, but the iron gate at the end of the driveway was left open so cars and partygoers could enter. The house was all glass and steel, a blocky modern design, perched above a perfectly manicured lawn. Beyond the lawn, the majority of the property was trees: tall, thick pines that hid the house amongst their boughs and gave it some privacy.

"Fuck, there she is." Juniper stopped abruptly. I followed her gaze, expecting to see Victoria. Instead, I spotted a tiny woman with short black hair, dressed in an orange shirt and sweater, giggling as she clung to her friend's arm and they entered the house together.

"Raelynn," I said softly.

"I don't suppose your little buddy, Leon, still has any interest in protecting her, does he?" she said. "Sure would save us a lot of trouble if he was keeping an eye on her."

"Yeah, I don't know if we can count on that tonight." I'd seen Leon days ago, but it was hard to get him to disclose the most basic shit, let alone how he felt about protecting the mortal he'd gotten obsessed with. He had his own problems going on, the kind of problems that had me worried he'd get himself into an even worse situation than he had been in with Kent.

Leon didn't know when to leave things alone. Adversely, he often didn't know when *not* to leave things alone.

"Alright." Juniper took a deep breath, straightening her jacket for the dozenth time. I slid my arm around her shoulders, tucking her up against my side. She stiffened for a moment, before she leaned into it. "Let's do this."

"Knock, knock, Hadleighs." I grinned as we joined the crowd squeezing inside. "There's a wolf at your door."

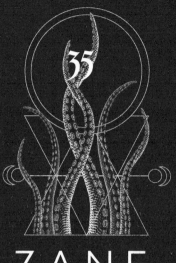

ZANE

THE SCENT OF liquor, sweat, and dozens of artificial fragrances hung heavy in the front room. The crowd was packed around us, their hormones creating a pungent cocktail in the air, telling me who was aroused, who was afraid, who was angry. Music pounded through the walls, heavy bass vibrating from a sound system at the other side of the room. Marijuana and tobacco wafted through the air, and I caught the sharp scent of cocaine. In the corner, two women downed pills with tequila shots. They locked eyes with me from across the room, their gazes heavy, their intentions clear.

"Everyone keeps staring at you," Juniper said, her arms folded as she looked around the milling crowd.

"Do you have a problem with that?" I came around in front of her, leaning my arm against the wall beside her. "If I decided to kill everyone who looked too long at you, I would have murdered half the party by now, and be well on my way to shredding the rest."

She gave me a mischievous smile, the same kind of smile she'd given me before she carved her name into my chest. "Honestly, I like it. It's kind of hot to see how many people can't keep their eyes off you."

I leaned down, brushing my lips against her neck. She sucked in her breath and clutched her hand around my wrist. "I like seeing them stare at *us*. Any one of them would be lucky to have us fuck them. But both of us? Together?"

She was barely restraining her smile as I pulled back to look at her. "We'd absolutely murder an orgy."

I tweaked an eyebrow. "Literally, or figuratively?"

"Depends on the circumstance." She used that hand on my wrist to reverse our positions, pressing her body up against mine, my back against the wall. "Under other circumstances, I'd bring those two women over here and get them on their knees for *me*. Maybe I'd even let them beg for permission to touch you."

"Goddamn. It's going to be really fucking hard to hide a boner right now, Juniper."

She giggled sadistically, groping me through my trousers. "Easy there, demon boy. There's only one reason we're here. We can fuck around later."

"I'll hold you to that. But right, right. Murder bitches, get fucked . . . or something like that."

She gave me a long, exasperated stare. "It's *fuck bitches, get money*, Zane."

"Right, yeah, that's what I said."

Couples were grinding on each other around us, and people had gathered around several tables hosting drinking games out on the large balcony that wrapped around the house. The kitchen countertop was lined with snacks, and the island bar was covered with bottles of liquor in every size and color.

There was no sign of Kent, and I had the feeling we'd have to wait for an opportunity to sneak away and find him. Once the sun had set, and everyone was too drunk to notice, we'd move.

I leaned down to speak over the noise, "Want a drink?"

She nodded her head. "God, yes please. Just don't make it dangerous."

"Oh, I always make them dangerous, love."

In the kitchen, I surveyed the bottles on the countertop before taking my picks from among them. The woman beside me kept staring at me over her drink, and when I glanced over, she swayed drunkenly and gave me a messy grin.

"Damn, Steph, you're looking fine as hell!" A man latched onto her, squeezing her ass as she squealed. I didn't need to see his face to know it was Jeremiah— the smell alone announced his presence. He brought his mouth close to the drunk girl's ear, but he made sure he was loud enough for those around him to hear, "I'm having a little private party in my room, why don't you head up there?"

She smiled and stumbled away as I began to shake the drink I'd concocted. Some humans considered themselves hunters too; humans like Jeremiah. But they preyed on the weak and vulnerable. They weren't hunters, they were trappers: baiting, luring, and *taking* whatever they could. They knew they were unworthy of their prey, but they wanted it regardless.

It was pathetic.

Jeremiah was still leaning there, staring at me as I twirled the shaker in my palm. "Are you a bartender or something? Bet that gets you a lot of pussy, huh? All the bartenders I know get bitches like crazy." He was pouring juice and vodka into a plastic cup. His shoulder kept bumping into mine, and I was really tempted to snap his arm from its socket. He was drunk and loud, all swagger and alcohol-infused confidence. "There's a trick to it, though, you know?"

I glanced over, because he'd held up his palm in such a way that I knew he wanted me to see something.

What I saw was a tiny white pill—right before he dropped it into the shaker and began using a muddler to crush it amongst maraschino cherries. He winked at me, poured the drink into a cup, and left the kitchen.

Motherfucker.

I watched him move into the living room and offer the drink to a tiny woman with bobbed black hair and large glasses. Raelynn Lawson.

I poured my drink, watching as she took the cup, smiled and sipped. Fucking hell, where was Leon? I'd told him to let it go, but damn, the stubborn bastard never listened to me.

Raelynn kept drinking. She wouldn't have a clue what

was happening once that pill hit her system, and something told me Jeremiah wasn't doing this just to convince her to join his "private party." He'd have something even more sinister in mind.

I found Juniper leaning against the far wall, surveying the crowd. I pressed the cup into her hands and said, "We have a bit of a problem."

"I saw." Her eyes were fixated on Rae, who raised her cup to her lips yet again. That girl was sipping down her own death and didn't even realize. "Why would she drink *anything* he handed her? We have to stop her."

"Can't exactly drag her away," I muttered. Jeremiah had moved away from her, but he'd be biding his time, keeping track of where she went. I hated pathetic little fucks like him.

Free will was inherent to existence, it was the one moral code we demons ascribed to. We couldn't claim a soul unless the human was willing. We did nothing with mortals nor each other that wasn't desired by everyone involved. To force one's own will upon another was considered deplorable.

Our target tonight was Kent, but I really wished it was Jeremiah instead.

"We have to get her to come to us then," Juniper said. The girl's eyes flickered toward us, as if she could feel us watching. She looked a little too long to hide her interest, and Juniper smiled. "I got this."

Juniper was a natural. I'd seen her flirt before—in those years when I'd stalked her, keeping my distance, I'd seen how quickly she could turn on her charm to get what she wanted. It had been my own self-inflicted plea-surable torture, to follow her into clubs and watch her dance, or lead a stranger to the bathrooms for a hookup. I'd never been one for jealousy—few demons were. I was possessive, but I liked watching.

The smaller woman was instantly flustered by Juni-per's approach, her cheeks going pink as Juniper leaned close to her ear, smiling, and lightly touched her arm. They both glanced back toward me, and I picked up the remote for the television so I could flip through the music playlists.

They were coming back, Juniper leading Rae by the hand. Rae's eyes moved over me appreciatively, but it was Juniper who'd captured her attention. As the song I'd chosen began to play, Juniper moved Rae between the two of us, her arms around the smaller woman's neck, their bodies close as the three of us danced. My woman could *move*. Her hips swayed, her body teasing close to Rae's as Raelynn moved closer to me.

Juniper whispered in Rae's ear, too softly for anyone else to hear over the music, "You need to stop drinking that, babe."

But not drinking didn't seem to be what was on Rae's mind, because she took another heavy sip. Juniper's eyes darted up to mine. I nodded, and Juniper tugged Rae by the hand, winding her through the crowd as I followed close behind. We found a bathroom around the corner and crowded inside, and I used my body to block the door as Juniper moved a very confused Rae over to the toilet.

"What—what are you—"

"I told you to stop drinking it," Juniper hissed, gripping Raelynn by the back of her neck as the girl stared at her with wide-eyed confusion. Juniper snatched the cup from her hands and set it next to the sink as she said, "Sorry, babe, it's for your own good."

Then she had her fingers down Raelynn's throat, and even I winced as the girl gagged, vomiting into the toilet. She was fighting, weakly, but Juniper was easily able to keep her bent over, gagging her again until nothing came up but a weak heave. Juniper let her go, and Raelynn sunk down against the wall, looking between us with wide, terrified eyes.

"What—what the fuck—is wrong with you?" she gasped, clutching her throat. She'd likely be sore for a few days; Juniper hadn't been gentle. It had also been hot as hell to watch my girl choke another until she gagged, and it made my human disguise slip a little.

Juniper was rinsing the cup out in the sink, filling it with tap water. "You're gonna need to get a hell of a lot smarter if you're gonna live, Raelynn," she said, shaking her head. "Don't you ever, *ever* consume anything Jeremiah Hadleigh gives you."

Rae sipped the water Juniper offered, looking at us like she expected us to attack her again at any moment. We needed to wrap this up. If the Hadleighs saw us hanging around their next victim, they'd be suspicious, and this entire thing could be ruined. Rae was really staring at me now, and recognition spread over her face.

"Zane," she said softly.

"Took you long enough to recognize me," I said, pouting. "Fucking hell, Leon wasn't lying about you being a chore to keep alive. Sucking down roofies like you don't have a care in the world."

"Roofies?" Her voice cracked in alarm. "What—"

"Your drink was drugged, babe." Juniper sighed. "The Hadleighs don't intend for you to leave this party, let me make that perfectly clear. And I've got shit to do so—keep drinking that water, get your head straight—I need you to get it together and leave."

As Rae gulped her water, looking utterly bewildered, I suddenly caught a familiar scent. Leon had finally decided to show up. His girl would have been passed out by now if we hadn't intervened. But Leon was built for killing things; he'd have a hard time keeping a pet rock alive, let alone a woman who seemed determined to throw herself into danger.

He was coming closer, and rapidly. He was searching for her. Best not to keep them separated.

As if something in her sensed him, Rae looked up at me suddenly and said, "Is Leon here?"

"He's around," I said, and nudged Juniper's arm. "Not watching you closely enough, that's for certain." I lowered my voice, leaning down so Juniper could hear, and said, "We need to start moving. Leon is here. He's looking for her."

Her eyes locked on mine, hard and instantly angry. I'd really been hoping I could continue to keep her and Leon separate, but it seemed that was no longer an option: Leon was right outside the door.

Oh, this was going to be *so* fun.

Juniper leaned down and grabbed Rae's arm, pulling her to her feet. "Look, we're gonna call you an Uber and you're gonna go the hell home. Or get the fuck out of town, preferably. I'm not about to have everything ruined because the Hadleighs' next sacrifice is ready to just lay herself at the altar."

Juniper didn't know Leon was close. Perhaps I should have warned her. But she nodded at me, and I opened the door—only to watch pure rage fall over her painted face.

JUNIPER

I KNEW HIM instantly. His face was covered with a black ski mask, but it didn't matter. I didn't forget. I couldn't forget.

Leon. The monster in the woods. The one who'd chased me in the dark. A living part of my nightmares.

Raelynn ran to him, throwing her arms tightly around his neck and drawing close. I didn't know her, but it was like watching a child get too close to a fire: it was instinctual to snatch them away. I wanted to jerk her back, I wanted to yell that he was dangerous. Who could possibly want to be close to a monster like that?

But Zane was a monster too. I'd seen a monster the first night I met him, and the first time I'd fucked him, and when I'd let him cut me. As much as I hated it, Zane's words to me about Leon hadn't been forgotten:

summoned by force—against his will—never had a choice.

"And here I thought you'd forgotten me, doll," Leon said, wrapping his arm around her and drawing her back, protectively, against his side. "It was a cute little show you put on grinding up between these two, but it gave me a feeling you've forgotten who you belong to." He gave Zane a heavy look, and I couldn't be certain if it was anger or begrudging thankfulness. Regardless, it made Zane chuckle and shake his head.

"Maybe if you'd paid a little bit closer attention, it wouldn't have been necessary," I snapped. Zane claimed Leon was "obsessed" with this girl, that he'd defied his master for her—but he'd let her waltz right into the Hadleighs' clutches.

Leon's gaze centered on me. His eyes were the same color as Zane's, but they were different in a way I couldn't put into words. They carried a coldness, a deadly suspicious hatred. "Juniper Kynes . . . so grown up now."

I never thought I'd stand there facing him without a gun in my hands. I'd also never thought I'd look at him and feel anything but hatred and fear. But the monster that had chased me through the dark had a name and a story now. He had pain, he had fear, he had . . . he had whatever it was that made him hold Raelynn like that.

But the memories were intruding, unbidden, forcing themselves to the forefront of my mind. *The forest. The ache in my lungs. My feet stinging with cuts from running barefoot through the dark. Those eyes tracking me, watching me, hunting me . . .*

"I'm not a scared little girl anymore," I said. "I'm a lot better armed than I was at fifteen."

Leon glanced cautiously down the hall, his eyes narrowing slightly. Zane nudged a little closer to me, his touch a small reassurance in my whirlpool of anxiety. When Leon looked back, he was smirking. "So glad you remember me. Hold on to that anger. It keeps you strong."

Rage blanketed my vision. It was half anger, half panic, and I barely knew what I was doing. I whipped out the knife from beneath my jacket and pressed it up against Leon's smartass mouth, fisting his jacket with my free hand. Zane muttered something, but I didn't care what the hell he had to say.

I wanted to use that blade to carve up Leon's face. I wanted to gouge out those awful, bright eyes. Rae was glaring at me as if she was about to start swinging, but I'd gladly take her down too.

But as soon as I'd done it, I knew I was wrong. These two weren't my enemies. Not even Leon, despite all the hate I had for him.

"You're lucky Zane has any affection for you." I tightened my grip on his jacket, the blade pressed hard against his lips. "Because you were first on my list."

My logical mind was telling me to stop. But the scared part of me, the dark part, was pounding my heart, squeezing my lungs, twisting my stomach.

Leon was standing there as if I'd offered to take him out for a drink, cool as a fucking cucumber, a spark in his eyes that was goddamn unnerving. "Easy girl," he drawled. "Don't threaten me with a good time."

He parted his lips and ran his forked tongue along my blade. His blood welled up, dripped over his lips and stained his teeth. He stepped back, smiling widely with Rae still tucked under his arm.

"Enjoy the party," he said. He winked as he turned, leading Rae back into the quiet parts of the house. I watched them go, shaking as the adrenaline left my system.

Zane slipped his arm around my waist. He led me without a word, and I allowed him. There was a glass door he slid open that led out into a garden tucked against the house. Paths of gravel meandered amongst the trimmed hedges, rose bushes, and arches of flowering vines, all planted around a tall, sprawling cherry tree.

There was no one else out there. The sounds of the party were muted, replaced instead with the trickle of a nearby fountain and the wind moving through the pines.

"I hate feeling out of control," I muttered. "I hate it. That feeling takes over and nothing makes sense. It's like everything goes dark and alarms are going off and—"

I went still, my breath sitting cold and heavy in my lungs. There, behind Zane, crouched amongst the hedges, was that awful blood-red, wide-eyed face.

I swallowed hard. The creature's eyes were locked on me, its long fingers tapping on its boney knees as it squatted in the shadows. Its body was red because it was *flayed*—the thing had no skin, just a reddish-pink network of webbed veins.

The panic in me was about to burst. My head was light, my muscles so tense they ached. I couldn't let this happen now. Not here. But I couldn't look away, and the longer I looked, the faster the darkness closed in, like a tunnel shrinking around my eyes.

"The Watcher," I whispered. All I could see were those lidless eyes. All I could feel was cold, sickening dread. "It's here. It's . . . it's . . ."

Suddenly, Zane's arms were around me.

It was warm against his chest. I could smell him with every breath I took. His chin rested on top of my head, tucking me even closer. My heart felt like it was going to beat out of my ribs, and my arms were crossed over my chest as if to protect it. The Watcher was back there, waiting, but without its eyes locked on me, the lightness in my head began to ease.

"It wants your attention," Zane said softly. "Don't give it what it wants."

I didn't dare close my eyes, for fear I'd open them and find myself someplace else, trapped in a nightmare. But as the silence stretched on and Zane kept holding me, I was able to take one long, slow breath.

"I'm broken," I said softly. "I'm fucked up. It's like I'm only getting worse."

His voice rumbled in his chest as he spoke. "I followed you for years, Juniper. I saw all your broken pieces. I saw the sharpness. It was like shattered glass every time I looked at you." His hand moved up, tucked against my neck, and his thumb pushed up my chin. "Have you ever seen shattered glass catch the light? Have you seen it reflect colors that a perfect, pristine pane never would? How it shines as bright as the sun?"

I didn't make a sound, but tears rolled down my face before I could stop them. I was going to ruin my face-paint if I kept this up. I hated crying in front of anyone; I always had. But instead, in that moment, it felt more like a relief.

"I don't think you need to be fixed, Juniper. I think you need to catch your light."

I lowered my face, pressing it back against his chest where he couldn't see me. The self-deprecating thoughts prodded at me, echoes of *Stop crying, you're weak, you're pathetic, stop.* But his arms, still immoveable, held them back like a wall I didn't need to build myself. His words were a callout to the lies that swirled in my head.

He was a demon who had everything he should have wanted from me. He had no reason to say that unless he meant it. It was a kindness that my brain couldn't twist. And if I couldn't twist it, I had to accept it.

I had to believe it.

"I'm . . . I'm sorry." I only got it out in a whisper, but I still managed it.

"For what?"

"He's your friend," I said. "I get it. I know . . ." I sighed heavily. I hated words. I hated trying to put the confusing things I felt into plain language. I hated trying to be understood, hated it so much I'd given up on it for years.

Somehow Zane had managed to change that. He made me want to try, even when it was hard.

Zane smiled gently. "Don't be sorry. He wasn't scared of you, and I wasn't worried for him. I was far more worried that little Raelynn was going to try to fight you, and that would've been a real mess. Like a chihuahua fighting a Doberman."

I laughed. "Oh fuck, that would've sucked. I mean, she wouldn't have won."

"Not a chance. But you know Leon wouldn't have let you beat on his toy."

I shook my head. "No. Probably not. I'd fight him too, though."

I wasn't sure how many minutes passed. I stopped counting them, stilling the eternally ticking clocks in my head. It wasn't about Leon, not really. It wasn't even about the Watcher, who'd retreated out of sight. It was the lack of control. It was the fear of letting go of fear itself. Fear had always kept me going, hatred kept me going. Letting that go, even a little bit, was like dismantling my own shelter.

But my shelter was crashing around me, it was a hazard as much as it was a defense. Maybe it was okay to dismantle it if there was another shelter there, something better, something safer. Something with a little light I could catch.

Strange that Hell's light could shine so bright.

EVEN WITH A light by my side, I waited in darkness, for something darker still. The party raged on into the night. We didn't return to the house, but instead lingered in the garden, and when too many people began to come out, we wandered back into the trees. We kept an eye on the house from a distance, watching through the massive glass windows.

"Maybe he's not here," Zane said, but I shook my head. Watching the party from outside was like watching a bizarre clockwork, all the characters going through their motions, deep beats replacing the clock's chime. Drink, dance, laugh. Perfect smiles and posturing gradually growing sloppy.

"If they intended to take Rae tonight, Kent will be here," I said. "He's here somewhere."

But as the time went on, I began to have my doubts.

It was after midnight, and the night had grown cold. Some of the crowds within the house had dispersed, but those that remained were trashed as hell. I could hear someone vomiting near the front of the house, and I adjusted my gun to rest a little more comfortably on my knee. I glanced up at Zane, but he wasn't watching the house anymore.

He was staring behind us, into the trees.

"What is it?" I followed his gaze, trying to make out anything in the dark.

"Probably nothing," he said, but his eyes were narrowed. "I thought I smelled . . ." He shook his head. "Doesn't matter. There's nothing back there."

I was about to insist he tell me what the hell he thought he'd seen, but sudden movement back toward the house caught my attention. I raised my gun, watching as two figures climbed over the railing on the deck. A small one was lowered down first, before the other leaped down, grabbed her hand, and ran with her into the trees.

"Leon," Zane said, watching from behind me.

"And Rae," I whispered. "What are they running from?"

Minutes passed as I watched the deck. Then the door opened again, and a familiar figure walked out across the deck. They came right up to the railing, staring out into the dark.

It was Kent Hadleigh, dressed in a gray suit. He puffed slowly on his cigar as his eyes scanned the trees, his other hand at his side, gripping a pistol. My vision shrank, everything else fading into the background. He was so goddamn close. I could make the shot from here.

Zane tapped my arm, right as I was about to raise the gun. "Wait. Not yet."

Kent strode down the stairway from the deck, the smoke from his cigar trailing behind him. I caught a whiff of it, rich tobacco and vanilla as he passed close by our hiding place in the trees. He stopped right at the tree line and clicked his tongue as if in disappointment.

Every inch of me was tense, my nerves tingling. The excitement coursing through me was almost too much to contain, a high that just kept rising. This was it. He was here, just like Everly had said he'd be. He was only feet away.

Tonight, Kent Hadleigh was going to die.

Zane glanced over at me, sharp teeth bright in his painted face. "Shall we?"

I nodded. "Get his attention. I'll take him down."

Zane moved quickly, disappearing from beside me. I stayed low, waiting until Kent's attention was turned away. I could see his face from where I crouched, even though it was cast in shadow. He looked older, tired. His hair was entirely gray, rather than speckled with it as it had been . . . back then. I understood why people trusted him—I understood why *I* had. His voice could sound kind, he could be generous. He could look at his children with affection, he could say all the right words.

It was all a lie.

He was a man who would do anything to get what he wanted. He was a man who saw cruelty and suffering as paths to glory. He looked at his own children and saw sacrifices to be made.

I looked at him and saw dead flesh.

He smirked and began to whistle as he turned away from the trees. But he didn't take more than a few steps before he noticed Zane. Kent stopped, and from my current angle, I could see a flicker of confusion across his face before cold, calculated calm settled again. He raised his cigar to his lips and took a slow puff, but I didn't miss the slight shake in his hand.

"Evening, Mr. Hadleigh," Zane said, his voice lowered to that deep baritone that never failed to make my insides shudder. "Lovely night, isn't it?"

Kent took the cigar from his mouth, tapping the ash into the grass. "Who are you?" His voice betrayed no fear. God, I wanted him to shake. I wanted him to feel his stomach drop. I wanted him to feel what I'd felt.

He would. Soon enough, he would.

"A friend of a friend," Zane said, still smiling. He wasn't trying to hide what he was: he was all golden eyes and sharp teeth, made even more unnerving with his painted face. "Why don't we take a little walk, Mr. Hadleigh? There's someone who's eager to see you again."

Kent's eyes narrowed, and his head jerked back toward the trees. He couldn't see me where I was hidden in the shadows, but his eyes moved over me for a moment and sent a chill up my back. I had to be patient. He was too close to the house.

"You can't touch me, demon," he said. "And I have no business with you."

"I don't need to touch you," Zane said. "Because you're going to turn around and start walking on your own accord back into those trees."

"And if I don't?" Kent's voice was sharp. I could have taken it as careless irritation if I hadn't spotted his hand shake again.

Zane tilted his head. "Do you really want to find out?"

I cocked the gun, and Kent's whole body twitched. He knew that sound, there was no mistaking it.

"What a clever little charm you're wearing around your neck, Mr. Hadleigh," Zane said. "Tell me, do your children have them too? Does your wife? How quickly can you get back in the house?" He took a step closer, and Kent stepped back.

"You're some friend of Leon's, aren't you?" he said and took another unsteady step backward, toward the trees. "Have you come here to take revenge for that snake?"

Zane's grin widened. "Oh, that's part of it. You've made a lot of enemies, Kent." He took another step forward, and Kent took another step back. He was almost under the trees now. "You've caused irreparable pain. Now, believe me, I do love to see chaos and destruction." Another step. Kent was under the trees. I began to creep closer. "I love to cause a fair bit of it myself. But there's a big difference between you and I, Kent."

"You're a demon," Kent snapped. "Your entire existence is meant to be bent to the will of your master—"

"There's the difference, Hadleigh." Zane's face had grown gaunt, and it wasn't just the makeup in the dim light. He looked truly haunting. "You harm those who are weak and vulnerable. You go after children. You prey on those who trust you. You make your own offspring into vile little monsters. You steal freedom. You *force* others to bend to your will under threats of pain and violence."

I was just behind Kent now. I raised the gun. He was too fixated on Zane to notice.

"You're a coward, Kent Hadleigh," Zane growled. "And tonight, you're going to die a coward's death."

I brought the gun down, slamming the butt against the back of his head. Kent grunted, his knees buckled, and he collapsed onto the grass. I hurriedly pushed him over, fumbled at his neck, and found a metal amulet on a chain. It was carved in the shape of a sword crossed with a wand, the surface mottled like dirty silver.

"Oh, that's a vile thing," Zane murmured, as I plucked it from Kent's neck.

I held up the amulet curiously. It didn't look particularly special, just old. But as I grasped it in my fingers, I found the surface to be stunningly cold. "Would this really protect him from you?"

"It's far more powerful than it looks," Zane said, grimacing in disgust. "The closer a demon is to it, the more it saps their strength."

"I'll keep it away from you then." Quickly, I dug a little hole in the dirt, dropped the amulet inside, and covered it. I had to remember to come back for it later, but I wasn't going to have that thing near Zane.

The demon kicked Kent curiously, frowning. "You didn't hit him hard enough. He isn't dead."

"That's the point." I stood up, high on the adrenaline coursing through my veins. I was gripped by a hunger I couldn't explain, a desire like nothing else. "Carry him. I saw a garden shed back in the trees. We'll take him there."

JUNIPER

KENT GROANED AS he began to stir. I'd hit his head hard enough to break the skin, so his gray hair was streaked with red. There wasn't much in the old shed: a bare bulb hung from the ceiling as our only light. A few rusty metal gardening tools were hung on the walls, and there was an old shelf covered with pots and bags of fertilizer. It was distant from the house, and with the loud music from the party, no one could hear if someone yelled in here.

No one would hear if someone screamed.

Kent shifted, and his shoulders stiffened as he realized his hands were bound. He blinked rapidly as his eyes opened, and I wondered what he took in first. Did he recognize the stone floor, did he recognize the walls enough to know where he was? Or was this a place he'd never even bothered to look inside, a place too below him? What did he think when he saw my boots standing in front of him? What did he feel, as he slowly raised his head and met my eyes—a skeletal woman in a dark suit—looking down at him?

He stared for a long moment, the wrinkles around his eyes and his forehead deepening. "Who are you?"

Zane was pacing behind me, like a rabid dog, eager to bite. The bloodlust was infectious between us. The more my excitement grew, the more he paced, clenching and unclenching his fingers.

"You know who I am, Kent." I thought back. I remembered, but I did it with intention, with my own free will. I softened my voice and said, "Please. Don't. The God isn't real. It's just an old story."

Recognition struck his face. "Juniper Kynes. Dear God . . ."

"It's been a long time." I crouched down, arms resting on my thighs as I looked at him face to face. Up close, his age was even more evident. He hid it well, but he was weakening. The monster in my nightmares—the face I saw looking down at me with sadistic joy—was now an old man tied up at my feet.

It was the greatest euphoria I could ever feel.

"Did you miss me?" I said. "You looked for me. You tried *so hard* to take me." I leaned closer as his eyes widened in trepidation. "But I was your greatest failure, Kent."

I whipped out my hand, my knife clenched in it. The blade caught him across the face, and at first, he didn't seem to realize what had happened. He blinked rapidly, looking at me in confusion, and then the gash across his cheek, across his lips, began to bleed.

"God," he whispered, his voice shuddering. "Dear merciful God . . ."

"What God are you calling on, Kent?" I hissed. "Certainly not the Deep One. You think that monster in the mines is merciful? You think It cares? I've heard It, Kent. I've heard It for fucking *years*, Its voice in my head. I've seen It in my nightmares. Your God craves pain and suffering. Your God would *revel* in this. But you already know that. You know what It wants. That's why you did this to me." I stripped off my jacket, and tugged open my shirt so hard that the buttons popped off. In the dim light, the deep, ragged scars on my chest looked even worse. The shadows settled in them, and not even the tattoos, not even Zane's mark, could hide them. "Do you remember, Kent? I screamed. I begged you. I was a *child*."

"I had to," he whimpered, and Zane snarled viciously behind me. "I had to, Juniper. You don't understand. You don't know what it's like to serve the Deep One, we—we do only—we do only as we are *ordained*—"

I slashed again, and this time, he felt the pain and screamed. His other cheek opened, welling blood down his face. He gasped, shuddering, trying to spit away the blood spilling over his lips.

"You should be honored," I said. "You're going to be a martyr. You're going to die for your God."

He began to shake his head, frantically, his breath puffing. "No . . . no, no, no, Juniper, you don't under-stand. *You don't understand.* I'm doing only what I must—only—only what we've been asked to do. Y-your suffering . . . it . . . it should have been beautiful—"

I widened my eyes. "*Oh*, I see. Suffering is beautiful." I nodded slowly and stepped back. "Zane, is suffering beautiful?"

I glanced back at him. His eyes were fixated on Kent, golden irises ringed with black. His eyes seemed to get darker with every passing day. "Oh yes," he said. "Suffering is beautiful; it's exquisite. Suffering is luxurious pain." His eyes darted to me. The tiny garden shed felt too small to contain his energy, as if he might burst, ripping everything apart. "Shall I demonstrate?"

"Please do."

My demon moved, and it was beautiful indeed. The screaming, the cracking bones, the tearing flesh. It wasn't all that different from butchering a deer, really. Even in the moment, with the rush of it all, it scared me just how numb I felt to what I saw. It didn't feel like I was watching a human being in pain.

This was just one of the monsters from my nightmares, screaming in defeat.

The scent of iron hung heavy in the air. Blood splattered across the stone wall, and the screams reached such a pitch they didn't even sound human anymore. It was an animal's scream, wretched in its primality, pathetically desperate, perfectly agonized.

Beautiful.

"Stop."

Zane stopped, immediately, Kent's leg gripped in his hands. The man was weeping, his shoulder torn from its

socket, his other leg snapped at the ankle, the bone protruding through the skin. "Oh, come *on*," Zane said, glancing
back at me with starving eyes. "Just let me snap the femur."

I sighed. "How can I say no to that face? Go on."

Kent tried to scream—the sound of his own bone
snapping cut him off. He seemed to choke, the sounds
that emerged from his throat little more than garbled
cries before he vomited all over himself.

"Ugh, come on, Kent," I said, as Zane rose up, licking
the flecks of blood from his lips. "At least try to maintain
some dignity."

"Please," the man's voice trembled, whimpering.
"Please, please, just—just kill me . . . just kill me—"

"Suffering is beautiful, Kent!" I reached down, grabbing
his jaw so he was forced to turn his reddened, bloody, tear-
and vomit-stained face up to mine. I laughed. "Don't you
see, Kent? Don't you understand? *Suffer for your God!*"

I'd waited so long for this. I'd waited so goddamn
long. Every inch of me was tingling; I felt giddy. Every
long night I'd laid awake, shaking in the cold, not daring
to let my guard down for even a moment because I knew
the monsters would close in—they'd led me to this. Every
day when I'd walked until my feet bled, with no food,
with nowhere to go—they had led me to this. Every intrusive memory, every time I'd curled up shaking, every
time I'd looked in the mirror and wept at the ugliness
he'd carved into me—it had led me to this.

I slammed my foot down on Kent's injured leg, elicit-
ing a cry that made Zane laugh. Kent Hadleigh had taken
a child and made her a monster. And I had no doubt

now: I *was* a monster, as much as Zane was, as much as Leon was. I was all jagged edges and broken pieces, scraped together into something sharp and ugly.

Zane took my wrist and kissed it. He kissed my palm, bloodying his lips, and then ran his tongue across my skin, his barbells caressing me.

"It's so good to see you smile," he said, looking up at me as he licked his lips. "It's goddamn sexy."

I pulled myself closer to him. All my senses were heightened, every nerve on fire. I was hungry—hungry for him, for how hot and hard his body felt as I ran my hands over his chest and around his neck. I traced my fingers over his lips, over the silver rings of his piercings, and he caught my finger in his mouth and sucked, his tongue moving around me so deliciously that I moaned.

"You're hard," I said, grinning up at him as he popped my finger from his mouth. Kent, moaning weakly on the floor, just had to watch. He had to watch me smile, watch me feel good, watch me *live*.

I hoped it killed him in a way physical death never could.

Zane looked truly monstrous in the dim light, with his painted face spattered with blood and his teeth stained with it. "How could I not be hard watching you like this, love? You look so fucking good with blood on you."

He ran his claws over my cheek, down to my throat, which he gripped before he kissed me. The taste of blood mingled between us, our tongues moving together. I wanted him, right there in front of Kent. I wanted the vile old man to die knowing he'd failed, utterly and in every way. He'd wanted me to suffer for his God, he'd wanted to take my life away.

But he didn't get my life, and he wouldn't get my suffering for even another moment.

Before he died, he'd only see me in joy. He'd only see me in pleasure. I'd given his God enough of my pain.

I turned back to his bleeding and broken form on the floor. Zane held me from behind, his lips on my neck, his body moving eagerly against mine. I held up my knife, so it caught the dim yellow light.

"Your God likes blood, doesn't It, Kent?" I said, as the man sniveled and Zane ground his cock against my ass, too eager to control himself. "If you truly want to be a good and loyal servant, I think you'd bleed for your God."

I didn't know if Kent even understood what I said. He was weeping and sniffling, snot and blood running down his face, shaking his head. "No . . . no . . . this isn't—this isn't how it's meant to be. You wretched . . . wretched bitch!" Spittle flew from his lips as he looked up at me, adrenaline forcing one final fight out of him. "You can't stop this! You . . . you'll never . . . *never* stop this!" He was breathing hard, panting as he squirmed uselessly. "The God will have you! You can't stop it—"

"I want to fuck you over his corpse," Zane groaned against my neck, claws digging into my hips as Kent carried on. "He's too loud. Bleed him like a fucking pig."

I leaned down. Kent babbled on, cursing me, his voice breaking and weakening. He looked at me with hatred, with disdain—with terror. Finally, after so long, he looked at me and was afraid. It was the expression I'd always dreamed of seeing on his face. I let the sight brand itself into my mind, covering the memory of his smile as he cut me so many years ago.

I leaned down closer, closer, until I could whisper in his ear. "All is as it should be."

I slit his throat. I wrenched the knife deep, slicing through his skin, blood spurting out over my hand, staining my white shirt and streaking down my chest. Kent gurgled, his body jerking, his strength sapping away. He kept staring up at me, like he couldn't look away, his curses dying on his tongue.

Zane gripped me, wrenching open the button on my trousers. He tugged them down as I stood over Kent, watching him with cold curiosity. I wasn't sure where my mind went in those moments. It was surreal. It was beyond joy; it couldn't be described as happiness. I wasn't sad. I didn't regret what I'd done.

It was satisfaction: pure, unadulterated satisfaction.

It was revenge. Cold, callous, unfeeling *revenge*.

And God, it felt so good.

Zane's fingers stroked over my clit as the life in Kent's eyes dimmed. "You failed, Kent," I whispered. "You failed, and your children will fail, and your followers will fail." Zane's cock stroked between my cheeks, his movements rough and eager, and I grinned. "You should have fucking made sure I died, Kent."

Zane entered me in one long, hard stroke, and I moaned at the stretch. I was already wet as hell and ready for him, and I arched my hips back, taking him deep. Kent's eyes had gone dull. The pulse of blood from his neck was slowing. Zane pressed against my back, biting my neck, then kissing the tender marks he left behind, fucking into me with primal need. I was already so on edge that every stroke had me shuddering, my breath coming in gasps.

He gripped my jaw, kissed my neck, and whispered, "I love to see my little wolf with blood on her teeth."

I leaned my head against the stone wall, gasping as he quickened his pace. Kent lay dead beneath me, his blood going cold, but my heat was only increasing. This was what I'd waited for. This was the reason I'd lived. This was why I breathed.

To destroy those who dared to fuck with me. To reclaim my life over their cold, dead bodies.

My muscles tightened, and I gasped as Zane dragged his claws down my back, leaving stinging scratches across my skin. He bit down on my shoulder, jerking my hips back against his cock. My eyes fluttered closed, my cunt throbbing on his cock as I got closer . . . closer . . .

"Fuck, you feel so good," Zane murmured against my ear, his body warm on mine, my moans heightening as he continued to rub my clit and fuck into me with hard, rough strokes. "My beautiful killer. Sick little fuck."

His words pushed me over the edge. I cried out, not caring how loud I was. If no one had heard Kent scream, then they wouldn't hear me moan. I came, and Zane followed soon after, his cock throbbing inside me and filling me with his cum. It dripped down my legs, into the pool of Kent's blood as I murmured, "Fuck your God, Kent. It can't kill me."

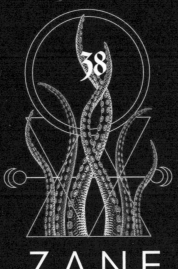

ZANE

MY LITTLE WOLF had broken her chains, and she was running free.

She jogged ahead of me under the cover of the trees. We were headed back toward the isolated side road where we'd parked her Jeep. The night air was crisply cool, the clear night sky peppered with stars and a waning moon. She'd glance back at me every few steps, a smile on her painted face, blood spattered across her jacket. Her button-up shirt hung open, and the sight of her tattoos and scars made me want to snatch her up and run my tongue over that soft, beautiful skin.

She was exquisite, she was built for Hell in every way. Most humans I'd taken over the years needed to adjust to Hell's oddities—it had been a strange and confusing transition for them. But Juniper? She would thrive. I knew she would. When her mortal life was over and her soul made the crossing, I couldn't wait to see her face when she beheld those first wondrous sights.

I wanted to be there every step of the way. I wanted to introduce her to a new life, at the end of this one.

I wanted to show her now. I wanted to give her a taste of what waited.

"How does it feel, little wolf?" I said as I spotted her Jeep ahead. She was breathless, her eyes wide in the dark. She smelt of blood, and sweat, and that sweet, wild aroma that was so uniquely hers.

"Satisfying," she said, but then she shook her head with an uncertain smile. "No, more than that. I don't think there's a single word for it. Vindicating. Amazing. Confusing." We stood beside the Jeep, and she turned to me. Her smile was hopeful, but it was frightened too. Like she feared this victory would be snatched away. "I've waited so many years for that. So many years to kill a man, Zane." She looked down at her hands, bloodstained and shaking with adrenaline. "And I did it. We did it."

"You did it, love. And it was sexy as hell to see you." I reached for her face, but she playfully dodged back, her smile turned mischievous.

"Oh? You think you can outrun me?"

I let her get a few steps before I caught her from behind, picking her up and throwing her over my shoulder so she dangled over my back. She struggled, beating at my back, and she shrieked as I turned my head and bit her ass in retaliation.

She laughed as I set her down, this time keeping an

arm looped around her back so she couldn't run away again when I caressed my claws down her face.

"I'm never using *bite my ass* as an insult again," she said.

I chuckled. "It was always a welcome invitation." I paused as I admired her in the dark. We needed to get some distance between us and this party, but I didn't want to go home. No, Juniper deserved more than that. This was her night, her moment. I wanted to take her somewhere she could celebrate, somewhere she could feel comfortable.

I wanted to give her a night where she didn't constantly feel like she had to look over her shoulder. A night to feel free.

"I want to take you somewhere," I said. She raised an eyebrow in an unspoken question. "Do you trust me?"

She blinked rapidly. Questions like that were unpleasant for her; any question that forced her to examine her feelings was. But I needed to know before I committed to doing this. I needed to know she felt secure with me. If she didn't, well . . . there were much bigger wolves than her where we were going.

Wolves with far sharper bites.

Finally, she raised her eyes to mine again. "Yes. I trust you."

Her declaration made me feel far more sentimental than I'd expected. I'd frankly never cared if I was trusted or not—it simply wasn't something that occurred to me as a necessity. I'd only ever needed humans to trust me enough to make a deal with me, and even then, they rarely *actually* trusted me. Why would they?

It felt like an honor to hear her say that. It felt like I'd earned something, like I'd been given a gift. I pulled her closer, tucked her hair behind her ear, and said, "I liked watching you tonight. You were ravenous. Merciless. You're powerful, Juniper. You're a rare soul."

"Oh, come on." She tried to look away, but I caught her face. I couldn't see it beneath her paint, but her skin was hot as she blushed. It made me grin. "Don't get all corny on me."

"Sorry, I can't help getting a little poetic about the most beautiful murder I've seen in years. My woman is an artist."

"*Your* woman?" She smacked at me, but she was smiling again.

"Yes, *my* woman." I held her tight as she playfully squirmed, snapping my teeth near her ear. "All mine. Every beautiful, murderous, perfect inch of you." I smiled at her, the very idea of where I was about to take her making my erratic heart pound just a little faster with excitement. "I want to take you somewhere Hellish."

She shook her head, smiling but confused. "Isn't Abelaum hellish enough?"

"No, *true* Hellishness," I said. "The Hell I know, the Hell you're bound for; not the Hell humans have concocted in their storybooks. Hellish in freedom and depravity."

"Okay, enough being vague!" She leaned up against the Jeep, arms folded, eyes narrowed at me. "What is this *Hellish* place? And do they have liquor?"

"Only the best of it."

"Is a bloody suit appropriate for their dress code?"

"You'll be the envy of everyone there."

"Let's go then!" She reached for the door, but I caught her wrist. As excited as I was, I needed her to understand.

"There will be demons there. Many of them."

She paused, her face growing serious. "What . . . what kind of place is this exactly?"

"Demons on Earth need a way to blow off steam," I said. "We need places where we can be ourselves, let loose without worrying about being seen. We need places to socialize, places where we can meet playmates we don't have to worry about accidentally killing."

"And where is this place?"

"The locations never stay the same for long. It wouldn't be a good idea to linger and draw too much attention. But an old acquaintance contacted me a few days ago and told me there was one nearby."

"One . . . what?"

"We call them Clans," I said. "Clandestine places. Think of a nightclub, but with no rules, no restrictions, watched over by a single host who ensures the liquor keeps flowing and everyone keeps fucking."

Her eyes widened, her lips parting slightly. She was intrigued. "Is it . . . I mean . . . is it safe for me?"

"Of course. Demons know better than to fuck with another's property." I gave her a wink, before her pride could flare up too much. "And you won't be the only mortal in attendance. You can relax there. You won't have to hide anything." Her eyes still flickered to the side.

She would be thinking through everything that could go wrong, assessing every potential threat. But that was exactly what I wanted to free her from. I didn't want her to feel threatened.

I wanted her to feel free.

"You can say no," I said. "It's up to you. But I'm only offering because I think you'd enjoy yourself. I think it would be something different for you, somewhere you don't have to worry about hiding. You could speak openly there. You'd be surrounded by beings that understand the strange side of life."

She gulped, chewing the inside of her cheek. This was for her, and if she said no, we'd find some other way to celebrate. But I wanted her to have this. I wanted her to have a place to let down her walls for more than just me.

She took a deep breath, lifted her chin, and said finally, "Okay. Let's go."

I DROVE, AND she sat beside me in the passenger seat with her feet up on the dash, tapping her legs to the beat of the music as "Friend of the Devil" by Adam Jensen played through the speakers. An old friend had sent me the Clan's coordinates a few days prior, and I didn't need a map to find my way. Most demons had an instinctually good sense of direction, but I'd traveled around Earth enough that mine was better than most.

I drove southeast, until we were deep in the forest. I kept my senses alert, sniffing the air through the open window for any signs of dangerous creatures.

But the only scent I caught was that of dozens and dozens of demons. I pulled off the road, grateful now that we were driving her Jeep. My car was fast, but it wasn't built for roads like these. I wound down the over-grown road until we reached a chain-link fence, barbed wire coiled along the top, with a large *No Trespassing—Government Property* sign secured to the locked gate.

I turned off the engine and hopped out. "We'll walk from here. Can you make it over, or should I toss you?"

She looked up at the fence, hands on her hips, before she pulled off her jacket and tossed it back into the Jeep. "It's not even an electric fence. I'll be fine."

I jumped over the fence easily, landing crouched on the other side. By the time I'd turned around, she'd al-ready climbed halfway up.

"Not bad," I said, as she carefully pulled herself over the top, gripping the wire between its barbs and turning herself so she could leap to the ground. "Not bad at all, little wolf. Although I still think it would have been fun to throw you."

"Of course you do," she snickered, shaking her head. We walked together back into the trees, the demonic scent growing stronger as we went. The cold air smelled of wood-smoke, sweet demonic blood, marijuana, and alcohol.

It smelled like home.

Juniper stopped abruptly, eyes wide, staring upward. I smiled at her awe over the massive structure ahead, and said, "Welcome to Hell on Earth, love."

JUNIPER

THE HUGE STRUCTURE before us, nestled amongst the trees, looked like an old gas power plant. The exterior was rusted metal and concrete, giving the structure a red-tinged color. Massive steam stacks lined one side of the building, and the forest had begun to overtake them, their sides draped in vines and moss. Lights flashed from the windows, and heavy bass rumbled through the metal.

"I'm glad you wanted to come," Zane said, and slipped his arm around my shoulders. My stomach was light with anticipation as we walked closer, my hands twitching. I'd left my guns in the car, but I still had my knife. I hoped leaving them hadn't been a mistake.

I trusted Zane, but I didn't trust other demons. I just had to reassure myself that if anyone tried to harm me, Zane wouldn't stand for it. I had no doubt he'd go absolutely ballistic on anyone or anything that got invasive with me.

It was the first time I was sincerely entrusting him with my well-being. I was walking into a place where every single other being there could crush me like a bug. I was walking into a party full of predators, and *I* was their favorite prey. So I took a deep breath to steady my nerves, and shoved my shaking hands in my trouser pockets as Zane pulled open a thick metal door.

The moment the door was open, the sounds and smells of the party within were unleashed.

The interior of the power plant was massive, reaching up several stories. The upper floors were made of grated walkways, and abandoned machinery was scattered around—massive generators and turbines.

Everywhere, crowded onto every available inch of floor, were demons.

Their bodies twisted with the music, dancing, grinding up against each other. Golden eyes shone in the dark, sharp teeth caught the blacklights' glow. Most of them were at least partly, if not fully, undressed. There was bare skin everywhere I looked, most of it adorned with piercings, tattoos, and scars.

Couples, throuples, and more fucked against the machinery, on the leather chairs and couches, on the floor. Dancers swung from the chains that dangled above, some of them restrained, contorting themselves into positions that should have been impossible. The air smelled of sex, musky and sharp. It smelled of liquor, tobacco, and weed.

It simultaneously reminded me of the dirtiest underground clubs I'd ever set foot in, and the classiest, most exclusive ones.

Zane and I waded into the sea of bodies, and he kept me tucked close to his side. I expected it to be a struggle to make our way in, but without even glancing at us, the crowd parted as if on instinct. The music blasted from every angle, massive speakers tucked away amongst the rusted old machinery, playing some dark, heavy beat. As we went deeper, I noticed more and more eyes turning our way. Their gazes landed first on me, then slid to Zane and quickly looked away.

"They're scared of you," I said. He chuckled.

"They respect me," he said. "Although I suppose there isn't much difference."

Phantom touches caressed lightly over my back, over my head. They were quick and cautious—almost curious. It was impossible to tell who was doing it, but I kept glimpsing hungry smiles through the crowd.

Zane must have felt me tense. "Don't worry. They're just curious."

"They're getting a little too touchy," I said, gritting my teeth as a particularly adventurous phantom touch stroked over my lower back. "Whoever the fuck just did that is gonna get their face rearranged."

"Oh *good*, you've got a vicious one, Z!"

There was laughter from above us, and I looked up. A demon was seated between the blades of a huge turbine, her feet dangling down. Her brown hair was cut short, her ears pierced with so many silver rings it was impossible to count them all. She smiled widely, and that particularly eager phantom touch returned, trailing up my spine.

"Scared to get too close?" I yelled up at her, and the touch turned into a very distinct sensation of claws on the back of my neck.

Zane was shaking his head. "Don't tease her too much, Hana. She'll throw something at you."

The demon leaped down, landing just inches away from me. "I'd be more than happy to play with her sharp toys if she has any she wants to point my way."

I didn't step back. She was my height, her claws painted so they glowed green in the black lights. She was wearing a leather jacket with nothing beneath, and there were dermal piercings just below her collarbone, the jewels appearing deep violet in the light. She wore tight, tiny jean shorts and laced up boots.

I looked too long. "Like what you see?" she said. Right as I opened my mouth to retort, a woman came bouncing up through the crowd, her long blonde hair disheveled and her lipstick smeared, a big smile on her face and a drink in each hand.

"Hana, someone just invited us to— Oh!" She looked between Zane and I, and Hana wisely took the drinks out of her hands before she bounced excitedly and said, "Oh, hi! Nice to meet y'all! I'm Sadie!"

She was human. She had big blue eyes and an easy smile, and she squeezed me into a hug before I could say a word. She was so damn peppy I could barely hold back a laugh as she took her drink back from Hana and started slurping it down.

Zane was laughing. "Cute, Hana. Real cute." Hana rolled her eyes, pulling Sadie a little closer.

"Yeah, a sweet little dumbass is what she is." She shook her head as Sadie began to dance, still sipping her drink. A little more seriously, she looked at me and said, "Sorry about that, didn't mean to freak you out. I'm Sathanas, but that's a mouthful, so call me Hana."

"Juniper," I said. "Sorry I threatened to destroy your face."

She shrugged. "Not the first time, hopefully won't be the last. Good to see you here, Z. Been a while."

"Been busy," Zane said.

"I see that." Hana scraped her claw over a bloodstain on my shirt. "Nice costumes. Really authentic."

"Very." I smiled.

"We'll be back," Zane said, squeezing my upper arm. "We still gotta check in with Azzi."

Hana rolled her eyes. "Have fun. We'll be upstairs on the couches. Come join us." She gave me a wink as she and Sadie turned away, disappearing into the crowd.

"Friend of yours?" I said. Zane tapped a finger near the piercing through his eyebrow.

"That's hers," he said. "It's been a long time. She got me into hunting souls."

"Damn, you really like assholes, don't you?" I said. Seeing her, and having met Leon, and taking an honest look at myself, I was beginning to see a pattern. Zane laughed out loud.

"Figuratively and literally, love."

We made our way through the crowd, toward the other side of the factory floor where a massive platform had been erected out of machinery and bent steel beams.

Even over the music, I could hear moans of pleasure and sharp cries of pain.

"This is what Hell's like?" A particularly tall demon brushed past me, their golden eyes flickering down to me, their white hair long enough to brush their thighs. "Were they carrying a whip made of barbed wire?"

"You'll see every variety of pleasure and pain here," Zane said. "Whether your desires are sweet or wicked, dangerous, unusual, disgusting—you can satisfy them here, just as you could in Hell. But listen up." His voice took on a serious note. "Azriel is this Clan's host. He watches over everything here; he makes sure it all goes smoothly. No one gets to stay without his approval, so watch yourself around him."

We'd reached the foot of the metal platform. Speakers were clustered around the base, the music thumping hard through my body as we stood in front of them. Above us, a being sat in a swinging chair constructed of thick chains, his long dreads hanging over his shoulders as he peered down at us. His deep brown skin was adorned with ink, the lines of his absurdly defined muscles clear beneath the tight, thin fabric of the black shirt he wore.

"Lucifer Almighty, if it isn't Zane!" He smiled down at us, the chains around him jingling at his movement. "And Zane has brought a little mortal soul, eh?" One moment he was seated in the chains—the next, he was off the platform, beside us, walking between us as he looked us up and down. "Been a long time, Z. Where's Leon? Still bound up with that awful magician?"

"Nah, he's got other problems to deal with," Zane

said. "Juniper and I were looking for some place to have a good time, if you'll welcome us."

"You know I'd always welcome you," he said, but his eyes were on me. "Ooh, you're an interesting one, aren't you? That soul of yours has bled." His gaze moved over my shirt, his smile widening at the bloodstains. But then his eyes lingered on my chest, and goose bumps prickled across my skin as he stared at my scars. "Oh yes. You've bled. Body and soul. You smell a little nervous, human. Are you scared?"

I was rigid, my back so tense it hurt. But Zane gave me a little nudge, and I forced myself to exhale. "Sorry. I'm . . . I'm nervous, yeah. It's weird to not be the scariest person in the room." I paused. "It's weird to be one of the only . . . people . . . in the room."

He nodded in understanding, circling me, his eyes stroking over every inch of me. "We predators enjoy the hunt, but we'd never hunt what belongs to another. Zane has claimed you, and there isn't a single being here who won't respect that. We're here for one thing, and one thing only." He spread his arms. "To have the most fucking depraved night we possibly can." He leaped away, back atop his platform, and reclaimed his seat amongst his chains. Another demon crawled eagerly to his feet, pressing their head up against his leg as if begging for attention. Azriel waved his hand at us, using the other to grip the demon at his feet by their hair. "Enjoy yourselves. If anyone bothers you, mortal, come to me. I'll take care of it."

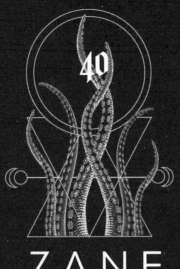

ZANE

NOTHING ON EARTH compared to demonic liquor, and it was being served here by the gallon. It was pungently sharp on the breath of every demon we passed, and I was eager for a drink. Human liquor did nothing for me—but Hell's alcohol certainly would.

"So, what do you think?" I spoke right in Juniper's ear as we wound through the crowd, making our way toward the large round bar that had been set up in the middle of the factory floor. A massive, shining pyramid of glass bottles was the bar's centerpiece, towering precariously above us. The bartenders, some of them blindfolded, handled multiple bottles at once, tossing them between each other as they poured libations into silver shakers.

Before I'd begun hunting souls, I'd wanted only to spend my time in places like this, concocting drinks in

Clans around the world. It was exactly the kind of environment I liked: crowded and chaotic, wicked and filthy. The challenge of serving so many demons, while maintaining perfect form and pulling off the absurd drinks these bartenders managed, was one I'd been eager to perfect.

"It's wild," Juniper said. "It feels . . . it feels *good* here. There's so much happening!" She laughed, shaking her head as if she couldn't really believe what she was seeing. We stepped around a couple fucking roughly on the floor, both of them bleeding and panting, the crowd around them cheering for more. I didn't miss the redness that tinted Juniper's face, the rise in her body temperature, the scent of her arousal.

She liked to watch. Perhaps she liked to perform too.

We got up to the bar, and I held up two fingers to the bartender.

"What are we getting?" Juniper yelled over the music. She didn't need to: I could hear her fine. "Do they have whisky here?"

"The bartender gives you whatever you need," I said. "You don't choose; they do." It was a difficult art, even for demons: determining what would suit someone best from a mere glance, everything concocted on an individual basis. Two glasses slid across the bar toward us, and I caught them, handing the lighter one to Juniper. She reached for it eagerly, and I snatched it back out of her reach at the last moment.

"This is *Hell's* liquor, Juniper," I said. "Be *careful*. It hits hard."

She twisted up her mouth skeptically. "I can hold my liquor, Zane."

"You've never had liquor like this."

I handed it over, and she took a large sip. The bartender was watching eagerly, and so were a few others clustered around the bar. Juniper's eyes widened and immediately began to water, and she coughed as she stared at the drink in shock.

"What—what the *fuck*—" She coughed again, barely holding the drink steady. I couldn't stop laughing, and the bartender shook his head with a grin.

"How is it?" he yelled to her, already in the midst of preparing three other beverages. Juniper wiped her tears away, staring at the drink like it had bitten her, but she still took another sip.

"Fucking *Christ*, this might kill me." She giggled, raising the glass to the bartender with a smile. "It's good!"

She giggled again, the alcohol already giving her a buzz. Fuck, I liked that laugh of hers. I rarely heard it, but it was so damn cute it made me feel vicious; it made me want to turn that giggle into a moan.

I took her wrist, pulling her after me into the crowd. She stood close against me, the press of bodies all around us, swaying to the music in rhythm with those around her. I tugged the elastic from her hair, letting it flow loose down her back. She shook it out, hair falling in her face, her eyes half-closed as she moved to the beat. It was hot amongst the crowd, so many demonic bodies rapidly raising the temperature even on a cold night like this. I stripped off my shirt, smiling at the refreshingly cold kiss of the air. Juniper had her back to me now but she moved close, her hips grinding back against me as she took another sip of her drink.

The way she moved was beautiful. Rhythmic and sensual, every movement smooth, perfectly in unison with me. It got me hard as fuck in just a few seconds, but no one was going to be horrified by that here. This entire crowd was horny as fuck and wasn't going to hide it.

She turned and stroked her hands down my bare chest as she danced low, leaning close, biting me softly as her nails dug into my hips. The eyes of the demons around us had turned to her, savoring her, forked tongues moving hungrily over their lips. But she was mine, all mine; and tonight, I wasn't going to share.

They could look all they wanted, and I hoped they did. They desired her, and it gave me a fucking head rush. She draped her arms around my neck, and I squeezed my hand around her throat. She smiled as she sipped the drink again, leaving a wet shimmer of liquor across her full lips.

"You look like you want to eat me," she rasped huskily.

"Oh, love, trust me, I do. I want to rip you apart."

I kissed her mouth, those sweet liquor-tinted lips. I knotted my hand in her hair and claimed her, my tongue dancing around hers as her body danced close to mine. She knew exactly what she was doing with the way her hips were moving: the sly smile on her face as our mouths parted confirmed it.

"I'm glad you brought me here," she said, her eyes bright as she looked up at me.

"I'm glad you're enjoying it, love." I still hadn't let go of her throat. I liked holding her like that, feeling how her heartbeat raced under my fingers. "Are you enjoying getting to tease me in front of everyone? That ass of yours is really starting to tempt me."

She smiled wickedly. "Tempt you? I hope so. It would be *such* a shame if you lost control in front of everyone."

She'd gone from tempting to demanding, and I wasn't going to deny her. I turned her roughly, so her back was to me again, her ass grinding against me. The demons around us were watching more eagerly now, their excitement rising. I leaned down, and whispered in her ear, "I'm going to make you lose control before I do, love. I'm going to make you come on my fingers, right here, in front of everyone."

She shuddered from head to toe, but she didn't stop dancing as I moved my hand down her body, sheathing my claws before I slipped my fingers below her waistband. She gasped softly as my fingers traced lightly between her legs, teasing her, her movements slowing as she began to focus her attention on my fingers.

"Everyone is watching," she whispered. I bit the tender curve of her neck, hard enough to make her whimper.

"Damn right, they are. They want to see how beautiful you look when you fall apart."

I slipped my finger between her legs, and groaned when I found her already wet. She was so soft, so deliciously warm, and she began to shudder as my fingers massaged her clit. She ground her hips down, rubbing herself on me, demandingly seeking the stimulation she was so desperate for.

I was too eager for her. I could have taken my time—but I didn't want to. I wanted to pleasure her, hard and fast. I wanted to see the ecstasy rush over her and overwhelm her.

She reached back, her fingers clawing at my neck as her back arched against me. I alternated between massaging her clit and pressing two fingers inside her, stretching her throbbing pussy with every thrust.

"Fuck, Zane—" Her words were breathy, trembling. She looked so fucking good, and I growled as I bit her again. The pain made her cry out, and several of those watching us cheered in response, a few of them inspired enough to seize their partners and begin their own rough games. Cries of pleasure and pain rose around us, and Juniper's eyes widened as she looked among them.

"Fuck, you like watching, don't you?" I murmured hungrily, fucking her with my fingers as a demon was forced onto his knees in front of her, his partner mercilessly stroking his cock as he shuddered. Her breath was coming rapidly, and she was shaking as she held me. "You're so wet, love. Do you like it when they watch you too?"

She nodded quickly, eyes hooded with heat and passion. The temptation to fuck her right there in the middle of the crowd was strong, but I could wait. Now that I knew just how much she liked it, there was no way we were leaving until I'd fucked her to complete mind-numbing ecstasy in front of every demon here. The walls of her cunt tightened around my fingers, and I rubbed my palm against her clit, loving every tiny whimper it brought out of her.

She moaned, shaking as she leaned back heavily against me. "Fuck, *fuck*, I'm gonna come—"

"There's my good girl," I murmured, keeping my pace steady, holding her tight as she gasped. "Come for me, love."

My words broke her, and I had to hold her up as her legs shook. The scent of her had gotten those around us into a frenzy, and the chaotic pleasure humming around us felt like a drug in the air. My head was buzzing with it, my body tingling with lust. I kissed her cheek as her tension drained away, and I brought my fingers to her lips. She sucked them clean, licking her own taste from my skin as she swayed.

I began to guide her away, back to the edges of the crowd. "Let's take a break, love, and allow you to catch your breath."

JUNIPER

MY ENTIRE BODY was tingling as Zane led me from the crowd. My legs shook, the afterglow of my orgasm leaving me warm and relaxed. My stomach was light with the almost-instant effects from the alcohol, giving me a buzz that made everything appear brighter. I felt high—calm, but eager, satisfied but somehow still desiring more.

I'd fantasized about playing in public, but I'd never done it before tonight. I'd allowed myself to be vulnerable in front of that massive crowd. I'd watched as those around me were frenzied by my pleasure, my bliss the center of their attention. I felt as if I'd ripped down another wall, like I'd overcome a fear without even realizing it.

Letting go felt good; it felt even better than I'd imagined. This place was like a bubble, isolated from the dangerous world outside. It truly was a little Hell on

Earth—a peek beyond reality, where there were no rules to be followed, and I had no fear of being mocked or rejected for who I was.

Zane led me up a metal staircase to the floor above. There were more couches here, a lounge where everyone could look down on the dancefloor and watch the pulsing crowd. That was where we found Hana and Sadie again, cuddled up on the couch together.

"Satan's fucking *balls*, that was hot!" Hana exclaimed, as Zane flopped down on the couch and pulled me down with him, holding me on his lap. All I could do was grin, and Hana laughed.

"Damn, you finger-fucked the sass out of her." She laughed.

"It's the only way to do it," Zane teased, giving my face a little squeeze. "Don't worry, she recovers quickly. There's more sass in her."

"Oh yeah, there's more," I said, still a little breathless. "One orgasm won't shut me up for long. Just gotta . . . come down a little."

Hana shook her head, but kept her smile as she watched Sadie dance in her seat. The affection between them was undeniable: Hana watched her protectively, possessively.

It was nice to sit for a while and just observe the events unfolding around us. The orgies below, the dancing, the soft-spoken conversations from the others gathered here. It didn't matter how late in the night it was; the party showed no signs of slowing.

But I was curious about Sadie. She was the only other

human I'd met who'd sold her soul. I'd caught sight of the marks on her shoulder when she turned, the scars etched carefully into her skin. She noticed me staring at her and smiled, so I decided to go ahead and ask, "So, uh . . . what got you to sell your soul?"

"I needed help removing someone from my life," she said, matter-of-factly. "Best decision I ever made."

Hana leaned over her, giving her a quick kiss on the cheek before she said, "I killed her fucking husband for her. Sick bastard wouldn't stop beating her, so I beat his face in." Their eyes met, and a little blush rose up Sadie's cheeks before Hana gave her another kiss on the mouth.

"I thought I was going to suffer in the afterlife for it," Sadie said. "I thought selling my soul meant I was damning myself, that Hell would be torturous." She shook her head as she looked around. "But it set me free. It saved me." She looked down for a moment, but her expression wasn't one of sadness. It was soft, teary-eyed happiness. She smiled again as she looked back up at me. "What about you?"

"Shit, well . . ." I swallowed hard, and felt Zane's hand on my back. He didn't say anything; he didn't need to. His touch was his reassurance, his gentle push for me to speak. Even though it made instant anxiety bubble up in me, I said, "I was the victim of a cult. They tried to kill me years ago. I made a deal to take revenge."

Sadie nodded, wide-eyed but not disbelieving, as if cults and selling one's soul were simply an everyday occurrence. But Hana sat up suddenly, snapping her fingers. "I should have *known*! Of course. The cult girl. Damn, you had quite a few soul hunters on your trail. I heard Zane pulled some intimidation shit and claimed you early. No one dared even get near you."

"He what?" I stared at her in surprise, then snapped my gaze over to Zane when he shifted in his seat beside me. "Others were after me?"

"Not for long," he said. "I made it clear no one was to touch you."

"Why?" The question slipped out before I was even sure why I was asking it. I'd known he stalked me for years, ever since I left Abelaum. All those months when I'd felt most alone, he'd been watching me secretly, waiting. But I'd thought it was just because he was curious, simply deciding if I was worth the trouble.

"I knew what I wanted," he said. "And even if it turned out you never wanted a deal with me, fuck . . ." He shrugged. "I still wouldn't have let another demon have you."

Hana was chuckling. "Aww, Zane found his soft spot."

"What's that mean?" I said.

Zane groaned softly, but Hana said, "It's when a hardass demon finds a human that makes them go all soft. The human that makes them wanna do sweet shit, the kind of human you'd take for long romantic walks around Hell. Sadie is mine." Sadie blushed again. "She loves roses so fucking much, she has me planning ways to get them to grow in Hell for her." She chuckled, shaking her head as she tugged Sadie close. "Didn't think I'd see the day, Zane. Damn, you've even let her carve you up a little."

I looked over at him again, expecting to see him protesting or shaking his head. But he was just looking back at me, his fingers tracing over the scars of my name on his shoulder. "I knew what I wanted, and I've been chasing it every day since."

Those words felt like a hand slowly squeezing around my heart. It wasn't painful, no—it was a comfort, an embrace within my ribcage. It stopped my breath for a moment. It made the ecstatic chaos around me slow to a mere blur.

It felt like walking into a familiar house and feeling warm, like sighing, like realizing you can rest after a long day. A little bit of light on my jagged edges.

"Have you marked her yet?" Hana's question cut through my soft thoughts, and the thump of music and cries of ecstasy around us roared back into my focus.

"Not yet," Zane said. I remembered him saying that marks—*piercings*—were used to signify loyalty and devotion amongst demons. It had a different connotation than the scars he'd given me: the scars were our contract, but a piercing, well . . .

A piercing was more than that.

"This is the perfect place to do it," Hana said excitedly. "Vian is here. They'd gladly give you some metal to use. And you know how good their pieces are."

"Not until she's ready," Zane said, squeezing his hand possessively around my thigh as he sipped his drink. His tightened grasp made me feel good—bold, even. It made all the fear I felt at the concept of devotion seem insignificant.

The scars were one thing, but to accept another mark, a mark in metal, meant so much more. They talked about it so casually, but there was an undercurrent of seriousness to it. It was intimate, almost somber.

It was like my name, carved into his chest. He could've healed it, he could have gone on like it was never even there. But he'd kept it by choice, not necessity. He'd wanted my name on him.

"I *am* ready," I said. Zane's eyebrows shot up, and Hana clapped her hands, leaping to her feet.

"Fuck yes! I'll go find Vian." She snatched Sadie's hand, dragging her along downstairs.

Zane was frowning. "Don't feel pressured," he said. "You don't have to do shit. I know Hana's really fucking enthusiastic, but—"

"I don't care if Hana's excited," I said. I traced my finger along his ear, along the rings and jewels pierced there. "This is about us. *Fuck,* it's about . . . " I took a deep breath. I could only say this because Hana and Sadie weren't around to hear it, and maybe the tiny sips of demonic liquor setting a fire in my chest helped too. "I don't know what you've done to me. I don't know why you make me feel . . . you make me feel safe. You make me feel like maybe everything isn't shit." God, I was bad at this. Putting fickle things like emotions into words was damn near impossible. "That's not something I ever thought I'd have, Zane. I didn't think I'd feel safe again. I didn't think I'd ever have any kind of relationship—"

I cut myself off abruptly, regretting my word choice. But Zane turned my face back toward him, and said,

"Don't be ashamed of what you want to say. I'm not going anywhere."

And that was the thing, wasn't it? That was the spark that lit up my dark, dead, broken soul—he'd seen all its sharp edges and hadn't left. He'd seen me as broken as I was and *wanted* me, regardless.

I'd always told myself I'd never rely on anyone else. I didn't need approval, or love, or support. I was fine alone. Yet here I was, surrounded by demons and twisted debauchery, and for the first time in years, I'd found something like home.

I felt accepted. I'd spoken my truth and been *listened* to.

Zane had listened first. He'd listened before anyone else had.

"I want your mark," I said firmly. "I'm ready."

I could tell he wanted to smile. "Are you sure?"

"Absolutely sure."

Finally, he let himself give me that sharp-toothed grin. "Let's introduce you to Vian."

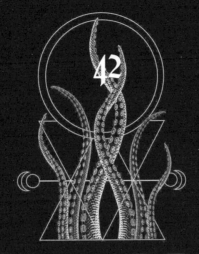

JUNIPER

VIAN NEEDED NO introduction; I knew it had to be them the moment I saw them.

They were easy to spot in a crowd: nearly seven-foot, broad-shouldered, and dressed in intricately braided, fine links of silver chain. There were few places on their face that they *weren't* pierced, fine metals and jewels decorating every inch of available skin. They were lounging upon the gaping maw of an old machine, the hunk of metal having been forcibly torn and pressed into a shape vaguely resembling a chair. They were surrounded by a dozen other demons, all adorned in similar garments of chains and carefully crafted metals, some of them restrained in cuffs that were as much works of art as their jewelry.

Vian smiled as we approached, sharp teeth shining with implanted jewels.

"My, my, has Zane brought a sweet little soul to mark?" they said, tapping white-painted claws upon the machine beneath them. They took a long look at me, their bright eyes scouring every inch of skin, lingering on my scars and the bloodstains on my shirt.

"Not very sweet, sorry," I said. "Pretty sour, mostly."

"You know I don't go for the sweet ones, Vian," Zane drawled, the pride obvious in his voice.

Vian stood, towering over us both. I automatically took a step back as I looked up at them, and they leaned down curiously to examine my face.

"Right then, *sour* little soul." Vian chuckled. "Where are you getting your metal?"

"Tongue," I said. I tried to keep my voice steady, but it still hitched at the end. I wanted this, there was no doubt in my mind. But the thought of a needle going through my tongue still made my stomach coil, like a snake trying to slither away into hiding.

"I think a simple piece will suffice," Zane said. "Something black, for her dark little soul."

"Mm, right, right." Vian nodded and grabbed a small metal box that hung from one of the chains around their neck. They opened it, poking around inside for an acceptable bit of jewelry, glancing up at me every now and then as if gauging what would suit me. My eyes flickered over the demons behind them, and I noticed several of the bound ones had needles through their lips and their ears: fresh piercings. But they didn't look as if they were in pain. They were breathing slowly and deeply, some of them with their eyes closed, limp as if they were in a trance.

"Do you make the jewelry yourself?" I said, trying to distract myself from my worsening nerves. A crowd was beginning to gather, other demons nudging closer, watching me curiously. Zane's hand slipped around my waist, tracing lightly over my skin.

"I make every piece," Vian said, with a little smile. "I find the materials, the jewels and the metals, and I form them myself. It's a passion of mine." They glanced back, their eyes softening with affection when they looked at the demons sitting behind them. "My beautiful creations are used to adorn even more beautiful beings. They solidify bonds. They bring pain . . . pleasure . . . catharsis."

They turned their attention back to the box and held up a black metal barbell—long enough to fit comfortably through my tongue. "Onyx from the Black Sea, metal forged by dragon fire. What do you think?"

My eyes widened as I looked at it and nodded. "Dragon fire? Do you mean . . . do you mean *real . . .*?"

Vian nodded, and Zane did too. Somehow, dragons actually existing managed to shock me, even after all the other shit I'd seen.

"It's perfect," I said.

Vian's smile widened at my nod, and they turned back to the demons gathered around and said excitedly, "Zane has brought a human to get her metal."

Every demon there immediately perked up. The ones in chains strained eagerly against their bonds, ready for a show, and those gathered at the edges pressed a little closer. I'd loved what we'd done earlier, I'd loved knowing that those dancing around us had watched Zane pleasure me. But now, I was faced with the anticipation of pain and the eager gazes of dozens. Above us, on the upper walkways, even more demons leaned over to get a better look.

"We don't have to do it here," Zane said softly, holding me close from behind. "It can be private, if you want."

I took a deep breath and turned toward him. "No. I want them to see. I want them to *know*." I wrapped my arms around his neck, bringing my body closer to his. "I want them all to know I belong to you."

He grinned, and I felt a hard, eager throb beneath his trousers. "Yeah? Shall we put on a show for them, love?"

"One they won't forget."

Vian turned back to us, this time offering a leather pouch. "Your equipment," they said, handing it to Zane and giving me a wink. Within the pouch were sterilized needles of varying gauges and metal clamps.

"Everyone seems so excited," I whispered.

Vian nodded. "Getting a mark, bestowing your metal upon another, is considered celebratory even when it's a private occasion," they said. "But when it's public? We eat that shit up. The tension, the blood, the pain, the ecstasy . . ." They chuckled softly. "This is what we live for."

The excitement was infectious. It rippled through the air, sending chills over my skin. The crowd began to murmur, and the music was a low, throbbing beat that thrummed through my body like a pulse. Zane grasped my face, blocking out everything around me for a few moments.

"Remember to talk to me," he said. "If you're overwhelmed, if it's too much, you tell me."

"I'll tell you," I said. "I won't just grin and bear it if you piss me off." I wasn't sure which I felt more strongly: the fear or the excitement. I lowered my voice, and added, "I trust you, Zane."

He kissed me deeply, roughly. I could feel the metal in his own tongue in that kiss, and it made my abdomen tighten with anticipation. He grabbed my ass, squeezed, and then turned me toward the crowd and forced me down to my knees.

I let out a slow, trembling breath as I knelt there. Zane leaned down and kissed my temple, his teeth snapping together hungrily near my ear. Then slowly, he pulled open my unbuttoned shirt. He pulled it down my arms, kissing my shoulders and my back with every inch he eased it down.

I'd never let so many people see my scars before. I'd always hidden them. Even after I got the tattoos, I still rarely wore anything that would allow a stranger's eyes to glimpse my chest.

I'd been ashamed of those scars for so long. I'd had to bear the marks of someone else's violence, someone else's cruelty, for so long. And every time I looked in the mirror, it became a reminder of what they'd done, a reminder that my will had been overtaken, that I'd been used, that my life had been reduced to insignificance.

But Kent Hadleigh was dead. These scars were my own. I didn't feel such horror when I looked at them now. I didn't feel such hatred for myself when I saw them.

I didn't have to be ashamed of what had happened. I'd been brave. I'd survived. I'd gotten this fucking far.

I took a deep breath and loosened my nerves. I forced out the instant urge to cover myself, the automatic twitch that told me to hide. It wasn't looks of disgust I saw around me: it was lust, awe, hunger, envy. And as Zane walked around in front of me, I saw pure adoration.

He crouched down, brushing my hair out of my face. He ran his claws over my chest, following the lines of my tattoos and then bringing his lips down to kiss my scars, and whispered, "You're so fucking beautiful."

I shuddered under his touches, gasping as he found every little spot that made me weak. Right beneath my ear, the hollow of my collarbone, my inner wrist—he kissed, and licked, and nipped with his teeth. Every tiny touch, no matter how soft, awakened my body and sent my nerves into high alert. My face was growing hotter, and more eyes were lingering now, more demons pausing to watch me. I spotted more humans amongst the crowd too: not only Sadie, standing next to Hana, but men and women who watched me with wide eyes, fascinated and fearful, envious and longing.

"Do you see the way they look at you, Juni?" Zane's voice tickled in my ear as he moved behind me, grasped my hair close to my scalp, and pulled me up from resting on my heels to my knees. "They long for you. Some of them wish they were you. And I'm honored you'd kneel for me."

I looked back at him, and reached up my hand to trace my fingers over my name on his chest. A jagged, messy scar—not unlike mine. Not unlike *me*.

"Before I hurt you, love, I'm going to pleasure you."
He tugged my head back, dragging his claws along my
exposed throat. Then he shoved me down, my face to
the ground and my ass in the air. He tugged down my
trousers and pulled them off my legs as I remained in position. My face was blazing hot—embarrassed but eager,
nervous but excited.

Only my panties covered me now. Zane's fingers
rubbed over the cloth, lingering where my arousal had
dampened it. Then they traced down my thighs, appreciatively squeezing me, causing goose bumps to spread
over my skin.

"Fuck, you smell so good."

Murmurs of affirmation rippled through the crowd
and my face grew even hotter. God, I'd gotten used to
Zane saying he could smell my arousal—but they *all*
could. There was no hiding it from them, no pretending I wasn't absolutely dripping over what was about to
happen.

Zane brought his head down and ripped the side of
my panties apart with his teeth. Louder growls were
heard as he pulled the cloth away and tossed it aside,
laying me bare, the cool air kissing my skin. My breath
began to shake, my eyes flickering over the faces around
me. I was already overthinking how I looked, how I
sounded, how I smelled—

But all that was entirely forgotten when Zane's mouth
closed over me.

His forked tongue licked over my clit, caressing
around it, teasing and flicking the bud until every touch

sent waves of overwhelming stimulation through my every nerve ending. He used his piercings to his advantage too, massaging the smooth, rounded head of the barbells over my clit. Every touch of the warm metal made me gasp, and then my abdomen began to tighten, and I eagerly arched my back.

"Feels so good," I whimpered, my words trembling. "Please . . . fuck, please . . ."

"Mm, I love it when you beg," he murmured right up against me, the vibration of his words making me shudder. He gripped my thighs tighter, claws digging into me as he pressed his tongue inside. I swore he could elongate his tongue at will—it was pressing deep, caressing my inner walls, a sensation altogether unique from his fingers or his cock. He could manipulate that tongue in ways I'd never even imagined, the forked sides working independently of each other to stimulate me until I was shaking, my cries completely unhinged.

I couldn't hold back anymore. I couldn't make myself worry about appearances or shame or pride. I was drunk on pleasure, terrified yet longing for the very thing that frightened me: the anticipation of that needle through my tongue. I wanted it so badly that not even fear, not even pain, could keep me from it.

Dread and longing intertwined in my mind's darkest places, fear becoming lust. The pain was part of the pleasure—the inevitable moment of destruction was inseparable from my desire.

Zane and I bled with each other, and for each other. Flesh and blood were the promises we couldn't put into words—they were the emotions language couldn't fully encompass.

My body was tightening, I could barely draw a steady breath. The music, the eyes of those watching, the crackling energy in the charged air around us—all that faded into the deep recesses of my mind. I was riding the edge of an orgasm, dragged carefully along its precipice, not allowed to fall but not pulled away from it either.

Zane's mouth parted from me and I groaned, left shaking and twitching, vision blurred with overstimulation. He pulled me back, held me tight against his chest, and growled in my ear, "Open your mouth, love."

I did as he said. He stood up, leaving me there on my knees, watching me as I remained in position for him. The eyes of the crowd and their eager smiles didn't matter as he stood in front of me, smiling at me with the metal clamps in his hand. He squatted down in front of me, and said softly, "Are you ready, love?"

I nodded, my mouth still open. My clit was pulsating, my body eager for more. Zane clamped my tongue, positioning it carefully, taking his time to make sure the piercing would sit comfortably. I was so giddy, so nervous, that I felt like laughing. I could barely hold myself still.

Zane held up the needle, the metal flashing in the blacklights. It appeared terrifyingly thick up close, and Zane clicked his tongue softly, demanding my attention back on his face.

"Don't be afraid, love," he said softly. "You're safe with me."

I almost closed my eyes, but I forced myself to keep them open. I watched his face instead of the needle. He moved with perfectly calm, careful control as he lowered the needle down.

Perhaps it was the pleasure still flooding my body, perhaps it was the adrenaline. But I felt the pressure of the needle going in and only the briefest pinch of pain. The demons around us howled, they cheered and yelled their enthusiasm. But I could only see Zane. There was a slight tug as he fit the jewelry in my tongue, secured it, and set the clamps aside. Then he held my face, cradling it, smiling at me as the head rush eased, and I smiled in weak, stunned ecstasy.

"How do you feel, love?" I just nodded and smiled, because it felt too strange to talk with the metal in my tongue. He kissed my forehead, and his grip moved from my face to my throat. "You did so well. You were so fucking brave."

He pulled me forward, and he laid back. I straddled his head, and he gripped my hips, holding me against his face. I could taste blood, and my tongue ached with the strange new metal. But those sensations were shoved aside as his ravenous mouth consumed me. Ecstasy spread through my veins like a drug, every stroke of his tongue bringing me higher.

He groaned against me, looking up at me from between my legs as he eagerly sucked my clit. The orgasm crashed over me so hard I cried out, my voice shaking with the force of it. My thighs squeezed around his head, and yet, *he just kept going*. Even as my orgasm gripped me so tight I could barely draw in a breath, he kept sucking and licking at me for more, holding me in place, not satisfied until he'd taken every possible second of mind-shattering bliss. Not until he'd made my shaking voice scream his name.

I WAS TOO drained, too overwhelmed to remember much after that. I remembered saying a few good-byes, Hana and Sadie embracing me. But mostly, I remembered Zane carrying me, because my body was at its limit, and every step I took nearly tripped me over my own feet. I remember him sitting with me in the Jeep, holding me on his lap with my head resting on his shoulder.

I felt safe. God, after so long, I'd found home.

JUNIPER

"I DIDN'T CRUSH half that old bastard's body to be discredited like that. Fucking hell."

I closed out the news site on my phone, chuckling at Zane's disgust. It had been a few days since the Halloween party, and the local paper had finally blasted its headline: *HEAD OF LOCAL HISTORICAL SOCIETY DEAD IN APPARENT SUICIDE.* It was the first and only public mention I'd seen of Kent's fate, and I had no doubt the remaining Hadleighs had made every effort to ensure that was the case.

"This is better for us," I said. "The last thing we need is for everyone in Abelaum to be on edge because they think a murderer is on the loose. The Hadleighs have never liked the police snooping around. I guarantee you they paid someone off to make Kent's death look exactly how they want it to."

Zane snorted. "I was looking forward to all the chaos. Terrified humans scurrying inside the moment the sun begins to set, locking their doors, trusting no one. It's *fun*."

"Abelaum is already close enough to that anyway," I said. "Everyone knows this place has monsters, they just don't have names for them. And now, one of those monsters is finally dead."

"I wonder if the family knows we did it." Zane leaned against the counter, naked except for a tight pair of black briefs. "I didn't notice any cameras around the house."

I really appreciated his habit of walking around nearly nude. It was a distraction, but a pleasant one. Every time his large hands tightened their grip on the edge of the counter, my insides tightened too. The demon had Pavloved me into getting hot over *hands*.

Strong, veiny, choking hands.

"When Kent saw you, the first thing he suspected was Leon." I shrugged. "Something tells me that's where they'll pin the blame, and probably a big reason they don't want anyone looking into it too deeply. Can't have some nosey journalist uncovering all the demon-summoning, human-sacrificing, occult shit from Abelaum's dear model family."

Zane chuckled. "Leon is going to be jealous as hell that you got to kill Kent. He's been talking about murdering that bastard for years."

"He's got his hands full with Rae. I doubt he needs the distraction of trying to murder the Hadleighs on top of that," I said, stretching my arms above my head.

"Hey, I'm gonna take the car and go get breakfast. I'm starving."

He snatched me as I got up from the table, tugging me over against his chest and tracing his thumb along my lip. "Well, don't take too long. I wanna see how that metal in your tongue feels on my cock."

I stuck my tongue out at him teasingly. It was still tender, but the swelling had gone down and it looked like it would heal well. "I'm supposed to wait six to eight weeks, Zane. *Weeks.* That means no blowjobs."

"Fucking hell," he groaned dramatically. "You humans heal so slowly. Thank Lucifer I'm flexible enough to suck it myself."

I laughed, disentangling myself from him to snatch up the car keys from the counter. "Okay, I'm going to hurry back *just* so I can watch you do that."

THE DAY WAS gray, a gentle mist drizzling as I drove down Main Street. I wasn't entirely sure what it was, but I'd felt different since Halloween night. Killing Kent, claiming my power in that, then partying with demons, meeting so many others who didn't balk at my past, letting Zane pierce me—it was a different kind of power than what I was used to.

Power had always simply meant survival: was I strong enough to make it through the day, strong enough to overcome whatever tried to kill me? But this power . . . the power I'd felt even when I'd relinquished control and let Zane pierce my tongue . . . that was something wholly different. I'd spoken the truth and been believed, I'd let down my mask without fear of retribution. I wasn't used to that. It didn't feel like the power of holding a weapon or taking a life.

It was a calm, quiet power. Like the sun rising in the morning, like the ocean eroding stone, like the strength of the oldest, tallest trees. It wasn't power for fighting, it wasn't power that could be stripped away. It was natural, inherent.

I stopped at a little cafe in town. Their breakfast sandwiches were pricey as hell, but they were the only place in Abelaum that would give me a sandwich with candied bacon on it. I'd pay anything they wanted for candied-fucking-bacon. With my sandwich and a cup of hot black tea, I sat in the car parked along the road and ate, enjoying the soft sounds of the rain.

I understood why people were drawn to Abelaum. Of course, with the university down the road, new people came and went all the time. But there was a quiet charm to this town that couldn't be ignored, something that promised to be welcoming—even though that sweet welcome could turn deadly the moment one accepted it.

I wanted to leave Abelaum as soon as this was over, but I had no idea where to go. I'd never thought of myself as being able to settle anywhere: getting a house, a home, putting down roots. But maybe, when this was all over, maybe there was somewhere safe out there for me.

Maybe it would be somewhere Zane would like too.

I nearly choked on my tea, ducking low in my seat. Victoria Hadleigh was coming up the sidewalk, the hood

of her raincoat pulled low over her face. She was on the
phone, talking rapidly, glancing nervously over her shoulder every few steps. There were bags under her reddened
eyes, and her face was pale.

She looked worse the closer she got. When she tucked
her phone back into her pocket, I noticed several of her
long acrylic nails were broken off. Those bags under her
eyes weren't just dark circles either.

They were bruises.

What the *fuck* had happened?

She was almost even with the car when she spotted
me. Her eyes fell on me and she stopped, blinking slowly
before her confusion cracked into open terror.

She ran, and there was no way in hell I was going to
let her get away.

I followed in the car, keeping at a distance but not
giving her a chance to hide. I expected her to return to
her vehicle, but she kept going on foot. She left Main
Street, jogging down a winding road that curved around
the new apartment buildings near the bay. She reached
the park and sprinted across the lawn, so I couldn't follow her in the car.

I had to make a choice: Risk her telling the rest of her
family she'd seen me or . . .

Or kill her. Here. Now. All I had on me was my knife,
and when I fumbled around for my phone to call Zane, I
realized I'd left it at the house.

Fuck. It was just me and the knife then.

But right as I was about to get out of the car, right as
Victoria reached the far side of the park and was about

to cross the street toward the beach, a black SUV pulled up alongside her.

I eased my door closed again, watching as she stopped and stared at the vehicle. Only when the passenger side door opened did she begin to back away, as none other than Jeremiah himself walked toward her.

So much for making sure she didn't blab about seeing me.

But Jeremiah didn't seem interested in what she was saying as she frantically pointed back in the direction she'd come. Her hands were moving wildly, and she was backing away faster, the closer Jeremiah got to her. The back door of the SUV opened, and two more men got out of the vehicle. The moment they did, Victoria tried to run. She didn't get far.

Jeremiah grabbed her roughly and she managed one brief scream before he slapped his hand over her mouth. The other two men moved to help him, and she was fighting them hard—fighting them like she feared for her life.

Without Kent in charge, what the fuck had the Libiri become?

They dragged her into the SUV, shoved into the back with the two men as Jeremiah got back in the front. They began to drive, and I started the engine again. I had to see where they took her. But as I followed, doing my best to keep a distance from the vehicle, a cold, hard feeling settled in my stomach.

When the SUV drove out of Abelaum, heading north along the bay, I realized where they were taking her.

This was the road to White Pine.

I should have driven back to the house. This wasn't something I should have gone near without Zane. But I didn't want to risk losing them. I had a suspicion about what they were going to do, and if I was right . . .

If I was right, things were going to get very bad, very quickly.

Three lives spared, three souls given, and one of those souls was meant to be Jeremiah or Victoria. Jeremiah had already made it clear he had no intention of laying down his own life.

My trepidation grew, and I widened the distance between my car and theirs. Zane was soon going to wonder where I was, and with any luck, he'd track me out here by scent. If the Libiri sacrificed Victoria, there was no telling how strong the God would become, and in turn, how much more power the cult would have.

I'd never thought it would come to this, but I couldn't let Victoria Hadleigh die. Not like this.

By the time I made it to the end of the narrow, twisting dirt road in the woods, the SUV was already parked and empty. It wasn't the only vehicle there either. At least a dozen others were parked along the road, all of them empty.

I pressed my back against the seat, gripping the steering wheel. I had to stay calm. I couldn't lose my nerve. My memories—those flashing, intrusive, painful bursts of memories—had to stay firmly in the past where they belonged.

Moving as quickly as I dared, I followed the path toward St. Thaddeus cathedral.

JUNIPER

THE AIR WAS heavy with the scent of a bonfire and the damp, rain-muddied dirt. The smell of the smoke triggered harsh, demanding stabs of fear inside my chest—fear that weighed me down like anchors hanging from my shoulders. But I couldn't go back, not now. I couldn't let another sacrifice happen.

Muddy footsteps covered the old wooden stairs to the cathedral's tall front doors, the chain that usually bound them unlocked and set aside. There was a murmur of voices within, but I didn't dare get too close to the doors. I had to find another way in.

When we were teens, Victoria and I used to sneak through the back door that led through the kitchens. If you were any kind of young deviant growing up in Abelaum, you'd end up at St. Thaddeus eventually. We'd come here to smoke, drink, or fuck our latest crushes in the dark corners behind the pulpit. It had felt blasphemous and edgy, our own little taste of stolen freedom. We'd been here a dozen times before the day Victoria led me through those doors and I found out our secret place wasn't so secret at all.

The old kitchen smelled of dust and mold. Puddles of rainwater sat stagnant on the destroyed wooden floor, and dust covered the empty shelves. Another door separated me from the nave: just one door, between me and the cult waiting outside. My heart was pounding, nausea rising. The more I thought about where I was, the heavier the wave of light-headedness that overtook me.

This wasn't a memory, this was reality. This was the here and now. But God, I wished Zane was with me. His presence would have calmed me, it would have given me the net of protection I so desperately needed.

The old boards creaked behind me, and a ragged breath sent a shiver up my back. I swallowed hard, squeezing my eyes shut tight for a moment. I didn't need to look back to know the Watcher would be there. Stalking me, waiting for its opportunity. Waiting for the moment when my fear would become too much, and it could push me into that deep, dark, dangerous void of my nightmares.

Zane had said to ignore it. I wasn't even going to fucking *look* at it.

I exhaled aggressively. I was in control. I just had to stay calm.

I crept toward the door, and slowly eased it open to just the slightest crack. The dancing light of a fire filled the nave, casting eerie shadows up the old walls and over the steep, broken ceiling. I couldn't see anything toward the front side of the church, but I could see the pulpit. It was surrounded by lit candles, perched upon a mountain of their own wax that had built up through the years. There was a murmur of voices and shuffling feet from the nave, the crowd of congregants just out of my sight.

Jeremiah leaned against the pulpit, dressed in a crisp white suit, looking out upon his congregation. It was his now, there was no doubt of that. I'd known killing Kent would throw them into chaos, but I hadn't anticipated Jeremiah would react so quickly and so . . . violently.

It was like he'd been ready for it. Like he'd been waiting. This wasn't the outcome I'd been looking for. I'd been anticipating a few weeks of power struggle within the Libiri, as all those vying for the top spot tried to make their move.

But Jeremiah had already put himself into position as their leader. He had his men behind him, young men who I assumed were his classmates; people he'd sucked into his lies, who craved the kind of power he offered. The power to snatch a woman off the street with no repercussions.

I hated Victoria, but it made me sick to see her tied up at their feet. Her jacket was gone, her shirt was torn and she was covered in mud, as if she'd fallen on the way here. She was gagged with a dirty cloth in her mouth, and her lip was bleeding. She was behind the pulpit, surrounded by people. There was no way in hell I could get to her.

"Brothers, Sisters," Jeremiah suddenly spoke, his

voice echoing around the cathedral and silencing the crowd's murmuring. "It's time."

I had no way to stop this. If Zane were here, we could have slaughtered them all, we could have laid waste to this mess once and for all.

But it was just me and my knife, and that wasn't enough. God*damn it*, it wasn't enough.

A hush fell over the church. All that remained was the sound of the rain and Victoria's soft, desperate whimpering. Jeremiah's eyes moved slowly over the crowd I couldn't see, narrowed, his hands gripped tightly onto the edges of the pulpit. I could still envision his father standing there, all too clearly. I could still hear the way Kent had addressed his followers, how earnest he'd sounded, how he'd spoken like a man who truly believed what he was doing was right.

That had made it all the more horrifying—how truly they believed they were doing the right thing.

"A few days ago," Jeremiah said. "We all suffered a great loss: the loss of our father, our guide, our shepherd. Outsiders will be told he killed himself, as they must be, to protect what we have. But we know the truth, don't we?" There were murmurs of ascent from the crowd. "We know that Kent Hadleigh was *murdered* for his devotion to God!"

Louder cries began, jeers of anger and cries for justice. My hand tightened on the doorframe, making the old boards creek, and I instantly held my breath, shrinking back. But Jeremiah was too absorbed in his speech to notice me.

"But we will triumph, Brothers and Sisters!" he said. "I will lead us forth. I will ensure our oaths are fulfilled. And I will ensure my father's death is avenged. I will ensure his murderers suffer for their blasphemy, as God wills."

"As God wills," the congregation murmured. I needed to leave. There was nothing I could do here. I had no way to stop this that wouldn't put me in imminent danger. But then Jeremiah crouched down, seized his sister's arm, and dragged her up beside the pulpit.

"As God wills, my dear sister Victoria will go to join the Deep One," he said, as Victoria strained against him. "Three lives spared must be three souls given. Here, today, we shall send the second soul to God, in thanks for Its mercy, in hope of the new world to come."

"Three lives spared, three souls given," the congregation repeated. Victoria wasn't looking at them—she was looking at Jeremiah, her eyes wide in accusation, in horror, in hatred. Gripping her so tight that his fingers dug into her skin, Jeremiah leaned down and kissed her forehead, murmuring something I couldn't hear as she began to frantically shake her head. Then he released her, and two of his men stepped forward to restrain her before she could crawl away. She was screaming again, muffled by the gag. Jeremiah returned to the pulpit, and lifted up a blade so it caught the fire's light.

I knew that knife. The dark curved handle was textured with little bumps, like the underside of a cephalopod's arms. I wanted to back away, I wanted to leave; but I was rooted in place. The knife held me fixated as

Jeremiah stood before Victoria and said, "Our Sister Victoria is afraid, but are we not all afraid of the mightiness of our God? Are we not all afraid of what It may demand of us? But we are no less devoted. We are no less determined. This is as it should be."

"This is as it should be."

"We will not allow Victoria's fear to keep her from her devotion to the Deep One. We will be strong for her. We will ensure her duty is fulfilled."

He was like his father—it was like Kent reborn.

The floorboards behind me creaked again. Cold breath sent a chill over my neck. In my peripheral vision I could see the blood-red figure standing there, but I refused to turn toward it. I swallowed hard, cold sweat dripping down my back as those stiff, flayed fingers brushed over my shoulder.

"No," I whispered. "This isn't a nightmare. I know where I am."

As Jeremiah leaned down with the knife, I saw myself in Victoria's place. I saw myself screaming, weeping, struggling, begging. I saw the masked faces that had surrounded me, watching me in silence, offering no help.

With the taste of bile in my mouth, I watched them cut her.

She was screaming, but the sound was muted. Everything felt hazy. I focused on the texture of the old doorframe beneath my fingers. I tried to lose myself in the scent of the smoke and the sound of the rain. I was falling, closer and closer to that dangerous vulnerable place.

The Watcher's gaze was cold on the back of my head.

It still had its vile fingers on my shoulder. I couldn't let it suck me back into the dark. I bit my lip, hard; I bit it until it bled. The pain kept me grounded, but only barely.

It seemed to last forever. When Jeremiah stood up straight, the knife dripping blood onto the floor, everything rushed back to speed with startling clarity.

"Let us take her up the hill," Jeremiah said, and it was like a light had gone out in his eyes, leaving only vast, cold darkness behind. "Let us take her to God."

I stood slowly. I backed away, as carefully as I could, until I'd reached the doorway through which I entered. Then, and only then, did I glance over. Only then did I look at the Watcher face-to-face, now crouched in the shadows in the corner, staring at me.

Its fingers twitched. Its wide eyes didn't leave my face for even a moment.

It wanted me. It wanted my terror, my pain. It wanted the endless screams in my nightmares.

I shook my head. Not this time. Not *fucking* this time.

I slipped out the door, and with the cool rain on my skin, I ran.

I was halfway back to the car when my stomach revolted. I doubled over, vomiting into the dirt. Victoria's muffled cries were still ringing in my ears. They sounded like mine. That awful place, the knife, the smell, the cold . . .

I'd stood and watched in silence. I'd done nothing—but I couldn't have. Victoria deserved to die, she'd done the same to me. She'd led me in to be slaughtered. She'd abandoned me to be tortured.

I spat, wiping my mouth on the back of my hand. I needed to get the hell out of there. I needed to get back to Zane, back to safety. The wind whipped through the trees above, and with it came the wretched stench of death.

As I looked ahead, down the trail that would lead me back to the car, I noticed something I hadn't before: numerous clusters of pale white mushrooms. They were everywhere, sprouted from the dirt, clinging to the sides of the trees, burrowing up from among the roots. Hundreds . . . thousands . . . they were everywhere.

I looked down at my shaking hands. Hands that had drawn blood, hands that had killed, that had helped me survive. Hands that had once clawed me out of the very mine Jeremiah and the Libiri were about to throw Victoria into.

I'd been thrown down alive. They'd throw her down alive too. There was still time to stop the sacrifice.

JUNIPER

I KEPT OFF the trail, sprinting through the trees. I had my knife out, at the ready—God, I was a fool to come out here without a gun. But I was going to lay low. I knew what I had to do. Once they threw Victoria down, I'd wait for them to leave, then bring her out. What the hell I'd do with her then, I didn't know. I'd always thought I'd kill her without hesitation. I'd *tried* to kill her, years ago, and gotten locked up for it. I wanted her dead.

But not like this. Not when I'd done the same shameful, hypocritical shit as the rest of those cowards. I'd watched them cut her and done nothing. As much as I hated her, as much as I wanted to put a knife to her throat and bleed her out, I wasn't going to let her vile God have what It wanted.

I wasn't like them. I was better than them. I was better than watching horror in silence.

I wasn't going to let the Libiri succeed. I wasn't going to stand by while they pleased the Deep One with even more suffering.

I was soaked to the bone, but I was close: numerous talismans dangled over my head, suspended on bits of knotted twine, spinning in the wind. It was truly storming now—the rain coming in torrents, thunder rumbling. I could see white cloaks ahead, stark between the trees.

The mushrooms covered nearly every inch of ground here. I crouched down, creeping slowly forward, crushing them underfoot with every step. They released a pungent scent of rot, squishing disgustingly under my shoes.

"Come on, Zane," I whispered to myself. "Find me. Fucking find me so we can kill these bastards."

If he could get here in time, we had all of them in one place. We could take them all out, we could end this and destroy them all.

I kept to the shadows as I tried to get into a position to see past the sea of white-cloaks. They all had their masks on: bone-white stag skulls, the eyes black pits. It was haunting how still they stood, how calm they were, all gathered around a place so drenched in evil it made my skin crawl just to be close to it. Had they convinced themselves this feeling of disgust was beautiful, like they had convinced themselves suffering was noble?

I was thankful for the rain and thunder muffling my footsteps as I crawled through the underbrush. The smell of rot and death was unbearable, thick in my nose and cloying in my throat. Finally, I could see Jeremiah standing before the open maw of the mine shaft. He wore his mask too, and Victoria was on her knees at his feet. She was bleeding, her shirt ripped away to make room for the awful, ragged marks cut into her skin. They'd removed her gag, and although her voice was raw, she still screamed at them.

"You can't do this to me! I know you, *I fucking know all of you*! You're wrong, you're all fucking wrong!"

"Keep carrying on, Sister, and we'll start to think you're defying God," Jeremiah said.

"Fuck this! Fuck all of you! Dad would have never let this happen—"

"Oh, you don't think so?" He knelt down, and Victoria jerked away from his hand. "Dad told us since we were in the cradle that one day, one of us would go. You're *blessed*, Victoria." It was hard to tell with the mask and the roar of the rain, but I could have sworn I could hear laughter in Jeremiah's voice.

He knew it was all a lie, but he carried on because it gave him power. It allowed him to stand there proudly with his sister in the mud. It allowed him to feel untouchable. My hand tightened on the knife. It didn't matter what God he served. It didn't matter if he thought he was blessed or chosen or whatever other bullshit he concocted.

He was going to die like his father.

"Is she not blessed?" he yelled toward the crowd as he stood. "Who among you would rush forward to offer yourself to the Deep One? Who here isn't a coward before God?"

There was a beat, then another, and for a moment, I

thought no one would step forward. I hoped I was about to watch them all turn their backs on this. But then . . .

"I would!" A white-cloak stepped forward. Faceless, nameless. "I would give myself to God in a heartbeat. I would be honored to be so blessed—"

They didn't get to finish. Jeremiah sunk the knife into their chest up to the hilt. He caught them as they fell to their knees, holding them close. "Then you're blessed indeed. The Deep One has blessed you. The Deep One will take you into eternity."

Not one of them moved. There were a few fervent murmurs of "All is as it should be" as Jeremiah dragged the bleeding acolyte toward the mine. He stood before the shaft and pulled off his mask, holding up his victim with his fists knotted in their cloak.

"God! Hear me!" His voice cracked as he screamed. "I offer you a soul, unbidden! I offer a soul in devotion, in worship! I ask for nothing except your blessing!"

He shoved his victim into the dark. There wasn't even a scream, and the rain covered the sound of them hitting the water below. It was as if they simply fell into an abyss, and would be falling for eternity.

Victoria was weeping now, shaking her head. Jeremiah's cronies kept her from crawling away.

Jeremiah spread his arms before the dark. He was breathing heavily, his white suit stained with blood. He closed his eyes, tipped back his head, and yelled, "Deep One! Bless me!"

It was as though everyone there collectively held their breath. Waiting . . . watching. I stayed low next to the trunk of the tree, but movement at my feet made me look down.

Mushrooms, sprouting up rapidly around my feet. A shudder went up my back, like a cold finger trailing along my spine. The wind howled around me, and with its howling came something horrifyingly familiar, a voice I'd heard too many times before.

But this time, It wasn't calling my name.

It was calling Jeremiah's.

The worshippers were murmuring. A tremor ran through the ground, and they began to shout. Jeremiah turned back to them, arms still spread. "You see? Do you all see? God is here! God has heard us! It has received our offering!" His wide-eyed, wild smile fell on Victoria. "And It will receive another."

I barely even had time to process what I was seeing as he dragged her up from the ground, screaming, fighting—and sliced her throat.

I had to swallow down the vomit that wanted to rise up in me again. Her blood spilled across the ground, and Jeremiah threw her into the dark, carelessly, roughly, her body flinging into the depths like a ragdoll.

Holy shit, I'd been wrong. I'd been so wrong. There was no saving her from that.

The ground rumbled again, a pulse thrumming beneath my feet. The air felt thick, sitting so heavy in my lungs that I had to desperately suppress the urge to cough. My body flushed cold as I realized that *something* was moving in the mine shaft. The shape of it was morphing, constantly changing—the darkness itself moved, like ink being stirred.

That ink was spreading, it was seeping out. Black tendrils tested the edges of the shaft's frame, reaching out into the air as if grasping for something. There was a gasp and a cry from one of the white-cloaks.

The murmurs passed through the crowd, "God is here. God is here."

They began to fall to their knees. As Jeremiah looked over them, the veins in the whites of his eyes turned red, like blood cracking to the surface. He faced the dark again, his chest heaving with the effort to breathe in the atmosphere's sudden thickness.

"Bless me, God," he said again. "Bless me."

The tendrils shot out. I clapped my hand over my mouth as they coiled around his limbs like snakes, moving rapidly, wrapping around every inch of skin as if cocooning him. He watched them with an expression somewhere between horror and fascination, and more of the crowd fell to their knees, throwing up their hands, crying aloud.

"God is here! The Deep One rises!"

But the God couldn't get out . . . It couldn't . . . surely It couldn't . . .

The tendrils enveloped Jeremiah's head. He jerked, and suddenly his mouth gaped open and the tendrils pushed inside him, down his throat, making it bulge as he choked. He bent backward, his spine curving to such an angle that he could look back on the congregation upside-down, his eyes rolled back in his head.

He began to rise off the ground, and I couldn't even fathom what the hell I was witnessing.

The black tendrils held him suspended in the air, pushing inside him with such violence that his chest enlarged and his throat swelled. His body began to twitch, then to shake, and black ooze leaked from his mouth . . . his ears . . . his *eyes* . . .

The rumbling stopped, and Jeremiah dropped heavily to the ground. All that remained was the rain, pouring around us. The tendrils were gone, disappeared inside him. No one spoke, no one got up. They merely extended their hands, trembling, toward Jeremiah's limp body.

Something seized me from behind, one hand clapped over my mouth and the other grabbed my wrist. I thrashed, panicking, but only until a deep voice whispered harshly in my ear, "No stabbing me this time, little wolf. We need to get the fuck out of here, *now*."

Zane. He dragged me up, giving no chance for protest or explanation. He was tense as hell and breathing hard.

Jeremiah began to rise. He raised his head from the ground, every movement a bizarre twitch. It reminded me of those things—those Gollums who had taken Marcus's body. But Zane didn't stop, no, he only moved faster. The last thing I saw of Jeremiah was him jerk fully to his feet, black goop seeping from his lips. He said something I couldn't hear, but from the way his lips moved, I could have sworn he said, "Someone is here."

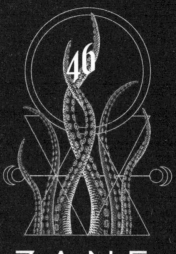

ZANE

OH, THIS WAS *fucked*.

Abelaum was fucked. Earth was fucked. We were absolutely fucked. But I wasn't about to stick around and wait for maximum fuckery, no sir. I was getting Juniper and myself the hell out of there and putting as much distance between us and that *thing* as possible.

I should have come looking for her sooner, but damn it, she liked having time alone and I wasn't trying to fucking smother her. My mistake—I left her alone for a couple hours, and I found her in the midst of the Libiri, watching Jeremiah-fucking-Hadleigh get possessed by a God. I wasn't leaving her alone for a second from here on. I was going to chain her to my goddamn wrist.

We reached the car, and I rummaged through her pockets for the keys. "Get in. Get in *now*."

She looked shell-shocked, her eyes wide. She was

far more confused than afraid, and I needed her to understand what the hell she'd just seen. I needed her to
understand why we were running.

"I couldn't save her," she said, her voice monotone,
deceptively void of emotion. "I couldn't . . . I wanted
to . . ."

"Save who?" I pressed the gas pedal to the floor the
moment we were off the dirt road. I felt far too tense to
be driving. It wasn't fast enough. God, the *smell* in those
woods. Rot and brine, blood and terror—a deep and ancient terror, the kind of thing that built up over centuries,
the residue of hundreds and *thousands* of suffering souls.

"Victoria," she said. "Jeremiah killed her. He made
the second sacrifice, Zane."

I slammed my palm against the steering wheel, wincing when it cracked beneath the impact. The God was
too close to getting out, far too close.

Juniper's eyes were on me, wide and uncertain.
"What the hell happened back there? What happened to
Jeremiah? Did you see it?"

Oh, I'd seen it. I'd seen the God's essence leech out of
the dark and seep inside Jeremiah. It was a mere *piece* of
the Deep One, a fragment and nothing more. There was
no way a mortal body could contain a God. Jeremiah
was likely already rotting from the inside out. But the
God's power would keep him moving, talking, killing. He
was a zombie to the Deep One's will, strengthened even
as he fell apart.

I hoped Leon had Raelynn far from here by now, hidden away. If Leon had any goddamn sense, he'd have

that woman locked in a bunker somewhere. The only thing standing between the Libiri and unleashing the God was one final sacrifice: Raelynn.

"Zane." Juniper's voice was firmer now. She'd gone from shock to determination. "What the fuck just happened?"

"Part of the God is in Jeremiah," I said. "Those sacrifices gave It enough strength to get a little bit of Its essence out of the mine and inside his body. It can live inside him like a parasite, using his body to get around. His body will break down, eventually—mortal flesh isn't built to hold power like that. But he'll be very, very dangerous until he does. Who knows how long the God can keep him alive?"

She gulped. "He'll go after Raelynn."

"All his focus is going to be on achieving the final sacrifice," I said. "And I'm not going to let him do that."

"How the hell are we supposed to fight him? What's his weakness?"

"Not *we*, Juniper. Me."

She was silent for a moment, her eyes blazing as she looked at me. "What the fuck do you mean?"

"You're not going after Jeremiah, not now. I will. I'll finish it."

Shock . . . then fury. The threads binding our beings together trembled with how angry she was. "Like hell you are. Not without me."

"You're not winning this argument, Juniper. Not this time."

I pulled into the yard at the house. The rain was

coming down hard, and I paused as I noticed the cluster of pale mushrooms near the front door. I crushed them underfoot before I followed Juniper inside.

She was laying out her guns, checking her ammo. I shook my head. "Juniper, I mean it. You're not coming."

"Yes, I am," she said firmly, reloading her pistol. I took the gun from her hands, set it down, and grasped her shoulders so she had to look at me. Her jaw was set, her gaze hard.

"Jeremiah isn't just a mortal man anymore," I said. "He has the God's strength. He'll be strong enough to rival me."

"Then you shouldn't go alone."

"I don't want to put you in danger, Juniper—"

"I've always been in danger!" she yelled, thrashing away from my hold. "I get it, the risk is higher now. I don't care! I'm not weak. I'm not . . . I'm not a fucking liability." Her fists were clenched, but her voice was shaking. "I'm not going to let you run off and do this alone. I can help. I'm not weak." Her eyes shone with tears she refused to let fall, and she growled furiously as she scrubbed her palm over them. "I'm not going to let you fight alone, Zane."

I took her face in my hands, relieved when she didn't try to pull away again. She closed her eyes, shaking in my hold as I kissed her forehead and said, "You're not weak, little wolf. You're not a liability, or a burden, or any other fucked-up self-deprecating shit your mind can come up with. But I need you to listen to me. Please. When you're with me, my first concern is always going to be to protect you. Always. I know you can handle yourself. I know how strong you are. I know you got by for years without me. That doesn't change my priorities."

She sniffed, shaking her head. I pulled her against me, wrapping my arms around her. I needed her to get it. I needed her to understand. I respected her strength, but regardless of her pride, I wasn't going to risk her like that. I wasn't going to let her face something that deadly.

"So what if he kills me?" she muttered. "My soul is yours. You'll take me to Hell. Dying would just put an end to this crazy shit—"

"Fuck that." My arms tightened around her. "Don't you fucking talk like that. We're not going to throw away your life."

She pressed her face against me, burying it so I couldn't see her, her words muffled. "My life isn't special, Zane, don't pretend like it is. I was never even meant to survive this long. I didn't have a fucking thing until . . ." She drew in a shaky breath. " . . . until I made a deal with you."

"Juniper—"

"I mean it!" She looked up, and she wasn't hiding the tears now. Fuck, it was jarring to see her cry. Physical pain had nothing on seeing that. "You've made me feel like there's a reason to even bother! You gave me eternity. You gave me hope that there's a chance to start over! A chance to have a life that isn't so fucked up . . . even if it isn't really life at all. You showed me places where I felt welcomed, where I didn't feel like everyone just thought of me as a freak. You . . . you wanted me. I don't care about the bargain, Zane, I care about *you*. I can't lose you. I can't. You let me feel like I found home." She sniffed, roughly rubbing her eyes again. "I love you, okay? You did it, you fucking did. You broke the wall down and fucking smashed it to bits. You said you wanted all of me, so there it is. You've got it. How the hell can I risk losing that?"

It was like she lit a fire in my chest, stoking the flames with every word out of her mouth. But before I could get a word out, she said quickly, "You don't have to say it. You don't have to, just because I did. It slipped out, I . . ." She shook her head. "You don't have to. I don't expect you to."

I tucked her hair back, wiping away a tear before it could roll down her cheek. "Juniper Kynes, I fully intend to spend eternity showing you just how much I love you. I'll dance in the rubble of that fucking wall forever. A demon won't use that word unless we mean it." I chuckled. "I let you lead when you need to, but I've been telling you all along, love." She bit her lip, hard, but I eased it away from her teeth with my thumb. "Listen to me: there are things out there that can take you from me. There are monsters and magic that can rip us apart." I took a deep breath, forcing myself to calm so I wouldn't hold her too tight. "You've fought your whole goddamn life to survive. But I'm fighting this one for you. I swore an oath to have you as mine. I gave you my sigil. I gave you my metal. You won't lose me. You can't fucking get rid of me, get it?"

She nodded, but I knew some part of her mind wouldn't let her believe it. She'd seen too much destroyed. She'd had too much taken away to accept that she had me, that she could keep me, that I was one thing she wasn't going to lose.

I wouldn't let it happen.

"You're not alone anymore," I said softly. "Let me do this. Let me keep you safe. And when this mess is over, we'll leave this damned town and do whatever we please. You've fought for your life, Juniper. You deserve to live out the rest of it without having to fight another day."

She leaned against my hand. There had been ecstasy in taking her soul, but this? This went beyond words. The magic that bound us together could never mimic this feeling; no bargain of the soul could ever come close to a declaration like love. And a mere word couldn't encompass what I felt for her—it couldn't describe the surety that she and I were meant to be entwined. The wild energy that made up our beings was magnetic, there was no pulling that apart.

I'd lived for hundreds of years, and I knew how rare that was.

I knelt down and kissed her hands. "Just this one time, Juniper. Lay down your weapons, and let me use mine."

She took a deep breath, and let it out with a shudder. She looked at me like she was trying to find a lie, like she was trying to find a reason to deny me. But I wasn't budging on this. No fucking way. I took care of what was mine.

"I'll let you fight," she finally said. "But you're not going alone. I'm going with you. I'll stay back, I'll stay hidden. But if something goes wrong, I need to *know*. I need to *be there*." Her eyes were desperate; they were pleading. "I'll keep my distance. I'm not afraid of them, Zane. There's only one thing I'm afraid of—and it's losing you."

I knew she wouldn't budge on this. At least this way, if things went wrong, she'd know immediately. It would give her a head start to run.

I nodded slowly. "You'll stay back. You'll stay hidden no matter *what happens*. Agreed?"

She nodded in return. "Don't you fucking die, Zane," she said. "Don't you dare."

I smiled. "You know I wouldn't disobey you."

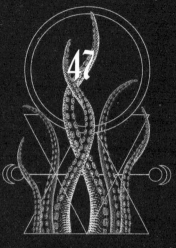

47

ZANE

THE SUN HAD set, and the smell of smoke was in the air. Something in Abelaum was burning; I could see the plume of smoke rising over the trees to the south. The air felt strange, it felt *charged*. Like a livewire sparking electricity through a pool of water.

We drove into Abelaum with the headlights off, and as we reached town, I spotted the cause of the smoke: the Food Mart on the corner of Main Street and 1st had been burned to the ground. I stared as we drove past, the parking lot closed off with ribbons of yellow tape.

Police were everywhere, and the sharp scent of blood and gasoline was in the air. As I glanced over, a body bag was lifted from the concrete and loaded into the back of the van.

"Shit is escalating fast," Juniper said softly.

"The God won't waste time," I said grimly. "Its

return to power is too close for It to start slacking. It's only going to get more vicious. More violent. And now It has Jeremiah to carry out Its will."

"Not for much longer," she muttered. I knew how badly she'd wanted to do it herself: she had wanted to end Jeremiah's life by her own hand, and I didn't blame her. But things had changed now, the danger was greater and far more urgent.

I needed to end this, and end it quickly.

Jeremiah had only a fragment of the Deep One's power, but even that made him a significant threat. The power contained in him had been palpable when I'd seen him in the woods, but it was also chaotic, difficult to grasp the true depth of.

I wasn't entirely sure what I'd be up against.

My own power was growing all the time, as all soul hunters' did. Every soul brought greater strength, and Juniper's had increased mine to levels I was still uncertain of. I rarely had a need to flex my full strength, so knowing what I was capable of at this point was difficult. But I sensed the changes in myself. Manipulating the energy and aether around me was easier than ever.

The whites of my eyes were darkening too. The golden irises I'd always had were deepening in color. If a demon grew strong enough, their eyes would turn black entirely.

Like the Archdemons. Like Callum.

I couldn't match beings like that yet. But damn, I hoped I was close. I was going to need it.

Everything just smelled wrong, and it got worse the closer we moved toward the Hadleigh house. Rain streaked over the windshield as we drove, the road briefly illuminated by a flash of lightning. I was glad for the rain; it would cool down my raging body temperature and keep Juniper better hidden.

When we reached the property, approaching it under the cover of darkness beneath the trees, we found it had changed since we'd last been there.

The huge lawn, usually pristinely trimmed, had grown long and wild. White mushrooms had sprouted up everywhere, so prolific there was a stringy, pale webbing spread across the lawn between the various clusters.

The driveway was packed with cars, and through the lit windows, I could see a crowd of people gathered in the living room. They were young men and women with tired, wide-eyed expressions. I spotted guns on the counter, but no one seemed ready for an attack. They were drinking beers, conversing quietly.

There was no sign of Jeremiah.

"I'm going to go find him," I said. Juniper nodded, her shotgun gripped tight in her hands. "If shit goes south, you *leave*. Understand?"

She narrowed her eyes. "If you need my help, then—"

"No," I said, crouching over her, my voice tight with the desperate hope she'd understand. "Juniper, if I can't kill him, then things are far worse than I thought. If I can't kill him, you need to get out of Abelaum. Get out of the country. Go as far away as you can."

She looked away, shaking her head. "I'm not making any promises, Zane."

It was the best I was going to get. She was smart, and

she knew what she was capable of. If it came down to it, she'd know when to run.

Even if it hurt.

Even if it meant leaving me to die.

"Stay hidden, and wait for me," I said. Crouching low, and moving fast, I made my way out of the trees and toward the house.

IT SMELLED EVEN worse inside.

Black patches of mold had grown on the walls, and the white carpet looked dingy and yellowed. I made my way down the hall, sniffing the air, assessing who all were in the house with me. There were eight humans in the living room, and half of them were deeply intoxicated.

"Tommy never should have gone with him," someone said, sniffling, a tremble in their voice. "I tried to tell him—"

"Sshh, shut *up*," another voice snapped. "Don't let him hear you talking like that. This is a bad time to start getting all sensitive about this shit, get it? We knew some of us would die. We've been told that from the beginning."

I eagerly licked my lips. Lives would indeed be lost— *all* of them. I still couldn't smell Jeremiah. There was just that overbearing stench of mold and rot tickling my nose. Maybe he was out. That at least gave me time to set up a lovely little welcome-home present for him.

Those eight humans didn't stand a chance. It was almost *too* easy. When I walked into the living room, their blank faces stared at me with utter confusion, unmoving. Their bodies tensed in their seats, their wide eyes blinking rapidly.

Not a single one of them had their weapons close at hand. And this was supposed to be Jeremiah's chosen few? What an embarrassment.

Slowly, one of the men stood. "Who the hell are you?"

I stretched my arms, gave a comfortable little groan, and said, "Me? Oh, I'm just a messenger."

They frowned, looking amongst each other in confusion. Some of them looked nervously at their weapons. More of them were getting to their feet.

"Messenger?" the man said. "What . . . what's the message?"

I cleared my throat, hands clasped politely behind my back. "Ah, give me a moment. I'll have to recite it from memory. Let's see: *To the evil human-sacrificing cunts that call themselves Libiri*"—I crossed the room before any of them could react, grabbed a man's head in my hands, twisted it, and ripped it off his body—"*fuck you.*"

Chaos erupted. They tried to reach their weapons, but humans were just so pitifully *slow*. I caught another, ripped open their throat, and flung their body across the room to crash against another one before he could make it out the door. Blood spattered across the walls, across the window, across the perfectly clean white couches.

There was something really satisfying about fresh blood against white cloth. It was honestly kind of poetic.

Within minutes, eight bodies lay at my feet. I cracked

my knuckles and waved out the window toward where I knew Juniper would be watching. I hoped she'd enjoyed the show, because there was more to come.

I got things tidied up. I moved the bodies up on the couch and smeared a little more blood around to make a lovely "*Welcome Home, J*" message on the wall. Then I took a seat, picking bits of flesh from beneath my claws, and waited for the guest of honor to walk in the door.

I didn't have to wait long.

Within minutes, I heard tires crunching on the gravel driveway. Tension knotted through my muscles, eager for what was to come. My foot tapped impatiently, the scent of the blood around me making my mouth water. Footsteps approached the front door—Jeremiah wasn't alone. At least three others were with him.

The door opened, and Jeremiah stepped inside, flanked by three men. The moment he saw me, he froze.

I smiled, wrapping my arm around the decapitated body beside me. "Hey, buddy. Welcome to the party."

ZANE

JEREMIAH'S PRESENCE SEEMED to swell in the space, pressing against the walls. He smelled rotten, vile—his scent wasn't remotely human anymore. When his eyes moved, they were too quick. They jerked from thing to thing, as if he was unable to take in all the things he was aware of at once.

"You're looking a little twitchy, Jeremiah," I said. "Feeling overwhelmed, perhaps?"

The men at his back were dressed in tactical gear: padded jackets, helmets, face shields, and of course, guns. They had their sights fixed on me, unwavering, far better prepared than their unfortunate comrades had been.

Jeremiah looked around—at the blood on the walls, the puddles seeping into the carpet, the intestines draped over the lampshade like cheerful party streamers. He took it all in, nodding slowly.

And he smiled.

"What do you think you know, demon?" The cadence of his speech was drastically different, easy to notice considering I'd followed him for a whole damn day. "How long have you been creeping around?"

"Long enough to know you're in over your head."

He narrowed his eyes. Recognition flickered in his gaze, and he said, "You were at the party. The . . . the bartender guy."

"Yeah, the one who gets all the pussy." I gave the body beside me a shove, pushing it away. The blood was getting cold and sticky. "Tell me, Jeremiah . . . how are your reflexes?"

I had already condensed the wall of energy in front of me. Right as his eyes widened in suspicion, I pushed it out, and it slammed into him and his men full-force. They were blasted backward against the wall, the impact so hard they burst straight through it, sending their bodies sprawling onto the lawn in a hail of splintered wood.

I chuckled as I got to my feet and strode over to the damaged wall. Jeremiah lay flat on his back on the grass, and two of his men were trying to roll over to their sides. The third seemed to have been knocked unconscious. Damn, and here I'd been worried. That blast probably shattered Jeremiah's ribs.

Or at least . . . it should have.

Maybe I got a little too cocky. Maybe I let my guard down way sooner than I should have. I walked across the lawn, ready to crush Jeremiah like the little bug he was.

But he leaped up, and he moved far faster than I'd thought possible. No human body should have been able to move that fast. His fist connected with my face, snapping my neck back—he gripped my shoulders, wrenched me down, and tried to follow up his fist with his knee. But I twisted, gripped his leg, and used it to wrench him to the ground.

His strength was shocking. He'd attacked me in a mere second, hitting me hard enough that I'd felt something crack. I tried to scramble into a better position and get on top of him, but he was grappling with me, somehow managing to hold me back.

"What—what kind of fucking—*freak* are you?" I snarled, squeezing his throat as he shoved against my face. His teeth were bared, his eyes were wild and bloodshot. Something thick and black dripped from his nose, and he snarled as he twisted, trying to switch our positions. I thrashed, breaking his grip and leaping back, putting some distance between us.

He got up, cracking his neck. He wasn't breathing hard; I couldn't smell any fear on him. Every inch of him was tense, his muscles bulging, veins rigid beneath his skin. He spat a thick glob of black stuff onto the ground, and I wrinkled my nose.

"So you're just fine with the whole rotting from the inside-out thing?" I said. "That's gross, dude. You smell."

He chuckled, shaking his head. "So carefree, aren't you? Not like the last demon I met. Honestly . . . I expected *him* to be creeping around out here. But you . . . what the hell is your game?"

"My game is simple: kill Rot Boy, go home, have a smoke. It's been a fun game so far."

I attacked again, but he was ready for me. He deflected my strike, slammed into my shoulder, and shoved me back, twisting my arm as he did. I barely managed to maneuver myself out of a nasty injury as I slipped away from him, pausing again to reevaluate my approach.

The popping sound of rapid gunfire sent me dodging back again, sprinting to avoid the bullets. Two of Jeremiah's men had found their feet, and they had their weapons aimed at me. It would take a hell of a lot of bullets to kill me, far more than they had. But enough bullets could still slow me down, and that was the last thing I needed.

Jeremiah was faster than I'd thought. *Stronger* than I'd thought.

I slipped around into the garden at the side of the house, and crouched down into the shadows. Footsteps ran past, with a second set walking slowly behind.

"You've run right past him, you blathering *fools.*"

Shit.

Jeremiah was on me before I could run again. I got my arm around his throat, gripping him tight as he flailed and tried to claw at my face. I squeezed his neck in my arm, until the breath was wheezing out of him and his movements became frantic. Fuck, he was hard to control. The strength I was using should have crushed a human's windpipe, and if that somehow didn't kill him, the lack of oxygen to his brain should have. But Jeremiah kept struggling. He thrashed his entire body against my hold, and I lost my footing, grappling with him on my knees—

More gunfire popped, and this time I couldn't dodge it. The bullets peppered my back, my neck. I flinched at the sting, and Jeremiah took advantage immediately. He twisted free and shoved himself back, right as more bullets peppered my back.

I could take out the two gunmen quick enough, but Jeremiah . . .

He didn't give me a chance for that.

He kicked me in the chest, so hard and so fast that it slammed me back through the garden wall. Bricks collapsed around me and I dodged his incoming fist, caught his wrist, and snapped it. But there was no satisfying scream of pain, no hesitation. It was like the pain didn't even register for him, and that caught me off guard. Off guard enough that his next strike made contact.

He slammed his fist against my back, right where one of the bullets had pierced into me. It was far more fucking painful than it should have been.

I tried to dodge back out of range and get some space between us, but I suddenly felt as if lead was pumping through my veins, every limb unbearably heavy. I shoved Jeremiah away, stumbled, and clutched at my shoulder where he'd hit me. But it hadn't just been a punch: my fingers encountered something small, something metal, sunk deep in my skin. And fuck, it was *burning*.

"I always knew my father wasn't using that thing the way he should have been." Jeremiah laughed, watching me gasp as I tried to pull the wretched metal thing out of my flesh. My fingers kept slipping on my own blood. Whatever it was, it was sucking up my strength so fast that my vision was darkening at the edges. Fuck . . . fuck this was bad . . . what the hell had he done?

"Tell me, demon: did you happen to leave something behind on Halloween? A trinket, perhaps? Something you stole, something you buried before you killed my father?"

Something stolen . . . something buried . . . *fuck*. The amulet Kent had worn. I hadn't even thought of it since then. I'd been so distracted—Juniper had buried it, and neither of us had thought to go back for it.

"Ahh, so it was you then," Jeremiah said, acknowledging the stunned look on my face. I glared at him and swallowed hard, trying to muster up any strength I could to go after him again. But the effects of that damned little amulet were nauseating. I couldn't even see straight.

"Boys, give him a few more."

The gunfire rang in my ears, and this time the bullets hit my chest and one struck my face. Their aim was terrible and I wanted to tell them so, but the sarcastic remark died on my tongue. I lurched, coughed, and spat up blood.

Oh, this was bad. Very, *very* bad.

I wasn't healing. I wasn't fucking healing.

I tried to grasp the amulet again, but when I reached for it, I could only feel its edge. It had sunk *deeper* into my back—it was burrowing into my flesh like a fucking leech. The damn thing was made to sap the strength of supernatural beings, and it hungered for it like a starving animal.

Jeremiah seized my throat and dragged me. I clawed

at his arm, leaving deep, jagged cuts in his flesh, but the gashes didn't seem to bother him in the slightest. He hauled me up, both fists knotted in my shirt, and pinned me against a tree.

"And here I'd been blaming the wrong demon all along," he said. He chuckled as he watched me struggle, thick black goop staining his teeth as he grinned at me. "I thought Leon killed my father, but he's too distracted doting on that little sacrificial lamb, isn't he?" He slammed me back so my shoulder struck the tree again and the amulet did too, pressing it in even deeper.

I blacked out for a moment. I felt like I was falling. When I dazedly returned to consciousness, Jeremiah was glaring at me with a look that was far too clever, far too shrewd. "Who do you serve?" he said softly. "Whose bargain are you fulfilling?"

I spat in his face, grinning as it hit his cheek. "Fuck you. You're a pathetic boy hiding behind a pathetic God. You can't even slow me down without some old witch's trinket."

He released his hold on me, and I fell to my knees. I didn't hear him give the order this time—the bullets struck me without warning.

"Tell me your name," he said calmly, as the gunfire finally stopped. "And who you serve."

The influence of the God slammed against my brain, screaming to get in. But It couldn't get my answers by force, not even as weakened as I was. Gods couldn't invade a demonic mind like They could with humans. I just laughed as I shut It out.

"How long can you keep this up, Rot Boy?" I said. "Your body can't take that parasitic God flexing so much strength forever." His face twitched, fury warping him as he leaned close to me. "Go on and keep trying. Your body will break down before you manage to kill me."

His expression turned cold. He tipped his head, squatted down, and reached out his hand to pluck at the tear his guards' bullets had ripped through my shirt. He narrowed his eyes, staring at me hard, as if he could find the answers he sought written on my flesh.

I stiffened. Shit. *Shit.*

I grabbed his wrists but he pinned me again, wrestling me to the ground. My limbs were locking up, the burning pain growing worse the more I tried to fight. Jeremiah's eyes fogged over, a thick mist clouding them as he shoved my arms down and ripped my shirt open.

He laughed, and it was the most vile, unnatural sound I'd heard come out of a human. When a God laughed, you could hear the screams of all the souls They'd taken, crying out in such agony it made one sick just to hear it. Those screams were in Jeremiah's laughter, too.

He traced his fingertips, blackened with rot, over my shoulder—over the scarred letters of Juniper's name. "So she's back after all," he said softly. "Victoria was right. Dear Juniper has come back to Abelaum . . . and got herself a demon."

"She's not here," I growled. "She's not even in Abelaum. Why do you think she'd come anywhere near this place?"

"Why indeed?" He pulled back his fist, and his

knuckles slammed against my face. I shook my head, dazed, and Jeremiah got off me, leaving me there on the ground. He paced around me, raising his voice. "Why indeed would Juniper Kynes come back to Abelaum? Could it be that she's a vengeful little bitch who doesn't know when she should just *fucking lay down and die*?" He screamed the last few words. He was staring into the trees, scanning the edges of the yard.

Fuck, Juniper had better be running. I knew she could see what was happening, and I could only hope she didn't get any brave ideas.

"I don't know what you're rambling on about," I said, shoving myself up to my knees. "You're getting boring. Try smashing my face again to spice things up."

But he didn't care about me anymore. His fingers twitched bizarrely as he continued to stare into the darkness, his breathing growing heavier. "I can smell her out there. Oh, Juniper, *Juniper*." He laughed. "I can fucking smell you."

My body felt so heavy. So goddamn heavy and weak. I had to get to my feet and find a way to dig the amulet out.

"She's out there," Jeremiah said coldly. "Find her. Find her, and bring her to me."

"Should we kill her?" one of the gunmen asked.

"No." Jeremiah shook his head. "Bring her alive. She needs to learn what happens when you defy God."

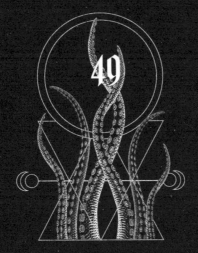

JUNIPER

THE CLOUDS WERE thick overhead, and I could barely see anything in the dark. The floodlights around the outside of the house were the only illumination as Jeremiah and his cronies launched backward through the wall in an explosion of shattered glass and splintered wood. But after that, the fight was hidden on the opposite side of the house. All I could hear was the destruction: crumbling brick, snapping wood . . . and gunfire.

Guns couldn't bring Zane down. It wasn't the bullets that concerned me. What worried me was how long it had been. I'd watched Zane annihilate a room of eight people within two minutes. Humans weren't difficult to kill.

If Jeremiah was truly a match for him . . . if Jeremiah was *stronger* than him . . . I didn't know what the hell I'd do.

I gripped my shotgun closer, my heart pounding faster as the minutes dragged on. I hated hiding there in the dark like a coward. But I'd agreed to let Zane handle it. I had to be patient. I had to be smart about this.

The floodlight at the back of the house flicked on. I sat up, narrowing my eyes as several figures walked into the open.

Two armed gunmen, thoroughly armored, were headed straight toward me, their guns at the ready. Behind them . . .

Behind them was Jeremiah, dragging Zane.

It felt like cold water had been dumped over my head. My breath caught, sick disbelief gripping my stomach.

"Oh, Juniper!" Jeremiah yelled, his voice high-pitched with wild, reckless excitement. "Come out, Juni! It's been so long!"

Shit, shit, shit! I began to creep backward into the trees, deeper into the darkness and the thick underbrush. I couldn't assess his injuries from this distance, but there was blood smeared across Zane's body. I had no idea how much of it was his.

Zane was one of the strongest beings I knew: the only thing I'd ever seen best him was that Archdemon, Callum. And I couldn't believe Jeremiah was that strong. If he was . . .

If he was, how the hell could I take him down?

The gunmen were quickly encroaching on the trees. I couldn't see Jeremiah now, but I could still hear him as he called out, "You can't hide, Juniper. I know you're here. Why don't you come out and play? Your demon couldn't handle the game. Why don't you come try to help?"

There was a sudden, ragged cry of pain, and my heart lurched. Fuck, what the hell had Jeremiah done to him? I crouched low and backed up even further. The gunmen had flicked on their flashlights, attached to the front of their vests. Those guns were no joke either. Jeremiah had them well-armed and well-equipped.

The bushes weren't thick enough to hide me from their light. I ducked behind a tree, my back pressed to the trunk, my shotgun ready. I took a few slow, deep breaths—I had to stay calm. Jeremiah was calling my name, his voice getting louder and more wild with every passing second.

"Juniper! The Deep One misses you, Juni!"

Laughter followed, sending a shudder up my back. My mouth was dry, and my cold hands shook on the gun. Behind me, the footsteps came ever closer, snapping twigs and crunching leaves as they closed in on my hiding place.

Zane would want me to run. He'd demanded it, he'd insisted that if Jeremiah somehow overpowered him, then I had to *go*. But I couldn't make myself do it. The very idea was repulsive. I could run from here, but what then? I'd go back to how I'd been before: running constantly, rarely resting, always looking over my shoulder. I'd go back to clawing my way through every day, surviving only for the sake of it, with no hope, no future, no light.

Ahead of me, in the darkness, there was a blur of red. Wide eyes stared me down. The Watcher waited for my fear. It waited for me to fall apart. I had no doubt it could hear my pounding heart and taste my adrenaline rush in the air.

I'm sure it would have loved to see me run.

I clenched my jaw. I'd promised myself I was done running. Zane had come back for me when my life was on the line; I wasn't about to abandon him, not now, not after we'd come this far.

A home isn't just a place—sometimes a home is a person; sometimes a home is flesh and blood.

And I'd defend the home I'd found to my last breath.

Slowly, carefully, I eased my shotgun back into its holster on my back and took out my knife from its sheath. This wasn't the time to go in guns blazing. One missed shot in the darkness and they'd know exactly where I was. I had to take out these two as quietly as I could, and then . . .

Then I'd figure out what to do about Jeremiah.

I huddled low to the ground, my back still against the tree, as one of the gunmen passed by my hiding place. The other one was about a hundred yards away, his back to me, shining his light into a thick tangle of bushes. The man's head and face were protected, but there was a small gap beneath his helmet. In the dim light, I caught a flash of bare skin: the back of his neck was exposed.

I rose up, stepped behind him, and jabbed the blade sideways into his throat.

He made a small sound, a whimpering gurgle as he collapsed against me. God, he was heavier than I expected, I could barely hold him up. I could only ease him slowly down, and drag his body under some bushes as quickly as I dared.

"Hey, you hear that?" the other guy shouted. I remained crouched, behind the tree again, the man bleeding out at my feet. "Hey, Anthony! Anthony?"

The footsteps came rapidly closer. His light swung dangerously close to my shoe, and I crept around one side of the tree as he came around the other.

"Oh shit . . . shit!" His light fell on the dead man and he began to rapidly back away. "Hey, J—"

He backed right into me.

I tried to stab him in the same spot, but my aim was slightly off. The knife ricocheted off the side of his helmet and he flailed, using the gun to try to strike me. But I gripped tight to his back, arms around his neck, and my weight was enough to throw him off balance. We collapsed backward, him on top, and his body knocked the air from my lungs. I gasped desperately, still clinging to him, refusing to let go. I began to stab frantically, wildly, but the knife couldn't penetrate his jacket, and he started yelling.

"Jeremiah! She's here, she's fucking—agh—"

"Just fucking *die*," I hissed as I sunk the knife deep into his neck, finally finding the soft spot. His blood spurted over my hand, the warm spatter flecking my face. I shoved him off and kept low, trying to see what the hell Jeremiah was doing now.

I couldn't see him.

I looked around nervously, scanning the trees. The Watcher had come close now. I never saw the damn thing move, it was just there, right behind me, standing over the body of the dying man. Its wide eyes moved slowly between me and him, as if assessing the better prey.

Crouched on the ground, I held out my bloody knife toward it. "Don't you try anything, you fucker," I whispered. "There will be plenty of fear for you to feed on tonight, but it won't be mine."

The creature's eerie eyes locked on mine. Just from looking at it, fuzziness was creeping up the edges of my vision. Panic was swelling in my chest like a balloon. But I kept backing away. The Watcher ducked down, its long red fingers curled around the dying man's skull as he stared up at it in horror. Slowly, it leaned closer, and there was a bizarre popping sound as its jaw began to open wide . . . then *wider* . . .

It took his *whole head* in its mouth.

I sprinted for the edge of the trees. Hopefully that would keep the monster occupied for a while. I began to crawl as I came up to the edge of the lawn, searching the yard for Jeremiah. It wasn't hard to spot him: he was crouched over Zane, his hand locked tight around my demon's throat.

I saw red. I stood, tucked away the knife, and pulled out the shotgun. It was fully loaded, and I had more ammo in my bag. If I had to put every last bullet straight into Jeremiah's skull to kill him, then that's what I'd do.

But he stood and faced me, right as I was about to shoot. He grinned and lifted his hand—dripping blood onto the grass.

Zane's blood. My demon's eyes were wide, their

golden light dulled, his lips parted as he gasped for breath. There was a roaring in my ears like ocean waves, a sea of dread rushing to drown me.

Jeremiah was muttering something I couldn't hear. I aimed right for his head.

"What the fuck did you do to him?" I yelled. "*What did you do?*"

"Careful, Juniper." He smeared the blood over his face, casually sucking a fingertip clean. "I've made your demon useful."

I looked down. For the first time, I noticed the strange ring around Zane, the grass burned down. More burn marks formed lines through the ring, creating a bizarre shape encircling his body.

The grass was still smoldering. In fact, the smoke was beginning to increase, but it didn't seem to be from any flames. The smoke was rising from the ground itself.

"What the fuck . . ." Plumes of black smoke rose from the ground, ashy and harsh as I inhaled it. Jeremiah stepped back, still grinning wildly as the smoke obscured him. I was coughing, my throat burning. I was about to start firing blindly into the smoke, but Zane turned his head to look at me and tried to lift his hand.

"Go, Juniper." His voice was rough, tight with pain. "It's a Reaper . . . he's summoning a Reaper . . . go . . ."

The smoke obscured him too. Then in the dark billowing smoke, something moved.

Something *massive*.

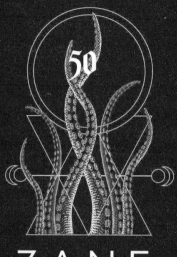

ZANE

THE PAIN ONLY got worse.

My entire body throbbed with pain, every muscle clenching, my limbs like heavy stones. That sharp, burning agony where the amulet had sunk into me was like a fiery-hot knife jabbed into my back—and not in a fun way. There was nothing even remotely enjoyable about this pain, despite my best attempts to make myself feel a little better.

I couldn't heal. Every ounce of my strength was sapped away, and my blood was seeping away with it. Jeremiah had sent his men after Juniper—they were walking straight into their deaths if she was still back there in the trees. He crouched over me, and in my blurred vision, all I could see was his smiling face, teeth stained with black rot.

"Bullets are expensive," he said, casual as fuck as

he looked down at my broken body. He was muttering, not talking to me so much as he was talking to himself. "And goddamn does it take a lot of them to even make you fuckers flinch. The amulet worked better than I expected . . . but there's too much risk . . ."

"Fuck you," I growled. "Fuck you and your fucking monologuing."

Perhaps I was lucky he ignored me. "But you know what's better than bullets and tiny charms? A Reaper."

He may as well have kicked me in the gut; I felt as stunned as if he had. Jeremiah shouldn't have even known what a Reaper was. They were Hell's executioners—massive, intelligent monstrosities with whom demons had formed a tentative pact. If a demon ever became so unruly that the Council decided to destroy them, a Reaper would be called in to do the job.

I laughed, but the sound was choked up with pain. "You're . . . fucking psychotic . . . if you think . . . you're going to get a Reaper involved."

"You think I can't?" His foot ground down on my chest. "Who do you think I *am*, demon?"

"You're just some pathetic—" Pain or not, I wasn't going to shut up. But what followed next wasn't pain. Not exactly. It felt as if something cracked open my head and wriggled inside the crevices, wrapped itself around my brain and began to *squeeze*.

Unbidden visions of a long dark tunnel flashed through my head. Visions of blood—of viscera—the sound of a thousand voices screaming in unison, in agony. At the end of the tunnel, a face . . . a figure . . .

draped in light and color, covered in a thousand blinking eyes, constantly morphing, ever-changing . . . tightening Its hold . . .

I forced It back, but he'd made his point clear: it wasn't *Jeremiah* who knew anything about Reapers.

It was the God.

His fingers poked and prodded my wounds, smearing the blood over my chest. "Demonic blood calls a Reaper to do its duty. I'm sure it won't mind if the blood doesn't belong to its intended victim. It can have you too, as a treat, once Leon is dealt with."

I was merely the offering. Leon stood between Jeremiah and Raelynn, but not for long. Leon couldn't win against a Reaper.

Jeremiah was going to execute him. He was going to kill Leon, and he was using me to do it. My nails dug uselessly into the grass, clawing at the dirt. I would have rather died. I would sooner let myself be destroyed than be the catalyst to Leon's death.

But there was nothing I could do. *Nothing.*

The haze clouding my vision became darkness. I was too weak now to even manage to send myself back to Hell. I didn't have the strength to open a gateway and escape this. Energy was gathering around me, Jeremiah's muttered words calling into the aether, beyond Earth, into the deepest depths of Hell.

He shouldn't have known the words to do it. No human being could.

Suddenly, even through the dark and the pain, I heard her. I could sense her near. I could smell her.

Juniper.

"What the fuck did you do to him? *What did you do?*"

I should have known better than to think she'd run. My little wolf didn't run. But fuck, she needed to. She couldn't possibly understand what was about to happen.

"Careful, Juniper." Jeremiah chuckled. "I've made your demon useful."

My nose filled with smoke, harsh and thick. It felt like a hand had reached between my ribs and was squeezing my insides, wrenching them around and tying them into knots. Flashes of light and feral growls emanated from the darkness thickening around me, and I managed to turn my head. Juniper stood there, wide-eyed and blood-stained, her shotgun aimed.

Fuck, it hurt to even try to speak. "Go, Juniper." My voice grated out of my throat, my tongue swollen. "It's a Reaper . . . he's summoning a Reaper . . . go . . ."

Then the darkness obscured her, and something massive moved through the smoke above me.

It was almost funny. All these years I'd been so determined not to do anything to piss the Council off, yet there I was, under the claws of a Reaper anyway.

Fucking hell.

There was a sound of cawing crows in the darkness, and the temperature dropped until my breath formed clouds in the smoky air. Worms and beetles crawled out of the ground beside me, frantically scurrying away as frost formed over the grass. The outline of a huge, bat-like wing moved over me.

Five blinking eyes, emitting a strange silvery light from behind the dark shroud that covered its face, looked down at me. Its voice was cold and deep, vibrating in my bones as it rumbled, "Hello, little demon. Do you submit to death?"

I sighed heavily. "No, unfortunately, I don't. Actually, I'd like to lodge a complaint. Killing me is . . . uh . . . severely uncalled for."

The Reaper chuckled, the sound unpleasant enough to make me shudder. Hundreds of sharp teeth hung from its neck, like jewels: trophies from its victims. They rattled together as it laughed, its armor of stone and black metal groaning as it moved. "Is that so? And yet, an Ancient Lord has called me with your flesh and blood."

"It's not his blood I've called you to spill," Jeremiah said, his voice far too loud for such a small, insignificant mortal. The Reaper's eyes jerked over to him and Jeremiah flinched, rightly so. At least he still had the sense in him to be afraid, regardless of what the God urged him to do.

"Not his?" the Reaper growled. "Then why, Ancient Lord, have you called my name? A Reaper does not appreciate its time being used frivolously."

"There's another demon," Jeremiah said. "His name is Leon. He's guarding someone, a mortal woman. I need him removed from her side. I need him broken."

The Reaper rumbled again—whether it was chuckling or merely breathing, I couldn't be sure. "Break him? And why would I not kill him, Ancient Lord? A Reaper arrives to take a life. I will not be denied that."

Jeremiah smiled, the expression twitching on his face. "Of course not. You may have the demon at your feet, as an offering. Once the other one has been broken, I'll take him for myself. But you can have this one when the job is done."

Great. I was a fucking bargaining chip between a Reaper and God—when it came to "places I wanted to be," this landed solidly last.

At least Juniper was gone. She'd run when the Reaper arrived, and it was my one sense of relief in this mess. Guns and knives wouldn't bring a Reaper down. She wouldn't have stood a chance.

Once the Reaper killed me, the bond between Juniper and I would be broken. Her soul would be free again. Maybe she'd find another being to take her to Hell; I hoped she did. A woman like her was too much for this world, too much for one mere mortal life. She needed more. She needed her freedom beyond this Earth.

Fuck, that hurt more than I'd thought it would: the melancholy, the . . . the loss. I wasn't afraid of dying—I hated leaving Juniper behind. I hated knowing that Leon would either die fighting this Reaper, or be broken and forced back under the Hadleigh's control. I hated that I'd failed to protect either of the beings I cared for most.

Juniper would survive; my little wolf would find a way. That was my only comfort.

"We Reapers are not servants to be given tasks," the Reaper growled. "But out of respect for an Ancient One, I will oblige your request. The demon, Leon, will be broken, and I will return for this one." It leaned down, its silver eyes gazing into mine. "You say you will not sub-mit to death, demon. But your body is poisoned. What a shame you will not be able to fight me, but you will be an easy meal."

A cold wind swirled around me, dissipating the lin-gering smoke and the Reaper with it. The night was eerily silent: no crickets chirped, not even the wind moved. Jeremiah walked back up beside me, casually picking at his teeth. "Too bad about your little bitch running away." He looked down at me with a cruel smile. "Did you think she'd save you? Running is what she's always done best. She'll run, and run . . ." His eyes hardened. "But you'll never escape a God."

He began to walk away. I was so goddamn weak I could barely lift my head to see him go. I couldn't run. I could only lie there and wait for my death to return.

"Personally," Jeremiah said, as he kept walking, "I hope she comes back. I hope she tries to fight the Reaper for you. I'd stay to watch the slaughter but . . . I have a sacrifice to attend to." He turned, looking back at me. His eyes were fogged, and when he spoke, his voice wasn't his at all.

"When I return, demon, I will be free. And it will be a very different world. It will be a world where no mat-ter where she runs, Juniper Kynes will never escape me again."

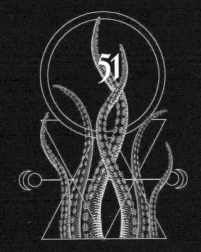

JUNIPER

JUNIPER KYNES WILL never escape me again.

Yeah, we'll see about that, bastard.

I'd watched everything from a distance, hidden behind the stone shed where we'd killed Kent. There was a chain on the door now, so I couldn't get in, but I'd needed *something* between me and that massive monster Jeremiah had summoned. The Eld, the Watcher, the Gollums—they were all bad enough. But this creature was no mere monster, it wasn't just a beast.

It was intelligent, and it was dangerous as hell if it regarded something a God had told it to do as merely a *request*.

I hated to keep hiding there, but even after Jeremiah had left, I waited. I didn't trust that the bastard wasn't watching from somewhere nearby, or that he didn't have other gunmen posted up somewhere. Zane lay still for

HARLEY LAROUX

several minutes before he began to struggle as if to get up. He kept reaching for his back, clawing at it as if something there was hurting him.

My hands shook, and my throat tightened as I watched. It made me sick to see him like that. Jeremiah hoped I'd come back to fight the Reaper, and he was going to get his fucking wish. If it could bleed and draw breath, then I could kill it.

I'd find a way.

Finally, after enough time had passed that I was almost certain no one was watching, I moved in.

Zane's eyes were closed, his breathing weak and far too slow. He was riddled with bullets, the wounds still bleeding. None of his wounds had even begun to heal. My hands hovered over him with uncertainty, furious tears making my eyes sting.

"What did he do to you? Fuck . . ." I brushed my fingers over his face, over the blood drying on his skin—and his eyes fluttered open.

"I should have known." He tried to smile, but it turned into a wince of pain. He lifted his hand and I caught it, holding his bloodied fingers against my face. "You couldn't just do the safe thing and stay away, could you?"

"Fuck no," I hissed. "As if I'd fucking leave you. Don't be ridiculous."

He shook his head. "You can't fight a Reaper alone, Juniper . . ."

"Watch me! Don't you dare tell me to go again: I won't. Just tell me how I can help you."

The few words he'd said had left him out of breath. He was silent for a minute before he managed to say, "The amulet . . . the one Kent had. Do you remember?"

I nodded, and a sudden stab of terror pierced into me. "Yeah. I buried it . . . I left it behind . . ."

Fuck. No, no, no . . .

"Jeremiah used it," he said. Slowly, painfully, he clenched his teeth and rolled over to his side. There on his back, beside his shoulder blade, there was something swollen beneath his skin. Horrifying bruises were concentrated around the area. "Stabbed me . . . I can't heal." He lay his head down, eyes closed. "Cut it out . . . cut deep."

It had been my mistake. *My* mistake had led to this. I'd left the amulet behind. I'd forgotten about it entirely. I pulled out my knife, shaking my head, cold guilt washing over me. "Zane, I'm so sorry. I forgot . . . I completely forgot it . . ."

"So did I." This time, he managed to smile. "Doesn't matter, Juni. Don't . . . don't berate yourself. Go on, love. Cut it out."

I grit my teeth, set my blade against his swollen skin— and cut.

Zane shuddered, but other than that, he didn't react as I cut open the wound. The wretched little amulet was deep; it twisted my stomach when I had to keep cutting deeper, digging the blade in until it hit metal.

"Ah, *fuck*," Zane hissed as I finally got my fingers on the amulet and tugged it free. The moment the metal was out of him, goose bumps ran over his skin, the bullet wounds pulsing like tiny heartbeats. He groaned, pressing his forehead against the grass. "Fuck, that is . . . extremely . . . unpleasant . . ."

I stared at the bloody bit of metal in my hand. It was hot, almost too hot to touch. "Does this work against more than just demons, Zane?"

He pushed himself up from the ground, head swaying dizzily. "Yeah. It would have an effect on most monsters . . . especially now." He winced as he stretched his arms and reached for his back. "That thing absorbed a hell of a lot of power from me. It uses the power it absorbs to make itself stronger. It's fucking dangerous."

I nodded, my mind turning. "Good. Perfect. Look, I know this is gonna suck, but . . ." I held it out toward him. "I need you to crush it."

He looked at the amulet like I'd just offered him a literal pile of shit. "Why?"

I tapped the muzzle of the shotgun on my back. "I need it small enough to fit in there. Jeremiah was so damn cocky, he left us a weapon without even realizing it." I grinned. "When the Reaper comes back, it's getting a face full of metal."

His expression was serious as he looked at me. "It won't be easy, Juniper. I've only heard of Archdemons killing Reapers, and that was during the wars."

"I don't need it to be easy. I just need it to work."

"Fuck . . . alright." He held out his hand, his broken claws slowly starting to regrow. "Let's get this over with."

I dropped the amulet into his hand, and his eyes immediately rolled back. He grit his teeth, inhaled sharply, and curled his shaking fingers around the metal. I hated to ask for it. I hated to make him hurt even more than he already was.

But when the Reaper returned, there was a good chance we were going to die. If there was anything I could do to reduce that chance, I had to do it. I wasn't going to go down without fighting.

Part of me already felt like it was too late. Jeremiah had sent that Reaper after Leon. He intended to take Raelynn tonight, and the last sacrifice would be made. Who could stop him now? The witch and her Archdemon? Did even *they* stand a chance?

Maybe it was over. Maybe we were witnessing the last breaths of a world about to fall to an ancient God. Maybe the Libiri would have what they wanted after all.

But I wasn't going to sit there and wait for death. I'd rather go out running toward it, arms open, than sit in the dark and wait to be killed.

"Here." Zane tossed the amulet toward me, shaking his hand as if burned. "Hopefully that will work."

I plucked up the bit of metal from the grass, now crushed small enough to fit in my shotgun. "It'll have to work. It's the only thing I can think of right now."

"If the Reaper would just wait a few days to come back, we could give it a real fight," Zane said. He was staring at his own shaking hands with complete exasperation. "So fucking weak. Now would be a really good time to . . . "

He stopped, his eyes fixing on something behind me. I looked back, heart pounding, ready to shoot.

But what he'd seen was a light, glowing in the upper window of the Hadleigh house. A shadow moved past the window and I frowned, but Zane was already on his feet.

"A soul," he said. "Now would be a really good time to claim another soul."

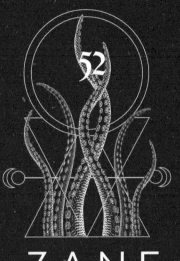

ZANE

JUNIPER STAYED CLOSE by my side as I limped into the house, guarding my back with her gun at the ready. She gasped when she saw the gruesome art I'd adorned the living room with: the gore spattered across the furniture, the blood on the walls and carpet.

"Damn, that's . . . wow . . ." She paused, having stepped onto something that looked like a liver. It probably *was* a liver.

"Jealous of my artistic talents?" I said. "I'd say I'm the next Jackson Pollock."

She shook her head. "Maybe if Pollock had a baby with Charles Manson."

We crept toward the back of the house, where I'd seen someone through the window. I could hear their pounding heart; I could smell their fear—they must have been hiding back there for hours. With the amulet torn out of me, my body was working wretchedly hard to try to heal, and it was making me dizzy. My body was a balloon and my head was an iron weight, making every step difficult. But there was no time for rest, no time for sleep. Thunder rumbled, and rain began to tap against the windows in the hall.

If I couldn't rest to recover my strength, then I needed something else. Something immediate.

I needed a soul, and I frankly didn't care how I got it. The Council would have to forgive me for bending the rules just this once.

I tried not to think of Leon. I tried not to think of what it would mean to be "broken" by a Reaper. He'd sooner die than submit to anything or anyone, but stubbornness can only do so much.

The house shook, but it wasn't with thunder this time. I paused, and Juniper looked at me in confusion—right before an awful, unnatural cry pierced the night.

"It's coming back," I said. "The Reaper is coming back." The lamps in the hall began to flicker rapidly, and a layer of ice stretched over the windows. Suddenly, with a pop and a shatter of thin glass, the lightbulbs in the hall all burst.

"It took down Leon." Those words felt too thick in my mouth. They were poison, so bitter I wanted to spit them out. "It took him down. Fuck."

"We'll look for him, Zane," Juniper said. "We're going to get the fuck out of here, and we'll find him. Both him and Raelynn. We're not letting the Libiri have this."

"I admire your hope, Juniper."

Cracks formed in the ice as it coated the windows. I wanted to shatter the glass, I wanted to rip this place apart. Leon was out there somewhere, probably on the verge of death. I had to get to him somehow, but right then, I was damn near helpless. The thought of his life being snuffed out, shattering the bond we'd had for so long, enraged me to the point of madness.

I grabbed a decorative vase and hurled it toward the wall with a cry so loud it rattled the glass.

Juniper gripped my arm, yanking me back as hard as she could to make me look at her.

"I only have hope because you gave it to me," she said fiercely. "You gave me hope when I had *none*, Zane. Jeremiah told the Reaper not to kill Leon. We'll get to him. He's strong."

I brushed my claws over her face, tucking back her hair. It was wild and tangled, a mane around her face. As beautiful as I'd ever seen her. "But I'm not. I'm not strong enough to protect you, Juniper. I'm sorry."

She grasped my hand and held it tight against her face, her dark eyes hard. "I don't need your strength, Zane. I just need you. Don't fucking leave me."

Her storm hadn't lost its strength, not even now, not even with death bearing down on us. I pressed my forehead to hers, her eyes locked on mine in the dark. "Never."

Another roar split the night, and she took a deep breath. "Let's keep moving. We need to get you that soul."

We found a locked door at the back of the house—an easy obstacle to get past. The lights had all been turned off in the bedroom beyond. Whoever was hiding there seemed to have realized they weren't alone, and had plunged the room into darkness.

"Come out, Meredith." Juniper shut the door behind us. There was a shadow on the other side of the bed, and it gasped sharply when Juniper spoke. "We know you're here."

Slowly, on the other side of the bed, a woman stood. Her white blouse and skirt were disheveled, her blonde hair messy, her face pinched into an expression somewhere between terror and fury. She looked between the two of us, wiping her hands repeatedly on her skirt.

"Get away," she hissed. "You . . . you *monsters*!" She jabbed her finger accusingly—not at me, but at Juniper beside me. "You've ruined everything, you *bitch*! Victoria offered you! *She made her offering*!" Her voice increased in volume and in pitch, nearly hysterical. "My daughter . . . my beautiful daughter . . . she did her duty." Suddenly she screamed, seized a mug from the bedside table, and launched it at us. It exploded against the wall, shattering porcelain to the floor.

"Your daughter is dead," Juniper said coldly. "Soon, your son will be too. Did you all think there'd be no consequences? Did you think no one would ever try to stop you?"

Meredith sneered, looking at Juniper with disgust. "Imagine a pathetic girl like you, shunning your destiny. No future to speak of. A trash girl from a trash family." She shook her head. "To think you're still standing here, while my daughter . . . while my daughter is . . ."

I wasn't going to stand there and listen to her talk to Juniper like that. I would have happily ripped out her tongue, but she still needed it.

She needed it to make a deal.

I lunged across the room, seized her by the throat and pinned her to the wall. She shrieked, cursing as she clawed uselessly at me. The house rumbled again, creaking with the force of the Reaper's supernatural cry. We were running out of time.

The Reaper would be here within moments. I had to make this quick.

"Death is coming for you too, Meredith," I growled, snapping my teeth near her face. "Which murderous beast would you rather face? The monster your son has released, or the monster your son has become? Or . . . would you rather face me?"

Her eyes widened, darting between me and Juniper in confusion. I grinned, letting her get a good look at the fangs. "All I need is for you to agree. Offer me your soul, and I won't kill you."

"What good is a demon's word?" she snapped, but I could see the desperation in her eyes.

"I swear it," I said, laying my hand over my heart as if that meant fuck all concerning my honesty. "Offer me your soul, here and now. Guarantee yourself some peace in the afterlife. And I'll let you go."

My claws hovered over her skin, eager to dig in. All I needed was her word. Just one little agreement and . . .

"Fine," she snapped. "Fine, take it. I—" she shrieked as my claws dug in. I made my mark hurriedly, roughly, the strings of her soul binding to mine within moments. It had been a long time since I'd taken a soul from pure desperation, especially one so vile as hers. Cruel souls felt so *sticky,* like they were covered with a slime that could never be wiped away.

But claiming her did what I needed it to do. Power flooded through me, my vision flashing for a moment as my body healed, bullets pushing out of my flesh and dropping to the floor. I gasped at the rush, breathing rapidly as my strength returned. It wasn't really pleasure so much as it was simply relief.

When I opened my eyes, I felt alive again.

Meredith was staring at me with absolute horror. "Black eyes," she whispered. "Merciful God . . . Deep One, deliver me . . ."

I stepped aside, motioning toward the door. "Run while you can. Your *Godly* son will be back soon."

That seemed a horrifying enough prospect to get her moving. But she only managed a few steps. Juniper grabbed her from behind—and slit her throat.

I'd promised *I* wouldn't kill her. Juniper hadn't been part of that bargain.

"See you in Hell," Juniper said, kicking her over onto her back and standing over her as she bled out across the white carpet. As the light drained out of the Hadleigh woman's eyes, Juniper looked back up at me, uncertain wonder on her face. "She's right, Zane. Your eyes are black. They're solid black."

I didn't have time to contemplate what that meant for me. Juniper's face fell and she raised her hand, pointing behind me. Her eyes were wide as she yelled, "Zane! It's back!"

The window behind me shattered, glass bursting around me. A massive hand encompassed me, crushing me in its grasp, and yanked me out into the night.

ZANE

THE REAPER'S FINGERS squeezed tight around me, my ribs aching under the strain. It hurled me out into the night, and I managed to curl myself up before my back struck a tree. The wood splintered, and I rolled out of the way the moment I hit the dirt as the pine toppled over and crashed to the ground.

The wind howled around me, the rain coming down in a torrent. Claiming that woman's soul had left a bitter taste in my mouth, but if the Council wanted to come for me over a breach of rules in a circumstance like this, then I'd gladly offer a *fuck you* to their smug faces.

It wasn't just about me. If it meant being able to protect Juniper, if it meant being able to fight beside her, I didn't care what rules I had to shatter. I'd use any means necessary. I would twist, destroy, and manipulate anyone and anything in my path for her.

As the Reaper lurched above me, its eerily glowing eyes blinking down at me, I smiled.

"Looking a little worse for wear," I yelled. One of the beast's arms hung down limply, and its bones were protruding from its wrist, its gray skin torn. It made me proud to know Leon had done it, to know the murderous bastard hadn't gone down without making the Reaper fight for it.

Demons didn't fucking lay down and die. If this was the end, then this Reaper would go back to Hell with the marks to prove I'd fought.

"You're strong after all, demon," the beast rumbled. "I look forward to a challenge I don't have to gentle myself for."

There was a rapid popping noise, and the Reaper flinched, turning its shrouded head in confusion back toward the house. Juniper was there in the broken window, down on one knee as she took aim again. More shots popped off, striking the Reaper in its numerous blinking eyes, and I immediately took advantage of the opening.

I launched myself up, straight for that injured arm. I got my teeth in its shoulder, ripping through taut muscle and sinew, tearing down to the bone and cracking it in my teeth. The beast roared, swiping for me with its other arm as Juniper continued to rain gunfire at it. The bullets likely felt like nothing more than a stinging annoyance, but even a tiny wasp could send a full-grown man running.

I dodged its swipe before it could hit me, and rolled under its armored legs. But its arm followed me around,

striking me hard and throwing me back, tumbling me
across the ground. In fury, it looked back for Juniper, but
she had climbed down from the house and was sprinting
toward the trees.

"Foolish human," the monster growled. "You have
no idea what you've done."

I lunged for it again, but it was ready for me this time.
Its claws slashed across my face, cutting open my cheek.
It dazed me for a moment, and that gave the Reaper the
chance to throw me down, pinning me under its hand.

I struggled, biting its fingers and tearing off chunks of
flesh. But the massive creature nudged off the shroud covering its face and opened its massive mouth. Seemingly
endless rows of teeth, long and sharp as needles, came
down for me. It could snap through my neck and
consume my entire head in one gulp—

There was a loud pop, and one of the Reaper's glowing eyes burst, blood spattering my face. The Reaper
roared, flailing back, freeing me from its grasp. I didn't
need to see it to know what had just pierced the Reaper's
face was no ordinary bullet: it was the amulet, now
lodged deep inside the beast's head.

From the looks of it, the Reaper hadn't been exagger-
ating when it had called the thing "poison."

The Reaper kept thrashing, slamming into trees, into
the side of the house, cracking limbs and sending glass
flying as it screamed. Juniper ran up to my side, her eyes
wide, somewhere between terror and elation.

"It worked," she gasped. "Holy shit, it worked!"

The creature lunged, and before I could get her behind

me, the Reaper snatched Juniper from the ground and lifted her into the air.

"Foolish, pathetic little human!" Its voice reverberated through the air, shaking the trees and shattering more glass with its volume. Juniper was struggling, but her arm was pinned to her side and she couldn't get the gun up. The Reaper's massive wings whipped down, sharp spurs on their edges slashing toward me. I dodged them and leaped up the Reaper's side, using its armor and flesh as handholds, climbing until I was on its back and nearly to its neck. The only arm it could use was occupied with Juniper, and that gave me the opportunity to crawl around to the beast's throat and sink in both claws and teeth.

Juniper screamed as the beast roared back, dropping her as it tried to pull me off. But I'd dug in deep, and though the charm's magic wouldn't be as effective against this monster as it had been against me, there was no recovering from a wound like this.

It knocked me off, and I caught myself before I hit the ground, landing in a crouch. My mouth was covered in its blood, dripping down my chin, and I watched with satisfaction as the beast stumbled back and roared furiously.

"I won't forget your face," the Reaper screamed. "Watch where you wander in Hell, demon. No Reaper who encounters you won't know your name."

The darkness intensified around it, shrouding its form as it dissolved. It gave up its physical body, bursting into fluttering ashes. It would go back to Hell, and perhaps it would indeed survive and tell all the others what I'd done. It didn't matter. Let them hunt me. Let them hate me.

Not fifty feet away, Juniper lay limply on the ground. As I sprinted to her side, a trickle of blood leaked down from a gash on her head. I squatted beside her, quickly covering the wound with my hand.

"Juniper?" I pressed my fingers carefully along her spine before I dared touch her, checking for any breaks. She groaned softly at the touch and I pulled her up, holding her close against me.

She stirred, her eyes slowly blinking open as she groaned again. "Fuck." She clutched her chest, squeezing her eyes shut again. "God . . . that—that fucking hurt—"

"What hurts?" Any injury dealt to her was one I'd deal to someone else. Someone was going to pay for this—someone would pay dearly.

She shook her head. "I think I—I'm okay—knocked the air out of me when I fell. Fucking hell." She sat up a little more, still breathing heavily as she looked around. It looked as if a bomb had gone off around us: the lawn had been ripped up in massive chunks, trees had been blown to bits, the quiet garden with all its neatly trimmed bushes was flattened. The house itself had nearly been split in two, water spraying from broken pipes and a distinct smell of methane in the air.

"Is it gone?" she said softly. "Did it work?"

"You're brilliant, love," I held her face in my hands, kissing her. Fuck, I'd never tire of that mouth. Every time her lips touched mine, it was like another band pulled tight around my heart, binding me to her. "Using the amulet like that . . . you brought it to its knees."

She grinned. "Glad to know you're not the only monster I can bring to its knees."

I kissed her again, lingering, savoring the taste of her. It was only when I pulled away a second time that I realized I was smearing blood across her face, and yet all she could do was smile at me.

"You've got a little something on your mouth," she said cheekily. I wanted nothing more than to scoop her up and get the fuck out of here. We could go find Leon, then leave this place behind and never set foot in Abelaum again—but the sound of tires crunching on the gravel driveway drew my attention.

"He's back," I growled. "Jeremiah is back."

JUNIPER

THERE WAS NO point in trying to hide. There was no need to be stealthy about it, not now. We walked across the lawn toward the front of the house—battered, bruised, and covered in blood. Lightning flashed in the clouds, briefly illuminating Jeremiah and his white-cloaked followers as they stepped out of their vehicles.

When Jeremiah looked at me, I felt the hateful cold of the Deep One's gaze in his eyes. He grit his teeth, fists clenched at his sides as those gathered behind him looked at us warily. I wondered how many of them remembered me, for I remembered them. There were new ones too, of course, but so many who stood behind him now had been there that night.

They'd stood in the church and praised the killing of a young girl who begged for their help. They'd watched in silence. They'd seen me thrown down into the dark.

Now, several of them were looking at me as if I were a ghost. Their sordid pasts had come back to haunt them.

Jeremiah was shaking with fury. His white suit was stained, flecks of blood across his jacket. Black liquid leaked from his nose and over his lip.

"How the *fuck* are you still alive?" he snarled. "*Where is my Reaper?*"

Zane grinned beside me. It was strange to see him like this, with the golden color in his eyes completely gone. He was black-eyed now—like the Archdemon. The air itself was hot around him.

"Where's your *new world*, Jeremiah?" he said, tipping his head curiously. "I could have sworn you said you'd be *free* when you returned." Jeremiah's face contorted with fury.

"The final sacrifice is done," he hissed. "It's *done*! Raelynn Lawson has gone to God, and it's thanks to me! All thanks to me!" He laughed shrilly, the sound far from joyful. "I did what my father couldn't, I did what my sister couldn't. Me! Me, me, me!"

"Someone sounds like they were spoiled as a child," I muttered. Jeremiah took one lurching step toward me, but his movements were strange. They were too rigid, as if something was fighting against his own attempts to move.

"You say the sacrifice is done," Zane drawled. "Yet here you are, still trapped in the broken body of a pathetic mortal man."

Jeremiah snarled like an animal. His head twitched violently, his shoulders tense and hunched. The followers behind him were backing away, their eyes wide with fear, their cloaks drenched with the rain.

I stepped forward, staring at them one by one. Young and old, some familiar, some strangers. Some had been my teachers, my neighbors, some had gone to my brother's funeral and comforted my mother as she cried. Some didn't know me at all.

Did they do this because they were afraid? Because they were hopeful? Because they were desperate, or cruel?

Did it matter?

I lifted my gun. "This is your only chance. You have three seconds. Start running. One . . . "

There was a split second of indecision. The white-cloaks looked amongst each other, murmuring.

"Two."

Some began to flee, sprinting back to their vehicles. Others lingered, staring at Jeremiah as if he would protect them. I smirked, my finger tightening on the trigger. "Three."

The crack of gunfire destroyed whatever courage the white-cloaks had left. They all fled, as the man I'd shot collapsed to the ground. They shoved each other in their rush to run, more than willing to push their fellow worshippers into the line of fire to save themselves. I picked off another, then another, before Zane leapt into the frenzy.

Even with the chaotic screams ringing out behind him, Jeremiah stared only at me, his lip curled in disgust. He shook his head, his eyes bloodshot as he said, "Dispensable. All of them. Wastes of cowardly flesh!"

His voice deepened to a monstrous roar. There was a rumble, and the ground behind him burst open. A massive gray tentacle exploded from the dirt, lashed out, and seized one of the white-cloaks as he fled from Zane. Zane leapt back, and the man screamed in Jeremiah's grip as the tentacle tightened around him. It squeezed tighter and tighter until there was a sickening snap of bones, and his crushed body was dropped limply to the ground.

"I will not be defied!" Jeremiah roared. He gripped his head in his hands, his eyes gone purely white as if they'd been filled with fog. "You will not defy me, Juniper Kynes! You're mine!"

His body hunched, then began to contort. I aimed and fired, pulling the trigger again and again. The slugs hit his body, tearing holes in his flesh and exposing gaping wounds full of black muck. He screamed, his body growing, his limbs elongating and new appendages bursting forth from his ribs. Thick tentacles sprouted from his body, as black liquid bled from his eyes and mouth.

I fired again, and this time the bullet struck his face. The side of his skull burst apart, but his eyes rolled in his head and focused on me again. His tongue darted out, hungrily licking his lips.

"Try again, Juniper." He giggled. The black muck swelled to fill the space left by my bullet, and I was so shocked I could only stare.

"Juniper, move!"

Zane shoved me out of the way right as a massive tentacle shot forward. It grabbed Zane instead, coiling rapidly around him and squeezing as it lifted him into the air. He strained, thrashing wildly against it, and managed to get one arm free from its clutches. He dug his claws into the slimy flesh, nearly severing the tentacle in two. It dropped him, coiling back, but more were coming.

Jeremiah had lost all the humanity he had left. His arms and legs were gone; his body now supported by a mass of thick, coiling tentacles. His face kept warping, as if something else inside his head was trying desperately to get out. He lunged for us, the tentacles shooting out in every direction. I fired rapidly, hitting the first one, and then the second, but the third—

The third snapped around my chest. It dragged me down to the ground, my arms pinned to my sides. I tensed my limbs, fighting against the crushing hold before it could crack my ribs. But it was so strong that my arms were beginning to shake. The tentacle coiled tighter and tighter, the massive suckers squeezing against my arms and coming dangerously close to my throat.

Jeremiah stood over me, grinning widely. "No more running, Juniper." Hundreds of voices were speaking in unison from his mouth, some of them rough and cruel, others screaming in agony. It felt like my brain was being squeezed, like my head was caving in. I kept struggling, all my effort going to keeping those awful gray limbs from crushing my chest. But at the same time, unbidden images were flashing in my mind.

The mine shaft. The dark. The tunnel. The Gollums waiting silently in their cavern. Tentacles coiling toward me out of the shadows—

"You never really could escape the dark." Jeremiah laughed, his contorted face filling my vision. "All these years later, but you're still just the little girl lost underground."

A sudden force blasted against him, sending him skidding across the ground until he slammed into the side of the house. I gasped, scrambling to my feet as Zane put himself between me and Jeremiah. Everywhere the suckers had touched me, bruised rings of broken blood vessels remained, stinging my skin. My arms were shaking, my muscles cramped, but I growled through the pain and hurriedly reloaded the gun. I took aim, blasting chunks off the tentacles as they coiled wildly across the ground, and Jeremiah rose back up.

Zane's black eyes stared him down. He stood lightly on his feet, and when he went in for another attack, he was too fast for my eyes to follow. Gashes ripped open across Jeremiah's sprawling, monstrous form, Zane's claws and teeth leaving trails of blood as he dodged around the flailing tentacles.

Jeremiah roared, and Zane leaped away just before a tentacle struck him in the chest. The massive limbs were as thick as the trees themselves, and when they struck the side of the house, they shattered the concrete and burst pipes, sending water spraying out across the ground. I sprinted through the mud, braced myself, and fired, striking Jeremiah right in the head.

He roared again, twisting and flailing on the ground. I tumbled out of the way before one of his limbs could strike me.

"No!" Jeremiah's face was morphing rapidly: human one moment, beast the next. Some of his limbs were shrinking, shriveling up and going limp like dead leaves. "This isn't over! It isn't . . . ah . . ." He shuddered, more black liquid oozing out of him. "God . . . why . . . don't . . . don't leave . . ."

"Your God won't stay in a dying vessel." I looked up, and Jeremiah did too. Zane had jumped onto the top of the house and stood right at the edge of the ruined wall. The air around him shimmered with energy and rippled with heat. Zane gave Jeremiah a bloody grin. "You're broken, Jeremiah, and the Deep One is cruel and merciless."

"No!" Jeremiah snapped, stumbling as his limbs returned to normal. All his wounds were visible now, bleeding thick black muck. I readied my aim again, advancing on him.

"Did you think the Deep One would be kind to you?" I said as he leaned heavily against the house, panting, his eyes darting left and right for an escape. "You and your family thought you could buy your way to power with the price of others' lives. Your own *sister*, Jeremiah! You waited for your own father's death to take his place! *You murdered my brother!*"

He grinned at me cruelly, stumbling away, toward the inside of the house. "Your brother begged me for mercy." He laughed, barely able to keep his feet. "I'll never forget how it felt to see the life go out of his eyes."

"He trusted you!" I fired, the slug hitting him in the throat. Jeremiah choked, gurgling as he retreated into the ruined house, like an injured bug scuttling into its burrow. "You made him think you were his friend. I saw the photos of you together! He was kind! Marcus never deserved this!"

The tears streaming down my face were hot with fury. Jeremiah shrunk back into the shadows of the house, groaning, leaving a trail of black blood behind him. Zane jumped down behind me from the roof.

"He's got no fucking power left," I said. "Let's end this."

JUNIPER

THE INTERIOR OF the house was flooding from the rain and burst pipes. A brief flash of lightning was my only illumination as I stepped into the ruined hall. Zane was close behind me, and I could hear Jeremiah gurgling and coughing close by.

"Why . . ." He was muttering, crouched somewhere in the darkness. "I did what you asked . . . I *did* . . . I brought the sacrifices to you . . . I did everything . . ."

There was a sudden agonized, contorted cry. I spotted him, hunched over in the darkness, surrounded by the bodies of the followers Zane had killed earlier. He looked up at me, eyes wide, shaking his head. "Juniper . . . Juniper, don't . . ."

"You fucking dare," I ground the words out from between clenched teeth. "You dare to beg *me*? You're a fucking *coward*, Jeremiah!"

He laughed again, and Zane muttered behind me, "He's already dead, Juni. He's falling apart."

Zane was right—Jeremiah's limbs barely moved, and he was surrounded by a puddle of black rot. He twitched on the ground, staring up at me, his face furious one moment, terrified the next. Thunder rumbled overhead, and a sudden burst of lightning was accompanied by a horrifying crack—

And then a boom. Then another.

I kept the gun aimed at Jeremiah as Zane hurriedly flitted from my side, then back again.

"It struck the house," he said. "The gas lines are broken. When the fire spreads, things are gonna get really hot, really quick."

I nodded and looked back to Jeremiah—only to find him crawling away from me, dragging himself along the floor. I walked after him, shaking my head as he dragged himself down the ruined hall.

"Don't make me shoot you in the back, Jeremiah," I said. "It's over. Face me."

His voice growled into a high-pitched screech. "Nooo! No . . . it's not . . . I'm blessed . . . God will . . . God . . ."

I pressed my boot against his back, pinning his weak body down. "Everything the Libiri did has failed," I said. "You didn't kill me. Your God couldn't take me. Your sister died for nothing. You may have killed my brother, but he's buried somewhere safe."

Zane came up behind me. I felt his heat on my back. I took a deep breath and kicked Jeremiah over onto his side. He stared at me, but there was no light or recognition in his eyes anymore.

"Your God will never rise, Jeremiah. It didn't have to end this way." I took aim. My finger tightened. "You thought you threw a lamb down into the dark. You didn't. You threw down a wolf, and I came back biting."

I pulled the trigger.

THE FIRE SPREAD, quickly and violently. Zane had just enough time to throw the mangled bodies of the white-cloaks inside before the house was consumed. Explosions rattled the walls as the flames hit trapped pockets of leaked gas.

Zane and I watched from a distance, silent in the grass. Smoke was heavy in the air, but the pouring rain kept the fire from spreading too far.

"It's over," I said softly. "It's really over."

It had been years. So many years with the threat of them hanging over my head, so many years in fear. Years of hatred, of anger and pain. Those things didn't simply go away, no, not after so long. Not even with them dead.

But I could breathe again. The unbearable weight that had dragged me down for so long was finally lifted.

This didn't feel like an ending. It felt like a beginning. The beginning of a story not shadowed by pain, a story that wasn't warped by terror. It was a story I didn't even know how to begin; a life I had no idea how to live.

Zane leaned closer to me, tucking back my hair. Both

of us were bruised and bloodied, ash smudged around our faces. Zane's entire mouth and throat were drenched with blood from the fight. But the tension had gone out of him. His eyes were bright and golden again.

"As fierce as a wolf," he said, and I rested my head against him. "You can rest now, love. You can rest."

Fuck, that did it. I wept against his shoulder, my chest tight, the tears burning. It was overwhelming. It was freeing. He laid his head on top of mine, and when I finally had cried all I could and wiped my face, he said, "You can lead wherever you want to go, and I'll follow. And, fuck, if you don't know which direction to take, then I'll lead for you."

I shook my head, laughing softly through the last escaping tears. "I'm a mess, Zane."

"Enough of a mess for this lifetime and the next. Every bright, sharp piece of you . . ." He kissed my bloodied hand, and then the other. "Your hunt is over, but mine isn't. It never will be. Not for you."

I leaned close, as if the words were still too tender to be loud, too intimate to be heard. "I love you."

"And I love every messy piece of you, Juniper. I won't tell you not to doubt it. I'll just prove it to you every day until you can't."

The flames were beginning to die down. Little remained of the house now. "We should go," I said softly. "Someone's going to call the fire department over all this smoke."

Zane nodded, getting to his feet and offering me a hand up. But as I stood, his eyes darted to the side, and instant panic shot through me. I lifted my gun as I turned, aiming—

But there, across the lawn just outside the trees, stood Leon.

Just Leon, alone. Then Raelynn . . . Raleynn was . . .

Zane put his hand on my shoulder. "Easy, Juni." His voice was gentle. "You know he won't hurt you."

I forced myself to lower the gun. He was right, I *knew* he was right. I didn't want to keep being afraid. I didn't want to keep clinging to awful memories. I wanted to start over, even if I didn't know how yet.

And I could see the relief on Zane's face. He and Leon had left their own marks on each other, and they had their own eternity they'd promised. If it was for Zane, then I could figure out how to take one tiny step.

I could figure out how to forgive.

Leon put up his hands as he walked toward us. His clothing was torn, and there were angry purple bruises along his shoulder, his chest, his face. "You beat me here," he said. "Got to have all the fun before I could, eh?"

I stepped closer to him, away from Zane's side. He regarded me cautiously, but not as coldly as I'd thought he would. He looked at me with a cool air of respect—and, somewhere within those bright eyes, even a little sadness.

Someday I'd ask him about that night. Someday I'd try to understand the things Zane had said about him. I'd try to understand his side, his pain, his fears. I wasn't the only victim in all this. I wasn't the only one with nightmares.

"Someday" didn't feel like much . . . but it was a way forward. It was another tiny step into figuring out how to live.

"Where's Raelynn?" I said.

"Close by. Hidden. She's safe." His tone became immediately guarded, but I gave a heavy sigh of relief. He had her. The Libiri truly had failed. Their last sacrifice was alive, and who the hell would dare try to take her now? I didn't know Leon well, but there was no doubt in my mind—he'd kill anyone who tried to take Raelynn from him.

"We left no one alive," I said. "The Hadleigh family is gone. The Libiri are gone."

He looked over at the house, silent for a long moment as he watched the lingering flames. "Jeremiah, too?"

"He died like a coward. You would have loved to see it."

"I would have loved to do it."

I chuckled, but I understood. He probably felt the same as I had for so long, except his revenge was claimed by another. I would have felt even more lost than I did now if I were in his place.

"I sold my soul for revenge. It was mine to take." I nodded slowly. "But it's over. It's over."

For a moment, I just watched the flames die with him. It was the end of years of pain, smoldering into ashes. The burning of the chains that had bound us both. Then, in the distance, I heard the wail of a siren.

"We should go," Zane said, coming up beside me and tugging lightly at my hair. "This place will be swarming with people soon."

I nodded and turned away—but it didn't feel quite right yet. I took a deep breath, turned back around, and offered my hand.

Leon stared at my open hand as if he didn't know what to do with it, as if he expected a trap and was trying to figure out where it would hit him. Damn, we really weren't so different after all. But slowly, with narrowed eyes, he grasped my hand.

"I forgive you," I said. "I really hate to say that, but I do."

His eyes widened for a moment, confusion mingling with his uncertainty. He barely gripped my hand, as if he was afraid to hold too tight, as if he needed to be ready to move away in an instant. He didn't say anything, but I didn't expect him to.

I let go, gave him a nod, and Zane tucked me back under his arm. The sirens were growing closer as we reached the edge of the trees, and Zane paused to take one last look back.

"You didn't say anything to him," I said. "Why?"

"I didn't need to. Leon . . . well . . ." He chuckled. "Leon isn't great at processing the touchy-feely things. They scare him too much." We moved under the trees, walking deeper and deeper into the darkness. "Funny, isn't it? A being that dangerous is most afraid of what he feels. Afraid to let anyone in, afraid to be vulnerable. He needs some time to process all this."

I understood that. Processing what had happened would take days, months, probably years. I didn't know exactly what Leon had been through, but he probably felt like I did. I felt raw, like my cocoon had cracked open and left me exposed. I had wings, but I had no idea how to fly.

"But I . . . fuck, to see him alive, I . . ." Zane's eyes brightened, a smile barely touching his mouth. "I'm so fucking glad he made it." He squeezed my shoulder, leaning over to press a kiss against my head. "Where to now, little wolf?"

There was only one thing I could think of. One place I felt calling to me.

"The ocean," I said. "I want to go to the ocean."

JUNIPER

IT WAS DAWN by the time we made it to the coast, but the rain hadn't stopped pouring. The ocean stretched out before me, lapping upon the shore in the morning's dim gray light. The water reached into the distance, seemingly endless until it met the sky. A great expanse of the unknown, vast and churning.

I stumbled down the sand, right to the water's edge. The waves lapped over my feet, cold foam gathering around my ankles.

I'd made it. As I stood there in the waves, the clouds parted just enough to let the morning sun shine down on my back, even as the rain kept falling around me. A new day had dawned and somehow . . . *somehow*, I was still alive.

I walked deeper into the waves. I walked in until they were nearly up to my waist. I dipped my hands into the water and watched the blood wash away. I listened to the wind and the crashing ocean. I listened to the cries of the seabirds overhead.

There was nothing left to call my name from the woods. The darkness that waited at the edges of my consciousness was gone. All that remained was an ache—one of uncertainty, of confusion.

I could hear Zane's footsteps behind me in the sand. I kept washing away the blood and dirt on my arms. I dunked down my head and scrubbed the salt water through my hair. It all washed away, all the filth trailing into the water.

The stains were gone. So what remained . . .

"I didn't think I would live," I said softly, but I knew he could hear me. "I never thought I would survive this. That was why I made the deal." I laughed, shaking my head. "The only reason I kept going after Marcus died was to get my vengeance. And now . . . it's done." I turned back to him, my arms wrapped around myself as the cold made me shiver. "It's over, Zane."

He nodded. The golden color had come back into his irises, but the darkness remained where the whites of his eyes had once been. He'd changed since I'd met him; he'd changed irrevocably.

I'd changed too. Except I didn't know what those changes meant.

I didn't know who I was now. Who I was meant to be.

"What now?" I whispered. I was weeping, tears streaming down my face, and I wasn't entirely sure why.

Zane waded into the water. He wrapped his arms

around me, held me close within his warmth and chased the cold away. "Whatever you want, love. Anything in the world. This life is yours."

He held my face in his hands and wiped my tears away. My carefully constructed walls were gone. I'd opened the door to my shelter and found myself terrified to step outside. The light was too bright, the world outside too vast, and I was simply *safer* in my shelter.

But Zane stood outside, with his hand outstretched as if to lead me out, as if to make the journey a little less terrifying.

"I don't know what my life is supposed to be," I said, closing my eyes because it was all too much. In the darkness behind my closed eyes, it was only me and him. In the dark, I could pretend I felt no fear of the future. I could imagine I didn't still feel chained to the pain, like it was an anchor I was trying to drag with me even though I longed to leave it behind. "This world isn't meant for me. I don't think it ever was."

He grinned, still holding me. "You weren't made for this world, love. You're too much for it. As am I. But that doesn't mean you can't make it yours." He pressed his forehead to mine. "You deserve to live. Eternity will be yours, but until then, I'll be beside you for whatever life you want to live."

I swallowed hard. "What if I'm too broken? What if . . . what if I can't . . ." What if I couldn't heal? What if I couldn't put myself together enough to *live*? What if I knew only how to survive, what if I could only desperately drag myself through every day? What then?

What if revenge was all I'd had, and now that it was over, I didn't know how the hell to go forward?

"You can be broken," he said. "You'll never be too broken for me. We can be monsters, you and I. We can be wretched, messy, strange things. If you're afraid, then you can be afraid. When you lose your light, I'll still come back for you in the dark. You're not alone." He kissed my forehead. "You'll never be alone again."

He looked at me like I was something treasured, like I was something beautiful, something rare. Things I'd never thought about myself, I saw in his eyes. "You deserve to live, Juniper Kynes. You deserve to be happy. You deserve to come out of the dark, when you're ready. It's alright if you don't know which way to go. I'll be beside you. I love you, Juniper Kynes, exactly as you are."

Fuck, I hated to cry. But that broke down the last measly defense I had. I let him hold me in the water, and I cried with relief, with hope, and yes, with fear.

But it was okay to be afraid. It was okay to be lost.

I wasn't alone anymore. I wasn't hopeless anymore. No matter how vast the world seemed, I could light the path ahead. I could gather up my broken pieces and start putting them together again.

I could find my way, with him by my side, into eternity.

Epilogue

ZANE

MONTHS LATER

I LIKED VERMONT in the spring. The green fields, the yellow flowers, birdsong—it wasn't usually my type of scene. I was partial to grime, chaos, and noise, and we could find that here too if we went to the right place. But Juniper needed the quiet, she needed the wide-open spaces. At least for now, I was trying to keep her away from anything too dreary.

A change of environment was good for her, at least that was what the therapist had said. I didn't know much about psychiatry and all that, and Juniper had been hesitant as fuck about the whole thing—understandably, given her history with doctors. But Hana had insisted the woman was a good fit. I had to admit she was uniquely qualified to help Juniper.

Hana had claimed the woman's soul years ago. If any therapist was prepared to deal with Juniper's tangled history, it was this one.

The office was tucked down a quiet street lined with trees. I never went far during Juniper's appointments, so I waited in the alley just next door as I smoked.

I felt her coming before I saw her. Juniper's presence had a way of vibrating over my whole being, the force of her nearly uncontainable, especially when she was emotional. She came down the office steps, peering around for me. It was still strange to see her walking around unarmed.

"How was it today?" She turned, smiling as she saw me. She walked over, and I stubbed out the joint so I could put my arms around her. "Your eyes are red, love."

"Yeah, well . . ." She tried to sound hard, but she still sniffled. "I might have spent most of the appointment crying. *Again*," she groaned. "Dr. Pierce says I bottle up my emotions too much. So I guess it's . . . cathartic . . . or something."

I chuckled at how disgusted she sounded. "You? Bottling your emotions? Shocking." She glared up at me, and I nudged her chin playfully as I walked her a little further down the alley. "It's good for you. It gives you an outlet to express yourself."

She wrinkled her nose. "I didn't punch any walls this time. That's probably . . . good."

"It's a step in the right direction." I paused and turned her, pressing her back up against the wall. I trailed my claws along her neck, smiling when goose bumps prickled over her skin.

"Here?" she said softly. "It's broad daylight!"

I shrugged. "I'll hear anyone coming before they see us. I just want to give you another outlet, love. To express yourself."

"To *express* myself, huh? Is that what you—ah—is that what you call it—" Her own gasping breaths cut her off. I had my hand slipped down her jeans, massaging over her clit. I loved the way her legs began to tremble. I loved pleasuring away her tension. I loved to feel her get wet on my fingers.

"Zane . . ." She wrapped her arms around my neck, nails clawing at my back beneath my shirt. Her arousal was slick on my fingers, and I slowly pushed one inside her, chuckling against her neck as her breath hitched.

"What is it, love?" I said. "Go on, use your words."

She groaned, her nails digging into me a little harder as I added a second finger. "Feels so good . . . fuck . . ." Her legs tried to squeeze together, and I nudged my knee in between them to keep them apart.

"Mm, don't bottle it up now," I said, nipping at the tender skin of her throat, leaving my marks there for all to see. I'd never grow tired of that—marking her, anywhere and everywhere that I could. Just seeing that flash of my metal in her tongue as her lips parted made my cock throb against my jeans. "I want to hear those pretty sounds you make."

I wasn't satisfied just getting my fingers in her. I jerked down her pants, just low enough to give me access, and knelt so I could get my tongue on her.

"Oh . . . fuck!" Her nails scratched over my head, her hips moving eagerly against my mouth. I lifted her easily, letting her legs rest on my shoulders and holding her ass as her back rested against the wall. I pressed my tongue inside her, groaning as her muscles pulsed.

"Come for me, love," I said it right up against her soft skin, savoring every drop of her hot arousal on my tongue. She stiffened, no longer holding back her desperate whimpers. They increased in volume and in need, and I squeezed her ass in my hands.

She cried out as her thighs squeezed around my head, her body shuddering with pleasure. I looked up at her from between her legs, grinning at her dazed face. "Just a little therapy after your therapy. To help you unwind."

"Fucking . . . hell . . ." she gasped as I stood and set her on her feet. She had to lean against me a moment, but she lifted her head again as she rubbed her hand over my cock through the denim.

"My turn now," she said, the look in her brown eyes absolutely devilish. I picked her up, tossing her over my shoulder as she shrieked.

"You can use your tongue in the car, love," I said. "I'm a little too eager to get you home and do a hell of a lot more than just eat that sweet pussy of yours."

She laughed, and I felt that was better than anything. Her joy, her safety, her freedom to live without fear— that was what I was after now. That was the hunt over which I obsessed. Her soul alone had never been enough; it never would be. I was always going to want more of her.

My own little wolf, with sharp teeth and stormy eyes. All shattered pieces and jagged edges that shone brighter than the sun. A soul as dark and strange as my own.

She was mine, and I was hers, for the rest of eternity.

Bonus Chapter

JUNIPER

ONE YEAR LATER

ATTEMPTING TO RETURN to a normal life after murdering a cult for vengeance was difficult. I'd spent so long on the move, sleeping out of my car, doing odd jobs—it was strange to know the bed I'd return to every night, the house that would shelter me. I wasn't built to live domestically.

Part of me still felt the urge to run. To abandon all my things and keep moving, keep hiding. My therapist, Dr. Pierce, said it was a symptom of trauma and that it would take time to work through.

But I wasn't a very patient person.

Instead of being snuggled safely into bed like a good girl, I was seated at a bar, with a whiskey sour in my hand. I was a regular at this place; the bartender knew me well enough to groan in despair when I walked in the door.

The walls, floor, and ceiling were all the same variety of waxy wooden panels; the air smelled like cigarettes and stale beer. Neon signs advertising beers and liquors flickered on the walls in between the mounted heads of deer, goats, and buffalo.

It was like old times. I was alone, in a bar full of strangers sizing me up, staring, cracking jokes, and brushing up against me to see how far they could push my boundaries. I played darts and won, then played pool and won again. As usual, a little cheating may have been involved at the pool table, but my opponents didn't notice.

Again and again, my eyes were drawn toward the door.

Waiting. Antsy with anticipation.

Zane and I had opened a tattoo shop a few months back. I managed the place, Zane tattooed, and a few other artists rented out a chair in our space. It kept me occupied, and gave Zane an outlet for both his creative and masochistic desires.

He was with a client late tonight, working on a large piece. He should have known better than to leave me bored and alone for so long, but it was only a matter of time before he realized I wasn't at home.

A shiver ran up my back at the thought of my demon hunting for me. It was a cold night, pouring rain. I kept checking my phone, imagining that I'd felt it buzz only to find no notifications waiting for me.

Finally, at a quarter after midnight, my phone chimed with a text from Zane.

You'd better not be causing trouble, love.

With a grin, I replied, What else is there to do?

Dr. Pierce was going to sigh *heavily* when I told her about this on Monday.

Draining my drink, I raised my hand to get the bartender's attention for another. But I jostled the man beside me, spilling his beer. He huffed and swore, and crowded my space when I ignored him.

"Least you could do is apologize, missy," the stranger said, leering too close. "You could learn to be a little nicer. Why don't you give me a smile, be a good girl and apologize?"

The door swung open. A tall figure filled the entrance, rain pouring behind him. Heavy boots stomped into the room.

Heat flooded my veins, and my heart beat faster.

Rain dripped down Zane's face. His shirt was damp, clinging tightly to his skin. His eyes were fixed on me, dark with irritation—almost black.

Patrons moved hurriedly out of the way as Zane approached. But my harasser didn't notice he was there until Zane's hand dropped heavily on his shoulder.

In his opposite hand was a dart, which Zane rapidly brought to the man's throat. The metal tip pierced into his flesh, a single crimson bead rolling down his neck. The man froze, his eyes wide.

"Consider yourself lucky that I'm in a good mood," Zane said. The man gulped, sweat breaking out on his forehead as he held up his hands. "And that I don't want to ruin the good bartender's night by leaving a corpse in his pub."

The bartender was watching without saying a word, slowly wiping down a glass with a rag. Zane jerked the man closer, and everyone in the bar flinched.

"If I see you in here again, I'll kill you," he said, giving the man a cheerful smile. "If I see you within a hundred yards of my woman . . ." He nodded toward me, and everyone took a large step further away from me. "I'll kill you. If I so much as get a whiff of your horrendous odor on the breeze, I will rip you limb from limb, starting with your cock. Do you understand?"

The man rapidly nodded. Several other men in attendance did too. Zane mockingly patted the man's head, slowly withdrawing the dart's metal tip from his throat.

"Fantastic. Since we have an understanding, I'd appreciate it if you'd all go ahead and *fuck off.*"

There was a scramble for the door. Within seconds the place was cleared out, leaving just Zane, me, and the bartender.

The bartender shook his head slowly. "Why is it that every time you two come in, there's trouble?"

"Trouble?" Zane took aim and launched the dart, hitting the bullseye perfectly despite the board being on the opposite side of the room. "No one's dead. No grievous injuries. The cops didn't show up. Looks like a good night to me."

The bartender set down his glass with a heavy *thunk*. "May as well lock up for the night then," he grumbled.

Zane clicked his tongue in disappointment. "I've had a long day, buddy. Just one drink before we go?"

He held up a twenty dollar bill, and although the bartender complained, he took the cash and made Zane his drink.

"Y'all holler if you need anything," he said, sliding Zane's cocktail across the bar. "I'm gonna work on these damn dishes."

Then he retreated into the kitchen, and it was just my demon and I.

Steve Wright was singing over the speakers, to the tune of "Wild, Wild Woman." Zane didn't say a word, but bobbed his head along to the music as he sipped his drink: a cosmopolitan.

I walked over to the pool table and picked up a ball, rolling it back and forth. "How'd you find me?"

"I tracked you like a dog," he said, tapping the side of his nose with a playful smirk. He was wearing far too little for a cold autumn night. "I could smell you and your bitchy attitude miles away. I knew you'd go out looking for trouble."

I tried to look offended as I sat on the pool table. "Trouble? Me? I'm shocked you'd think such a thing."

Leaving his drink on the bar, he came to stand in front of me. He tucked his fingers beneath my chin, tipping my head back so I was looking up at him.

"I should spank you," he said. His eyes turned almost entirely black, with merely slim golden rings where his irises should have been. "Going out in the middle of the night. Not telling me where you are. Nearly getting yourself hurt."

"I'm just keeping you on your toes." I stared up at him with wide, fake-innocent eyes. "I have to test you every now and then. Make sure you're paying attention."

His hold on my chin tightened, his claws lengthening and digging into my jaw.

"I see. This was a cry for attention." He pressed me backward, practically climbing on top of the pool table as he loomed over me. "As if I don't worry over your safety every time you walk out the door, every time you're out of my sight. Shit, Juniper."

His words were sharp, with just enough anger that goose bumps prickled over my arms. He noticed my chills, his hand trailing down my side.

"Do I see excitement in your eyes, love?" His sharp nail pricked beneath my chin, the same spot he'd threatened the man who'd been harassing me. "Do you like the thought of me hunting you through darkness and rain? Obsessing over you? Growing more feral with every passing second that I couldn't find you?"

The air was heavy, and grew even heavier as Zane's presence swelled. He leaned down and placed a chaste kiss on my cheek, tender and gentle despite the painful intensity of his grip.

"Is that what you want?" he whispered. The anger in his voice was gone; all that remained was love. "A reminder that I'm here for you? Do you need to feel safe, Juni?"

I almost swore at him for daring to touch my feelings with those quiet words.

"Shut up," I whispered. He was so close, I could have kissed him. He drew me closer like a magnet, irresistible. The air was vibrating around him, hot and eager with desire. "I don't need anything. I'm fine alone, as always."

The demon grinned, all sharp teeth and wicked charm. "Is that so? I think you're forgetting something, my beautiful lone wolf. All those years you were watched. You were stalked. You were protected. During the years you were running, I was paying attention. I had only one thing on my mind . . ." He pressed his forehead to mine, dark eyes burning into me. "Claiming my woman, no matter how long it took."

His kiss was rough. He consumed me, his tongue playing with mine and the jewelry pierced through it. His knee nudged between my legs, keeping them spread as he scolded me in between kisses.

"Your pride makes you so goddamn foolish. You've had to be strong your whole life. You've had to be alone. But that's not how it works anymore, get it? I have you. I'll always have you. Don't underestimate eternity, love. Don't forget that there isn't time, distance, or danger that could keep me from you."

He paused, and I tried to gasp for air without making it obvious. But he could read me like an open book.

"You think you're fine alone?" he said, in a teasing whisper that made me shiver. "Show me. Demonstrate how good it feels to do it all by yourself."

"The bartender could come back any second," I warned. I trailed my finger down my chest—over the scars of his sigil, between my breasts, past my navel. "You really want him to see me like that?"

"Like what?" he crooned. "Splayed out and begging for the pleasure only I can give you? I like to show off. That's exactly how you should be seen."

"So cocky." I made a show of popping open my jeans and sliding my hand between my legs. I gasped and moaned, and he rolled his eyes at me. He straightened, his loose joggers tented with the monstrous cock within.

Suddenly, to my surprise, Zane yanked me off the pool table. My hand was still squeezed down my pants as he turned me and bent me over the table, my cheek pressed against the felt, my boots barely touching the ground.

"Don't stop," he ordered. "Keep touching yourself."

He pulled down my jeans, and my underwear with them. I could be seen at any second. Someone could walk in the door, or the bartender could return from the kitchen.

But I didn't care. All that mattered was the feeling of Zane's fingers trailing teasingly over my hips, gripping me for a moment—before he gave me a stinging swat.

"Ow! Fuck you, asshole!" He pressed me down, one palm between my shoulderblades ensuring that I couldn't get up.

"What did I just tell you?" He leaned over me as I glared at him, his demonic strength useless to fight against. "Touch yourself. Make yourself feel good. And while you do . . ." He lowered his voice. "I want you to think about how much *better* it would feel if it was me."

His words inspired rebellion, but it couldn't last forever. I worked my finger over my clit, trying to lose myself in the pleasure despite the sharp, stinging spanks he was unleashing. I wanted to swear at him again, to yell, but I also didn't want the bartender to hear me making a fool out of myself.

As if he couldn't hear the sharp sound of Zane spanking me. My face burned.

"Finally quieting down?" Zane's palm smacked soundly against my thigh. "How does it feel? Was this what you wanted?"

"Ooh, fuck—yes!" I arched my back, pushing my ass toward him. He smacked me again, and I hissed at the stinging pain. "Feels so good."

"Does it? I'm sure this is what you prefer then: being bent over the table and spanked, rather than bent over and fucked?"

I grit my teeth. "Absolutely. My fingers feel . . . better than . . . aah . . ."

"What was that? Speak up, Juni."

I didn't even get a chance to respond as he spanked me again. Pressing my forehead against the table, I focused solely on keeping quiet. I felt feverish—too hot, too needy. My own hand wasn't enough, but I'd known that from the start.

"I want you." My voice was soft, little more than a whisper. Zane's warm hand rubbed over my stinging skin, and his hips pressed against me. The massive outline of his hard cock made my breath catch.

"I'm going to need more than that, love." Although I couldn't see him, I could tell Zane was grinning. "I want to hear you beg for me. I want to hear you say *please.*"

His hand squeezed between my legs, covering my own. He moved my hand, and my breath shuddered at the stimulation.

"Tell me, Juniper," Zane's voice was low. "Is it better alone?"

"No."

"What do you want, love?"

"You." I sucked in my breath as his fingers squeezed inside me, pumping slowly. "I want you, please."

He kissed the nape of my neck as he bent over my back, his hips gyrating against me. He'd taken his joggers down at some point; his bare flesh was so warm against mine.

"Please," I whispered, turning my head so I could catch his mouth for a kiss. He thrust against me, not yet pressing inside but taunting me with his closeness. I was teetering on the edge of ferality, choking on my need. "Fuck me, Zane. I want your cock to destroy me."

"Need me to fuck the attitude out of you?" he said. "I can do that, love."

With one hard thrust, he was inside me. I clapped my hand over my mouth to muffle my cry, but the pain was already melting into pleasure. My body clung to him, his girth overwhelming me. I'd already worked myself up, but he knew exactly how to work my body.

He moved in long, slow strokes, at first. Then harder, deeper, faster. He wrapped his hand around my face, and hooked his fingers into my mouth. Every thrust made me gasp, then whimper, then moan.

"That's it, my love," he growled. "Take it for me. Is this what you were waiting for? For your demon to find you and take care of you?" With two fingers still hooked in my mouth, he gripped my hair with his other hand. He was fully sheathed inside me, deep and aching. The most exquisite pain. "I'll always take care of you. Always. Don't ever fear that I won't find you."

He turned me, lifting me off the table and into his arms. Chest to chest, with my legs around his waist and his arms around me, he impaled me on his cock once more. My head fell back, growing pleasure snatching the words from my mouth. My core tightened, and I saw stars. Every nerve was alight as I came, eyes rolled back, my nails digging into his shoulders hard enough to draw blood.

"Say it." His voice was low, his sharp teeth clenched as he looked into my eyes. "Will I always find you, little wolf?"

"Yes," I gasped, breathless. "I know you'll always find me."

His head dropped against my shoulder when he came inside me. He rocked against me, our breathing in unison as we melted into the afterglow.

I was exactly where I needed to be: claimed, cared for, safe in his arms. For a few blissful moments, I was soft. Vulnerable, like a hermit crab out of its shell.

Zane's fingers stroked through my hair, tucking it behind my ear. "I'll always keep you safe. I know it's going to take years for you to get used to that, but you and I have all the time in the world." He set me slowly on my feet, helping me to get my clothes back on before adjusting his own. "But until then, no matter where you go, I'll follow."

I jumped when the door behind the bar swung open, and the bartender poked his head out with a heavy frown.

With a voice weighed down by exasperation, he said, "Are y'all done? I'm gonna lock up."

"We'll head out," Zane said. He finished his drink in one gulp, never taking his eyes off me. Then, with one arm around me, we walked together out the door and into the night.

"You didn't have to save me back there," I said, as I walked under his arm.

"Oh, I know that." We stopped at a crosswalk, rain pouring down on us as we waited for the light to change. "But I like saving you. It makes you blush."

My cheeks were instantly hot, and I shoved his arm. "I don't blush. Christ, you're so annoying."

He pulled me close, kissing my reddened face as I squirmed and protested. When I kept struggling and he finally pulled away, I grabbed his shirt collar and dragged him back.

"Don't let me fight you off," I muttered against his mouth. Then I shrieked as he picked me up and flung me over his shoulder, carrying me down the sidewalk like a sack of potatoes.

"Never," he promised, and I knew he meant it.

THE END

Keep reading for a special excerpt of
the next book in the Souls Trilogy!

SOUL OF A WITCH

Everly

I am the servant of a merciless God. I am the daughter of Its preacher. All my life, my power has been controlled by others. They raised me to be meek and stifled my magic.

But no more.

A brutal murder led me to discover a mysterious house full of magic—and the ancient, powerful demon within. He says my power can change the world, that I can kill the evil creature I once worshipped.

But at what cost?

Callum

For two thousand years, I've been alone. Slaughtering fallen Gods as I searched for the witch that haunted my dreams, begging for my help.

Now that I've found her, I will protect her with my life. But when the fate of Earth, Heaven, and Hell hangs in the balance, not even her soul is safe from destruction. If a choice must be made, I'll let the world burn if it means having her as my own.

Soul of a Witch *is book 3 in the Souls Trilogy. Although all the books are interconnected, they are stand-alone and can be read in any order.*

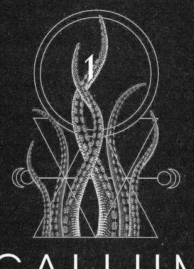

CALLUM

HELL—2,000 YEARS AGO

A MORTAL MAN once told me, "Only the dead have seen the end of war." But I, being infinite, was doomed to see it all. Every great battle, every raging conflict. The fall of every kingdom on Earth, in Heaven, or in Hell. The endless loss of lives in an ever-churning machine of bloodshed.

The curse of the immortal.

I took up arms, I witnessed the destruction of great cities and the deaths of so many—and yet, I went on. Hell was the domain of the immortals, but even we could be snuffed out.

So many of us were already lost.

There was a soft sound as the flap of my tent was

brushed aside. It was my second-in-command, Kimaris. "A scout has returned, my lord."

"A scout?" I turned. "We sent three."

"Yes, *dux*. Only one returned." Her voice didn't betray the pain in her golden eyes.

The fields were covered in ash. Cities leveled. Young ones snuffed out. And still, we went on. Infinite.

I couldn't recall the last time I'd mourned. There was no time for the ceremonies with which we bid farewell to the dead. We couldn't celebrate the freedom of their beings, nor could we come to terms with the horror of their fates.

To die by the hand of a God was to become Theirs for eternity. Your essence, sucked into Its own, the wretched suffering of your immortal being feeding Its gluttonous power. A horror beyond words, beyond what even we demons could imagine.

"How much time do we have?" I said.

"They'll reach us before dawn."

Then we would fight in the night. We were the last line, the final defense before the city of Dantalion. If the High City was taken, then Hell was no longer ours. It would become the realm of Gods.

"Callum . . ." She hesitated, staring at the grass but seeing something else entirely. Something that made her lip curl as she said, "There are Reapers with them."

Sharp, cold fingers of dread gripped my chest. But I kept my face utterly blank. I imagined myself as a chiseled stone, unmovable, unchanging. Unfailing.

"I want every warrior ready. Go through the camp,

get them sobered up. We don't have time for their com-
forts."

"Yes, *dux*." Kimaris turned to go, but there was a
final thing to be done.

"The scout," I said. "Are they well? Able to travel?"
She nodded. "Take them aside and select two others. I
want them to stay back from the battle. If the line is broken, they are to go back to Dantalion and give word. A
little time to flee is better than none."

Kimaris looked stricken. "The High City has never
fallen," she said sharply. "Never."

"Pride will make us think we're untouchable. But the
Gods advance. We are the last line. Dantalion will not
fall while I still live." I paced across the tent, snapping
my fingers. "Tell them, Kimaris, but let no one else know
of this. Keep the conversation private."

A GREAT WHITE fog was growing on the horizon, rolling toward us over the vast plains. Lightning flashed
within, briefly illuminating the gargantuan shapes of
beasts as they advanced.

Behind me, in the distance, the High City shimmered
in the dark, its lights extending far into the heavens. I
longed for her warmth, her twisting streets, the shining
onyx towers of her keep. But I cast away the feelings; I
forced my heart to harden.

If I hesitated, if I allowed myself to long for anything
other than bloodshed, Dantalion would be taken.

Hell's army was gathered at my back, demons young

and old. Dark clouds gathered overhead, obscuring the night sky and the silver light of the twin moons.

"And so comes the rain," Kimaris said, as the heavy drops began to fall. She whispered, "How many do you think?"

We gazed at the nearing fog. It was faint, at this distance, but I could hear the screams within. Agonized, tortured screams of all those beings the Gods had consumed. Mortal or immortal, it didn't matter. Their souls were locked into eternal torment for the Gods, creatures that thrived and fed upon suffering. Their forms were massive and ever-changing.

Flying before them, like great black shadows, were the Reapers. They were adorned in bones, their multiple eyes glowing beneath their shrouds. Their cries pierced the night, animalistic and hungry. The howls of the Eld creatures mingled with them, the lesser beasts crawling at their masters' heels, gnashing their teeth.

"It doesn't matter how many," I said. "We don't stop until there are none."

Turning my back on the encroaching fog, I faced my warriors. Fangs clipped eagerly, the sound of snapping teeth our battle cry. Many of these demons had sharpened their claws, or fit metal spurs on their fingers. Some held massive weapons made of aether, metal, or stone, their blades shimmering in the night.

Looking upon them, with the lights of the High City glowing at their backs, I could see the end of this war.

Whether I would live to see it, I didn't know. But the end was here.

"Hellions!" My voice roared over the landscape, loud enough to reach even the furthest line of demons. "Some among you have lived as long as I. You've seen the world change, you've seen wars come and cities fall. But some of you are seeing war for the first time. You've seen friends and lovers die, you've seen blood fill the streets of our cities."

They shouted in response, chanting, "Honor the dead! Honor the dead!"

When had I last seen a funeral pyre? When was the last time we'd had enough peace to send the ashes of our kin free to the winds?

As I looked upon them, I saw fear, I saw fury. I didn't see hope. I saw hundreds of beings bracing themselves to die.

Straightening my shoulders, I said, "Dantalion relies upon us and we will not let it fall! I've seen you, fought with you." I paced along their line, meeting their eyes, touching their shoulders. Making it clear they had a leader who was not afraid. "I've seen you tear out the hearts of Gods, drenched in the blood of the Eld! I've seen your viciousness! Today, we go into battle with the names of those we lost on our lips. Honor the dead! But do not forget the living. Do not forget the lives of those beside you, and those behind you. Honor them!"

Weapons slammed, howls broke out across the ranks. Lifting my hand, I drew the edge of my blade across my palm so the blood ran down my wrist. Many of the warriors followed suit, for no demon wanted to give their enemy the satisfaction of drawing first blood.

"We'll see the sun rise on their corpses!" I yelled. "These fields will be fed with their blood! For no creature, no God, will take Hell from its true keepers!"

The cacophony of their shouts and howls was deafening, loud enough to drown out the horrendous screams of our enemies. Stretching my wings toward the sky, I watched them come. The white fog reached out long tendrils toward us, and the screaming grew louder. Massive beings stirred in the darkness.

"Death calls!" I yelled. "But today, you will not answer! Today, you fight, and death will feed on your enemies! Hell is ours!" I slammed my blades together with a crack like thunder, beat my wings, and launched into the air. The first tendrils of mist touched my face, cold as ice and bringing with it whispers of agony.

I bared my teeth. Above me, a massive form loomed.

"Death calls," I murmured. "Death calls."

I raised my weapons and faced the Gods.

THE SUN BEAT down, a blood-red yolk floating in a pale gray sky, as I walked among the fields of the dead.

The odor of burned flesh and rot permeated the air. Corpses riddled the landscape as pools of blood seeped into the dirt. Dead Gods were scattered across the field, their massive forms melting into lumps of quivering flesh, surrounded by clusters of phosphorescent fungal growths. Dying Reapers with ruined wings and broken bodies roared curses at me as I passed.

All around me lay the bodies of my kin. Demons I'd

known, fought beside. Demons I'd loved, who wore my metal and jewels in piercings I'd given them with my hands.

One by one, as I found them, I took out the metal they'd given me. The jewelry pierced through my ears, lips, and eyebrows, covered in glittering jewels—I ripped them out. I didn't feel the pain. Physical pain was nothing in comparison to this.

One wing dragged behind me as I knelt before another body. They'd been gored, but I knew their face. Ryker. They wore my metal pierced through their lip, and I could remember how joyous they'd been when I gave it to them. We'd spent all night in rapture before rising in the morning to fight another day.

If this was what it took to save Hell, perhaps I shouldn't have saved it.

I closed their wide, glassy eyes. Then choked down the pain, swallowed it whole, let it sit like a knot of agony in my chest. I wouldn't stop until I'd seen them all. Every single one. I would not allow even one of my warriors to go unwitnessed into the Void Beyond.

Through the lingering smoke, I could see the High City. Its spires and glittering towers of onyx and emerald pierced the sky like a beast's teeth. Lucifer's great citadel overlooked it all, the tallest of its towers disappearing into the clouds.

They would call me a hero. There would be feasting, debauchery, orgies. Liquor would flow for days. Hell's future was secured, the war was won.

Lucifer would grant me his favor. He would mark me,

just like I'd wanted for so long. My ascension would be complete.

Archdemon.

Royal.

Revered.

I wanted none of it.

Turning my back on the city so many had died for, I trudged on. There was a voice in my head, screaming my name like an endless echo. The cries of my warriors were trapped within my own mind.

Amid the swirling smoke ahead, a figure appeared.

It was a woman. Not a demon, not a beast. A mortal woman, with long blonde hair that was damp and dirty. She wore boots and trousers, but the make of her clothing was unlike anything I'd seen on Earth or in Hell. Her head was bowed, her shoulders hunched as she clutched at her side.

I sniffed the air.

Blood, sugary sweet, spring berries and honey, nectar on my tongue . . .

She was a witch.

Witches only sought demons for one purpose—to control us. They would force us to bend to their will if they could discover our true name.

Something about this witch was familiar. Like the face of an old friend, warped by time. But that was impossible. I did not keep company with witches.

Then she lifted her head and looked at me. Her eyes glittered like sapphires, bright and beautiful amid so much gore. We faced each other in silence across the open field, her scent wafting over me like a heady perfume.

Intoxicating, irresistible, the most alluring ambrosia. Then she spoke, and my entire world changed.

"Callum . . . please . . . help me . . ."

**Look for *Soul of a Witch*
coming soon in paperback!**

ACKNOWLEDGMENTS

First and foremost: to my husband. Thank you for making sure I (mostly) kept my sanity during this whole process. Thank you for dragging me out of the house when I worked one too many weekends in a row. Thank you for your amazing meals, for listening to me ramble on and on about book problems, and as usual, for being the voice of reason when I feel like things are a mess. I wouldn't be able to do this without you.

To Zainab, my lovely editor, thank you all your hard work and determination to make this book the best that it can be. I can usually think of a million things I need to fix in my drafts, but your critiques get my head in the right place to make the improvements that are *actually* necessary, instead of just rewriting forever. And you know I always look forward to your teaser highlights!

To Shimaira, for your fantastic work proofreading this big book, I can't thank you enough. You're incredibly kind and thoughtful, and you've helped me with more than just catching typos. Thank you for everything.

To my reader group and my ARC readers, I LOVE YOU ALL! On my hardest days, our wild little group gives me the determination to keep going. You've brought me so much joy, my internet haven is right there with you all in Wicked Dark Desires.

To every reader, whether this is your first read with me or not, thank you so much for picking up this book.

Thank you for stepping into my weird little world for a while. I hope we can meet again, in the next adventure.

Until next time,
Harley